"You could kiss me again."

Her own words surprised her. . . . Imogene didn't realize until she'd said them how much she wanted it. A kiss to make her feel wanted and cherished.

But mostly—oh, mostly what she wanted was to keep that light shining in his eyes, to kiss away the darkness and keep it away. Forever, if she could.

He looked down at her, and she felt his hand at her waist, felt his heat through her mantle, through the cold damp air. The snow fell into her eyes, catching on her eyelashes and melting there so she saw his face in prisms.

"A kiss," he murmured, and with a sharp stab of relief she saw that radiance grow even stronger in his eyes, dazzling her as he bent and brushed his mouth against hers. . . .

D1115639

Also by Megan Chance

MEGAN CHANCE

THE PORTRAIT

A DELL BOOK

Published by
Dell Publishing
a division of
Bantam Doubleday Dell Publishing Group, Inc.
1540 Broadway
New York, New York 10036

The trademark Dell® is registered in the U.S. Patent and Trademark Office.

ISBN: 0-440-22080-7

Printed in the United States of America

Published simultaneously in Canada

October 1995

10 9 8 7 6 5 4 3 2 1

OPM

To my sister, Robyn
For all those years of love and pain and joy,
And for the best gift of all: Morgan
And to Rob Cohen
For years of believing

In a dark time, the eye begins to see,
What's madness but nobility of soul
At odds with circumstance? The day's on fire!

—Theodore Roethke

Chapter 1

She was finally here.

Imogene Carter paused in front of the door. The astringent fumes of turpentine and paint filled her nostrils, along with the scents of musty halls and crumbling plaster and dust.

The smells of possibility.

Her stomach tightened. Possibility. The word was as frightening as it was exciting. Her entire future hung on this interview. She wiped her sweaty palms on her skirt, trying to ease her nervous tension. She couldn't afford it—not today. She had to be clear-headed and calm. Her father would never forgive her if she failed.

"Are you sure about this, my dear?"

Her godfather spoke from beside her, and she turned to look at him, noting the lines of worry marking his face, the concern in his expression.

She nodded shortly and tried to give him a reassuring smile. "I'm sure. I want this. Really I do."

Thomas hesitated a second too long. For a moment she was afraid he would refuse to go through with this, but finally he ran a hand through his snowy white hair and sighed in resignation. "Very well then," he said. "As you wish." He rapped sharply on the door. There was no answer.

He frowned and rapped again.

Still no answer. Imogene held her breath, waiting. "He knows we're coming, doesn't he?"

"Yes, of course." Thomas knocked more impatiently. "Whitaker! Whitaker, are you in there? Speak up, man!"

"Come in." The voice that came from behind the door sounded far away and harsh with irritation.

Imogene threw an uncertain glance at her godfather, but he only gave her a quick shake of his head and pushed the lever, swinging open the door to usher her inside.

Imogene stopped short, unable to keep from staring. The scents of turpentine and paint were stronger here, along with those of linseed oil and must, but now there were more than just smells. Cold sunshine filtered through the windows at one end of the large room, lighting the paint-spattered planked floor and a huge table laden with half-finished canvases and stretching wedges and jars of fixing oil that glowed like honey in the sun.

There were paintings everywhere—hanging on the high-ceilinged walls, leaning in corners, piled one against the other. Some were even painted directly onto the plaster—there was a roughly drawn scene of an entwined couple and a fully realized still life that covered the bottom half of the far wall, so beautifully colored that the pears seemed to loom out of the plaster, ripe and succulent.

So many images, so many colors. It took her breath away, leaving her to stare in fascination and yearning.

This was what she'd wanted, what she'd hoped for. The dream her father had given her came rushing back, easing her nerves, so heady and magnificent she felt strong at the thought of it. She *could* become an artist here. She could be everything Chloe had been. She could make her father proud.

Smiling, she started to turn to Thomas, and stopped at the sight of the man standing in the light of the blindingly bright window.

Her excitement died as quickly as it had come; her tension came crashing back. The man—it had to be Jonas Whitaker—was staring at a huge canvas before him, his long dark hair straggling over his shoulders, his presence filling the room even though he didn't look at them. In fact, he seemed oblivious to the fact that they were even there. His concentration was focused on the easel, his brow furrowed between heavy, dark brows.

He was nothing like she'd expected. She'd imagined someone like . . . like . . . Nicholas. Someone charming and beautiful and artistic. Someone with grace in every movement and smiles in his eyes. But this man was nothing like her sister's fiancé. This man was overwhelming. Somehow unnerving.

Beside her, Thomas spoke in his smooth, comforting voice. "Whitaker, this is Imogene Carter, the student I told you about."

Jonas Whitaker didn't look up. He didn't move. Finally Thomas cleared his throat and stepped forward again. "Whit—"

"You said the name was Carter?" Whitaker kept his eyes on the painting. His voice was deep, so melodious it surprised Imogene when she heard words instead of music. "Of the Charleston Carters?"

She shook her head. "No. Of Nashville."

"Nashville." The artist eased the word past tight lips, lifted a brow, tilted his head. "Ah. The little Rome of America."

With an oddly stiff motion he set aside his pallet and turned to face them. His profile had been sharp—a straight hawklike nose, a short chiseled chin, deep-set eyes—but when he faced them that sharpness seemed to fade. His nose became only straight and well shaped, his jaw long, drawing out the oval of his face. Yet his cheekbones were still high and distinct, and his thin lips had an air of arrogant amusement in their set —as if he were aware of some cruel joke even as the rest of the world was foolishly naive.

And his eyes seemed to pierce right through her.

She stood steady beneath his gaze even though her heart was pounding, even as she saw the judgment in his eyes, the unwavering scrutiny in his expression. It was absurd how closely he studied her, as if he could somehow gauge her talent just by looking.

She straightened her shoulders and lifted her chin. The moment she did, he turned away.

He glanced at Thomas. "Can she draw?"

His dismissal of her was humiliatingly complete.

Thomas didn't seem to notice. "She's spent the last three years at Atkinson's in Nashville."

"Atkinson's? What's that? Some finishing school?"

"There's not much else in Nashville, I'm afraid," Imogene interjected apologetically. "But I've studied watercolor—"

"I don't teach watercolors."

"Her father thinks she may find her real talent in oils," Thomas put in calmly. "Even tempera."

Jonas Whitaker looked at him quizzically, a small

smile on his lips. "Her father? Has he studied art then? He knows something about talent?"

His tone was insulting. Imogene resisted the urge to wince and glanced at her godfather. Thomas didn't look at her. His gaze was focused unflinchingly on Whitaker, and when he spoke she heard a hard and unfamiliar tone in his voice. "Samuel studied art in Rome when he was a young man. He trained his oldest daughter, Chloe, and she was well regarded as an artist in her own right."

Imogene felt a stab of pain at his words, a wave of grief and guilt that only grew more intense when Whitaker frowned and looked at her.

"Chloe?" he asked, looking confused. "If she's the artist, why isn't she here?"

Imogene felt Thomas's hand on her arm, a reassuring presence. "Chloe died five years ago," he said in a quiet voice.

Whitaker said nothing. His lips tightened, and his eyes grew even more assessing as he looked at her. He was going to refuse her, she thought. He was going to say no, and the knowledge brought desperation surging into her blood, a despair so great she couldn't stand it.

Anxiously she tried to think of something to change his mind. Chloe—of course, what would Chloe have done? Imogene brought the image of her sister firmly into her mind, pictured Chloe's vibrance, her smile, her radiant blond beauty. Chloe would step past him and grab the brush from the easel and show him she could paint. She would force him to say yes.

In Imogene's mind, she saw it. In her mind, she felt it. She pulled the image to herself and took strength from it, imagined she *was* Chloe as she looked back at him, right into those clear green eyes, and took a step toward him—

Whitaker turned back to his easel.

The vision fell away. But before she could speak or plead or do anything at all, Whitaker spoke.

"Monday morning, nine sharp. Bring your own supplies."

She stared blankly at him, sure she couldn't have heard him correctly. But then she glanced at Thomas and saw his smile, and she knew she hadn't been imagining things. It was no dream.

Relief made her so weak she grabbed on to the back of a chair for support.

"Well then, we'll leave you to your work," Thomas said.

Imogene glanced at Whitaker. He had forgotten them already. He was looping his palette back over his gloved thumb, and she knew he wouldn't say another word, that in his mind they were already gone. It didn't matter; she didn't care. He'd given her the chance she wanted, had done what she needed him to do. She imagined what her father would say when he found out Whitaker had accepted her, imagined his smiling expression, the warmth of his words. *"You have made me very proud, Imogene. Why, you've done as well as Chloe could have, damn me if you haven't."*

They were the words she'd waited her entire life for, words of acceptance, of love, and Imogene knew this was finally her chance to hear them, her chance to be the daughter her father had always wanted, the daughter he'd lost when Chloe died.

This time, she wouldn't fail.

Not this time.

Jonas stared at the canvas before him, trying to concentrate on the sketched lines and curves, trying to ignore the footsteps hurrying down the warped floorboards of the hallway. But each one grated, every squeak accentuated his anger and blackened his thoughts until the painting before him became nothing more than a collection of lines—all flawed, each one mocking.

It was supposed to be his masterpiece, the vision he'd held in his head for years—a reclining nude, a wash of pale color against a dark background, an unforgiving, uncompromising courtesan. He'd dreamed about it, blended colors in his imagination, pictured the perfect subtlety of chiaroscuro in his mind, and now he was finally turning years of dreaming into the smooth, liquid reality of paint.

But it was a failure already. He had just finished the underdrawing, and yet his passion for the idea was gone, the fire had left him. He'd attributed it at first to the model. She was a silly little coquette, the dancer-mistress of a friend of his, who liked the notoriety of posing nude but contributed little else to the portrait. There was certainly no flash of intelligence behind her eyes.

Though he didn't need intellect. She was fine for his purposes; she had the right curves and the dark, lustrous hair of his vision. No, the problem wasn't her.

It wasn't his skill that was lacking either. He was ready for this, had been ready practically since the idea first came upon him at Barbizon four years ago.

No, neither of those things was the problem. Before today, he had known that something about the painting wasn't working, but he hadn't known what. Now he did. Now he knew exactly why his vision had left him.

It was because of the footsteps fading down the length of the hall. It was because of Gosney. It was because of Imogene Carter.

The thought brought a quick, burning surge of anger. Jonas jerked the palette from his hand, throwing it aside, hearing it clatter to the floor with a grim sense of satisfaction. Christ, he hated this. Hated it with an intensity he couldn't remember feeling in a long time. Gosney, in his elegance, had made it all seem like a grandiose favor, as if Jonas had volunteered to teach Imogene Carter out of the kindness of his heart, as if it were a generous and unselfish gesture.

But then, he supposed blackmail was too nasty a word for a gentleman like Thomas Gosney.

Jonas snorted. No, Gosney would never use the word blackmail, but there was no other way to describe what the man had done to him. Today's interview was a farce, nothing more; it was just a way for Jonas to pretend he had some sort of power, a way to maintain whatever dignity he had left. He had kept them waiting because he wanted to make Gosney uncomfortable, and he'd ignored them because he hated to be interrupted.

In the end, these little manipulations meant nothing. Both he and Gosney knew he had already acceded to Gosney's "request." He would teach his patron's goddaughter because Gosney had threatened to withdraw his patronage if he didn't, and they both knew the effect that would have on Jonas's career. Though Jonas usually preferred to forget that Gosney had created him—or at least, created a market for his work—it was the truth. New Yorkers were like sheep; they didn't know what they were supposed to like until they were told to like it. Two years ago Thomas Gosney had told them to like Jonas Whitaker.

Jonas frowned. Gosney was an important and influential man. If he removed his support, Jonas knew his other patrons would melt away as well, the money would disappear. He had already lived his starving artist years, and he had no desire to do it again, despite the contempt he felt for most of the well-heeled, well-padded men who paid him to ensure their immortality.

The follies of the rich, he thought, absently rubbing his aching left arm. Unfortunately, he made his living from those follies, and the hell of it was, before a few weeks ago, he'd liked Gosney well enough. The man was generous with his money and his praise, and he demanded little enough in return: a portrait of his wife, a landscape of the Hudson River covered with ice. Jonas had been lucky. Gosney's patronage had been a blessing. Until now.

Until Imogene Carter.

Jonas studied the canvas before him without seeing it, thinking about the woman who had just left. Imogene Carter. He couldn't say now what she looked like, even though it had only been moments ago that she'd stood in the middle of his studio. She was nothing but a bundle of gray wool and pale violet, and a wan oval face with big brown eyes that stared out at him from beneath an atrocity of a puce satin bonnet.

He didn't need to know more to know what kind of a woman she was. He'd seen her kind before, the cossetted, easily dismissed ladies of society—women who played at watercolors and drew pretty little houses in the country. Women who believed they had talent even though they were, at best, remedial sketchers who understood nothing about proportion and less about art. Women who swooned at the sight of a nude.

Yet he had agreed to teach her how to paint. The idea was absurd. Laughable. Infuriating. Christ, he didn't have the patience to deal with some coddled goddaughter, especially one who would faint the first time he brought a live model into the studio. One who would run at the first harsh word. . . .

Jonas closed his eyes and took a deep breath, wondering—again—why the hell Gosney had chosen *him* to be Miss Carter's tutor. Though Gosney had never been crass enough to say it, Jonas assumed his patron had heard the rumors; maybe even passed them along himself. God knew everyone else had.

Perhaps Gosney believed Jonas felt some kind of obligation to him. An obligation that would make him think twice before he harmed the sweet, bland Miss Carter. If so, it was most unfortunate. Patronage had never made a difference to Jonas when it came to his behavior. Nothing did.

That was the hell of it.

He pushed the thought away. Damn, he was trapped. He couldn't afford to lose Gosney's patronage, and yet he couldn't stand to be controlled by the man either. Not over some untalented watercolorist who knew nothing about the world except what she'd learned in some backwater finishing school.

Jonas thought back to the way she'd looked standing there beside Gosney—shapeless and nervous, spoiled and too sheltered—and he thought again: *the kind of woman who would run at the first harsh word . . .* He stared at the window, frowning. Imogene Carter *was* the kind of woman who would run. Whatever she'd learned in that finishing school in Nashville, it wouldn't be enough to prepare her for his lessons. One day of honest criticism, maybe two, and she would fly nervously back to her watercolors and her mama.

The thought was compelling. As compelling as the knowledge that if Miss Carter left his tutelage on her own, he would owe nothing to Gosney. If she made the decision not to continue, Jonas could not only keep his reputation—as marred as it was—he could also keep Gosney's patronage.

The beauty of it was that it would require nothing of him except that he be himself, that he treat her no differently from his three other students—the young men who had studied in Rome or at the Ecole des Beaux Arts in Paris before their parents had cut short their support and they had come to him. Students who had seen the great Dutch and Italian masters. Students who had a passion for art and a talent, but who still felt insecure enough to squirm beneath his exacting eye.

There was not a finishing-school watercolorist among them.

He remembered Imogene Carter standing there, exuding fragility, one of the delicate flowers of Nashville society.

He could destroy her with a word.

And he would even enjoy it.

Chapter 2

*H*e woke to the sound of whispering, to murmurs that stole through the thin walls separating his alcove bedroom from the studio, to hushed movement that sent the tapestry guarding the entrance swaying slightly. Jonas glanced at the pocket watch dangling from the scarred wooden post of his bed, groaning silently when he saw the time. Nine-ten. Christ, he'd overslept.

Wearily he struggled to one elbow. The creaking of the bedstead stabbed into his head, and he covered his eyes with his hand, trying to remember exactly what had happened last night—and whether it caused the pounding pain behind his eyes. He hadn't had that much to drink, he was sure, but then again, maybe he had. He'd stopped noticing the wine the moment that little actress entered the room.

Not so little, he amended, remembering Clarisse's bounteous charms. He'd gone out looking for something to bring back his inspiration, and instead the only inspiration he'd found was in the generous breasts of a redhead with a passion for painters and a hungry curiosity about false hands.

He groaned again, sitting up and grabbing his polished wooden hand from the night table. Clarisse had not been able to take her eyes off it, he remembered, studying the curved, immobile fingers, the leather straps dangling from the worn padded wrist. Cynically he wondered what had been going on in that libidinous little mind of hers, and then he realized that he already knew. She was no different from the others. Since he'd lost his hand four years ago, he'd been amazed to discover just how many women found it . . . intriguing.

Intriguing, he thought derisively, keeping his eyes averted as he strapped the hand to his stump of a wrist, buckling the leather straps and jerking a soft kid glove over the rigid fingers with an ease born of practice. *As if it were nothing more than an affectation.*

The thought made his head pound harder.

He took a deep breath and got to his feet. He should cancel today. He was drained and exhausted, and he still felt edgy, still felt the thin vibration of anxiety he'd hoped a night with Clarisse would ease.

It hadn't. It was there, flourishing deep inside him, biding its time, waiting to spring.

Jonas grabbed a pair of stained and spattered trousers from the floor and pulled them on. The voices of his students grew louder, he heard their worry, and he knew they were wondering if they should wake him or not, or if it was going to be like last spring all over again. . . .

He banished the memory, viciously jerking a shirt from the bedpost and pulling it on without buttoning it. Yanking aside the tapestry, he hurried out into the blazing brightness of his studio.

"Christ." He covered his eyes, wincing as the light sent pain shooting into his skull. "It's too damn bright in here." He tried to adjust to the sunlight, to see the figures standing before him. "McBride, remind me to ask that bastard Tate for some curt—"

He stopped short. A woman stood between Peter McBride and Tobias Harrington, a woman Jonas had never seen before. She was short, and—except for the voluminous folds of her skirt—delicate looking, with light brown hair that was pulled back in a barely fashionable, too-loose knot and skin that looked impossibly pale against the unflattering light pink of her gown.

He opened his mouth to say Who the hell are you? but then she lifted her chin and looked at him with steady, unwavering eyes, and the expression brought her sharply into focus, the memory came racing back.

Imogene Carter.

Irritation surged through him, and he realized he hadn't really expected her to show up, had hoped their meeting two days before was enough to scare her away.

He gave her a cold smile. "Well, well," he said slowly. "Miss Carter. I'm pleased to see you're so prompt."

She didn't look away, though a faint flush moved over her cheeks when he began to slowly button his shirt over his bare chest.

"You said nine sharp," she said.

"So I did." Jonas nodded, enjoying her obvious embarrassment. "It's a pity you caught me by surprise. I was looking forward to introducing you to the others." He motioned to the three students standing uncomfortably beside her. "But I can see you gentlemen have already met our little neophyte."

Peter McBride stepped forward. His tall, lanky frame made the movement seem clumsy. "Well, yes, sir, we've—"

"Good. Then go ahead and set up."

They didn't move, just stood there looking sickeningly anxious—except for Miss Carter, who watched expectantly, as if she were waiting for some great revelation.

Annoyance tugged at him. She was so damned naive. Some art school somewhere should have beaten that dewy-eyed idealism out of her before she even thought of coming to him.

Daniel Page stepped forward, running a nervous hand through his coal-black hair. "Uh—sir—" he said hesitantly.

"What is it?"

"The lesson, sir. What—what're we to paint this morning?"

Jonas stared at him, uncomprehending for a moment. *What're we to paint this morning?* Damn, he had no idea. He glanced around the room, searching for something, trying to remember if he'd given any thought at all to this week's lessons, and knowing he hadn't. He'd been too busy cursing at the portrait of the courtesan, too busy trying to wring inspiration from a canvas that mocked him with its silence.

The reasons for that empty canvas brought anger rushing back again, strong and vibrant, and he glanced at Imogene Carter and wondered how much it would take to send her running today, wondered if he should give them a statuette from his collection to paint. Perhaps the ivory carving depicting the "Hovering Butterflies" position, or maybe the large-breasted, round-bellied South American fertility goddess. How would she react to those? The thought was compelling, but Jonas dismissed it. It was too easy, and he had to admit there was a part of him that looked forward to the game—a small, sadistic part that enjoyed exacting punishment for Gosney's gall, that wanted to see the embarrassed flush on her cheeks, to see her face fall at his first harsh criticism. No, he wanted more of a challenge, something less obvious. Something so subtle she couldn't run to Gosney with it.

His gaze lit on a vase of dying red dahlias just beside the door. Dimly he remembered that Marie had left them there the last time she modeled for him—a week or so ago—and now they were wilted and faded. They were innocuous enough, and in any case, there was nothing else. Jonas crossed the room in a few strides and grabbed the vase, slamming it down in the middle of the table. Petals fell to the marred surface.

"Those," he said tersely. "Paint those."

They didn't question him. They never questioned him. Jonas stood back, watching as Peter and Tobias and Daniel propped up their easels and began preparing their palettes, working with an economy of movement, a familiarity that seemed graceful and efficient.

It was then that he noticed Miss Carter was just standing there, frowning with concentration as she watched the others' activity.

"Miss Carter," Jonas said softly.

She turned to him with a hesitant smile. "I'm not sure how to start," she said. "I'm afraid I don't have an easel."

Ah, how precious. How perfect. Jonas heard the winces of the others as palpably as if they'd been words, and he smiled coldly and walked over to her, pausing only a foot away, close enough so that she took a step back. He saw a flicker of apprehension in her eyes.

"You don't have an easel," he said.

Her smile wavered. She shook her head. "No, sir, I don't."

"Do you have a canvas?"

She laughed slightly and looked down at the case in her hands. "We worked mostly on paper—"

"Do you have a canvas?" he repeated.

This time her smile died. She looked up at him, and her fingers tightened on the case, her eyes shuttered. "No, sir."

Jonas struggled for patience. "No easel. No canvas. Tell me, Miss Carter, what did you intend to do this morning? Watch?"

Silence. Her jaw tightened; she glanced at her hands.

Suspicion crept into Jonas's mind, a dismal certainty. She was even more inexperienced than he'd imagined. Jonas suddenly knew she'd never worked a canvas in her life, was suddenly certain the colors in her case would be completely wrong for oil work. He wondered briefly, gloomily, if she even knew how to draw.

"Have you ever primed a canvas, Miss Carter?"

She shook her head. "No, sir."

"You've never ground colors."

"No, sir."

"Have you ever made an amber varnish?"

She licked her lips, and when she spoke her voice was so quiet he had to strain to hear it. "Never, sir."

"Christ save me." Jonas turned abruptly on his heel.

At his quick movement, the other students jerked to life, hastily ducking their heads, studying the dahlias as if the flowers had suddenly burst to vibrant life before their eyes. Jonas ignored them, striding to the space beside Tobias Harrington. Quickly, with the efficient one-handed movement he'd developed over the years, he unfolded an easel and grabbed a primed canvas from a pile leaning against the wall, slamming it into place so violently the easel rocked.

"There," he said, motioning to it, not bothering to keep the derision from his voice. "Miss Carter, why don't you show me if you can do anything at all? Perhaps we could even see if your drawing skill has progressed past stick figures."

Her head jerked up, and Jonas waited, waited for her to burst into tears, to wilt before him. But she only took a deep breath and nodded—a short, quick nod—and into her expression came a determination he hadn't expected, a willfulness he didn't want. He knew suddenly that she wasn't going to run, that she was going to sit in front of that canvas and try to impress him with a drawing ability he had surpassed by the time he was ten.

He knew all that, and so when she squared her shoulders and walked toward him, he stood back and waited for her, trying to control the disappointment coursing through him, the surprise that there was any steel to her at all.

He wondered if Gosney had told her, if she knew how bound Jonas was to his promise to teach her. He decided not. There was too much resolve in the way she eased past him, in the way she seated herself on the stool and took the piece of charcoal he offered her.

Too much acknowledgment of risk. She wanted to succeed, he realized suddenly, and he wondered why.

He stepped behind her, scowling at the pristine canvas. She had strength—he couldn't deny that. Though how much, and just what it was, he didn't yet know.

But he would find out. And he would find out soon.

He crossed his arms over his chest and leaned forward, breathing over her shoulder, feeling a twinge of satisfaction when she stiffened and moved away. "So, Miss Carter," he said slowly, in a whisper that sent tendrils of her hair dancing around her ear. "Draw me a dahlia."

Jonas Whitaker did not like her, that much was obvious. Imogene settled back against the padded seats of the brougham and stared out the window, watching the passing brick town houses of Washington Square with a grim sense of futility. His dislike surprised her. She knew that sometimes people were disappointed when they first met her, people who knew Chloe or her father and expected the entire Carter family to be as charismatic. Imogene knew the looks, the way the joy of meeting her faded with her first soft hello, the way they turned back to her father or to Chloe to continue a conversation that did not include her, that could never include her.

She was used to watching them, used to wishing she could be what they wanted her to be, that she could entertain them with a word or a smile. Until Chloe died, Imogene had been the one who faded into the background, the one forgotten when the talk came around to the Carters. *"Olive is so sweet, and you sim-*

ply must meet Samuel—and Chloe—ah, darling
Chloe. . . ."

It was true she was used to being ignored, used to
being passed over, but she didn't think she'd ever been
disliked before, at least not like this, not with such
. . . intensity.

She told herself she was imagining it, that it couldn't
be disdain she'd seen in his eyes, but the illusion was
impossible to maintain. She had not mistaken his
scorn, she knew. She'd seen it in his every gesture and
look, heard it in every word he'd spoken to her.

She didn't know how she'd offended him or what to
do about it. She couldn't quit—the thought of it nauseated her. She thought of her father's words to her before she left Nashville, his familiar disdain. *"Nothing
like getting away from those milk-and-watercolorists,
eh, daughter? Whitaker's exactly what you need, I
think. Something to put a little steel in your spine."*

Even with the buffer of distance the words stung.
Imogene put them out of her head, thought instead of
yesterday, of the glowing pride she'd imagined would
be on his face. She knew exactly what she would see
instead if she stopped the lessons and came home now.
Disappointment. Anger. There was too much at stake
to fail. This was her one chance to redeem herself in
her father's eyes, in her own.

Her one chance to make up for surviving Chloe.

Imogene swallowed and turned away from the window, closing her eyes against the quick ache of memories: the sight of her sister twisting in pain and her
father's misery, the touch of Nicholas's hand . . .

No, she could not go home to Nashville a failure,
regardless of how Jonas Whitaker felt about her. He
might dislike her, but he could not drive her away, not

until she'd learned the things she had to learn from him.

Not until she'd lived up to her sister's promise.

The resolve gave her strength, and by the time the carriage cleared the north end of Washington Park and stopped in front of the gothic pillars of the Gosney house, she felt better, composed again. When Thomas met her at the door, she gave him a reassuring smile.

"Join me for some tea, won't you?" Thomas motioned toward his study. "I was just getting ready to have some when I heard the carriage. I've been waiting to hear how things went."

She felt her smile falter, braced herself for the lie that things had gone well. From the beginning, her godfather had protested this whole idea. He had gone along with it only because her father insisted, because she had promised him she wanted it. But Thomas truly worried about her, she knew, and if he thought Jonas Whitaker had treated her badly, he would stop the lessons in a moment and send her home. She swallowed and hung her mantle and hat on the peg by the door. She couldn't take the risk of telling Thomas about Whitaker. Not yet.

"Of course," she murmured, following her godfather through the huge double doors that led to his private sanctuary. She took a seat in one of the deep burgundy chairs that flanked the pink marble fireplace.

"So, what happened today?" Thomas asked, his voice deceptively light. She saw the concern in his deep blue eyes as he poured her a hot, fragrant cup of tea.

She searched for the right words; words that would ease Thomas's worry, words that would make the morning successful without being a complete lie. She took the cup and looked down into it, swirling the pale golden liquid until it released its flowery aroma in steam. "We painted dahlias."

"Dahlias?"

"Red ones."

"I see." Thomas sat, holding his own cup delicately between long, well-shaped fingers. "Red dahlias. How interesting."

Imogene nodded; she felt the fine edge of tension between her shoulder blades, in her face. "He's a fine teacher."

Thomas gave her a quick look, and Imogene had the sudden feeling that she'd said the wrong thing. He didn't answer her, and the silence grew between them, along with her tension, until Imogene wondered if she should think up an excuse to go to her room. But before she came up with one, Thomas broke the silence.

"Imogene," he said slowly, and then he took a deep breath, his fingers pressed so firmly against the fine china of his cup she wondered if it would break. She had the thought that he was going to say something that pained him, but he only repeated what he'd told her before. "Imogene, I—I just want you to know that I'm here for you, my dear. If you have any problems at all, if Whitaker does anything—"

"No, of course not. What could he do?" Imogene spoke quickly—too quickly. When she felt Thomas's eyes on her, studying her, Imogene played at a nonchalance she didn't feel. "He's done nothing. Nothing at all."

She forced self-possession through the words. Thomas had always been good at seeing through her, ever since she was very small and he had come visiting every few months, bringing her a special book, or a doll, because *"A sick little girl needs reasons to get better, don't you think, dear heart?"* Almost as if he knew that even her own parents never made time to visit her sickroom, as if he knew he was her only friend.

She lowered her eyes and stared at the thin leaves floating to the bottom of her teacup and hoped he would believe her, hoped he wouldn't see how afraid she was of failing, how afraid she was of disappearing completely in her father's eyes the way she had in her mother's.

She looked up at her godfather, forced a smile. "It was fine today, Thomas, really it was. I'm sure I'll learn a great deal from Mr. Whitaker."

He frowned slightly. "You're sure?"

"I'm sure." She nodded and took a sip of tea, struggling not to choke as the hot liquid burned her tongue, scalded her throat. "You—you shouldn't worry so much about me."

"Oh, my dear." He leaned forward, putting a hand on her knee, and his eyes were soft and kind and as comforting as they'd been all those years ago, when he'd sat beside her sickbed, reading her a story. "If I don't, who will—eh? Who will?"

She tried not to feel sad at the words.

Chapter 3

"We're drawing hands, Miss Carter, not lumps of clay."

"Look at the delicacy of Clarisse's fingers, Miss Carter. Do you see even a semblance of that in your sketch?"

"Miss Carter, you do understand the rudiments of proportion, don't you?"

His words were like small slaps, each one stinging a little more, until Imogene thought she'd go mad if she had to hear him say *Miss Carter* again in that sneering way of his. *Miss Carter, Miss Carter, Miss Carter* . . . Coming from him, her name seemed familiarly profane, like a curse that had been uttered so often it lost its meaning, though not its wickedness.

Imogene leaned closer to her easel, clutching the charcoal in her fingers more firmly. From the corner of her eye she saw Whitaker make the rounds again, and she set her jaw and squared her shoulders and forced herself to concentrate, wishing he could move past her even one time without jabbing her with his words.

He never did. Jonas Whitaker stalked the room like

a restless cat, peering over shoulders, scrutinizing the sketches on each easel and finding fault with every one, firing out criticisms with the lethal force of a cannon. The only consolation was that no one escaped it.

Though that was hardly a consolation. His words to the others were edged with respect, while his comments to her held only derision. Imogene worked harder. She added veins and sinews and texture, she worked at visualizing the hand from the inside out. It didn't matter. She couldn't begin to make it perfect enough for him. Imogene frowned at the blowzy, coarse model sitting before them, struggling once again to find the delicacy he kept talking about, some hint of elegance, but there was nothing. Not even the woman's hands, draped as they were over a wooden pedestal for the benefit of the class—could make any claim at all to grace.

Chloe could have done this. The thought breezed through Imogene's mind, increasing her resolve. In her mind she saw Chloe, the way her sister worked a sketch, the clean, spare lines she drew, the pretty little frown she made when she concentrated. Imogene knew just how Chloe would have drawn the woman sitting before them today, how her sister would have found a graceful form even where none existed.

Imogene closed her eyes briefly, taking strength from the vision before she tried again. Perhaps a line here, a bit of shading there—

"That's it for today. Go home."

Whitaker's voice boomed through the studio, startling her so completely Imogene dropped her charcoal. She bent to retrieve it.

"Except you, Miss Carter. I want to talk to you a moment."

Imogene forgot the charcoal. She stiffened slowly and twisted to face him. "You wish to speak to me?"

He was in the middle of lifting the pedestal away from Clarisse, and he turned and eyed her coolly. "Is there something you didn't understand, Miss Carter?"

She shook her head and turned quickly away. "No, of course not. I understand."

"Good." He turned back to the model.

Imogene looked at her sketch, staring at the awkward lines, the amateurish form, and felt a sick sense of dread that only increased as the others began packing up their things. There was no reason for Whitaker to want her to stay after class, no reason for him to want to talk to her.

No reason except dismissal.

She inhaled deeply, tried to tell herself that wasn't it, that he simply wanted to point out some small thing —a more subtle way of shading perhaps, or a quick lesson on form. But she didn't believe it, not after the way he'd criticized her today, the ruthless needling. Dismissal explained everything much too well. She closed her eyes against the images that were too clear and too brutal for comfort. Jonas Whitaker towering over her, those green eyes glittering with contempt, his melodic voice harsh and discordant. *"You may gather your things and leave, Miss Carter. I don't have time to waste on dilettantes with no talent—"*

A touch on her shoulder made her jump. Imogene's eyes snapped open, she jerked around to see Peter Mc-Bride standing behind her.

"Don't worry," he reassured her in a quiet voice. He cast a glance at Whitaker, who was talking with Clarisse a short distance away. "You're not as bad as he lets on. He's a hard master, that's all."

It was impossible to smile at him, but Imogene tried. "You're very kind," she managed.

"I'm serious." Peter's pale blue eyes were concerned beneath the sandy wings of his brows, his expression was sincere and intense. He leaned closer, his voice lowered. "Some other time, I'll walk you to your carriage—we'll talk. There're a few things you ought to know about him."

Imogene frowned, but before she could ask a question, he smiled a good-bye and hurried away with the others. She stole a glance at Whitaker and wondered what Peter meant by the words, wondered how they could help her.

"Go on now, Clarisse," Whitaker said impatiently, a little harshly. "Go home. I'll see you tonight."

"Don't forget, you promised," Clarisse whined. "I'll be performin' at the Bow'ry. I'll leave a ticket at the door. Don't forget."

"I won't."

Clarisse giggled—it was a high, annoying sound. "Good then." She pressed against his gloved hand, and her voice came low and throaty. "And don't forget *that* either."

"I never go anywhere without it." There was sarcasm in his tone, a bitterness that puzzled Imogene, and she tore her gaze away, feeling suddenly embarrassed and intrusive, wishing he would end this now, wishing he would dismiss her, or chastise her, or whatever he intended to do.

She heard a quiet whisper and then Clarisse's annoying laugh, and Imogene looked up to see him escorting the woman to the door.

"Later, darlin'." Clarisse blew him a kiss, and then

she was gone, swishing from the room in a flurry of burgundy skirt and glaring red hair.

Whitaker spun around so quickly Imogene had no warning, and no time to look away.

"I didn't realize you were possessed of such prurient interests, Miss Carter," he said, raising a brow.

She couldn't help it—she flushed. "Sir—"

He ignored her. He crossed the room, stopping by the window. "Come here."

Imogene forced herself to breathe evenly. She got slowly to her feet, smoothing the silk of her pale lilac gown, willing herself to face him with equanimity. If she really tried, she might be able to talk him out of this decision. The thought faded as quickly as she had it. She didn't have Chloe's silver tongue; she didn't even know the first thing to say.

He pulled a large canvas from the wall with quick, impatient movements, then set it on a worn, paint-spattered chest nearby. "Here," he said shortly. "You're going to prime this."

The words didn't register for a moment. Imogene stared at him dumbly, sure she hadn't heard correctly, sure that what he'd actually said was *"Miss Carter, you are dismissed."* But then he lifted his brow and gave her that derisive little smile, and she heard herself stammering in surprise.

"You—you want me to prime this?"

"I believe that's what I said."

"But I don't know how."

"Really?" he said in a tone so heavy with sarcasm it sank through her like a stone. "Why do you suppose I asked you to stay, Miss Carter? To discuss theory?"

She licked her lips, afraid to say the words, afraid that saying them might make them come true. But she had to know, had to be sure, and so she spoke quickly, before she could change her mind. "I thought you were going to dismiss me."

"A tempting idea." He smiled thinly. "But not today. Today you're going to stay until you prime this canvas for me."

She worked to disguise her relief, grateful when he turned away to grab something from the table beside him. It gave her a moment to compose herself.

But he seemed oblivious of her. With sharp, decisive movements, he laid items on the chest beside the canvas: a thick, twisted tube of white lead paint, a small bucket holding thin sheets of a hardened, cloudy substance, a palette knife and a slab of glass, one jar containing turpentine and another full of oil. Then he crossed his arms over his chest and looked at her.

"I've already done part of your job for you," he informed her. He waited for her nod before he went on. "The linen's been wetted and stretched on the frame. Now it's dry."

"I understand," she said.

Ignoring her, he went on without pausing. "Your first job is to make the glue."

She nodded. "Very well. What do I do?"

"What do you do? You listen to me carefully. There's isinglass there—" He pointed to the bucket. "Boil it in some water until it's the consistency of jelly. There's a pan on the stove."

He said nothing else, merely leaned back against the window, arms still crossed, the fingers of his gloved hand tense and curled, eerily shadowed against the gray-white of his shirt. His whole body seemed stiff, as if there were some energy within him that he worked hard to check. But he didn't succeed completely. That energy blazed from his eyes despite his stillness, and she had the peculiar sensation that he missed nothing, that he saw her every movement as she grabbed the bucket of isinglass and added pieces of the fishglue to water.

The knowledge made her slow and careful. She set the pan on the small stove. "Until it boils?" she asked.

"Until it's like jelly," he answered.

"And then?"

"We'll get to that in time," he said calmly. "Now I want to know something about your education, Miss Carter. Who didn't bother to teach you how to prime a canvas? What was the name of that school? Allen's, or something?"

"Atkinson's."

"Ah yes. Atkinson's. What did they teach you there? Besides sketching pretty little houses and painting watercolor sunsets."

Imogene forced herself to ignore his ridicule. Just because he hadn't dismissed her yet didn't mean he wouldn't. He was watching for mistakes, and she could not afford to make any, could not afford to let him humiliate her. She called on her reserves, spoke in a quiet, controlled voice. "It was a very good school."

"No doubt," he said, and if anything, the irritation in his voice was stronger. "What did they teach you? The classics? Perhaps you read Shakespeare or Milton? John Donne?"

She shook her head. "No."

"You studied Greek then? Or Latin?"

The fishglue was starting to boil. Imogene focused on it, on the thickening, cloudy bubbles, the putrid smell, and wished she knew how to answer him, wished she were quick and clever, the way Chloe had been. Chloe would have tossed back her head and given him a challenging stare and said *"We learned deportment, Mr. Whitaker. Manners. You would do well to study them yourself."*

"Well, Miss Carter? What did you study there? Please, enlighten me. I'm dying to know."

Imogene kept her eyes averted. "Deportment," she murmured.

"What did you say?" His tone was insistent, relentless.

"The glue is boiling," she said.

"Let it boil. I asked you what you said."

"Nothing. It was nothing."

"Deportment—that's what it was, wasn't it?" There was amusement in his voice now, unmistakable and painfully harsh. "What the hell is deportment?"

The words came to her again. *"Manners, Mr. Whitaker. You would do well to study them yourself."* She opened her mouth to say it, to answer him. She heard a bare squeak of sound.

But before she could speak he pushed away from the wall. "Is the glue thick yet?" he asked impatiently, dropping the subject of Atkinson's so completely she wondered if she'd imagined the entire conversation.

She peered into the pot, gathering her composure. The fumes stung her eyes; the grayish bubbles were popping with loud smacks. "I think so," she said, relieved at his sudden disinterest.

"Then bring it over here. Now."

Imogene wrapped a rag around the pan's handle and carefully lifted it, bringing it to where he stood. He gestured to the chest, and she set the pot on it and stepped back. Her palms were damp again, she felt tension in her shoulders, in her face, as she waited.

He gave her the thin half smile she hated. "It's an easy enough job. Even you should be able to handle it."

She pretended to ignore the insult, pretended he hadn't spoken at all. "What do I do?"

"Brush the glue on the canvas. Do you think you can do that, Miss Carter?"

She was beginning to hate her name.

He pointed to the thick brush beside the canvas. "Use that one to spread the glue. There's nothing hard about that, now is there, Miss Carter?"

It was annoying how melodious his voice was, how that thread of amusement clung to it like a faintly unpleasant smell. Imogene picked up the brush and dunked it in the glue. The thick isinglass adhered to it stiffly, plopping off in globs when she lifted the brush.

"It's too thick," he said. "I told you to cook it until it was like jelly, not to boil it dry."

"You told me—" She stopped. Her fingers clenched on the brush. She set her jaw.

"You'll have to use it anyway. There's no more." He moved away from the wall. "Spread it on thinly, Miss Carter. Thinly."

She grabbed the canvas with her free hand. It slipped from her fingers, but he was beside it instantly, holding it steady until she could take it again. Imogene grasped it tightly, digging her fingers into the wood frame. She clutched the brush, touched it to the canvas tentatively, slowly, feeling his scrutiny, wanting to do at least this right.

Glue plopped in huge, gelatinous drops, skidding down the fabric to pool on the trunk. She dabbed at it determinedly, trying to spread it, but the isinglass was too stiff. It wouldn't spread, she couldn't make it behave. It just kept glopping on the canvas.

"Thinner, Miss Carter."

She clenched her teeth, dipped the brush again in the glue. This time, the sticky mass dripped down her skirt, puddled on her shoe before she got it to the canvas.

"Keep it even. Spread it thinner." His words were sharp. He moved closer, until he was right behind her.

She dipped the brush again. This time the glue dropped down the middle of the canvas. Quickly she tried to spread it out, swishing the brush through it, streaking glue in criss-cross patterns.

"Even strokes," he snapped. "You're ruining it."

She struggled for patience. "I can't—"

"Christ." He wrenched the canvas from her grip, flinging it away. It cracked against the wall, clattered to the floor. He grabbed another one from the pile beneath the window, a smaller one, and slammed it in front of her. "Do it again."

He would not break her. He would not. Imogene dipped the brush, stroked it once, twice, over the fabric.

"Thinner!" he demanded.

She tried again.

He yanked the canvas away. It crashed to the floor beside the other. He slammed the next one down so hard the chest shook.

"Do it again."

Imogene felt tears of frustration press behind her eyes, and she bit her lip and hoped the pain of it would make them disappear. She felt the drip of isinglass on her shoe, the hard press of the brush handle against her fingers. *No, he can't make me fail. He can't make me.* Angrily she swiped at her tears with the back of her hand, tried to focus on the canvas he'd set in front of her.

"Again!"

Imogene bit her lip so hard she tasted the salty, metallic taste of blood. Doggedly, clumsily she set the brush to the canvas. Too hard. The canvas shifted. She grabbed for it, but it fell back, out of reach, clattering against the chest, slipping to the floor.

He lunged for it. She saw him grappling with the frame, saving it just before it hit the floor, one hand curving around it, the other strangely ineffectual, and there was something about the movement, something about the way he grabbed the frame, the way he set it back on the chest, that was vaguely peculiar, a little disturbing. Imogene frowned, ignoring the canvas, the brush, staring at his gloved hand, at the way the fingers were curled yet rigid, oddly stiff . . .

His hand was not a real hand at all.

Imogene caught her breath, shock and surprise brought her heart into her throat. Her frustration faded away. *He had a false hand.* She couldn't believe she hadn't seen it before—it was so obvious. The single glove, the always-tense fingers, the way he favored his left hand. How strange that she'd never noticed. She found herself wanting to look more closely. It was all she could do not to stare at it, and so she lifted her eyes and tried not to look at it, to look instead at his face, at the wall behind him, at anything but that hand. But it compelled her and she found herself staring at it again, feeling strangely reassured at the sight of the fixed fingers, somehow . . . connected. . . .

"What are you waiting for, Miss Carter?" he asked sharply, looking up at her. "Do it—"

He froze. His whole body stiffened, his eyes locked on hers, glittering and green and so bitter and cynical she couldn't look away, even though she wanted to—Lord, how she wanted to. But his gaze wouldn't release her, and she had no choice but to stare as he brought his gloved hand up, infinitely slowly, inch by inch, finally cradling it in the other with an intimacy that was somehow both gentle and sensuous. Imogene felt the heat of embarrassment flood her face, she felt disconcerted and ill-bred, repulsed and curious at the same time.

"They didn't tell you," he said bluntly.

She shook her head. "I'm sorry."

He made a small sound, a rush of breath, an aborted laugh. "What the hell for?"

She didn't know what to say, what a person was supposed to say. Miss Atkinson's lessons in deportment had never covered this; even thinking of Chloe brought her no answers. Imogene dug her nails into the brush handle and finally said the first thing—the only thing—she thought of. "Because you must wish you still had it."

He didn't answer. Just stood there, running his fingers over the leather glove, looking at her with that odd expression on his face, and in that moment, she had the strange and startling notion that his false hand was the most real thing about him, that it somehow kept him human. She thought suddenly, *We're not that different.* He was no more perfect than she was. She opened her mouth to offer—she didn't know what—comfort, maybe, or perhaps only simple understanding.

But before she could speak, he nodded at the glue.

"We haven't finished," he said abruptly. "Until you get that canvas right, you'll be priming one every day."

The moment dropped away almost before she knew it was there, dissipated in the warmth of the room, spun away in steam. Imogene watched Whitaker grab another canvas, watched his graceful movements. It surprised her, and she realized she'd somehow expected him to be clumsier now that she saw he had a false hand. But he wasn't, and she realized nothing else was different either. The moment had left no lingering resolution, no sudden inspiration.

Or had it?

Imogene looked at his smooth motions and the arrogant expression on his face, and realized she was wrong. Something *had* changed. Something was gone. When she looked at him now she no longer saw the teacher with the power to break her. Now when she looked at him she saw just . . . a man. A man who could teach her if only he would. A man who could not force her to leave if she didn't want to go.

The realization brought sudden calm, a strength that fed her resolution. She had as much power as he did over her future, maybe more. He could not make her leave, and she would not go. The thought made her smile.

Imogene dipped the brush again and turned to the canvas. "Very well, Mr. Whitaker," she said calmly, not flinching from his gaze. "Exactly how thin shall I spread it?"

Chapter 4

She was not what he'd expected.

The thought plagued him all afternoon, circled in his mind like a tiresome nursery rhyme. He couldn't forget it, couldn't forget her, even though he'd deliberately visited Tommy Chen's in an attempt to do just that, even though he was surrounding himself now with loud voices and music and people. Too many people. The Bowery Theater was crowded tonight.

Jonas squinted and rubbed his eyes. The opium he'd smoked earlier was wearing off; he was beginning to feel the sharp edges again, the buzz of energy invading his languor. He could still taste the lingering traces of wine on his tongue, and the voices around him stabbed into his brain, the movement of the men pushing past him to scream at the stage made him slightly dizzy.

The Bowery. Christ, why was he here, instead of sinking into a well-padded chair at the Century Club— or even crawling into bed? He should be home, he knew, but he didn't want to go back to the studio. Not back to the mockery of the half-drawn courtesan, not back to the room where Miss Imogene Carter had looked at him with pity in her big brown eyes.

Pity. Jonas made a sound of disgust. It had been so long since anyone had looked at him with pity that he'd forgotten how unpleasant it was, forgotten how it made him feel dirty and helpless. As if he were some beggar who needed a penny or a word of comfort. As if he had more in common with the hot-corn girls who haunted the streets, selling their bodies and their wares, than with the men who spent their evenings in the plush tranquility of the clubs on Fifth Avenue. And the fact that it had come from *her,* a nothing little no-talent watercolorist, made him sick.

He should have let her go with the others instead of keeping her behind. He wished now that he had. But he'd been so confident that today would be her last, that he could make priming that canvas so humiliating and unpleasant she would have no choice but to quit. Certainly it had started out that way.

But then he'd tried to catch that falling canvas and everything changed. Not only was she not humiliated, she had found a strength he hadn't anticipated and didn't want, and he knew it was because she perceived his false hand as a weakness, because when she looked at him she saw a man who wasn't a whole man at all.

And he couldn't argue with that.

Jonas took a deep breath, banishing the thought, forcing the visions of Imogene Carter from his mind. He tried instead to concentrate on the actors cavorting on the battered stage. He searched the lights for Clarisse's buxom figure, suddenly feeling hungry for her crude but honest sexuality, for the avaricious look that came into her eyes when she looked at his false hand. There was no pity in Clarisse, and no pretense, and he wanted that tonight, wanted smooth skin and hot, wet softness, wanted to bury himself in her and let her moans and her curses fill his mind.

God, it sounded good. Jonas scanned the stage. He felt the vibration starting in his blood, the anticipation, the impatience. He would bring her back to the studio, maybe even press her to the floor and take her in front of that damned unfinished odalisque—a kind of sacrifice to the muse. He chuckled slightly at the thought.

How much longer until this damned melodrama was over? He tried to pierce the shadows of the wings, irritated when he saw nothing but figures he couldn't identify, people moving in fuzzy outlines.

Then he saw her. She was half hidden by the curtains, just stepping into the pool of light at the edge of the left wing. Her face was harshly lit by the lamps on stage, and it seemed sharp and almost feral, her whole body was tense as she waited for her entrance. Then he heard a loud "Better hide, b'hoys! Here she comes now!" from one of the actors on the stage, and Clarisse stepped onto the proscenium, breasts outthrust, hips grinding. He heard her coarse, guttural voice. He was close enough that her expressions seemed exaggerated both by overacting and makeup, close enough that he saw the sweat gathering on her temple, the outline of her nipples through her too-thin, too-tight costume.

He grew hard just looking at her. Yes, she was what he needed tonight. A rough, lusty coupling, a woman who tired him out physically, who involved him enough to make him forget Imogene Carter's misplaced pity and her incomprehensible smile and the fact that he hadn't been able to break her as easily as he wanted to.

He leaned forward on the bench, rubbing shoulders with the men sitting on either side of him, waiting impatiently. The smells in the pit were beginning to get to him, the scent of sweat and tobacco, the sickeningly sweet aromas of liquor and rotting oranges. The shouting was loud in his ears, the high-pitched whistles of hecklers pierced his skull.

When was this damned play going to end?

Almost in answer to his thought, he heard laughter and applause, and Jonas looked up to see the players taking their bows—a motion that nearly pushed Clarisse's breasts out of the low-cut bodice.

His hunger intensified. With a muttered curse, he lunged from his seat, crashing into the man beside him and nearly knocking him to the floor. Jonas ignored the man's glare and kept going without a word of apology, pushing his way through the crowd in the pit, past the vendors hawking apples and ginger beer. He glanced at the actors who were still bowing, laughing good-naturedly as they dodged the apples thrown onto the stage,

He took the last steps quickly, jumped onto the proscenium without effort. He saw the other actors turn to look at him and then look away, used to such interruptions, and he heard the shouted comments of the milling crowd. Clarisse was at the other side, and he strode toward her, not hesitating when an apple hit him hard in the thigh. He was beside her in moments.

"Jonas, darlin'!" she breathed, and he saw the streaks of sweat through her makeup, smelled her musky scent beneath her overpowering perfume. "You did come."

He grabbed her hand without saying a word, dragging her off the stage, to the wing, back to where the ropes controlling the scrims and sets and curtains ran in straight lines down the rough wall. There were a few people back there, moving sets and pulling props, but he ignored them and pushed her back into a corner half hidden by moth-eaten velvet curtains, into the shadows.

"Oh, Jonas," she said, giggling and pushing at him with her hands. "Not here, darlin'. Wait till I change my costume—"

He couldn't wait. The hunger raged inside him. He moved closer, pressing his hips against hers, his hand closing over her breast. He let go of her for a moment, long enough to pull her skirts up, long enough to free himself from his pants, and then, before she could pro-test, before she could say anything at all, he was inside her, and just as quickly she surrendered, pumping against him, her breath steamy in his ear.

She was everything he'd wanted, wet and hot and easy, and he thrust into her over and over again, wait-ing for the soft forgetfulness to take over, waiting for numbing mindlessness to descend.

He felt Clarisse's heated skin, the fullness of her breasts, heard her excitement and her gasps of plea-sure mingling with his own. Her eyes were closed, and he wanted her to open them, wanted to lose himself in them and forget today. But she didn't open her eyes, and he felt the pulsing rise of culmination and knew he was too far gone to control it, too aroused for finesse.

"Look at me." He heard his own desperation in the words, and hated it—and hated it even more when she obeyed him. When she looked at him and instead of her face he saw a different face altogether. He saw brown eyes wet with compassion, dark with pity.

Brown eyes.
Clarisse's eyes were blue.

Imogene groaned silently as the gesso splashed out of the bucket once again, splashing the once-pristine blue of her watered-silk gown. It was already stained past repair—spots of yellowish white dotted the skirt and trailed in streaks near the hem.

It was a small enough price to pay. For the first time in two days, she was doing something other than brushing glue on linen. She glanced up at the tiny one-foot square canvas in front of her. It was the only one she'd managed to do to his satisfaction, and she was grateful for that at least, because it meant she could go on to the next step—as painstakingly slow as it was.

She glanced at the woman posed in the middle of the room, baring her arms and legs and most of her back to Peter and Tobias and Daniel. It reminded Imogene of the days she'd spent in her father's studio, watching from the doorway as he and Chloe painted and laughed and talked about light and perspective and color. Imogene sighed and turned back to the bucket. She wanted to be doing that now, wanted to be drawing instead of priming, choosing colors instead of adding white paint to glue and water.

"Look at the shadows, Mr. McBride." Whitaker's voice boomed from the other side of the studio. "Clarisse's skin is more pink than yellow—see how the light breaks over her shoulder? What the hell is that sickly brown you're using? Try ultramarine for the shadows—or purple, if you're still struggling to copy Da Vinci."

Imogene winced involuntarily at Whitaker's harshness, feeling relief that she wasn't the focus of it—a relief that died the moment she heard his footsteps coming toward her. Her shoulders tensed; Imogene tried to keep her motions smooth and calm. *He's just a man,* she reminded herself, remembering yesterday, remembering that brief moment when she'd seen his vulnerability, his weakness. *He can't force you away.*

Though he seemed anything but weak now. She felt his presence long before he reached her—a stirring energy, a rush of thought and movement that seemed to make the very air shiver—and when he stood behind her she felt his gaze as strongly as a touch.

"You're doing a remarkable job mixing the gesso, Miss Carter. It usually only takes minutes, yet you've managed to stretch it out to nearly an hour. Truly amazing."

Imogene kept her eyes steady on the canvas, dipped the brush into the gesso.

"Like this, Miss Carter." He snatched the brush from her hand and leaned over her shoulder, spreading the milky liquid onto the canvas with clean, efficient strokes, each one even, each graceful. Then he handed the brush back to her. "Try it."

He stood so close she felt his breath rustling her hair, felt the warm moistness of it against her cheek. Imogene took the brush without looking at him, concentrating on keeping her movement steady and assured as she worked the canvas.

"You're dripping gesso down your skirt, Miss Carter." His voice was soft and mocking in her ear. "I hope you pay your laundress well."

He cannot force you away. Imogene gripped the brush more firmly, spreading the gesso over the canvas as evenly as she could. The liquid dripped onto the fabric, and hastily she swept it up, spreading it across, trying to imitate his clean, even strokes—and failing miserably.

"I told you to give it only a thin coat of gesso, didn't I? That will take all day to dry." His voice dropped to a whisper, he turned to walk away. "It looks like you won't get the chance to paint Clarisse after all."

Deliberately Imogene brought back the image of him yesterday, the way he'd stood there cradling his false hand, that moment of clumsiness and vulnerability, and it gave her strength. She spun around to face him. "Mr. Whitaker," she said, and her voice came out breathy and a little too desperate. She winced at the sound of it. "Mr. Whitaker—"

He stopped, looking vaguely surprised. "What is it?"

"Do you—do you think I might at least sketch her today?"

This time his surprise was too obvious to misinterpret. He frowned. "You want to sketch Clarisse?"

Imogene nodded. "Yes. Please."

He hesitated, and Imogene knew without a doubt that he was going to say no, knew he would condemn her to another day of dripping gesso down a canvas, of keeping her chained to these uninspired, unfulfilling tasks that taught her nothing about proportion or colors or form, and she clenched the brush in frustration, tried to think of what Chloe would do now, what she would say.

But then he smiled—a nasty, disturbing smile—and chuckled quietly. "Ah, well, I would hate to see you miss the lesson completely. You brought your sketch pad, I take it? I suppose you can draw Clarisse—or make an attempt, at least."

Her frustration vanished in the clean joy of relief, of victory. Quickly, before he could change his mind, Imogene grabbed the sketch pad she'd left leaning against her case and went to her chair. She felt the apprehension of the other students in the air, knew they were watching her, waiting to see what Whitaker's game was. She met Peter's gaze with her own, saw his uncomfortable smile, his mouthed "Careful!" But she only smiled back at him and sat down, determined not to let his warning keep her from taking advantage of Whitaker's sudden boon. This was the first time she'd ever been allowed to join other artists, the first time she'd ever been made a part of things, and she wasn't going to let anything spoil it. Not even Whitaker himself.

She looked up to see him coming toward her, his step slow and menacing. Imogene took a deep breath, ignoring him as she reached for a short and crumbling stick of charcoal. She worked to still the excited, nervous trembling of her fingers and focused on Clarisse, looking for the form as her father had taught her, considering shading.

Then she felt Whitaker behind her, leaning close, felt the heat from his body against her back. Imogene pressed her lips together, determined not to let his presence ruin her concentration, and suddenly he was leaning over her shoulder, bending close to her ear.

"To draw her, you need to truly look at her, Miss Carter," he whispered. "Look at her with the eyes of an artist—a lover. Can you do that, do you think? Can you see the line of Clarisse's leg, the muscles in her calf? The way the shadows fall across her ankle? Can you see?"

His voice was deep and quiet; she heard again the

rhythms she'd heard the first time she met him, the
music, and it was seductive somehow, so much so she
found herself following the gentle instruction of his
words, found her gaze following the line of Clarisse's
leg, the softly rounded calf that led to a dimpled knee,
to the fullness of thigh. Found herself seeing pale flesh
and ash-colored shadows she'd never noticed before.

"I—I see," she murmured, fascinated.

"Do you?" He was so close she felt the heat of his
breath against her ear, the tickle of his hair trailing
over her shoulder. "Look closely, Miss Carter. Do you
really see the form? Do you see the texture? There are
a hundred colors there. Do you think you could match
even one?" He said the words, and she saw every detail, the play of light, the colors, the smooth skin that
roughened at the knee. She saw things she'd never
seen before, in a way she'd never seen them. And she
thought suddenly, *I could paint this.* She felt the full,
perfect force of inspiration, the elation of vision and
the power of skill, and she listened to the soft murmur
of his voice and was mesmerized by it.

"When you look at Clarisse's leg, do you think of
Michelangelo? Do you wonder how he had the
strength to go into the morgues, to slit open corpses?
He wanted to study their anatomy, Miss Carter. He
wanted to see how muscles and bones and sinews all
come together, to show that in his art. Do you think
you could do such a thing—for art?"

The loud rapping at the door startled them both.

Whitaker straightened with a bitten-off curse.

The spell was broken. Imogene blinked; for a moment she wasn't sure where she was or what had happened, for a moment she couldn't believe it was over.
She opened her mouth, started to say, *No—no, please,*

don't stop now, but Whitaker was already striding angrily to the door.

"No interruptions," he muttered. "How many times do I have to say it?"

She felt numb with disappointment. She watched him walk across the room and wished he would come back, wanted so badly for him to keep talking. He'd made her see something—truly see it, the way she never had before, and this interruption now was unwelcome, as trivial and unimportant as his dislike and his contempt now seemed. She wanted back that moment when his voice and his nearness had mesmerized her and made her feel she belonged, that moment of artist's sight. For it, she would gladly bear his impatience and anger. He'd made her feel like Chloe in that instant, vibrant and alive and passionate, and it was something she'd never experienced in her life, something she never even thought was inside her. Oh, she would give anything to have it back, anything at all.

Imogene felt the keen edge of frustration as he reached for the door, flinging it open without regard for the nearly nude woman posing in the middle of the room.

"Childs," he said irritably. "It's before noon, isn't it?"

At his words, the man who stood in the doorway smiled broadly.

Imogene caught her breath in surprise. He was beautiful, with features so fine they looked almost feminine. Blond and tall, he was the perfect foil for Jonas Whitaker's darkness. He walked confidently, almost arrogantly, into the room. "You're overwhelming me with your affection, Whitaker," he said dryly, pulling off his gloves. "I knew you'd be ecstatic to see me, especially since I've just returned from Paris with some of that cognac you're so fond of." He glanced around the room, taking a cursory inventory of Clarisse, of Daniel, Tobias, and Peter, before his pale gaze came to a stop at Imogene. He stared at her for moments, long enough that she felt uncomfortable, and then his brow furrowed in surprise. He turned back to Whitaker. "Well, well. You have a new student? I didn't realize you were planning to take on another."

Whitaker shut the door. His frown deepened. "You're interrupting my class, Childs."

"Send them home early." Childs shrugged. The motion made the bright strands of his long hair catch the sunlight. It seemed impossibly golden against the dark blue of his coat, gold as a new coin. "Besides, you've got the key to my studio, and I need it now, before my trunk arrives."

Whitaker's mouth was set in a thin, disapproving line. His green eyes burned. His gaze swept Daniel, Tobias, and Peter before he jerked his head toward the door. "Very well then. We're done for today."

Immediately the three got to their feet. Imogene waited for him to exclude her, to tell her to stay, that there was some other project he wanted her to work on, another canvas to prime. But it was as if he'd forgotten her, and she felt a brief, embarrassing wave of disappointment as he crossed the room, disappearing behind the tapestry-hung doorway, seemingly oblivious to the bustle going on around him.

The last thing she wanted to do was leave now. But she dropped the charcoal stick into her case and gathered up the rest of her things anyway, heading distractedly toward the door, still thinking about that moment with Whitaker, the artist's sight—

"Not so fast, *chérie*."

She felt the soft press of a hand on her arm. Imogene jumped and spun around, nearly falling into Childs, who stood there with a small smile on his lips. "Stay and talk to me a bit, won't you, while I wait for your moody tutor?"

She stared at him, too surprised to do more than gape. Childs was the kind of man who never looked twice at a woman like her, the kind of polished sophisticate who noticed a Chloe but never an Imogene. He was like the men who had haunted her parents' parlor in Nashville, men who hovered, smiling and too kind, while they waited for her sister to make an appearance. A man practiced in flirtation and games.

A man like Nicholas.

She had no idea why he was standing next to her. A man like this always had a reason. It made her uncomfortable that she didn't know what it was, and she was too muddled to think it through, was still too stunned by Whitaker's teaching to care. Imogene stepped away. "I'm afraid I can't," she said uneasily. "I'm sorry, but I must go."

"You must? Whyever for?" Childs asked casually. He didn't release her arm, and though his touch was light, Imogene felt the slight pressure, the insistence in his long, slender fingers. He lifted a dark blond brow, looked at her with that pale blue gaze. "Is it because we haven't been properly introduced? I assure you I can amend that error, *ma chérie*." He made a slight bow. "I am Frederic Childs."

Reluctantly Imogene offered her hand. "Imogene Carter," she said.

He let go of her arm long enough to take her fingers in his. "Imogene." On his tongue the name sounded like the finest French delicacy, smooth and luscious. Vaguely obscene. "How lovely. So tell me, Imogene Carter, what you're doing in my friend's studio. I must admit I find it . . . curious . . . that Jonas is teaching a woman."

"My godfather knows Mr. Whitaker quite well."

"Your godfather?"

"Thomas Gosney."

"Gosney?" Childs's eyebrows rose in surprise. It disappeared quickly, melting into thoughtfulness. "How intriguing." He released her hand and gave her a captivating smile—one so bright it left her feeling dazed. "Well then, Miss Imogene Carter. If you ever decide you've had enough of Jonas, I hope you'll consider taking up with me."

So much like Nicholas. The thought made her a little sick, and she stepped away from him, wanting suddenly to leave. She grasped her case more tightly and looked toward the door. "Mr. Childs—"

"Ah, I've shocked you, Miss Imogene, and I didn't mean to," he said, smiling. "Please say you'll forgive me." Then before she could answer, he looked past her. "Here comes your teacher now."

"Tormenting my students, Childs?" Jonas asked mildly, holding out a large key.

Childs took it and stuffed it in his pocket. "I was just telling Miss Carter that she could come to me when she's had her fill of you."

"Take her now if you like," Whitaker said. He glanced at Imogene and raised a sarcastic brow. "I'm sure she's more than ready to be rid of me, isn't that so, Miss Carter?"

Imogene looked at him in startled surprise. "No, of course not."

Frederic Childs laughed. He touched her arm again, bent so close his fine hair brushed her cheek. "Ah, *ma chérie*," he said in a low voice. "I would be most happy to teach you how to paint—or anything else you desire."

His touch, his voice, the flirtation—it reminded her too much, too sharply, of Nicholas. Without thinking, Imogene jerked away—so quickly she bumped her easel with her hip. It scraped across the floor with a loud squeak that made her feel more disoriented and uncomfortable than ever.

"It's . . . all right," she said. "I should go." She grabbed her sketch pad and glanced at Whitaker, and was surprised to see the thoughtfulness on his face. A deep, quiet thoughtfulness that was somehow disturbing.

"Please, not so soon," Childs murmured.

"Jonas, darlin'!" Clarisse called out from behind the changing screen. "I can't find my stockin's. Are they in the bedroom?"

It was Imogene's chance.

She fled for the door.

Chapter 5

Childs stared at the door, slapping his gloves together in the palm of his hand. "Interesting," he murmured, and then he turned to look at Jonas. "Gosney's goddaughter, eh? How did that come about?"

Jonas's irritation grew. "He asked me to take her on."

"He asked you?" Childs smiled. "And you said yes —just like that?"

"That's right."

Childs shoved his gloves in his pocket, sauntered to the window. "Now why do I find that so hard to believe?"

"Because you're a cynical bastard, that's why." Jonas glanced at the door, wishing Childs would leave, wanting to be alone for a minute—or, at least as alone as he could be with Clarisse whining about. Something was at the edge of his mind, nagging him, something about the way Imogene Carter had reacted today, the way she'd gone running out—

"Is she any good?"

It took a moment for Jonas to remember what Childs was talking about. "She's adequate," he said, distracted, then cursed himself when Childs's brows rose in surprise.

"Adequate?" he asked. "You've never taken on an adequate student in your life."

"There's a first time for everyone."

"Perhaps for some. Not you." Childs regarded him steadily, his pale blue eyes burning with curiosity. "Why do I think there's more to this than you're letting on?"

"I have no idea." Jonas gestured to the door. "But you're taking up my time, and I have things to do—"

"Ah, yes." Childs glanced toward the changing screen, where the silhouette of Clarisse's lush body jiggled on the thin fabric. He smiled and raised his voice. "Clarisse, love, are you still there?"

"Bugger off, Rico," she cursed from behind the screen.

Childs laughed. "Still as gracious as ever, I see." He glanced at Jonas. "When did you take up with her?"

"A week ago," Jonas said tersely.

"Only a week?" Childs turned back to the screen. "Were you mourning me, *chérie*? Is that why it took you so long to find a new protector?"

Clarisse didn't answer.

Jonas stepped forward. This had gone on too long. He wasn't in the mood to deal with Frederic Childs now, even if it had been months since he'd seen his friend. He couldn't stop mulling over this morning long enough to concentrate on meaningless chatter. The image of Imogene Carter's face wouldn't leave him. It bedeviled him, nagged him; he kept seeing how ill at ease she'd looked when Childs was flirting with her. There was something about it, something that tugged at the edge of his mind. . . .

"I suppose it's too much to hope for fidelity from those you love." Childs sighed.

"Ha!" Clarisse grunted. "Like you didn't have yer little tramps in Paris!" She stepped out from behind the screen, her generous breasts crammed into the confines of her green satin gown, her feet bare. She glared at Childs, then turned to Jonas with a superior sniff. "Where're my stockin's, darlin'? I asked you to bring 'em."

"In the bedroom." He gestured to the doorway, waiting until she disappeared behind the tapestry before he looked back at Childs. "It's not that I'm not glad to see you, Rico," he said. "But get the hell out of here."

Childs grinned. "It's good to know some things never change," he said, settling onto the windowsill with languid affection—much to Jonas's dismay. "But I'm not ready to leave yet. Not until you tell me the story behind the intriguing Miss Carter."

Intriguing. That was one word for her. Jonas remembered the way she lifted her chin and asked him if she could sketch Clarisse today, the way she'd stared at the model instead of looking away as he'd expected. He had wanted to embarrass her, and she'd refused to be embarrassed, had instead been . . . interested. Not vulnerable at all, not frightened as he'd anticipated. He frowned and looked at Childs. "There is no story."

"Au contraire." Childs shook his finger. "I can see it in your eyes, *mon ami,* and even if I didn't, the idea of Gosney asking you to take her on—and you acquiescing—is simply too delicious to resist."

"It's not what you think," Jonas said dryly.

"How interesting, since I'm thinking nothing. I simply don't know what to make of this, Whitaker, so you must fill me in." He looked toward the bedroom. "And if I remember correctly, it will take Clarisse a full fifteen minutes to recall how to put on her stockings, so there's plenty of time."

Jonas said nothing, wondering if he could get Childs to leave by simply ignoring him.

"If you don't tell me, Jonas, I'll start the rumors at the Century myself. Let's see, how should the story go? Ah yes, how about this: You saw the girl and wanted her, and so you blackmailed Gosney into bringing her here."

Childs tilted his head, a gleam came into his eyes. "Or perhaps you've already compromised her?"

Jonas glared at him. "I haven't touched her."

"Why not?" Childs grinned. "She's a woman, and you have a certain reputation—"

"Not for innocents."

"Ah yes, she *is* that, isn't she?" Childs sighed melodramatically, leaning his blond head back against the window. "Rather delightful, isn't it, for a woman to be so uncomfortable at such harmless flirtation? What is it, Jonas? Are you all right?"

Uncomfortable. Harmless flirtation. That was it, the something that had been eluding him all evening. Everything clicked into place.

Of course. The idea came into his head full blown, so clear and simple he couldn't believe he hadn't thought of it before, couldn't believe the solution had been there, in his grasp, the entire time. Childs was right; Imogene Carter would run at the slightest flirtation—she'd done exactly that today. It was what had been nagging him since she left, the vulnerability he'd been waiting for, the weakness he needed.

He stared at the window, not seeing the wavering glass or the buildings beyond. Instead, he saw Imogene Carter as Childs smiled down at her, flustered and embarrassed and uncomfortable, stepping back from his touch. Miss Imogene Carter could bear criticism, she could withstand Jonas's impossible demands. But when it came to sex . . . well, that was another thing altogether.

He licked his lips, remembering her nervous clumsiness and imagining how she would react if he got her into a corner, the way she would try to back away, how she would grip her skirt or push at her hair. It would take nothing more than that to send her running, he was sure. Nothing more than a few well-chosen words, a look or two, maybe a touch.

It would be the easiest seduction he'd ever tried— and that was saying something.

Jonas crossed his arms over his chest, feeling a deep sense of satisfaction. Yes, it would work. By next week, Imogene Carter would be nothing more than a faint and vaguely unpleasant memory. By next month, he wouldn't remember her at all. The thought made him smile.

"What the hell is it?" Childs's irritable voice cut into Jonas's thoughts. "Either share your little joke or stop looking so pleased with yourself. It's quite annoying."

Jonas looked at him, and his smile deepened. "It's nothing, Rico," he said. "Nothing at all." He suddenly felt a great and strong affection for the man who'd been aggravating him intensely only moments before, and he motioned to the door, ignoring Childs's frown and Clarisse's rustlings in the bedroom. "Come on now, and show me to that cognac you were talking about earlier. I find I'm suddenly quite thirsty."

Imogene stumbled distractedly down the last flight of stairs, nearly tripping over the hem of her gown. The day spun through her mind in a kaleidoscope of images: Frederic Childs, Nicholas, Whitaker . . . Especially Whitaker. The thought of him eclipsed the others; Childs's flirtation was nothing more than a small and insignificant irritation, the memory of Nicholas was easily forgotten in the brilliance of those brief moments when Whitaker had shown her the artist's vision, when he had made her *see* . . . Lord, it sent her heart racing, made her breath come shallow and too fast. Excitement sped through her blood; she could hardly wait to return tomorrow, to learn more, to see more.

The thought of it absorbed her so entirely she barely heard the voices coming from the studios ringing the bottom-floor exhibition hall, bumped into two artists making their way toward the entrance, and hardly gave more than a nod to the man who held the door open for her. She hurried down the stone steps toward the brougham, anxious to get home, to describe the day to Thomas.

"Miss Carter! Miss Carter!"

The voice pierced her distraction. Frowning, Imogene slowed and turned.

It was Peter McBride.

"Mr. McBride," she said. "I didn't expect to see you."

He'd been leaning against the building, but now he

hurried down the stairs toward her. "Did he hurt you?"

"Hurt me?" Imogene stared at him in surprise. "Of course not. Why would you think—"

"You're sure he didn't harm you?"

The intensity of his tone was a little frightening. Imogene frowned, puzzled by his concern. "No. No, he didn't."

"Good." He sighed with relief, released her arm. "I should have waited upstairs. I planned to. But then Childs came in, and you were talking to him . . ." He looked chagrined. "I thought it better to wait here."

"You were waiting for me?"

He nodded. He took her elbow and steered her away from the steps. "Where's your carriage? I'll walk you to it, if you'll allow me."

Imogene motioned down the street, to where Thomas's shiny black brougham stood waiting.

"I told you yesterday that there were some things you should know about him," Peter continued, leaning closer, as if he didn't want anyone to hear, even though there was no one near—only a few people across the street, strolling in the cold autumn sunshine, and an old man who walked ahead of them with quick, shuffling steps, his booted feet rustling the few fallen leaves the wind had blown onto the walk. "I think you should hear them now."

The memory of the last hours faded in the rush of curiosity. There was such secrecy in his tone that for a moment she heard her mother's voice in her ear, chiding her to turn away from gossip, but Imogene pushed it aside. The truth was, she wanted to know more about Jonas Whitaker, now more than ever. She wanted to understand him, to understand why he'd been able to make her see Clarisse with nothing more than words, to understand his mercurial brilliance.

She turned to Peter, unable to keep the urgency from her voice, the demand. "Yes, please. Tell me."

His hand tightened on her elbow. Peter hesitated as if trying to find the rights words. "Jonas Whitaker is a —a brilliant painter, one of the geniuses of our time. Some of his earlier works are such pure inspiration. I'm sure you've felt the same way."

Imogene looked down at the immense flagstones beneath her feet. Peter sounded so reverent she couldn't bring herself to admit that the only paintings she'd ever seen by Jonas Whitaker were the ones on his studio walls.

"Though I have to say I was surprised to see *you* in his class," Peter went on. "Most women—well, they don't care for him much. I've seen works of his that even make me blush. He is a bit controversial . . ."

The word grated on her nerves. Yes, Jonas Whitaker was controversial, but she'd heard that word associated with him too many times. For her father, for Thomas, it had become a justification somehow, something that didn't quite explain him, that excused rather than questioned. "I've heard that too," she said.

"He's controversial for more than just his paintings, I'm afraid," Peter said. "There are rumors that he was thrown out of Barbizon a few years ago. They say he offended one of the other artists there, someone important, though no one knows who. The talk is that it was Jean Millet, that Whitaker was too friendly with his—uh—" Peter threw her a sideways glance—"his wife. They say Millet—or whoever it was—asked a friend to get rid of Whitaker. The two of them got into a fight. That's how Whitaker lost his hand."

Imogene frowned. The story sounded too easy, somehow, a little too pat, but she couldn't say why, didn't know why it suddenly made her think of the way Whitaker had cradled his hand yesterday, that strangely gentle touch.

"Do you believe that?" she asked.

Peter looked at her as if he'd forgotten she was there. "I don't know. I guess I do." His expression hardened. "Yes, I'm sure I do. He is . . . You haven't been around him long, you haven't seen the things we've seen. He's never the same. He's—" He took a deep breath. "I've been studying under Jonas Whitaker for a year now, and I don't know him at all. He's the . . . moodiest man I've ever known." His tone was perplexed, as if the words weren't quite right but he didn't know why.

"It's true he's always angry," Imogene offered.

Peter laughed shortly. "Today he was," he said. "And yesterday, and maybe he'll still be angry tomorrow. But not forever, I guarantee you." He looked down at her with an expression so intense it sent a shiver creeping up her spine. "I should tell you about last spring, I think. It's not an easy story to hear."

Imogene felt again that sharp needle of curiosity. "Tell me anyway."

He hesitated, and then he nodded. "One day—it was March, I believe—and it was a Monday. I remember because we hadn't seen Whitaker for a few days. We got there at nine, as usual. Daniel and I. Tobias hadn't started yet—he came a few months later. Anyway, the door was locked. Tightly locked, which was odd, you understand, as he'd been expecting us, and there was no note on the door, nothing to tell us where he'd gone or what to do.

"So we waited. Well, first we pounded on the door, but there was no answer, and so we thought maybe he'd gone to Goupil's for supplies. We waited an hour before we decided to leave, and we were on our way down the hall when Childs came up the stairs. He asked if class was over early, and when we told him that Whitaker wasn't there, that there'd been no answer, well—he looked so odd. He paled, I think, and then he raced past us and started pounding on the door, screaming bloody he—" Peter cleared his throat. "He was yelling, you know. Shouting at the top of his lungs.

"Daniel and I were just standing there watching, not knowing what was wrong, and there was Childs, making all this noise. . . ." Peter shook his head at the memory. "It didn't take long before two or three others came racing up the stairs. They all seemed to know what was happening; they were throwing themselves at the door until someone finally found a key, and then we all went inside."

He paused, and Imogene felt inexplicably nervous as she waited for him to continue. But Peter seemed lost in his thoughts, and finally she had to prompt him.

"Go on," she said in a low voice.

"It was like nothing I've ever seen." Peter's gaze was distant. "There were empty bottles everywhere, and one of the walls had been . . . smeared . . . with black paint. It was like a big dark cloud on the wall . . . It was on the floor—big black footprints . . . and five or six paintings that were all the same. They all had a single pattern on them—it was like a . . . a tornado, I guess. I don't know what else to call it. Nothing but blacks and browns. So . . . bleak."

Peter swallowed. "But the worse part was that he

was there. He'd been inside the entire time, just sitting in a chair, staring out the window. When we came in he barely moved—it was like he didn't even see us. He was just sitting there. . . . Then he looked at Childs, and he said, 'The madness is waiting for me, Rico. Should I give in to it?' That was all, just 'Should I give in to it?' as if he would if Childs said the word."

The horror of the moment reverberated in Peter's voice; Imogene heard it as clearly as if she'd been there in the room with him, as if she too had heard Whitaker's voice, that deep, melodious voice, flat and deadened with pain. She squeezed her eyes shut.

"How awful," she whispered, though the words were inadequate and she knew it.

"The worst part is that I keep hearing his voice. You know, I can't forget the way it sounded. It was . . . eerie, almost. Otherworldly." He shivered, shaking his head as if trying to lose the disturbing image. "He was like that for two weeks," he said. "Class was canceled. Then, suddenly, we got the message that he was back. That was all—just a note telling us to be in class the next day. And when we came back, he was like a different person. He was just . . . I can't explain it. It's the only time I've ever really liked him. It was inspiring to be around him. He was like a shooting star, I guess, I don't know. So brilliant it was hard to look at him. . . ." He trailed off as if the admission embarrassed him.

They were nearly to the brougham, and he stopped and turned to look at her. "I wouldn't stay with him except for those moments. He is . . . quite mad."

The words surprised her, disturbed her, but not for the reasons Peter gave her. Jonas Whitaker was insane. Imogene wondered why the thought didn't frighten her. She should be frightened. She should be horrified at the idea of studying under a madman.

But instead all she felt was the same surge of recognition she'd had the day she'd discovered he had a false hand, the same sense that he was like her, that there was weakness inside of him, and pain.

She thought of Peter's story, of Whitaker's words— *"The madness is waiting for me, Rico. Should I give in to it?"*—and she understood them better than she wanted to. She could make no claim to madness, or to the kind of passion Jonas Whitaker felt, but she understood those words. She understood the feeling of helplessness, the intangibility of will. She knew what it felt like to lose yourself, to search so hard for an anchor that any certainty at all was enough.

She had felt that way before. When Chloe died. When Nicholas left . . .

Imogene swallowed, pushing away the memories and the pain that came with them. Oh, yes, she understood. And there was something else she understood too, something that gave her strength, that made her want to rush back to the studio, to see Jonas Whitaker again, to talk to him. Jonas Whitaker had turned pain into genius, had dredged inspiration and redemption from suffering, and she wanted to know how, wanted to understand the secrets he held, the passion she saw on his face—the same kind of passion she'd often seen on Chloe's.

She was suddenly sure he could give that to her. After all, he'd already given her that moment today, that moment when she'd seen in colors and brushstrokes, that split second when she'd found the form Chloe had always seen.

Jonas Whitaker was touched with fire, and Imogene

had the strange and curious feeling that his madness only added to that, that the streak of brilliance her father and Thomas talked about somehow came from there. It was nothing to be afraid of, that madness; instead it was something to embrace, the price for genius.

The thought filled her with anticipation, with a stronger determination than ever. The things Jonas Whitaker could teach her if she could only get close enough, the things he knew. . . .

"Miss Carter?"

Peter's voice broke into her thoughts. Imogene looked up at him, at his long, drawn face, his unsure expression, and felt such a wave of gratitude for his candor that she gave him a bright, reassuring smile.

"Imogene," she said. "Please, Peter, call me Imogene—all my friends do."

Chapter 6

Jonas watched her enter the room with Peter McBride. She was laughing at something McBride had said, and her cheeks were flushed, ruddy from the cold, her small nose touched with red. She still wore that puce monstrosity, but her eyes sparkled beneath the stiff fabric, and she untied the bonnet and set it aside with a shake of her head that caused a few more strands of light brown hair to loosen and dangle against her throat.

She seemed . . . different today, Jonas thought. More confident, somehow. He watched as she unfastened her mantle and shrugged out of it, hanging it on the peg next to the door. She never stopped talking to McBride, who was also strangely animated, his hooded eyes unusually bright.

Something had happened between them, Jonas thought, watching the couple from the corner of his eye while he pretended to study the canvas before him. Something that had caused them to band together. He wondered what it was, wondered if he should be concerned. Perhaps Peter wanted her. . . . Jonas frowned at the thought, but then he dismissed it when he saw Peter follow her to her chair. McBride didn't spare a glance for the sway of her skirts or the subtle turn of her waist, he didn't watch her from behind the way a man does when he wants a woman. Granted, she looked pale and too delicate in that pink-striped satin, but there was still a shape there, still the soft rounding of hips and breasts, still the sensual indentation of waist.

No, McBride didn't want her; the knowledge eased Jonas's tension. It made it easier to implement his plan if there was no suitor about—though the idea that McBride might be any competition at all was ludicrous.

A sudden commotion at the door put an end to Jonas's thoughts, and he looked up to see Clarisse enter, Tobias and Daniel just behind. Jonas lifted the palette off his stiff thumb and put it aside. It was time to put things in motion. He made his way to Clarisse, his anticipation sharpening with every step.

She was fumbling with her cloak, and when he approached she glanced up, frowning. "What're you so happy about this mornin'?" she snapped. "My head is poundin', and it's all your fault. You and that wretched Rico Childs."

Images from last night flickered through his mind—warm cognac and deep red wine and tangled bodies—and Jonas smiled more broadly and held out his hand for her cloak. "I didn't hear any complaints then," he said, hanging the rusty black velvet on the peg. "You seemed to enjoy yourself."

She put a hand to her eyes. "I didn't know I'd have a headache this bad this mornin'," she complained. She glanced at the class and sighed. "So what d'ya want me to do today, darlin'? Somethin' that lets me sleep, I hope."

He leaned closer, brushing his lips against the coarse, hennaed hair at her temple, catching a whiff of unwashed, smoke-scented skin. "Your breasts, Clarisse," he said in a low voice. "They're exquisite, quite perfect. Will you show them to my class today?"

She giggled and pulled away, her blue eyes glinting. "You are a wicked man, Jonas Whitaker. A wicked, wicked man."

He lifted a brow, chucked her under the chin. "But you like it, darling, don't you?"

"I like it," she said simply, and Jonas felt a tug of satisfaction. *Ah, Clarisse, how simple you are. How very, very simple.* He smiled as he watched her make her way across the studio to the changing screen and disappear behind it, and then he looked over at Miss Carter and saw the gentle flush on her cheeks as she talked to McBride. A flush he hoped would soon become much harsher, much redder.

He moved away from the door and his students fell silent waiting for him. Slowly, aware that their eyes followed his every move, Jonas grabbed a chair from the big table and set it before them, positioning it on the platform Clarisse had posed from yesterday.

"We'll continue with life studies today," he said casually, deliberately turning his gaze to Miss Carter, smiling inwardly at her wide-eyed attention. "Miss Carter, I believe you should continue with charcoal this morning. The rest of you prepare your palettes. And let's forget about using raw umber for the flesh tones, shall we?"

He waited while they worked, waited until Clarisse emerged from the changing screen, wrapped in a rumpled piece of white linen. She tossed back her red hair and seated herself in the chair, and then, with the aplomb of a woman who'd dropped her gown for many men before, she let the wrap fall to reveal her breasts.

Jonas smiled. He refused to look at Miss Carter, at least just yet, preferring the keen edge of anticipation, allowing himself the luxury of imagining her expression instead, the way her face would turn scarlet with embarrassment, how her hands would shake. Ah, he could picture it so easily. He felt liberated already, and he concentrated on positioning Clarisse to emphasize her breasts even more, turning her body slightly, lifting her chin to elongate the line of her throat, raising her arm to cause her breasts to lift. He allowed his anticipation to grow, waited for the right moment, savored every lingering second.

"Notice the color of the skin," he instructed as he posed her. "Try starting with vermillion for the veins, then glaze over with the lighter colors. Remember Titian's *luce di dentro*—the internal light. Clarisse's skin glows with life—it radiates."

He touched Clarisse's cheek, ran his finger over her jaw, down her throat, a slow, caressing touch. "Remember that a silk woven of blue and red threads can't be duplicated by any silk simply dyed purple. Like the silk, there are different colors in Clarisse's skin. See here, the pink of her cheek, the bluer shadow of her jaw." He dropped his hand lower, skirting her collarbone. "See how it shines here; it's almost white in the light, but the sun adds just a bit of Naples yellow—"

Almost time. . . . He felt a surge of expectation, could barely contain himself as he touched the top swell of Clarisse's breast. *Now.* He smiled broadly, turned to Miss Carter. "And here, the—"

He froze in surprise.

She wasn't scarlet with embarrassment, wasn't averting her eyes as he'd expected, as he wanted. Instead she was sketching intently, her fingers curled around the charcoal, her motions slow and deliberate. There wasn't a hint of mortification on her face, not a touch of chagrin.

Disappointment pricked him, annoyance came sharp and quickly on its heels. "Miss Carter," he barked, feeling no satisfaction at all when her gaze riveted to his. "Do you know so much more than the rest of us that you don't have to pay attention?"

She frowned, looking slightly confused. "I am paying attention," she said slowly.

"Oh?"

"Yes, I—" She turned her easel so he could see her sketch pad—a confusion of lines, a figure that was barely recognizable as a woman's form—and he saw that beside each spot he'd named, she'd scrawled a color. Naples yellow by the shoulder, vermillion for veins, ultramarine shadows . . . They were all there, every one he'd mentioned.

Behind him he heard an aborted snicker, a cough. Jonas stiffened. Miss Carter was watching him with same expression she'd worn that first day, when she'd looked at him and smiled that uneasy smile and told him she didn't have an easel. He saw that same naive expectation in her eyes now, only this time it was more intense. This time it seemed to demand something.

It made him uncomfortable, it made him think of yesterday, when she'd faced him and asked to sketch.

Like then, he felt the overwhelming urge to humiliate her, to weaken that innocent strength.

Slowly, deliberately so, Jonas smiled. "I see," he said in his coldest, quietest voice. "What a good idea that is, Miss Carter. Words for colors. I had no idea you wished to be a writer."

She looked taken aback. "I—I don't."

"No?" Jonas thinned his smile. "Then perhaps you could tell me how those words resemble art?"

She seemed confused for a moment, and then he saw the dawning in her eyes, the flash of awareness, along with a strange disappointment.

"Perhaps you heard nothing I said yesterday," he went on.

"No," she protested in a low voice. "I heard everything you said."

"Really? Then perhaps you should try utilizing your knowledge, Miss Carter." He drew his hand away from Clarisse's breast, pointed to the sinew of her throat. "For example, perhaps you'd care to tell us what color you see here."

There it was, that expectation again. She leaned forward, looking thoughtful, her eyes narrowed in concentration as she studied the place he pointed to. "It's pink," she said.

"Pink?" Jonas lifted a brow. "Pink how, Miss Carter? Pink-white or pink-yellow? Do you see blue there, or purple? Green or brown?"

It seemed to take her an eternity to answer. "Pink-yellow," she said finally.

"Pink-yellow?"

She nodded.

"And here, Miss Carter?" He moved lower, to the

hollow at the center of Clarisse's collarbone. "What colors do you see here?"

"Purple." Her voice was more confident now, a bit bolder. "Gray."

Not confident enough. Jonas smiled. He lowered his hand. "What about here?" he asked, stopping at Clarisse's nipple. "Tell me the color here."

He waited for her reaction. Waited for shyness and nerves and the pink heat of embarrassment. He wanted it. And for a moment, just a moment, he thought he had it. He watched her freeze, saw her stiffen almost imperceptively, and he felt the pure rush of elation, thought *This is it. She'll run now. She'll run—*

But instead she gave him an unblinking stare. Instead, she licked her lips and said easily, "Pink. And—and brown."

There was not a trace of humiliation in her voice. His elation fell away, and in its place came anger and disappointment. Damn, he'd been so certain she would run, and her stoicism now enraged him, the way she lifted her eyes to his, the determination and hope in her expression. It frustrated him more than anything else she could have done, sent the blood racing hot and furious in his veins, and before he could stop himself, before he even knew what he was doing, he stalked over to stand behind her.

"Draw," he demanded, hearing the harshness of his voice echo in the thrumming of his blood. "Draw Clarisse. Now."

She tried to turn to face him. But he grabbed her shoulder and kept her facing the easel, and after a few breathless moments she did what he wanted. She leaned forward and touched the charcoal to the paper, made one tentative stroke alongside the scrawled words, added another for shading. Before she could draw a third, he wrenched the charcoal from her fingers, ignoring her quick inhalation, her half-spoken protest.

He leaned over her shoulder, and with quick, certain motions he drew the lines—one and then a second, another to show the roundness of Clarisse's breast, a fourth for detail. He heard Miss Carter's breath pounding in his ear, felt the tension in her body. He finished in seconds, dropped the charcoal into her lap and drew back.

"Is that what you were going to draw, Miss Carter?" he asked, pointing to the breast he'd drawn on her paper. Just a breast, nipple erect, intimate in detail, without arms or chest or throat to give it proportion.

He looked down at the top of her head, at her honey-brown hair. "Well?" he asked.

She lifted her chin, he saw the deep rise and fall of her chest beneath the candy-striped satin. "I wish I could do it half as well," she said, and her voice was quiet and even and without a trace of fear.

Her answer took his anger; the soft wistfulness of her words left him standing there, suddenly cold and ill at ease. Jonas looked away, stiffening when he saw Clarisse's raised brows, McBride's castigating gaze. Daniel's face was set, and even Tobias—silent, servile Tobias—was squirming in his chair. Suddenly Jonas realized that he'd forgotten the plan he'd had spent most of last evening plotting.

He had meant to embarrass her with Clarisse's nudity. Had meant to send her running from the suggestion of sex. Had meant to see her blush and squirm because she was too innocent and too naive.

But it was that very innocence that disarmed him, and instead of humiliating her, he'd lost control and humiliated himself. Her naive determination defeated him as easily as she'd defeated him the other day, as cleanly as if she'd looked at him and said once again the silly words that had been ringing in his head since she'd spoken them. *"You must wish you still had it."* Christ, so absurd: that dewy-eyed pity, the misplaced compassion. As absurd as the wistful longing in the words she'd just said. *"I wish I could do it half as well."*

He stepped away from her chair and turned his back to them all, closing his eyes, trying to calm his racing heart. No one had ever done that to him. No one in a very long time, and it was intolerable that it was happening now, and with a woman who was nothing more than a pampered backwoods daughter, an innocent without wit or cleverness or beauty. It was intolerable that when he looked at her he saw everything he hated —the powerlessness that had forced him to take her on, his weakness—

His fear.

There was no more time for subtlety. It would take more than the suggestion of sexuality to make her run. It would take seduction itself. Much as it annoyed him, there was no other choice. Jonas rubbed his eyes, inhaled deeply, and waited for the drumming in his head to subside.

"Sir?" It was Daniel's voice, young and concerned and a little frightened.

Jonas waved his hand. "Go on," he said. "Continue."

He waited until he heard the scratching of charcoal on paper again, the hiss of brushstrokes and the wet suck of paint, and then he walked as casually as he could to the empty canvas in the corner by the window, to the half-drawn odalisque, and forced himself to remember what was at stake. He waited until he was calm enough to trust his voice, and then he sat on the windowsill, feeling the cold from the windows against his back, letting it soothe him before he spoke.

"Miss Carter," he said, and then he noticed that she hadn't moved, that she was sitting there watching him. He forced himself to speak evenly, quietly. "I would like you to stay after class today."

She nodded shortly, but she didn't look away, and when he saw the look in her eyes, the quiet speculation touched with pity, he felt the baffling rage growing again, and he made himself turn away to look at the courtesan. But the sight of the unfinished canvas only angered him again, and he closed his eyes and leaned his head back against the cold glass. The motion reminded him of Rico, of yesterday. Where the hell was Childs? He found himself thinking of last night's fine French cognac, wishing he had a glass of it in his hand. *A drink for courage.* The thought brushed through his mind, and he smiled derisively, wondering when things had degenerated so far that he needed a swig of cognac to attempt a kiss.

Not just any kiss, he reminded himself. A kiss calculated to frighten. A kiss for a woman for whom he felt nothing but anger and resentment, for whom he felt not the slightest attraction. And how best to go about it? He couldn't just go up to her and grab her. No, best to do it subtly, to approach things carefully, as if he were attempting to seduce one of the rich daughters who came to him to have their portraits painted, one of the silly, vapid creatures who simpered and preened within sight of their starched chaperones but watched him with knowing, too-wise eyes. They were easy to win over; he'd had enough of them to know. He knew how they changed the moment the chaperone's back was turned, how they talked of grand passion and rebellion when all they really wanted was wooing and romance and fops who professed their love with every breath.

But Imogene Carter was not like them, and his intentions were not the same. He didn't want consummation. He didn't want pleasure. He spent the rest of the lesson turning ideas over in his mind, wondering over the best way to approach her. He paced the room wondering. He criticized his students' work, offered suggestions, but by the time the class was over, he couldn't remember who had done well and who hadn't, who was the best at blending colors, who had drawn Clarisse with proportion and grace. He couldn't remember what Miss Carter had drawn at all.

He was aware that they were all watching him with wary eyes, and he almost felt their questions hovering as he moved from easel to easel. *What will he say? Why hasn't he yelled at her, at me? What made him so damned angry earlier?* So many questions, though they should be accustomed to his erratic behavior by now. It surprised him that they weren't, made him feel faintly ashamed, and that only increased his preoccupation—so much so that Jonas barely said a word when the lesson ended. He only waited while they all gathered up their things.

All except Miss Carter. She watched them leave, and Jonas saw the way she worked over her drawing with barely suppressed energy. Nervousness, he thought, feeling a stab of satisfaction that only grew when he saw a reluctant McBride walk out the door.

Clarisse stepped from behind the changing screen, buttoning her bodice. She turned to Jonas with a smile. "You want me to stay, darlin'?" she asked.

Jonas shook his head. "Go on," he said. "I'll see you later."

Clarisse's brow furrowed. She looked at Miss Carter, then back to him. "But—"

"Go on."

Her mouth tightened, a perfect little rosebud of red-stained pink, and resentfully she moved toward the door. But not before she brushed by him, not before her hand grazed the front of his trousers, her fingers tracing him through the cloth. It seemed she was not so upset about last night after all.

He waited until she disappeared through the door, until the heavy oak slammed shut behind her, before he turned to Miss Carter.

He said nothing. He let the silence stretch between them until it seemed nearly unbearable, and then he moved toward her, stopping just behind her, barely a hairsbreadth away. He felt the heat of her shoulders at his thighs. He glanced down at the easel in front of her, taking in the shaky lines she'd drawn, the tentative, minimal shadowing, the outline of Clarisse's body without detail—the swelling of breast without a nipple, with nothing but two-dimensional heaviness.

There was no talent in the drawing; or rather, there was some skill, but it was mediocre, passionless, technique without magic, like a mildly pleasing story without emotion or depth. She would never be a great painter; the most she could hope for was to become a decent portraitist—or perhaps even one of those traveling artists who went from town to town drawing prize pigs for awestruck farmers. But a great painter? Ah no, never that.

Still, there was enough to work with for now.

She drew a breath. "Sir?" she asked finally, and he heard again that strange hope in her voice, the slight giddiness that jibed badly with his earlier assessment of nerves. "Is there something you wanted?"

He refrained from making the most obvious answer, the lie he couldn't support and she wouldn't believe. Instead, he leaned over her shoulder, plucking the bit of charcoal from her fingers like before. But this time he pressed against her back, let his hair fall over her shoulder, felt it drag along her cheek.

He heard the sharp catch of her breath, felt the infinitesimal freeze of her body. He could almost hear her heart pounding against her chest.

"You're falling behind, Miss Carter," he whispered against her ear. "I thought, perhaps, a private lesson would be in order. Also, I wanted to apologize for today."

She turned to look at him; he saw the surprise in her eyes. He half expected her to say something, to make some coy little remark, but she merely nodded and turned back to face the easel. "It's quite all right," she said. "Shall we get started?"

Jonas frowned. Her composure was surprising, her calm acceptance. But then, he supposed she didn't know him well enough to know he rarely apologized for anything. "It was unforgivable. I should not have lost my temper."

A momentary pause. Then, "I understand."

"Do you?" He leaned closer; he could smell the heat of her, the fragrance of—what was it?—vanilla maybe, or . . . or almond. Very subtle. Almost masked by the harsh scent of paint. He whispered against her ear. "I confess I'm not used to having women in my class. Perhaps I'm a bit more . . . thoughtless . . . than I should be. Forgive me?"

He saw the erratic pulse in her throat, the quivering flutter beneath her pale skin. Slowly, slowly, he dropped the piece of charcoal he'd taken from her, stroked her clenched fingers with his thumb.

She inhaled slowly, pulled away. "Sir, shouldn't we start?"

He didn't budge. "Start what?"

"The lesson."

It amused him, her attempt to maintain the illusion. Jonas cocked a brow, smiled a tiny smile. "The lesson," he repeated. "But, Miss Carter, this *is* the lesson. We have started." He let the charcoal fall from his hand, and then he reached down again, curling his fingers around hers, stilling them. Again he stroked her fingers with his thumb. "This, for example, this is a lesson in how to touch." He raised her stiff hand to his mouth, brushed her knuckles with his lips before he let her hand fall again to her lap. "And this—this is a lesson in caressing." He laid his finger against her cheek, stroked the smooth, warm line of her jaw. The blood pumped into her cheeks; for a moment Jonas imagined he felt the heat of it.

He let his finger fall beneath her chin, felt her convulsive swallow as he stroked her throat, stopping at the high rounded collar. "And now, perhaps, we could try a kiss—"

She wrenched away from him, her shoulder cracking into his chest. He staggered back. She got to her feet so violently her skirt grabbed the chair leg. The fragile stool crashed to the floor. Jonas caught his balance just before he fell, awkwardly saving himself with his good hand, clumsily moving into a crouch.

She was staring at him, her breath coming fast and shallow, her eyes wary. She had grabbed something off a nearby shelf, ostensibly to protect herself, though she wasn't wielding it like a weapon, and she didn't try to use it against him when he got to his feet to face her. She didn't move at all.

He smiled at her, let his contempt show on his face. He gestured to the door. "Go ahead, darling. Run away. Run on home to your goddaddy and tell him all about it."

She flinched as if he'd hit her. Then something melted in her eyes, the wariness disappeared, replaced by something else that made her eyes seem too wide and too brown—almost black. Something he'd seen before. He stared at her, trying to decide what it was, startled when she laid the slender stone statuette on the shelf beside her and faced him with a strange equanimity.

"I know," she said. Her voice was calm and steady, soothing in its evenness. "You don't have to pretend. I know."

Jonas frowned in confusion. What the hell was she talking about? "You know what?" he asked.

"Peter told me."

"Told you what?"

She glanced toward the door, and then back at him. "I know what they say about you. That you're . . . mad."

He hadn't thought she could say anything to affect him, and for a moment he didn't understand her, thought she was talking about anger. But then he real-

ized her meaning, it translated itself in his mind: *mad
. . . insane.*

Insane.

He hadn't expected to hear that—not from her.
Most people never said it. Most people were afraid to
even think it. And yet here she was, offering it to him
as if it were an excuse for everything, begging him to
take it as if it somehow made everything all right. It
was startling, it was uncomfortable, and strangely, it
hurt. Not as much as it had when his brother Charlie
had said it, or when his sister thought it, or when his
father scrawled it on the papers committing him to the
Bloomingdale Lunatic Asylum. But still, it hurt, and in
the wake of that startling realization, he suddenly understood something else, suddenly he knew what he
was seeing in her eyes, why that look was so uncomfortably familiar.

It was that damnable compassion again, that
wretched pity.

It was unbearable.

"Well, if they say it, it must be true," he said, ad-
vancing slowly, angrily, feeling a vindictive pleasure
when she backed away. "It gives you even more of a
reason to run, doesn't it, darling?" He kept moving,
forcing her back and back and back, watching her trip
over her skirt. "Go ahead and run. Run for the door."
She was nearly to the corner now, nearly trapped. He
kept going. "Hurry now, before I change my mind."

She bumped into the wall behind her, jumping at
the contact, and he saw her nervousness, saw also the
way she lifted her chin to face him, her unflinching,
determined expression. He told himself to release her.
Told himself to stop, but he couldn't. The word was
ringing in his mind: *insane, insane, insane,* and he

wanted to punish her for saying it, wanted to punish her for the way she offered it to him, as if he weren't to blame, as if he couldn't control himself.

Because it was true, it was all true, and he hated that about himself, hated that she'd seen it.

He trapped her with his forearms, heard the dull thud of his wooden hand against the wall, felt the vibration of it into his wrist, his arm.

"Too late," he whispered. "You should have run."

He pressed against her, pressed his whole body against her, felt her legs and her hips and her breasts through the voluminous petticoats, the boning of her corset. She was stiff, inviolate in her armor, but he heard the harsh gasp of her breath, imagined he felt her fear shiver in the air around them.

Now, he thought, *now for the* pièce de résistance, and he bent his head to kiss her, to rape her with his mouth, to send her running away.

And stopped.

She was staring at him, her brown eyes soft, her mouth set, and though he saw the tiny vibration of the pulsepoint in her throat, there was no fear in her gaze at all. Nothing but a strange and fatal honesty, an empathy he could not imagine, a strength he could not endure.

"What?" he demanded, unable to stop himself. "What in the hell are you thinking?"

"I want to know what it's like to be you," she said, and her voice was thin and hushed and hard to hear. "I want to understand."

As quiet as her words were, they crashed through him, stole his breath, brought the anger and shock rising so violently in him that he jerked away as if her very touch were poison.

"I want to know what it's like . . ."

He pointed to the door, stunned to find that he was shaking, that his finger was trembling. "Get out!" He screamed the words, his voice was roaring in his head, painfully loud. He saw her cowering in the corner and he wanted to hurt her. "Get the hell out of here."

This time she did as he ordered. This time she picked up her skirts and ran, a blur of pink and white. He heard the door open and slam closed again, heard her steps on the warped boards of the hall, the creaking stairs.

It wasn't until she'd been gone a full five minutes that his rage left him. Without it, he felt sick and hollow.

"I want to know what it's like to be you."

Christ.

Chapter 7

"He had you paint what?" Katherine Gosney stopped in surprise, creamed peas dripped from the fork suspended in her hand. "A nude? Oh, good Lord. . . ."

"It's what artists do, love," Thomas interjected quietly.

"Artists yes, but not unmarried young women." Katherine's fine patrician features tightened in distaste. "Dear, shouldn't you have protested? It's so indecent."

Thomas spoke before Imogene could answer. "Whitaker's done more indecent things than that," he said calmly. "Remember last spring, when—"

"Really, Thomas." Katherine threw a glance at Imogene. "That's hardly appropriate dinner conversation."

"Oh, for God's sake. Imogene's a grown woman."

"Her mother would swoon if she knew what you were letting Whitaker teach her."

"I don't have any control over what Whitaker

teaches her." Thomas took a sip of wine. "You know I warned Samuel."

"I'm sure he didn't really understand."

Imogene stared down at her plate, letting the conversation pass over her. She was on the outskirts again, letting others discuss her as if she weren't in the room, and after today it felt unfamiliar and strange. After the morning she'd spent with Jonas Whitaker, she didn't feel herself at all. She felt as if she were on the verge of . . . something. Some new and stunning discovery.

"It's all right," she said. "It doesn't matter, really."

Her words brought sudden silence.

Thomas looked startled, as if he'd truly forgotten she was there, and then an embarrassed flush spread over his face.

Katherine's shoulders slumped beneath the violet moiré silk of her gown. She sighed, her features softened with real affection. "Oh, dear. I'm sorry, I didn't mean to exclude you. I'm afraid I was a bit overzealous. It's just that drawing nudes is hardly an appropriate pastime for a young woman."

"A young woman studying to be an artist," Thomas reminded his wife quietly. "Imogene can't waste her talent painting flowers and sunsets. She needs to learn classic forms. Do you know of any artist who hasn't attempted a nude at some point in his career?"

"I'm sure there are some," Katherine said stubbornly. "What about those men who paint landscapes? Those—what do they call themselves? The Hudson Valley painters?"

"Hudson River," Thomas corrected with a sigh. "And maybe Imogene's not interested in painting stilted landscapes."

"You only say that because you don't like them."
Katherine argued. "Maybe she does."

Imogene sighed. It didn't really matter; she was having trouble concentrating on the conversation anyway.

She could not get Jonas Whitaker out of her mind.
Since yesterday, when she'd seen his passion firsthand
and felt for herself how exhilarating art could be, all
she'd wanted was to feel it again, to taste it, to touch
it, to understand it. Peter's story had only added to
that fascination, and now not an hour passed that she
wasn't thinking about it, yearning for it.

She had wanted that today too, had gone to class
hoping it would happen again, praying he would lean
over her shoulder and show her how to find that artist's vision again. When he'd asked her to stay after
class, she was sure her prayers had been answered, and
the excitement that possessed her made her fingers
tremble so badly she could barely hold the charcoal.
When he'd leaned over her shoulder and started to
draw, she'd thought *Yes, oh, yes, let me feel it again.*

Instead she'd felt something completely different.

Instead she'd felt desire.

Imogene's throat tightened at the memory. It had
startled her, that desire. His caress, the warmth of his
breath against her skin, the curiously invasive way his
hair had brushed her cheek. . . . They were the kind
of touches she hadn't experienced for a long time,
touches she'd convinced herself it was better not to
remember, not to expect. Touches that spoke of an intimacy that didn't exist, an intimacy that reminded her
of other things. Of tangled sheets and loosened hair
and moonlight slanting across bare skin.

Of Nicholas.

It was why she'd jerked away from Whitaker this

morning, why she'd run. She could not bear to think of
Nicholas, could not bear to feel desire when Jonas
Whitaker touched her. Because she knew he was simply teasing her the way the men in her father's circle
teased, a flirtation that was insincere and painful when
she was the focus. She knew men weren't interested in
her that way. She knew it because Nicholas had told
her so, and even if he hadn't, she'd seen it every time
she'd stammered a coquettish reply or tried to smile,
had seen the small smiles that told her more clearly
than words that she was nothing more than a charity
case, an obligation to fulfill.

But in spite of the fact that she knew all that,
Imogene had watched the way those same men were
with Chloe, had seen their broad smiles and genuine
laughter—and she had wished just once that someone
would flirt with her the same way.

Well, she'd got her wish in spades. First with her
sister's fiancé, and then with Jonas Whitaker. And
she'd embarrassed herself both times. Today she
should have done nothing more than give Whitaker a
knowing smile, should have treated his flirtation as
something casual, should have responded as if he'd
said nothing more important than "I hope you're feeling well today."

She should not have felt desire.

Lord, what a fool she'd been. His flirtation meant
nothing. It was ludicrous—and dangerous—to assume
it meant more. Men like Jonas Whitaker did not look
twice at women like her, and she told herself it wasn't
what she wanted from him anyway. She told herself
she wanted an education in art, to understand his brilliance. Anything more was absurd.

She told herself all those things, but still she

couldn't get Whitaker out of her mind. His attention had been flattering. It had been . . . more . . . than that. Bewildering. Beguiling. As compelling as his brilliance.

Imogene squeezed her eyes shut. Thank God he had turned on her the way he had. His anger had saved her, had erased her embarrassment, had reminded her of her real purpose—

". . . Dear, what do you think?"

Katherine's voice shattered Imogene's thoughts. She looked up blankly.

"What do I think?" she repeated. "About what?"

"About studying someplace else. Perhaps the Spingler Institute. I understand they excel in teaching young women the basics of art."

Imogene stiffened. She glanced at Thomas, who was watching her carefully, his expression warm and concerned, and then she forced herself to speak flatly, to hide the fact that Katherine's words made her feel sick inside, hot and cold. "You want me to leave Jonas Whitaker?" she asked carefully.

"I'm only worried about your reputation," Katherine said, leaning forward. "If the word were to get out that Whitaker's using life models—well, you would be ruined, Imogene. Surely you realize that."

Thomas shook his head. "It's not quite that extreme, Katherine."

"It could be." Katherine threw a glance at her husband. "I'm sure Samuel didn't understand just how controversial Jonas Whitaker is."

"I think he understood perfectly," Thomas said dryly. He looked at Imogene. "But it's up to you, my dear. If you'd rather study somewhere else, we'll arrange it. I'll explain things to your father."

Imogene looked down at her plate, trying to focus her thoughts, to ease the panic she felt at Thomas's suggestion. Not because of her father—though he would never understand—but because the thought of leaving Whitaker's tutelage made her feel desperate. She couldn't leave him now, not now that she'd realized what he could teach her.

Katherine pushed back her chair, her rosewater scent wafted through the room. "I'll leave the two of you to discuss it," she said in her smooth, cultured voice. "Would you like tea, dear?"

Imogene shook her head. She waited until Katherine left the room before she turned to Thomas. Thomas, who would understand the way he always understood. She opened her mouth to tell him that she didn't want to go, but before she could say a word, he sighed.

"Katherine is worried about you, my dear," he said.

She frowned. "I know."

"She doesn't truly understand about artists." Thomas leaned forward, pressing his elbows into the ivory tablecloth, his expression intense. "But she makes a good point, one I hadn't thought of. Of course it's not so bad for young men to be studying from life, though it's still a bit scandalous. But a woman—an *unmarried* woman, Imogene—"

"He's brilliant, Thomas," she said, and though she saw her godfather's surprise at her interruption, she didn't stop. "I never really understood what that meant before now. I can't walk away from that. He can teach me so many things."

Thomas looked troubled. He folded his hands on the tablecloth, looked down at his fingers. "But at what price, my dear?"

She studied him carefully. "You mean his madness," she said.

She had startled him, she realized. Thomas sat back in his chair. "Who told you he was mad?"

"Peter McBride."

"One of his students?" Thomas asked heavily.

"Yes," she said, and then when she saw the skepticism in his face, "You don't believe it."

"I don't know." Thomas shrugged. "It depends on what you mean by mad. Do I think Whitaker would hurt someone? No. Do I think he's dangerous? No. No, I don't. I think he torments only himself. But if you're asking if I think he's touched . . ." He sighed. "I think he's a genius, my dear. And I think it takes a bit of madness to have that kind of talent. Maybe more than a bit." He looked up at her. His blue eyes seemed to pierce through her. "Does it frighten you?"

Slowly Imogene shook her head. "No," she said quietly. "No. It doesn't frighten me at all. Two days ago he made me prime a canvas. Over and over again until I got it right. That was why I was late coming home. He wouldn't let me go until I'd at least done one."

Thomas scowled. "I'm not sure I understand."

She regarded him steadily. "I can prime a canvas now, Thomas. It took me two days, but I can do it."

"Forgive me, but—"

"Yesterday was the first day the model was there." Imogene rushed on, trying to make him understand, and the words came tumbling out, too fast to control. "And he made me look at her—really look at her. He made me see things I've never seen before. He made me understand . . ." She took a deep, ragged breath. "Thomas, he asked me if I would do what Michelangelo did—if I would go into the morgues to study. He asked me if I would do that for art.''

Thomas was watching her thoughtfully. "And what did you say?"

She laughed shortly, shrugging. "I don't think I knew what to say. It didn't matter. Thomas, don't you see? What matters is the way he made me see. He may be mad, but I think you're right, his brilliance is . . . it's . . ." Her words trailed off in a sigh. "I want to learn from him, Thomas."

That was all. It was so simple, and so very, very difficult to explain.

Thomas was looking at her curiously, and for the first time in years, she couldn't read his expression, didn't know at all what he was thinking. She looked down at her plate, at the whiteness of the veal and the creamed peas, and felt tension knot her shoulders as she waited for his answer.

She heard his sigh. She looked up to see him rubbing his chin with his hand, looking at her with a thoughtfulness and care that made Imogene feel unexpectedly guilty. Guilty because he was worried about her, and she knew if she told him what had transpired between herself and Whitaker today, he wouldn't even be giving her the courtesy of a discussion. But then she thought of yesterday, of Michelangelo, and her guilt disappeared.

"Thomas," she began, hearing the edge of desperation in her voice.

He held up a hand to forestall her. "I understand," he said slowly. "Or at least I think I do. But I'm not entirely sure you're safe, Imogene. I still worry. If you change your mind . . ."

Relief washed over her. She shook her head and smiled. "I won't. And I'm safe enough, believe me."

Thomas eyed her thoughtfully and leaned back in his chair. "I hope you're right, my dear," he said in a slow, heavy voice. "I only hope you're right."

"Ah, darlin', yes—ah!" Clarisse's words caught in a moan; she arched against him, digging her nails into his back, tossing her head so the bright red strands of her hair played among the multicolored spatters on the floor. Her breasts jiggled against his chest, her legs tightened about his hips, urging him deeper, deeper while she moaned in rhythm to his thrusts.

She felt good, hot and wet, and Jonas plunged into her over and over again, looking away from her writhing body and focusing on the canvas looming above them. The unfinished courtesan watched with an unforgiving smile, and he grabbed Clarisse's hip with his good hand, feeling the cheap, dirty pleasure course through him, thinking fleetingly of painting the courtesan with spread legs, because between spread legs he could forget so many things.

Like Imogene Carter's haunting face, the too-soft words. *"I want to know what it's like to be you . . ."*
Christ.

His climax burst over him before he even realized it, the sharp, piercing gratification stealing his breath and his thoughts, the pure hedonism of feeling restoring his mood. This was what he'd needed since this afternoon; he'd spent the evening wanting it, barely able to control himself while he waited for Clarisse to make her way back to the studio.

Jonas took a deep breath and rolled off her, lying

back against the floor. The cold boards felt good against his back, the chill in the air soothed his skin. He closed his eyes and felt the heavy touch of sleep.

"It's cold in here."

Clarisse's whine startled him out of his half doze. Jonas opened his eyes to look at her. She sat up, tossing back her hair. The movement made her breasts bounce enticingly.

"Can't you build a fire? And where's Rico, anyway? You said he was bringin' over that lovely brandy."

"I don't know." He watched the way she moved, the way her hips shifted when she got to her feet, the firm roundness of her buttocks, and he felt himself stirring to hardness again. "Come here."

She tossed a smile over her shoulder. "Oh, you're just insatiable, darlin', ain't you?"

"It seems so." He patted the floor beside him. "Don't make me come after you."

"And why not? It's the least you can do, after makin' me lie on that cold floor. Why, I—"

The knock on the door startled them both. Jonas sat up, frowning. It was close to midnight, he was sure. Midnight on a particularly dark night; heavy rain clouds hid the moon and the wind rocked bare branches against the sky. Inside, the dim and wavering light of a candle barely held its own against the looming shadows of the room.

"Rico?" he called. "Childs, is that you?"

"No. It's—it's Thomas." The voice was hard to hear and hesitant. "Whitaker, open up, won't you?"

Gosney. What the hell was he doing here? Unless . . . Jonas scrambled to his feet, grabbing the trousers he'd left crumpled on the floor. He threw Clarisse her gown.

"Get dressed," he commanded tersely, pulling on his pants. He barely waited for her to fasten the gown before he opened the door.

Thomas Gosney stood in the hallway, the smoking lamps making his bundled shadow seem huge against the plaster walls, the top hat stories high. Gosney looked up, and then past Jonas, and when he saw Clarisse his shoulders slumped.

"Forgive me," he said. "It's too late to be calling, I realize. I was at the club, and I'm afraid I rather lost track of time."

Jonas stared at him, feeling a touch of dread. Gosney looked disturbed. The memory of today came crashing back to Jonas, the way he'd pressed Imogene Carter into the corner, tried to kiss her. It was why Gosney was here, he knew, and Jonas cursed himself inwardly, wishing he hadn't lost his temper, wishing he'd been as subtle as he'd first planned. Because he knew already that she'd told Gosney, and now it was all over, all of it. The thought sank into Jonas, filled him with a sweeping depression, a black despair. Funny, he had expected to feel relief. . . .

He stepped back, motioning Gosney inside. "Please. Come in."

Gosney hesitated. "I had hoped you'd be at the club."

"Not tonight."

"I don't want to interrupt."

"It's no interruption." Jonas jerked his head at Clarisse and was amazed—and oddly grateful—when she obediently hurried into the bedroom. He turned back to Gosney. "Can I get you something? Wine?"

"No, no." Thomas shook his head and stepped inside, taking off his hat and holding it in his hands. He made no move to unbutton his coat, didn't look for a chair. "I won't stay long."

Jonas shut the door. He caught Gosney's stare as he did so, saw the way his patron's gaze lit on his arm, on the leather straps at his wrist, before Gosney politely averted his eyes, and Jonas realized he'd forgotten to put on his shirt, that his infirmity was there for anyone to see. Shame uncurled in his stomach. Hastily he went to grab his shirt from the floor. He pulled it over his useless hand, shrugged into it.

Gosney said nothing. He simply stood there watching, waiting, and Jonas buttoned the lower fastenings of his shirt and turned to face his patron, crossing his arms over his chest, leaning back against the table in an attempt to regain his composure, to brace himself for the things Gosney was undoubtedly going to say.

"I assume you're here about your goddaughter," he said. There was no point in prolonging things, after all, and he was feeling the sudden and intense urge to get to Clarisse.

Gosney looked surprised for a moment, and then he nodded. "Yes."

"If it makes you feel better, know that I'm sorry for it."

Gosney made a dismissive motion. "Oh, there's nothing to be sorry for. I did insist that you take her on. I just didn't realize—"

"It's not your fault, or hers." Jonas cut him off impatiently, not understanding why Gosney hadn't lost his temper, why he wasn't calling him all the things he deserved to be called. "Don't be such a damned martyr. I shouldn't have done it."

Gosney shook his head. "I didn't expect you to do anything else," he said. "Imogene wanted to study art.

I assumed that meant nudes as well. There's no need to protect her from it."

Jonas stared at him in confusion. Nudes? What the hell was he talking about? "I don't understand," he said.

"The nude," Thomas explained patiently. "She told me you had them paint a woman the last few days. What did you think I meant?"

It took a moment for the realization to hit Jonas, a moment to understand that Imogene Carter hadn't told Gosney what happened today, that she hadn't run home and confessed that Jonas had all but attacked her. She hadn't revealed his rage or how he touched her and caressed her, how he trapped her in the corner and pressed his body against hers.

She hadn't told.

The knowledge made Jonas uneasy. He wasn't sure how to feel about it or what to do. Wasn't sure how to answer Gosney, so he said nothing.

Thomas continued. "Katherine is worried about her, however, and I thought I should come and talk to you, to make sure you're, well, to be honest, to make sure Imogene isn't being pushed too fast. She hasn't had a great deal of schooling, you understand, and I thought —it might be a bit much, you know—a nude after only a few days. . . ." He trailed off as if the subject made him uncomfortable.

"I see." Jonas said. "She's offended then."

Gosney shook his head. "No. Not at all. In fact, she says she wants to stay on."

Jonas stared in surprise. Nothing Gosney could have said would have shocked him more. "She wants to— what?"

"She wants to stay on."

"She told you this when?"

"Tonight, at dinner." Gosney sighed. "To be perfectly frank, Whitaker, I offered her entry to the Spingler Institute instead. Even though I understand the nudes are necessary, I can't help worrying about her reputation. And Imogene is so frail still, I fear she'll never truly have the strength of a normal young woman."

Jonas was too dazed to answer.

Thomas fingered the rim of his hat nervously. "But she refused me. She said she preferred to study under you, and though I don't truly understand her reasons, I defer to her desire in this. But—" He looked up, his eyes burning in the darkness."—I must ask you to treat her with delicacy. You must teach your students the way you will, of course—you know what suits them best—but if I hear a single word, even a hint of misconduct . . ."

He left the sentence unfinished, but Jonas heard the unspoken threat, remembered the words Gosney had coerced him with a mere month or so ago. *"I made you, Whitaker. Don't forget it. A word from me and your paintings won't sell for a halfpenny."*

But this time, Jonas didn't feel the choke of resentment. This time, he felt no anger at all. He felt—he didn't know what. Puzzled, relieved, disappointed. Those feelings were all there, and they all focused around Imogene Carter, around the "frail" young woman who had stared up at him with wide brown eyes and said *"I want to know what it's like to be you."*

And through it all was the keen edge of panic, the needling of fear. She had not told Gosney about today. She had not said anything and Jonas didn't understand why, didn't know why she wasn't running away, why she hadn't sought to punish him with Gosney's interference.

It scared the hell out of him that she hadn't. Jonas felt at her mercy now, and it made him dislike her more, made him want to be rid of her so badly he could taste it. None of this made sense. *She* didn't make sense. He'd behaved reprehensibly. She should have run long ago, and he didn't understand why she hadn't, didn't understand her motivations at all. What did she want from him? Talent he couldn't give her. Techniques could be learned from anyone. And sex. . . . Jonas remembered her frightened eyes, the way she jerked from his touch. No, sex was not what Miss Imogene Carter was after.

What then? What?

"Well?" Gosney still stood there, his gloved fingers closing tightly on the brim of his hat. "Do we understand each other?"

Jonas forced a tight smile, bowed his head. "Of course."

Gosney swallowed. "Good." He put his hat on his head, held out his hand. "I'll leave you then. Once again, I apologize for the lateness of the hour."

Jonas shook his hand. "It doesn't matter."

"I'll be calling on you next week. I have an idea I'd like you to try. I think it will interest you. An allegory, really. Greek myths and all that. Cupid and Psyche." He went to the door and opened it. "That new technique of yours—the flat colors—I think it will lend itself to this well."

"I look forward to it," Jonas said.

Gosney nodded. "Next week then. Good night."

"Good night."

The door shut. The hall creaked. Jonas stood there, watching the door, his thoughts churning in his head. He tried to order them, tried to get them to behave, but they were too scattered, too fragmented. He felt the buzzing in his blood; it raced through his heart in time to the words crashing in his mind: *"I want to know what it's like . . . I want to know what it's like . . ."* Louder and louder until he put his hands against his ears, felt the hard press of the hateful wooden fingers against his skull.

"Jonas?" Clarisse's voice from the bedroom. Low and throaty, breaking the rhythm in his head. "Darlin', is he gone?"

Jonas dropped his hands, felt the need rising up in him again, hard and fast. "Yes," he called. "He's gone."

"Why're you waitin', then?"

Why indeed?

Jonas strode to the bedroom, banishing the voices in his head. Tonight he would let Clarisse's soft heat and the erotic touch of her skin soothe him. Tonight he would forget about Imogene Carter and her reasons for not telling Gosney the truth, her reasons for wanting to stay.

But tomorrow . . .

Tomorrow he would find out why.

Tomorrow he would break her.

Chapter 8

"Today we'll be studying the female back." Whitaker stepped up to the platform where Clarisse sat, his long, elegant fingers unfastening the buttons at the back of the model's too-tight green gown. Slowly he eased the satin over Clarisse's shoulders to reveal her back.

It was seductive, the way he did it, the lingering motion, the way he brushed his fingers over the woman's skin. So tactile and suggestive Imogene shivered, feeling the fine hairs at the back of her neck rise. Too well she could imagine what that touch would feel like. Far too well.

Imogene swallowed and focused her gaze on Clarisse's back, trying to banish the thought, to forget about yesterday and the way he'd touched her. It was obvious it had meant nothing to him; this morning he'd graced her arrival with a single glowering look that reminded her of the way he'd ordered her to leave yesterday, of that black anger that darkened his eyes.

It was just as well. She didn't want him to touch her again. It only made it harder to concentrate, only

clouded her real aim. But still she wished she knew
what she'd done to make him so angry, wished she
knew how to ease it. As long as he was angry, he was
unlikely to be the teacher she longed for. As long as he
was angry, she doubted there would be a repeat of two
days ago.

The thought depressed her, but she held her charcoal tightly in her fingers and leaned forward when he
began to talk, hoping that maybe she would find the
magic anyway, that perhaps she could reach it alone.

"Now look closely," Whitaker said. He splayed his
fingers over Clarisse's shoulder blade. "See how
smooth the muscles are? Concentrate on just the
shoulder for now. In a moment we'll move to the
spine."

He stepped away, and Imogene stared at the model's
back, wishing she understood anatomy better, the way
Chloe had. She remembered her sister poring over
medical papers with their father, sketching for hours
in an attempt to get a single line right. Imogene narrowed her eyes, trying to see with her sister's vision,
working to follow the lines of the muscles.

She set the charcoal to the paper, drew the first
sweep of shoulder, and glanced up—just as Jonas
Whitaker stepped down from the platform. He was
looking directly at her. Imogene stopped, startled by
the bitter anger in his glare.

"Miss Carter," he said, his tone all soft menace. His
eyes glittered when he crooked his finger at her.
"Come with me a moment, won't you?"

She couldn't help her swift joy at his notice, no matter the reason. It was so intense she leapt clumsily to
her feet, knocking the easel with her arm. He was already striding to the far side of the room toward the

windows, and she hurried after him, ignoring the scowl Clarisse threw her way.

She followed him to the table where her primed canvases waited, stopping a few feet away from him.

He turned toward her. "It's time for another private lesson, Miss Carter," he said. He pushed the frames aside. They went clattering to the floor. Imogene tried not to wince.

He dragged a slab of glass and a short palette knife toward him. "I'm assuming you know nothing about grinding colors," he said, setting out a jar of oil and another of varnish. He looked up at her, a smug expression on his face. "Well, today is your day to learn. Come closer."

Imogene hesitated. Unbidden, images from yesterday came flooding back: the feel of his hair on her cheek, the press of his body against hers.

He smiled coldly at her. "Well?"

Imogene banished the images. She told herself she could ignore his touches, that she could control her yearning, and moved to where he'd motioned. Close enough to feel him beside her even though they weren't touching. Close enough to feel his warmth, the rush of air when he moved.

"Certain colors need to be ground more than others," he said in a low, compelling voice. "Some need to be washed as well. Ultramarine is one." He lifted a small bowl. A fine ultramarine dust clung to the bottom, the residue of a liquid that had long since evaporated. "This is color that's been washed already, first in hot water, then in cold," he said, tilting the bowl over the glass slab. He tapped it a few times with his other hand; she heard the hollow sound of his false finger against the ceramic.

"This is pure color," he said, his breath stirring the bright blue particles. He lifted the jar of oil and let a few drops puddle on the glass. "Add the oil a little at a time," he said, setting the jar aside and picking up a palette knife. With swift, efficient movements, he mixed the powder into the oil, kneading the mixture with the knife, spreading it over the slab and scraping it up again. Carefully, step by step, he added drops of oil and a few of varnish and blended, his movements so precise and rhythmic Imogene felt herself falling into a trance. *Pour, spread, scrape. Pour, spread, scrape.* How finely he did it, how gracefully. It was so measured and easy she had to remind herself he was performing all the motions with only one hand.

He straightened suddenly; she felt the brush of his rigid hand against her skirts, felt him move closer even as he seemed to be moving away. "Now you try," he whispered, and his breath was hot against her ear, she felt the shivering of the little hairs at her temple.

The air grew close and tight. She felt the press of him against her hip, and despite her resolution not to let his touches affect her, a shiver spun up her spine. Imogene struggled to control her reaction, to keep her breathing even, to cool the flush heating her skin. She stepped away, a single step, but it was enough to ease the tension in the air and steady her breathing.

She reached to take the palette knife and the oil, thinking he would hand them to her and move away. But instead he moved closer, and his fingers seemed to linger against hers as he placed the items in her hands.

Imogene tightened her jaw and tried to ignore his proximity. But her hands shook slightly as she poured the oil. A few drops only, but they puddled on the glass and spread, colorless and silky, into the paint.

Too much. Hastily she pushed paint into it, trying to catch it before he had the chance to berate her, cursing herself for not being able to do even this simple thing correctly. She waited for him to say something, waited for his impatient anger.

But instead he moved behind her and looked over her shoulder. Instead his voice was low and seductive in her ear. "Slow down," he said. "Slower, that's the way." Then his hands were suddenly on either side of her and he was against her back, his good hand holding her wrist steady, guiding her gently into the motion of kneading: back and forth, back and forth, *spread, scrape, spread, scrape.*

She stared at the glowing color, at the paint-stained fingers wrapped around her wrist. They were long and well formed, elegant. Bits of faded color—vermillion and ultramarine and Naples yellow—accentuated the wrinkles of his knuckles, the texture of his skin. She found herself entranced by the play of sinews in his hand, mesmerized by the rhythm, by the gentle pressure of his fingers, his heat at her back. But it was the rhythm more than anything, and it was so hypnotizing that when he released her wrist she kept moving the palette knife against the glass, loath to stop, taking pleasure in the way the paint built up, the way it thickened and gained body, the stiff wet sound of it. She was so focused on the kneading she almost forgot he was there.

Until she felt the touch of his fingers on her cheek. The spell shattered, so abruptly that Imogene jumped. But he held her tightly against him, and she couldn't move or pull away.

"Darling," he whispered, and his voice was low and seductive and heavy with loathing while his fingers

stroked her skin with the most delicate of touches. "I had a visit from your goddaddy last night, did he tell you?"

His words confused her, his touch, his voice. Bewildered, she shook her head.

"He kept it a secret from you? Tsk, tsk." His hair danced against her throat. "He wanted to tell me something. What do you suppose it was, Miss Carter, hmmmm?"

She felt the briefest of kisses against her ear, the light, heated brush of his lips.

"I—I don't know," she whispered.

"He asked me to treat you gently," he murmured. She heard the faint amusement in his tone, the derision. "I forgot to ask him exactly how gently he meant. Perhaps you know." His breath was heated and moist against her skin, his lips caressed her throat. "Is this gentle enough, darling?"

Lord, oh, Lord. She was dizzy and trembling and too hot. Desperately she thought of Chloe, but even imagining her sister couldn't bring to mind a single setdown, not a single course of action. *Move,* she told herself. *Step away.* But she couldn't move, couldn't do anything but stand there trembling in his arms, mesmerized by a touch she told herself not to want, seduced by words that stole her breath and her will.

"What is it you want from me, Miss Imogene Carter, hmmm?" he asked. She felt the cradle of his hips through her skirt, pressed to her buttocks. His voice was quieter than a whisper, his fingers played with the loose curls at her throat, stroked her jaw. "Why don't you run away, I wonder? Why—"

"Take your hands off her, you son of a bitch!" Clarisse screeched.

Whitaker started, his hands dropped, and Imogene sprang away, nearly falling into the paint, cracking her hip on the table in her haste. She'd forgotten all about the others, had forgotten everything but Whitaker, and now their faces filled her vision, all stiff with curiosity and fear. Heat rushed into Imogene's face, along with the ache of humiliation. They had been watching. No doubt they'd seen her lean into him, seen how easily she was persuaded, how simple it was to seduce her. Lord, what they must think.

She tried to catch Peter's eye, to explain with expression if not with words, but he wouldn't look at her, and she felt alone and abandoned until she suddenly realized they weren't staring at her at all. They were staring at Whitaker.

Frowning, she glanced at him. His face was so hard and cold and expressionless he seemed cut from marble. It was obvious he'd already forgotten her. He was looking at Clarisse as if the rest of them had disappeared.

Clarisse surged to her feet, her skin blotchy with rage, her eyes burning with self-righteous anger. She marched across the studio until she was even with Whitaker.

"How dare you touch her like that!" she spat out. She raised her hand to slap him.

He caught it easily. "Don't cause a scene, Clarisse," he said calmly. "Or you'll make me angry."

She jerked away from his touch. "Like I give a damn! I'll cause a scene if I like." She threw a glance at Imogene; it was so baleful Imogene stepped back, gripping the table to steady herself. "You must think I'm daft, makin' love to the girl right afore my eyes like that. Didya think I wouldn't see?"

"To tell you the truth, I didn't much care." Whitaker said, smiling coldly.

"Well, I won't put up with it," Clarisse threatened. "Get rid of her or I'm goin'."

"Don't tell me what to do, Clarisse." Whitaker's voice was soft, too soft, and so full of warning Imogene's heart stopped.

But Clarisse didn't seem to notice. "I tell you I won't put up with it," she said again.

He shrugged. "If you don't like it, you can always leave," he said lightly. "In fact, I'd prefer it if you would. Right now. And don't come back."

It took only a second for his words to register. Clarisse blanched. Her skin went sallow, accenting the shadows beneath her eyes, the creases framing her mouth. Then her expression tightened, her pretty eyes narrowed.

"You son of a bitch," she spat, spinning away from him. "To hell with you and your little whore both!" Her curses filled the air as she grabbed her cloak off the peg and yanked open the door.

It slammed shut behind her.

There was silence.

Then there was a frantic surge of activity. Tobias grabbed clumsily for his paintbox, Daniel suddenly found his palette fascinating, and Peter began painting furiously, even though there was nothing to paint.

Imogene stood there, stunned and disbelieving. She was the cause of this; her befuddled mind struggled with the knowledge. She—sickly little Imogene Carter —was the cause of a jealous rage. It was incredible, and oddly flattering. As foreign as the feeling was, it was rather exciting, almost heady. And it made her curious. She was a nobody, yet Clarisse had been jealous of her, and Jonas Whitaker had pressed against her, had kissed her ear, had caressed her throat. He had made love to her, just as Clarisse had said, and now Imogene wondered why, wondered what the two of them saw in her, wondered what he saw in her. It fascinated her suddenly, the simple question: What did Whitaker see in her?

From across the room came the sound of a throat clearing, Daniel's deep but wavering voice. "Sir, shall we—shall we continue? Or shall we . . . go?"

Slowly Whitaker turned to face him. "Go?" he asked, and Imogene heard again that amusement in his tone, the touch of contempt. "Ah, now, that is the question, isn't it?"

He turned to look at her, and the sharp speculation in his eyes, his small smile, made her wary. But she didn't look away, and it seemed that only made his smile broader.

"Miss Carter," he said, drawing the syllables of her name out until they sounded like a caress. "It seems we're in need of a model."

The suggestion was there, in his voice, startling and illusory. She couldn't believe it, told herself not to believe it. He couldn't want her to model for them. But she saw the query in his eyes as he moved closer to her, saw it when he stopped just before her, close enough that she could feel his heat and smell the scent of turpentine and oil that clung to him, the faint remnants of smoke. She found herself staring at his chest, at the open collar of his shirt, and with a shiver she noticed the dark curls that started there and disappeared beneath the threadbare cotton. Curls that Nicholas had never had.

She felt again that stab of desire, the sinking in her

stomach, the heat that started there and spun into her blood, clear into her fingertips, and she knew he was deliberately trying to make her feel that way, that his every move and word had been intended to seduce her, that his question now was a compliment meant to manipulate her, an insincere and calculated flattery. And she wondered again what he wanted from her, who he saw when he looked at her. The questions suddenly seemed more important than ever, somehow necessary. This was Jonas Whitaker, a handsome, brilliant artist. A man she wanted to understand, to learn from. She was nothing but an inexperienced student, a woman who could not possibly tempt him, a woman he could not possibly want. So why all the attention? Why?

Her throat felt dry; it took all Imogene's effort to keep her breathing steady when he reached out, cupping her chin and tilting it up, forcing her to look into his eyes.

"So what should we do, Miss Carter?" Whitaker's fingers stroked her skin, his voice was smooth and beguiling. "The others are waiting for me to show them a woman's back."

"Imogene. Genie—" Peter's voice, a quick protest. It seemed to come from miles away.

Whitaker smiled. "Genie?" he repeated, and then he said the name again, a tentative test, rolling it over his tongue as if he liked the feel of it, the taste. He bent until she felt his breath against her lips, the whispered accents. "Genie, darling, will you model for us today?"

There it was, the question he'd alluded to. But hearing the words startled her. For some reason she'd expected them to blast through the room, a loud and obscene declaration, words that would bring her to her senses, that would take away the possibilities and leave her with emotions and respectability intact.

But instead the words were soft, a forbidden temptation that cajoled with compliments. Instead, they seduced her, whispered against her skin, danced around her. *"Genie, darling, will you model for us today?"* Her questions came flooding back, leaving her weak and flattered and curious. *Why me? What does he want from me? How does he see me?*

Lord, she wanted to know, wanted to know so badly it was all she could think about. In the light of it, propriety didn't matter, nothing mattered but knowing more about him, answering those questions. And oh, she wanted to know the answers. She wanted it more than anything she had ever wanted.

Imogene took a deep breath and looked steadily into his eyes.

"Christ." The word was a harsh whisper, startled surprise. He dropped his hand so quickly it was as if she'd burned him. He stepped back.

"I'll pose," she said quietly, not taking her gaze from his. "I'll pose for the others . . . if *you* draw me too."

He stared at her, and she saw the wariness on his face, the suspicious question, and thought he would refuse, but he only frowned and said, "You want me to draw you?"

"Please."

He looked at her steadily, assessingly. Then finally he nodded, and that thin smile was back in place again, the faint contempt. "Very well then," he said.

She nodded, trying to control the excitement that soared through her, the fluttering in her stomach. She took a deep, calming breath and reached behind her neck, feeling for the buttons at the back of her collar. "You'll have to help me," she said, and it amazed her how calm her voice sounded, how unemotional.

Without waiting for his assent, she turned her back to him. It seemed an eternity before she felt his fingers working the buttons, slipping them through the fastenings easily, smoothly. She felt the loosening of her collar, the cool air of the room touching the back of her neck. She felt the unfolding of the material at her back, the soft scrape of his knuckles over the flimsy protection of her chemise, loosening her laces.

Then he was at her waist, and he stopped and moved back. She thought she heard his breathing grow more strained as she stepped away from him and went to the chair Clarisse had occupied earlier. It was a long distance; she held the front of her dress to her breasts, thinking of Clarisse and the way the woman had bared her nakedness without a qualm, the sheer confidence of the way she moved. Imogene felt disembodied, keenly aware of her movement without feeling it at all. *This is someone else entirely,* she thought. *Some stranger . . .*

But then she saw their eyes on her, saw their rapt attention: Peter's dismay and Daniel's flushed embarrassment and Tobias's unabashed stare. There was something exciting about their reactions, something insidiously decadent. They were watching her the way men never watched her, and with a start she understood what Clarisse had felt, and Chloe. Imogene felt the power of her movement, was aware of her body in a way she'd never been before, the sway of her hips, the dangling hairs bouncing against her cheeks, her throat. Excitement coursed through her, she felt its heat in her face, felt the tingle in her skin.

She felt . . . alive.

Her senses were on fire, the blood raced through her veins. She stepped up on the platform, letting her gaze rest on the others for a moment before she turned and sat with her back to them, closing her eyes as she lowered the sleeves of her dress, the chemise straps. She felt the brush of cool air on her bare shoulders, felt the hot touch of their collective gaze, and satisfaction surged through her, a strange and heady confidence that grew when she saw Whitaker reach for an easel and a sketch pad and join the others. He was going to draw her. He was going to draw her, and she would look at that sketch and know what he saw when he looked at her. She would see with his vision today after all.

The thought was intoxicating. She could imagine now what Chloe must have felt surrounded by the adoring suitors who crowded the parlor. For a moment it seemed her sister's spirit surged into Imogene. She straightened her shoulders and lifted her head, feeling, for the only time in her life, like a woman worthy of attention.

She heard the scratching of charcoal on canvas and waited.

Chapter 9

*J*onas stared unseeingly at the sketch before him, at his hastily drawn lines. He did not understand what had happened. Something had changed, something had wrested control from his hands, and it sent the blood racing through his veins, filled him with fear and dread and a disturbing euphoria.

He continually underestimated her. She was never what he expected. He thought of when she'd first arrived this morning, wearing the blue moiré silk that was as colorless and unflattering on her as everything else she'd worn. It made her look weak and frail, and he'd let that fool him, even though it shouldn't have, even though he knew she was stronger than she looked.

He was twice the fool, since he could not look at that moiré silk now without thinking of how it had looked peeling back under his fingers, slowly—button by button—revealing the virginal pointelle lace of her chemise, the smooth ivory of her flesh. He could not stop remembering how dark and dirty his fingers had looked against her pale skin, or the freckles spattered across her shoulders, or those fine light hairs at the nape of her neck, the pale down . . .

Jonas closed his eyes briefly. He was truly going mad. He had wanted to send her running, and instead he was the one who felt the need to run. Because he could not take his eyes off her. Because sitting there with her back to him, she was captivating and puzzling, a mystery he needed to solve. Because when she named her conditions for posing, he had wanted suddenly and completely to draw her, as she'd asked, and he could not figure out why.

He told himself she was too delicate, too pale, too fragile for his tastes. But the sunlight pouring through the windows added color to her skin, sent highlights flickering through that honey-colored hair, gave her a soft warmth, an ethereal, almost spiritual, strength.

He told himself she was plain, her face too angular for beauty, her jaw too long. But sitting there the way she was, with her chin lifted at an angle to him, he saw the delicate structure of her jaw, the rise of cheekbone, the fine symmetry of her features.

He was entranced by those expressive eyes and the smoothness of her skin and her scent, by the strange force of her words, the wistfulness he heard in them, the threat of intimacy. *"I want to know what it's like to be you. I want to understand."*

Why the hell wouldn't she run?

Jonas clenched the charcoal in his fingers, feeling overwhelming frustration. He didn't know what else to try, what to do, couldn't even remember why he wanted so badly for her to go. What was it about her? Why was it that she affected him this way? He couldn't remember the last time a woman had gotten so under his skin—

The lines on the paper seemed to congeal suddenly, to take form before his eyes. Not just separate lines, more than a two-dimensional plane, more than space and shadow. He looked down at his sketch pad and saw the woman he'd drawn in exquisite detail. The sketch took his breath away. He stared at it, at the sensuality of the form, the quiet eroticism, and felt a shock and dismay that went clear to his bones.

He shook his head. Ah, Christ. Christ, not this. Not so easily. He'd struggled for days with the courtesan, for weeks. She had never unfurled as easily as this. Every sketch had been a struggle, every line a defeat.

The buzzing in his blood grew. It rang in his ears, pulsed through him like a heartbeat. Jonas dropped the charcoal and stepped away until he could no longer see the drawing, wanting to deny it even existed. She was in everything. *Everything.* He didn't want her there, didn't want any part of her at all. He glanced up at her, sitting there on that platform, not at all the victim he'd wanted her to be, and his anger came fast and furious. He felt as defeated as the courtesan had made him. Viciously he tore the sketch from the easel, crumpling it and throwing it to the floor.

"Get dressed," he said harshly. He could barely get the words out, but they seemed to echo in the room, too loud and too brutal. "For Christ's sake, get dressed and go home. All of you go home."

She jumped, twisting around to stare at him. He saw her gaze drop to the paper he'd tossed aside, saw the question in her big brown eyes. Then color flooded her cheeks, and she was frowning, pulling up the sleeves of her dress, and McBride was on his feet and moving toward her, helping her with her gown. Jonas felt the stares of the others as well, turning on him, trapping him, and he didn't give a damn what they saw or what they thought.

He turned away, striding past them to the canvas against the window. He grabbed his palette on the way, determined to paint, determined to let his vision take over, to blank out Imogene Carter and her delicate curves and fragile features. Determined to draw the courtesan. Determined not to look at her again, not to think about her.

He heard the door to the studio open. Jonas kept his gaze fastened on the canvas before him, the muted underpainting, the lush lines of the whore. . . .

The studio door crashed shut. Jonas glanced over. It was Childs. The sight of him brought both relief and irritation. "What do you want, Rico?"

"It's past noon, *mon ami.*" Childs shrugged, a loose, beautiful movement that sent his golden hair tumbling over his shoulders. "Time for all the boys and girls to go home." He glanced over the room, and Jonas felt a surge of annoyance as Rico turned his smile on Miss Carter, who was stepping off the platform, blushing prettily, her dress done up again to hide those smooth, creamy shoulders, her pale throat.

"Ah, Miss Imogene," Rico said in his smooth, cultured tone. "How nice to see you again. I—"

"Leave her the hell alone." For a moment, Jonas didn't realize the words had come from him. For a moment, the intensity of his anger startled him. He saw Childs turn to him, a dark blond brow rising in surprise, saw the sudden interest flaring in his friend's eyes.

"Let's go, Imogene."

With a part of his mind, Jonas heard McBride's voice. It was too loud in the sudden silence. He saw the way the man took Imogene Carter's arm, the way he pulled her to the door. She hesitated for only an instant, long enough to grab the crumpled sketch Jonas had thrown away, and when Jonas saw the careful, precious way she held it, he lost whatever illusion of control he had.

"Yes, go, Genie, won't you?" he said, putting all of his anger and self-mockery into the words. "Get the hell out of here."

And even though he knew Childs was watching, even though he knew there would be questions about it later, Jonas couldn't take his eyes off her as Peter escorted her to the door. He expected to feel relief when she was finally gone, but all he felt was a confusing disappointment, and he could do nothing but stand there while the others left. When Tobias Harrington finally closed the door behind him, Jonas slowly turned his gaze to Rico, who was lounging on the model's chair, the image of careless indolence.

Jonas wasn't fooled. He saw the intense interest in his friend's pale blue eyes, the thinly veiled curiosity.

"Well, well. What was that all about, *mon ami*?"

There was no excuse he could offer. Briefly Jonas wondered what to tell him. What explanation would satisfy when he didn't understand himself what had just happened? He thought of a dozen offhand comments, vague disclaimers, easy lies, but he knew by the way Rico was watching him that he would never escape so easily.

"Well? Are you going to answer me, or shall I be forced to come up with an explanation myself? Let's see—I know—you've fallen madly in love with the girl—"

"Don't be ridiculous," Jonas snapped.

"*Pardon,* but it hardly seems ridiculous to me. I heard your last words to that little innocent—not to mention those charming endearments you sent my way. You hardly sounded disinterested."

"Words are easily misunderstood."

"Don't turn philosophical on me, Jonas, I can hardly bear it." Childs groaned, rolling his eyes. "Credit me with a little intelligence, won't you? There's not much room to interpret 'Leave her the hell alone.'"

Jonas worked to keep his face impassive. "Perhaps I was angry at something else."

"Perhaps Paris is in Germany."

"Don't start with me, Rico."

"You forget," Childs said with a limpid smile. "You can't threaten me. I've already seen you at your worst."

"That's what you think."

"And anyway, my curiosity has the better of me."

"I won't insult you by reminding you of the pitfalls of curiosity."

"Or I suppose I could simply ask Clarisse." Rico glanced at the changing screen, and then frowned and looked around the room. "Where is she, anyway? I thought you said she'd be modeling today."

Clarisse. Jonas had forgotten about her. Forgotten her so completely it took a moment for him to react to Childs's words. "Clarisse," he repeated slowly. "She's gone."

"Gone?" Rico's frown deepened. "You say that as if she's dead."

"Dead to me anyway. I'm done with her."

"You're done with her? After only a week?" Childs's scrutiny intensified. "Why do I feel as if I've missed something?"

Jonas tried to keep his words casual. "It's nothing, Rico. I was tired of her, that's all."

"Who have you replaced her with?"

The question stabbed through Jonas with surprising sharpness. It was a valid query, given that he was never without a mistress, but it startled him that he'd forgotten that, and he wanted to answer: *No one. I've replaced her with no one at all.* He wanted to believe it. But then he saw Imogene Carter sitting on the chair, lowering the straps of her chemise over her shoulders . . .

Jonas's mouth went dry. He swallowed, forced himself to make a dismissive gesture.

"I see."

The studied disbelief in his friend's voice irritated Jonas. He turned away, back to the table, to the glass slab loaded with half-ground ultramarine. "It's easy enough to find a woman. You know that."

"Yes, of course. How silly of me to suspect you're not telling me the whole truth."

Jonas winced. "Rico—"

"Please, *mon ami*, you sound so tortured. If you're so determined to keep everything such a secret, just say so and be done with it."

"It's a secret."

"Damn you." There was laughter in the words.

Jonas sighed. "It's nothing for you to be concerned about, Rico."

There was silence. Then Rico's voice came, soft and somber, all humor gone. "Isn't it?"

Jonas squeezed his eyes shut. Funny how that concern pierced through him. It almost undid him, and he opened his eyes and stared at the paint on the slab, forcing himself to gain control, trying to come up with some plausible lie, some way to explain to Rico what he could not explain to himself. How could he explain that the thought of a mistress suddenly seemed repulsive and coarse? That a virginal, colorless woman had suddenly taken on such vibrancy that it was impossible to banish or forget her?

He couldn't explain any of it. And he knew if he tried, Rico would just look at him with those too-perceptive, too-blue eyes, and see right through him the way he always had. It was why Jonas hated Childs as much as he loved him, why those months Childs had spent in Paris had been a relief for both of them.

Despite himself, Jonas remembered last spring. He buried the memory as quickly as he had it, forcing himself to speak gently. "It's nothing, Rico. Really, it's nothing."

"I've heard those words before," Childs said quietly.

God, the pain he felt at Rico's soft statement, the misery of memory. Jonas forced himself to forget it, to turn and smile, to pretend nothing had changed at all. He kept his voice deliberately light. "Tell me why you came over this morning."

Childs laughed, a short, dismissive sound, and Jonas knew it was more a response to the fact that he was keeping secrets than to his question.

Rico grinned wryly. "All right, my love, I'll play along like a good boy. I came this morning to invite you over. The other night I'd forgotten—I brought something back from Paris for you—a bit of the devil himself. I thought you might enjoy it—a lungful of wickedness to go with the rest of you, eh?"

Jonas didn't pretend to misunderstand. He closed his eyes, imagining the smooth, sweet heaviness of opium. Ah, it sounded good. It sounded like blessed peace, heady forgetfulness.

And he wanted to forget. He wanted to forget today. Wanted to forget the vision of her eyes and the tanta- lizing glimpses of her ivory flesh and how easy it had been to draw her. He wanted to forget today and last night and yesterday, wanted to calm the fierce buzzing in his blood that had grown stronger and stronger since she'd looked in his eyes and said *"I want to know what it's like . . ."*

Jonas shook his head slightly as if to clear it. "Yes," he said. "Yes, I'd like that very much."

Childs gave a little bow. "Then come with me. What was that poem? ' "Come into my parlor," said the spi- der to the fly'—something like that."

Jonas smiled. "You can tempt me all you want, Rico, but I'll tell you no secrets today, I'm warning you."

Rico laughed. It was joyous and sweet, and the stu- dio seemed to pulsate with the sound. "I've already told you that you can't threaten me," he said, and he led the way across the hall to his studio, like the Pied Piper leading children to the sea.

It was later, much later, that Jonas lounged on the huge bed in the corner of Childs's studio, his eyes bleary and his body drunk on smoke. He watched the golden and black shadows cast by the oil lamp dance over the walls and Rico's paintings, over the large trunk from Paris that still stood in the middle of the room, its lid thrown open to reveal the multicolored fabrics of Rico's wardrobe—waistcoats and morning coats and trousers spread all about, some crumpled on the floor, some strewn on the bed, some crunched beneath Jonas's legs.

It was like a Pandora's box, he thought, eyeing the quivering fringe of the bedcovers, the gold that looked more golden in the lamplight, the rich burgundies and greens that seemed to pulsate in the lying visions of the drug. Rico's chambers were much more opulent than his, but that was because Childs cared about fine things and Jonas did not. Childs loved luxuries, soft velvets and expensive liquors and fine perfumes. Even now the scent of incense hung in the air, mixing with the sweet opium smoke, heavy and deep with spice.

Jonas felt as if he were drowning in it, and he longed to close his eyes and stay here forever, but there was a thrumming in his blood that the opiate hadn't taken away, not yet, and he needed something else to ease it.

"More?" Childs's voice came to him, sounding languid and hopelessly far away, though it wasn't. Rico hadn't moved from where he sat beside Jonas on the bed, the picture of decadent languor, a pipe in one hand while he stroked Jonas's hair with the other, threading his fingers through the strands in an intimate, soothing rhythm.

Jonas reached up and took the pipe, sucking the burning smoke into his lungs, letting it curl around him. So insidious, he thought, closing his eyes. One never knew where the drug would take you, how dangerous it would choose to be, or how alluring.

Like Imogene Carter. The thought unfurled in his mind, slowly and without surprise. He hadn't been able to lose the image of her, not throughout the long evening and not now, in the dark hours of early morning. He remembered what he'd called her earlier, what Peter had called her. *Genie.* The name fit her. Like a genie in a bottle, she was magical, seductive, alluring. She was as dangerous as the opium, the way she haunted his thoughts.

He could not get her out of his mind, and though he'd smoked the opium to forget her, it only intensified his vision instead, brought back every detail of this morning in startling clarity. He remembered how much he'd hated her when she walked into the studio, how he'd been looking forward to destroying her today, to discovering her scheme and making her pay for her presumption. He remembered how he'd savored the words *"Genie, will you model for us today?"* and then how shocked he'd been when her small, slender hands went to her collar, how paralyzed he'd been by the smooth grace of her movements. She had never seemed so self-possessed, never so confident. And somehow that was seductive.

Ah, Genie. Genie turning her back to him so he could finish the buttons. Genie bending that long, pale neck, almost like an offering. That heated, almond scent, the silky warm flesh, the honeyed strands of hair dancing over his knuckles as he unfastened the buttons —one, two, and then three, and then clean white lace and freckled skin and smooth softness.

She was all fragrant intrigue, a huge contradiction— quiet and subdued, but with such startling power, a power that had radiated from his sketch, that had flowed from her into his hands. He wanted to savor the discovery of it, to think about that intoxicating conviction in her eyes. It had been so provocative, so alluring. It made him wonder for the first time what she would be like in bed. He imagined it; the smooth satin of her flesh, the soft trembling of her body, the harsh, moist little gasps brushing his cheek. He thought about the way that hair of hers would look tumbled about her shoulders, wondered how it would feel against his skin.

The image drove him nearly insane; he could not forget it, could not erase it. He thought of her and he felt the quick and savage thrust of desire, and it was different from what he'd felt for Clarisse or any of the others. It was more than just carnal lust, and he knew it had everything to do with that look in Imogene Carter's eyes. The look that turned the little brown moth into a beautiful butterfly. The look that had changed his intentions, took his original reasons for wanting her gone and sent them floating away, as elusive as the smoke wisping through the bed hangings. Gosney's threats, his own inability to paint—those things seemed so unimportant now, so ludicrously trivial.

They didn't matter—not in light of what he felt tonight. Because what he felt tonight was the elation of inspiration—the same inspiration that the threat of her presence had taken away just a few weeks ago. The ideas were crowding in his mind now, swirling though his head in the prismatic dance of opiate, pure and fuzzy and beautiful. Hundreds of them, spinning so fast and furiously he barely had time to think of one before another that was even more potent and compelling burst into his brain.

He looked at his hand, lying motionless on his chest, and it seemed to glow with brilliance. Long ago, at Barbizon, Jean-Claude Millet had told Jonas there was fire in his blood, and tonight he believed it. Tonight he wondered if there was anything he couldn't do. Everything fell into place. Abruptly he saw the courtesan he'd been trying to paint in all its vivid detail—his masterpiece, the *pièce de résistance* he'd intended to be the greatest, most sublime offering at the National Academy exhibition. He had wanted to show contradiction and desire, had wanted the woman to be disturbing, to show the power women had—that elusive power that controlled men whether they wanted to admit it or not. The courtesan's nakedness, her disdain, her strength would reflect all that—ah, God, it *would* be the greatest thing he had ever done.

Because this morning he'd realized what it needed, the thing he'd been seeking for weeks, the edge that eluded him. He had never been able to see the courtesan's face in his mind, but now suddenly it was there; the guarded eyes, the colorless beauty, the flat monochrome of her skin. Genie Carter.

God, he was so damned brilliant it amazed him. The exultation of earlier still burned in his blood, the fierce joy of inspiration grew until it filled his soul. He laughed at the pure wondrousness of it.

"Hmmm?" Rico stirred slightly beside him, and Jonas opened his eyes to see Childs leaning over him, his expression drowsy, his long blond hair falling forward like a lion's mane.

"Genie Carter," Jonas said, struggling to one elbow. He heard his voice; it was breathless, too fast, but he couldn't slow down. "She's the courtesan, Rico. Christ, can you see it? That face—it's the perfect face. Like a butterfly."

"Like a butterfly?" Rico leaned back against the headboard and closed his eyes, smiling. "You've lost me, *mon ami.* Her face is like a butterfly?"

"She's stunning, don't you see?" Jonas shook his friend's arm until Childs opened his eyes again. "I've got to paint her."

"Oh? I thought your little odalisque was nude."

"Yes, of course."

"And Miss Imogene is going to take her clothes off for you? Ah, you *are* clever then."

Rico's voice was languid, so slow that Jonas had already forgotten the beginning of the sentence before Childs reached the end. It didn't matter anyway; the only important thing was the nude—and all Jonas could think about was that it might be better if she were draped in some diaphanous material, something that lent an opalescence to her skin, the *luce di dentro*. Yes, perfect. A scarf or something. Rico must have something.

Jonas lunged off the bed, hardly noticing when Rico protested. He went to the trunk in the middle of the room, tossing out clothes—waistcoats and fine linen shirts and stockings—damn, there must be something. He spun around, staring at the room, at the heavy bed hangings and the mulberry-colored drapes and the pillows.

"What are you looking for?"

"A scarf," Jonas said. "A robe—" He spotted a length of mosquito netting draped over a table in the corner of the room. The finely woven cloth shimmered in the dim candlelight. He strode to it, pulling it loose with one quick tug, upsetting bottles and brushes and a few saucers holding color. He held it up, holding it so the candlelight diffused through it. Ah, yes. Like the cocoon of a butterfly—thin and cottony. It added another layer of meaning to the painting that he liked, and he smiled and looked over his shoulder at Childs, who was watching him with a laborious frown.

Rico took another tug on the pipe. He held the

smoke in his lungs for a moment and then exhaled with a sigh. "You want Miss Carter to wear that?"

"Yes."

"I see." Childs smiled. "I was right, wasn't I? You do want the little innocent."

The words blurred together in Jonas's mind. *Theliddleinnocent,* and they were as compelling as she was. Yes, he wanted her. Wanted her in a hundred different ways. Wanted her so badly it was all he could do to keep from hiring a carriage and racing to Gosney's house to get her.

But then he thought of the painting waiting in his studio, and it was even more compelling, the vision burning in his blood too tantalizing to deny or postpone. His fingers itched to get started. He threw the mosquito netting over his shoulder and started for the door.

From the bed, Rico laughed, and then he started humming, a slow chorus, a familiar and compulsive melody, "'I dream of Jeannie with the light brown hair . . .'"

Jonas turned from the door with a smile. A dream, yes. Genie Carter was that. She was a lovely dream, and the night was shimmering with color and vibrance, and even Childs, languid as he was, looked shining and beautiful as he lounged against the pillow, the candlelight glinting on his hair.

"Come with me," Jonas urged. "The night's still young."

"Ah, yes." Childs struggled from the bed and made his way slowly toward Jonas. "The night's young enough. It's only you and I who get older. Where are we going? Down to the Bowery? Maybe we can find

Clarisse, eh? She's probably over being angry with you."

"No, not there," Jonas said, yanking open the door and pulling Rico after him into the hall. "We've more important things to do."

"Oh? What's that?"

"We're going to paint, my friend," Jonas said, pushing open the door to his studio, feeling a surge of excitement and revelation so pure his whole body tingled with it. "We're going to paint a masterpiece."

Chapter 10

It had been two days since she'd been back to the studio. Two days since she'd received the note from a messenger she'd never seen before, a single line scrawled on a piece of paper torn from a sketch pad, the handwriting bold and black and nearly indecipherable. *No class until further notice. JW.* That was all. No explanations and no apologies, and when Thomas had gone to the studio to inquire, there had been no answer to his knock.

It reminded Imogene of Peter's story about last spring. She wondered if Whitaker had been sitting in his studio, listening to her godfather's summons, lost in his own visions. The thought was disconcerting and uncomfortable, and she found herself feeling that she should go to him, to look in on him if nothing else, to make sure he was all right. But she dismissed the notion. She didn't know Whitaker well enough to intrude, and more than that, she wasn't sure how he would respond if she did visit him—or even what she would feel upon seeing him again.

Imogene glanced at the sketch hanging above her

washstand. The paper still looked crumpled and worn, even though she'd worked painstakingly to smooth the wrinkles, hoping to bring out whatever secrets were hidden in the folds, hoping it would explain everything. She'd thought the drawing would explain why he paid her so much attention, what he truly wanted. But instead the sketch only raised more questions than it answered.

The portrait Imogene had rescued from the floor was of a woman she didn't recognize, a woman whose resemblance to herself lay only in the gown and the hairstyle. The rest . . . the rest was someone Imogene had never seen before, someone she didn't know.

The woman in that picture looked delicate and beautiful. She was half turned toward the artist, and there was something sublime in her profile, something peaceful and confident in her expression, poise and grace in her pose. She was exquisite and arresting, almost . . . sensual. She was everything Imogene was not. And Imogene couldn't help but look at it and wonder who it was he'd drawn, or why he'd thrown it to the ground in anger, as if there were something ugly in it, something profane. At the time, Imogene had thought maybe it was because she was such a poor subject, or that he saw nothing in her worth drawing. But the sketch was so beautiful that now she wondered if his temper had anything to do with her at all.

She sighed and turned away, going to the window to stare out at the park below. She wished she were the woman in the picture—a woman of mystery and grace, a woman who could interest him, challenge him. The longing frightened her. Jonas Whitaker was not the man for her; it was useless to feel desire or yearning. It was useless to want him. But she did, and she knew that was the most dangerous feeling of all.

She leaned her head against the window, feeling the cold glass upon her skin, along with sinking despair. She wasn't the kind of woman Whitaker would be attracted to, she never could be, and the thought filled her with a sense of loss that was impossible to bear.

As impossible to bear as the notion that she might not see him again.

"Imogene?"

Katherine's voice came from the hallway. Imogene's godmother had been solicitous and kind over the last two days, but for once Imogene didn't want kindness. She didn't want the busywork of embroidery and tea. She wanted to think through her confusion—for once she wanted the solitude that had been her life in Nashville.

But Katherine meant well, Imogene knew, and so she sighed and turned from the window. "Come in."

The door squeaked open, and Katherine peeked around the edge. "Oh, Imogene, you *are* here," she said. There was a breathless relief in her voice. "Haven't you heard me calling?"

Imogene frowned. "No. I didn't hear anything."

"Well . . ." Katherine stepped inside, holding out a piece of paper. "This just came for you. I think it's important."

Imogene stared at the note in Katherine's hand, feeling an odd dread at the sight of it. Odd because she knew it was about Jonas Whitaker, though she had no reason at all to think it. It wasn't torn from a sketch pad like the last message she'd received. This was a heavy, cream-colored stock that bespoke elegance and money, as different from the other as it could be. So different Imogene told herself it was absurd to think it had anything to do with Whitaker. But her breath caught anyway as she hurried toward her godmother, and her hands trembled when she took the note from Katherine's hand.

Katherine frowned, her deep brown eyes dark with concern. "Imogene, is everything all right? Is this— were you expecting this?"

Imogene shook her head. The paper felt thick and textured against her fingers. She unfolded it slowly, noting with part of her mind that the thin copperplate handwriting was not one she recognized. Her chest tightened with apprehension. It was bad news, certainly. A quick, impersonal statement telling her he would no longer be teaching her. That, or maybe something even worse, something informing her of his untimely death or . . . or . . .

An echo of Peter's words lingered in her ears. *"The madness is waiting for me, Rico. Should I give in to it?"*

She shut her eyes briefly, willing away the thought before she undid the last crease and read the words. Like before, the message was simple: *Jonas Whitaker requests the pleasure of your company immediately.*

There was no signature.

Imogene felt a sudden, fierce joy, along with an uneasiness that made her mouth dry. "Someone brought this?"

"He's downstairs now," Katherine said. "He insisted on waiting." She patted Imogene's hand, a gentle, reassuring touch. "Dear, is everything all right?"

"He wants to see me."

"Who does?"

"Mr. Whitaker." The questions rang in Imogene's

mind. He wanted to see her immediately, and she had no idea why, still could not begin to fathom what he wanted from her. She could not believe he meant to give her a lesson. It was late, already near dinnertime.

"Well, thank goodness," Katherine said. "So you'll be going to the studio in the morning, then?"

Wordlessly Imogene held out the note. Katherine read it quickly, the frown furrowing deeper between her eyes as she handed it back. "He can't be serious," she said. "Certainly he means for you to come tomorrow?"

"It says immediately."

"Yes, but—"

"Perhaps I should talk to the man who brought it."

Katherine motioned to the stairs. "He's in the hall," she said.

Imogene had to force herself to take the stairs with dignity and grace. Still she couldn't quite go slowly enough, though it seemed an eternity before she saw who waited in the foyer.

Frederic Childs. Imogene hesitated. He was quite possibly the last person she expected to see, and yet he stood as if he belonged there, lazily studying a framed woodcut, his long blond hair falling over the shoulders of his fine blue coat. Like Nicholas, she thought. Comfortable in any situation.

Immediately a smile curved his mobile mouth, his eyes sparkled. "Miss Imogene," he said, making a small bow. "I'm delighted to see you again."

"Mr. Childs." She didn't smile back. She gestured with the note. "You brought this?"

"Yes," he said, starting toward her. Then he stopped, and his gaze slid beyond her. *"Pardon,"* he said with cool aplomb. "I didn't realize there was another beautiful lady on the stairs."

Imogene half turned to see Katherine standing behind her. She'd forgotten her godmother was even there. Distractedly she introduced them.

Childs smiled again, that dazzling smile. "I've heard a great deal about you, Mrs. Gosney. You and your husband are quite well thought of in the art community."

"Oh, you're an artist?" Katherine threw a questioning glance at Imogene.

"He's a friend of Mr. Whitaker's," Imogene explained, hearing the edge of impatience in her voice. "Please, Mr. Childs. This message—"

"Ah, yes, the message." His smile stayed steady, the good humor in his voice didn't fade, but something came into his eyes, some expression she couldn't read. "I've come to escort you to the studio."

Katherine frowned. "It's nearly time for dinner. Surely he doesn't mean—"

"Oh, but he does."

"I know artists have strange hours, Mr. Childs," she continued reasonably. "But surely this can wait until tomorrow."

Childs shook his head. "Forgive me, Mrs. Gosney," he said, disagreeing with firm politeness. "But this can't wait." He looked back to Imogene, and his smile mellowed, his face softened. If possible, it made him even lovelier than before, added a gentleness that was more real than his smooth charm, more insidiously captivating. "Miss Imogene," he said softly. "Jonas would like to see you. Please come."

She wanted to. Oh, Lord, she wanted to, but it was

dangerous to want to go to him so badly. *Say no.* She
opened her mouth to say the words.

Then she looked at Childs, really looked at him, and
the refusal died in her throat. She saw the urgency in
his eyes, an urgency cloaked in smiles and nonchalance, and it made her think again of Whitaker alone
in his studio, staring out the window while the others
pounded on the door. Her reservation died, forgotten
in the strength of compassion and concern. There was
no question; of course she would go to him.

Imogene crumpled the paper in her hand. "Very
well," she said. "I'll get my mantle."

Katherine's frown deepened. "I don't know—"

Childs glanced at her. "I promise to keep her safe,
madame. You have my word she'll come to no harm."

Imogene heard her godmother's hesitation. "Perhaps in the daytime," Katherine said. "But at
night . . ." Her words trailed off uncertainly, her eyes
studied Imogene for a moment before she sighed and
nodded. "At least let me send you in our carriage.
Henry can wait for you then."

"By all means." Childs spoke with smooth, unemotional courtesy, but Imogene thought she saw relief in
his expression when he turned to her, as well as a
slight impatience. "Shall we go then, Miss Imogene?"

She nodded, hurrying to the small armoire at the
back of the stairs. She grabbed her mantle and glanced
down at her gown, wishing for a brief moment that she
had something fancier than the thick bayadere silk
with its stripes of darker lavender velvet and its un-
adorned flounces. She banished the absurd thought
quickly. Lord knew Whitaker wasn't summoning her
for her looks. She doubted he would even notice what
she wore.

She closed the frogged fastenings of her mantle and grabbed her bonnet by its ribbons as she hurried back down the hall.

Childs looked up and smiled. "Ah, there she is," he said. His blue eyes sparkled when he glanced back at Katherine. He took her hand and bowed over it. "It has been a delight talking to you, Mrs. Gosney."

"And you," Katherine answered. Her voice was slightly breathless, the way it always was when she was enjoying herself. "I shall talk to Thomas this evening about commissioning you."

"*Madame,* you are too kind. I await your word." He released Katherine's hand with a smile, and then he straightened, shaking back his hair with a quick, graceful movement before he turned to Imogene and held out his arm. *"Chérie?"*

Imogene nodded and clutched the arm he offered—in her haste grabbing a little too hard. He raised a brow at her, and she smiled weakly and forced her fingers to loosen, feeling the hard warmth of him through her gloves and his heavy coat, smelling his rich, spicy cologne. When the front door shut behind them and they were standing on the stoop, the cool, damp autumn air brushing against her skin, threading through his hair, Childs turned to her with a smile.

"Don't be so afraid, *chérie,*" he whispered. "You look as if you've just handed your soul to the devil for safekeeping. I assure you I am not so dangerous."

She looked at him in surprise. "I'm not afraid," she said. "Should I be?"

He blinked, and Imogene realized that he had expected some witty or clever remark. She glanced away again, feeling embarrassed and foolish, wishing once again that she was the practiced flirt her sister had

been, that she knew anything at all about captivating a
man. She half expected Childs would abandon her
there on the step and take back his offer of escort, but
he only chuckled and led her toward the waiting carriage.

"I don't know," he said. "Perhaps you should."

His words only added to the strangeness of everything she was feeling, the anticipation edged with
worry. But Childs's steadying hand on her arm as they
entered the brougham was reassuring and soothing,
and Imogene found herself trusting him despite the
fact that she hardly knew him.

"You are kind to do this, *cherie*," he said, looking at
her somberly. His voice was quiet and even, but there
was an undercurrent in the words, the same undercurrent she'd heard when he asked her to come, and she
thought of Peter's story, felt the keen stab of worry.

"What's wrong with Whitaker?" she blurted.

"Wrong?" Childs looked at the window, resting his
elbow on the narrow sill and his chin in his hand. She
could see nothing but the curtain of his hair and part
of his profile. "Things are never 'wrong' with Jonas.
They are only more or less normal." There was an edge
of something in his voice—grief maybe, or perhaps
nothing more than simple sarcasm.

Imogene frowned. "I don't understand."

He gave a small laugh and looked back at her, a
bitter smile on his lips. "No, I don't imagine you do,"
he said, and this time he didn't look away, but stared
at her thoughtfully. Imogene flushed beneath his scrutiny, feeling as if he were searching for something, as if
he expected to find something in her face, and when he
spoke again she wasn't sure if he'd found it or not.
"Ah, but you're such an innocent," he murmured—the

words so quiet it was as if he were talking to himself. "Why has he chosen you, I wonder?"

His question startled her, Imogene felt the soft seduction of fear. "Chosen me?" Her voice sounded harsh and too sharp. "What do you mean?"

His gaze stayed on her for another moment, and then he smiled—a light, self-mocking smile—and turned away. "It's nothing," he said, shrugging. "I have known Jonas a long time. Too long, perhaps. There are things you don't know about him—"

"I know he's mad," she said, wanting suddenly to show him she was not as naive as he thought.

He only laughed. "Mad?" he asked. "Who told you this?"

"Peter McBride."

"Ah, Peter. Well-intentioned, well-heeled Peter." Childs looked at her, his gaze piercing. "What else has he told you?"

Imogene licked her lips, feeling as if she'd said something stupid, as if she'd misunderstood something, though she didn't know what it was. "He told me about last spring."

Childs leaned his head back on the padded wall of the brougham, saying nothing, letting the silence fill the carriage until Imogene's head pounded with it.

The carriage slowed. Imogene looked out the window to see the familiar buildings lining West Tenth Street, and concern tightened her chest so it was suddenly hard to breathe. She leaned forward, half turning to look at Childs, and found herself touching his arm to get his attention. "Please," she said, hearing the urgency in her voice. "Please tell me—is he like that today?"

Childs's expression was so somber and questioning

it took her aback. "If I told you he was," he said
slowly, "would you run away?"

The words were familiar. She heard Jonas Whitaker's deep timbre in her mind, the haunting rhythms of
his voice. *"What is it you want from me, Miss
Imogene Carter? Why don't you run away . . . ?"*

She didn't take her eyes from Childs. She shook her
head. "No," she said. "No. I wouldn't run away."

The brougham lurched to a stop. She heard the
wheels splash through mud, the groaning squeak of
carriage springs. Frederic Childs sat up and leaned forward, reaching for the handle on the door. He opened
it and stepped down, holding out his hand to help her.
Imogene put her gloved fingers in his palm.

"Well?" she asked hesitantly. "Is he . . . ?"

Childs glanced at the building, at the top story,
where the fading sunlight glinted off the windows of
Jonas Whitaker's studio. Imogene felt his hand tighten
around hers.

"I think you'll find him changed."

It was all he said as he led her to the stairs.

Chapter 11

She had expected silence, or if not that, then at least respectful quiet. But the studios on the first floor hummed with activity. Artists scurried through the open lower gallery, hanging paintings and propping easels, laughing and teasing and toasting each other with glasses of deep red wine.

The commotion reassured Imogene. She told herself it would be silent if something was wrong with Whitaker, that the air would be heavy with fear and worry instead of fragrant with cigar smoke and the rich, gamey scent of roasting fowl.

But she had no idea if that was true.

She glanced up at Childs as he led her toward the stairs. "Is it always like this?" she asked quietly.

He shrugged. "There's a showing tonight."

Which told her nothing, Imogene realized. She tried to banish her nagging sense of worry as she climbed the stairs to the third floor. But it wouldn't go away; in fact, it only grew worse when they reached the top, because unlike the rooms downstairs, the studio doors up here were tightly shut, the hallway quiet.

Deadly quiet, she thought. Except for their footsteps and the rustle of her skirts, there was no other sound at all.

The stillness didn't seem to faze Childs. His step didn't falter as he guided her to the last door on the left; he didn't hesitate before he rapped sharply on the panel and pushed the door open.

"Jonas!" he called, ushering her inside and shutting the door behind them. "Jonas, we're here."

There was no answer. The studio was as still as the hallway had been. The only movement was the flickering lamp on the table and the growing shadows of sunset. Imogene frowned, glancing about her. The studio looked different, more crowded than before. She'd never seen so many brushes soaking in jars, and dishes of color were scattered everywhere. Propped against the wall were three sketches—wildly painted, uncontrolled swathes of bright color and bold forms—all similar, as if he'd tried repeatedly to capture the same image. When she looked around, she saw at least six others leaning against books and statuettes and upended pans, each frenzied, each like the rest.

She thought of the black paintings Peter had told her about. These were nothing like that. These were light and airy. There was no darkness in them, no bleak landscapes, and she was startled at the extent of her relief. She had not realized how completely she'd expected to find him as he'd been last spring, yet it was clear—at least from the paintings—that he was not.

"Lord," she breathed. "He's been painting."

Childs threw her an amused glance. "How observant you are, *chérie*," he said. "Yes, he's been painting like a demon. Now, if I could only figure out where the hell he—"

"Ah, you're here!"

The voice seemed to come from nowhere. Imogene jerked around to see Jonas Whitaker shoving aside the tapestry covering the far doorway. The sight of him startled her even more than his voice had. Whitaker was smiling as he stepped into the room. *Smiling.* A lightning-quick smile, one so foreign and strange it looked out of place on his lips, somehow bizarre. Imogene stared at him in stunned amazement, waiting for his smile to twist, to become the familiar thin sarcasm. But as he crossed the room to them, she realized that his smile was real. She thought again of Childs's words. *"I think you'll find him changed."* Yes, he was that, but except for his smile she didn't know why she thought it, didn't understand why she felt such a magnitude of difference. There was something about the way he walked . . . a curious energy in his motion. It pulsed from him, restless and fast and involving, and she couldn't take her eyes from him.

Not even when he came to a stop in front of her, his gaze caressing her as if he couldn't look at her enough, his green eyes glimmering and passionate and so intense they nearly burned. They paralyzed her. She felt that tense excitement again, the elation that had possessed her the last time she'd seen his eyes like this, the day he'd leaned over her shoulder and talked of Michelangelo.

Whitaker stepped closer. He took her hand—so quickly she didn't have time to pull away or protest—and tightened his grip as if he were afraid she would do just that. She felt the soft caress of his thumb against her fingers. There was a subtle energy in his touch, a quivering excitement, and when he looked at her she saw it in his eyes too, that same exhilaration. It was strangely heady. She felt trapped by it, mesmerized.

"Tell me, Genie," he said, drawing out her name the way he always did, so it sounded like a touch. "Are you ready to see the world with us tonight?"

His words, his touch, were overwhelming. *The world* . . . He made it sound exotic, enticing, compelling. Like everything she'd ever dreamed of, everything she'd ever wanted.

He leaned closer. " 'Stop this day and night with me,' " he quoted, and his voice took on the deep, rich tones of a song. " 'And you shall possess the origin of all poems.' "

His words sounded familiar, but she couldn't place them, and it wasn't the words that mattered anyway, but the way he said them, the way his fingers stroked rhythms on her skin. She couldn't look away, didn't want to look away, and when she felt again the soft shivers of desire, she told herself he was only playing with her.

But this time she didn't care. She wanted to lose herself in his eyes, to hear him talk and feel his touch. Without conscious thought she leaned toward him, wanting to feel that magic again, waiting for it, needing it.

But then that look disappeared from Whitaker's eyes —or . . . it wasn't that it disappeared, not really. It was more as if he'd cloaked it, banked it the way one banked a fire, covering the hot, dangerous coals with deceptively cool ashes, and when he finally released her hand, saying "So you'll come," Imogene felt a surge of disappointment. She stepped back, trying to compose herself, watching as he moved quickly across the studio, grabbing a shiny black beaver hat from a

table littered with tubes of paint and brushes. He settled it on his head and motioned to the door. "Hurry
now, or we'll be late."

He was confusing, bewildering. Imogene felt as if
some important part of a puzzle were missing, but the
spell he'd woven around her was still too strong, and
she couldn't think of what the missing piece was,
couldn't seem to gather her thoughts at all. She threw
a puzzled glance at Childs, who was watching Whitaker with detached amusement. "But where are we—"

"No questions," Whitaker interrupted lightly. "It's a
surprise, Miss Carter. Don't you like surprises?"

"But I—"

"Come along, *chérie*," Childs said easily. "Trust me.
You'll be in no danger."

No danger. Imogene looked at Childs, at his blond
hair gleaming in the last rays of light streaming
through the window, at his perfect features, and then
she glanced at Whitaker. *No danger.* He looked like a
panther, with his green eyes and that long, dark hair
falling over his shoulders, contrasting subtly and tac-
tily with the gleaming top hat. She realized suddenly
that he had dressed for this evening as well, but unlike
Frederic Childs's blue superfine and richly embroi-
dered waistcoat, Jonas Whitaker's clothes were starkly
black. A black frock coat and tight black trousers and
a broad black tie that covered his collar. The only relief was the white shirt he wore, the only concession to
decoration the gold buttons on his black waistcoat.

Yes, he looked very much like a panther. Sleek and
black and captivating.

No danger.

Oh, what a lie that was. What a terrible lie. She
thought of how she'd lost herself only moments be-

fore, how he made her forget who she was, forget everything. She was in the worst kind of danger, she knew it, and yet when he looked at her with those glittering, compelling eyes and crooked his finger at her, she found herself going to him, following him and Childs without a word out the doorway and down the hall, through the bustle on the first floor. And when he waved away her godfather's brougham—and Henry—in favor of a cab that waited just outside, she didn't say a word, merely got inside and settled her skirts and felt the press of him beside her and the warmth of Childs's leg across from hers.

But when Whitaker rapped on the ceiling and the carriage sped off, wheels spinning wetly through the New York streets, Imogene felt the danger again, a danger that shivered in the close, too-warm air, that hovered around Jonas Whitaker. She clenched her fists in her lap and looked out the window and felt a breathless excitement more terrifying than anything she'd felt before. Because though she felt the danger, it was warm and welcoming and tempting. More tempting than it had ever been with Nicholas. Impossible to resist.

She only hoped she could survive it this time.

He couldn't stop watching her, even though she didn't look at him, even though her shoulders looked rigid and her hands were clenched tightly in her lap. It didn't matter; she would relax once they got to Anne Webster's. Once they got to the salon it would all begin—the thought brought exhilaration shivering up his spine, sent the cold heat of adrenaline coursing through him.

He had dreamed of this, had thought of nothing else. He had struggled with the portrait the last two days, inspired but unable to truly capture the mystery he wanted. The essential core of her eluded him. It eluded him as he tried new forms and played with color. It eluded him as he tried to sketch the shadows of her face. Even though he could see her before him, the image shifted and changed, and this morning he had looked out the window and seen the gray streaks of rain and known—suddenly and completely—what was missing.

She was an innocent, untried and naive, still closed to the world. Why had he not remembered that before? He couldn't see the beauty of her soul because he hadn't found it yet. It was still buried beneath convention, wrapped in silks and wools and velvets. She was truly the butterfly of his vision, suffocated by society's strictures as well as its clothes, and he wanted suddenly to take those clothes off, to tear away the cocoon and bring her shining and newborn into the world, to liberate her.

He knew he would see her then, truly see her. Once she was released, he would find the soul that he ached so to capture on canvas. He would free her, and in turn, she would be his courtesan, his masterpiece. She would be his gift to the world. It was why he'd sent Rico to find her. He was too impatient to wait, and Anne Webster's Thursday night salon was the perfect place to start.

Ah, he could hardly wait to get there. He felt restless and on fire; his blood was pulsing in his veins, tingling in his fingertips. He glanced at her again, but she kept her gaze fastened on the window of the carriage, on the lights that grew brighter and brighter as the darkness of twilight began to fall. He tried to see what she was seeing, and found himself mesmerized by the way the light reflected on the window and the dark red of her bonnet, by the way it glanced off the satin to send a vibrant glow of color into her face. It made her look ruddy and alive, and he took it as a sign. Alive, yes. She would be twice as alive by the end of the night. Like the genie in Aladdin's lamp, she was a prisoner—a captive waiting to be freed with a gentle touch.

He smiled at the thought, and imagined he saw the swish of smoke surrounding her, smelled the soft rich scent of Arabian spice.

"Something amusing?" Childs asked.

Jonas glanced at him. Rico leaned into the corner of the carriage, looking every inch the cynical and jaded artist. It made Jonas laugh. "How dour you look," he said. "Dour and sour. You'll make Genie think we're going to a funeral."

She turned from the window. "Where *are* we going?"

He gave her a smile. "The world awaits us, Genie. Make your three wishes. Or should I make mine?"

He saw the puzzled look in her eyes.

"Three wishes?" she asked.

Jonas leaned forward. The red glow cast by her bonnet seemed to intensify, the dawn-pink of her skin was captivating. He wanted suddenly to take her just as she was; for a minute the urge was so strong he trembled with it. He wanted to seduce her, he wanted her to seduce him. And then he realized she *was* seducing him, though he didn't think she knew it. "I know what my first wish would be," he whispered.

She sat back, swallowing hard, and turned away so abruptly all he was left with was the back of her head, her impenetrable bonnet. He heard Rico's snort of laughter, and Jonas grinned and sat back again, ignoring Childs to watch the lights pass by. They were like fireworks, welcoming and celebratory, and for just a moment he forgot her and Rico, for just a moment he was caught up in the idea that the lights were for him, that they were a message from God. *"Change the world . . ."* The words matched the rhythm of the passing lights, the sharp burst of yellow that slowly melted away through the window. *"Show us what art can be. Mankind awaits your brilliance—"*

The carriage lurched to a stop.

"Looks like we're here," Childs said, sitting up straighter. He glanced out the window. "Ah, yes. Waverly Place."

Waverly Place. The words filled Jonas with anticipation and impatience. Without waiting for the driver, he wrenched open the door. The clean scent of rain-cleared air met his nostrils, along with the smell of mud and the faint hot odor of the gaslights lining the street. He stepped out, looking at the well-kept brownstones and brick town houses that lined the road, their steps guarded by pillared balustrades and wrought-iron gates. It was still early, and people were walking along the flagstones, their voices carrying easily on the cold air, echoing up and up until they filled the clear, dark sky with sound.

He tilted his head to follow them up. The sky wasn't dark enough for stars, not yet, but it would be soon enough. For now, the gaslights could be stars, their light seemed to penetrate his soul, to fill it with laughter and talk and warm, beautiful places. Prisms of color danced on puddles still left from yesterday's rain, and he stared at them, mesmerized by the changing patterns, the shapes, until he heard the creak of the carriage and turned to see Rico helping Genie from the step.

Jonas caught her gaze. He saw her puzzlement as she looked at the building before them, and it made him want to laugh, to taunt and tease her, to ease her uneasiness away, bit by bit, one piece at a time. Shoes first and then stockings, pantaloons and corset and chemise. One by one, until she stood in front of him, naked and ready to face the world . . .

He grinned at her and then laughed at the startled look on her face before he strode through the open gate of the brownstone in front of them. He took the steps quickly, stopping at the stoop to wait impatiently for her and Rico. When they reached the bottom step, he rapped sharply on the door.

It opened almost instantly, flooding the twilight with light and talk, with the tinkling notes of a piano. A man in a checkered waistcoat and heavy gray beard stood at the doorway.

"Whitaker!" he said, and there was a warmth in his voice that made Jonas smile in return. "Where the hell have you been lately? And Childs too! This *is* an occasion."

"It's good to see you, Webster," Jonas said. He looked into the hallway, into the press of people. "A busy night, eh?"

"Yes, of course. It wouldn't be successful if it wasn't too crowded to move," Leonard Webster said easily. "Come in, come in." He stood back until they'd squeezed inside, and then he shut the door and leaned against it. "Who is this you've brought with you? Have we met, Miss—"

"Allow me to present Miss Imogene Carter," Childs

said with his usual gallant charm. "Miss Carter, this is Leonard Webster, our host."

She smiled an enigmatic smile, and now that the street lamps were gone, her face looked pale beneath the harsh red bonnet, almost ethereal. "How do you do, Mr. Webster," she said.

Webster smiled politely, and Jonas knew the man was wondering who the hell she was. It was obvious she was no actress, and though she had her own quiet charm, she was not the kind of woman he and Rico usually brought to the salon. He could almost see Webster ticking off the possibilities in his mind: *Actress? No. Mistress? Not their type. One of those Bohemian thinkers? Perhaps, but . . . no.*

"Feeling confused, Leonard?" Jonas asked dryly.

Webster only gave him a bland look. "An original, I see," he said, and then he squinted at Childs. "A friend of yours, Childs?"

"A student of Jonas's," Rico said.

Jonas nearly laughed aloud at the look of surprise on Webster's face. "A student of mine, yes," he said, teasing. "She's a brilliant painter, Leonard, the next Raphael—so be kind to her, won't you? Where's Anne?"

"At the piano." Webster motioned to a wide doorway flanked with velvet curtains of red and gold. "Where else? That young musician from the Broadway is here tonight."

Jonas nodded, anxious to get into the crowd, to feel the energy of talk and ideas pulse around him, to see revelation flicker over Genie's skin with the candlelight. He glanced into the parlor. It was crowded tonight; people leaned against walls and filled every seat, and the rush of talk lifted over the piano, heavy and enticing. Anne Webster preferred candles to lamps on these nights, even though the house was piped for gas, and what seemed like hundreds of candles covered tables and the sideboards and the piano, dripping waxy and fragrant over silver and crystal holders, shivering in the drafts caused by movement and talk.

He saw Anne across the room, resplendent in pink satin, her dark hair caught up in a spray of roses. As if she sensed his gaze, she glanced up and smiled, motioning him over with a silent wave.

He looked over his shoulder. Rico was watching him, waiting for the next step, and beside him Imogene Carter stood, her brown eyes darting as she looked at the people talking in the foyer, her cheeks unnaturally flushed.

Excitement made him impatient and a little rough. He grabbed her gloved hand in his and heard her startled little rush of breath as he jerked her closer. She stumbled against him, a quick press of silk and wool and warmth, a whiff of almond, before she pulled away again.

"Where are we—"

"Shh," he said, touching his false finger to his lips, then glancing at Rico. "Coming?"

"As always," Rico said wryly. "Lead the way, *mon ami.*"

Jonas tightened his hold on Genie's hand, pulling her after him as he made his way through the crowd. Many people he recognized; they were the same artists and writers and actors who were always in attendance at Anne's little soirées, and he smiled a hello and pushed through them on his way to her, anxious to introduce Genie and set his plans in motion.

By the time they finally reached their hostess, his

excitement was at a fever pitch. He saw the way Anne looked at him, the speculation in her stare, but when they approached, she only leaned forward and gave him a brief hug, touching her lips to his cheek before she pulled away again, leaving in her wake the faint scent of roses.

"Why, Jonas," she said, smiling. "How good of you to come—and you too, Frederic. The two of you have been making yourselves scarce lately."

Rico took her hand and bent over it, his blue eyes twinkling. "Only because the longer we stay away, the more beautiful you are when we return."

Anne laughed. "You never change, my dear," she said. "It appears even Paris leaves you unaffected."

"Or perhaps too affected," Jonas said.

Anne's smile widened. She drew her hand from Rico's, her eyes were dark with curiosity as she looked at Genie. "I see you've brought a guest."

"Miss Imogene Carter," Jonas said. "One of my . . . students."

That surprised her, he noted with a smile. Anne's finely arched brow rose. "A student?" She looked at Genie again, more sharply this time, and Jonas imagined that she saw what he did, the pearl beneath the shell, a mystery hidden by the mundane. His heart beat faster when Anne turned her gaze to him and he saw a knowing look in her eyes and knew she understood. It made him feel vindicated and confident, so exalted he wanted to laugh out loud.

"I'm pleased to know you," Anne said, looking back to Genie with a small nod. "I hope you enjoy yourself this evening."

Jonas felt the nervous flexing of Genie's hand beneath his fingers, but she only smiled—a soft, quiet smile—and said, "I'm sure I shall."

"Come, let me introduce you all to a new friend of mine. I believe he intends to read from Whitman's new poetry collection this evening. It should be quite exciting." Anne took Jonas's arm, leaving Childs and Genie to follow. She leaned close as they moved through the crowd. "A student, hmmm, Jonas? Or perhaps—something else?"

Ah, she was clever. Jonas delighted in it, as he always did.

"You never miss a trick, do you, darling?" he asked with a quick laugh. He leaned close to whisper against her ear, and the words came spilling out, he couldn't say them fast enough. "She's my masterpiece, Anne. Can't you see it? She's so fresh, so untried, but I tell you there's something else there—a great mystery—"

"She's your new model, then," Anne said with amusement. "An interesting choice, Jonas. Though innocents are a bit passé, don't you think? And certainly not your style."

He was confused for just a moment. Innocents not his style? He'd been corrupting innocents most of his life, or at least women who pretended to be so. Now that he thought about it, he wasn't sure he'd ever had a true innocent. Not until now. Perhaps that was what captivated him so. Perhaps it was only that she was the real thing, naive and pure, something to despoil. . . .

The cynicism of the thought put his nerves on edge. No, he didn't want to despoil her. But to teach her— ah, yes, he did want that—to see the change in her eyes, from purity to sensuality, from naiveté to wisdom. His own Aphrodite, the most sensual of the gods.

"Help me find her divinity," he said urgently, and

when he saw the bewilderment on Anne's face, he plunged ahead, wanting her to understand. "I'm looking for a goddess, Anne."

Anne's brow furrowed. "You speak in riddles, Jonas. I—oh, excuse me, there he is." She pulled away from him, gesturing to a man in the crowd. "Davis! Davis!"

Jonas threw a curious glance at Rico, who came up just behind him, Genie in tow.

"Davis Tremaine," Rico explained in a low voice. "He was in Paris during the summer. An art critic who fancies himself another Ruskin." Rico lifted a brow and smiled. "He has a reputation for having a true eye for beauty—as well as an . . . unfortunate . . . hunger for it."

Anne stepped back, waiting for Tremaine to make his way through the crowd. She spoke *sotto voce.* "Tremaine's quite popular lately. He'll give the girl the cachet you're looking for." Then, when Tremaine reached them, she straightened, breaking into a practiced hostess smile. "Ah, here you are now. Davis, have you met Jonas Whitaker and Frederic Childs?"

"Childs, of course. Haven't seen you since Paris. Delighted." Tremaine nodded at Rico. He leaned closer, squinting in a nearsighted way, and held out his hand. "Regret to say I haven't had the pleasure of meeting Mr. Whitaker yet. I've heard of you, of course, sir. Saw that last exhibition—when was that, a year or so ago? Particularly liked that provincial thing you did—"Women with Sheaves,' I believe you called it."

An ass, Jonas thought, dismissing Tremaine summarily. He barely remembered "Women with Sheaves." He'd done it at Barbizon, years ago, and it was an inferior painting, a test of color, a minor work even to his own eyes. It offended him somewhat that

Tremaine hadn't seen anything of his new attempts, and the fact that he felt that way irritated Jonas even more. Normally critics mattered little to him—bad critics especially. And he knew instantly that Davis Tremaine, whatever his ambition, was a bad critic. Jonas wondered why the hell Anne had brought him over.

"And Davis, this is Imogene Carter," Anne continued blithely. "She's one of Jonas's students."

"Charmed, Miss Carter." Tremaine's words were short and clipped and rigidly polite. Dismissal rang in his tone, disinterest deadened his eyes. It only angered Jonas more. Tremaine was as stupid as he was pretentious. There was a living work of art in front of him, and he failed to even see it. Annoyed, Jonas took Genie's arm and started to turn away.

"Mr. Tremaine, I'm pleased to meet you."

Genie's soft voice stopped Jonas in his tracks. It was calm and even, and he released her arm, surprised. Even more surprised when he realized that, but for the flush in her cheeks, he'd never seen her look so calm, so self-possessed.

Except once. Jonas swallowed as the vision came into his head. A creamy shoulder, a knowing smile—

"My father admired your writings very much, Mr. Tremaine." She was smiling at the critic now, a quiet, shy smile. "He told me he thought you were insightful."

Tremaine stopped short. "Insightful?"

"He liked what you said about Hiram Powers." Her face wrinkled as if she were trying hard to concentrate. "That statue—the 'Greek Slave.' About how the chain she wore made it clear she was a slave, so no one cared about the fact that she was . . . nude."

Tremaine visibly puffed. "Yes, of course. Once you

saw the chain, you knew the story. Perfect sculpture for those too lazy to interpret truly great art." He leaned closer, pulling a pair of fragile glasses from his pocket and settling them on his long, thin face, scrutinizing her though the lenses. "So you're a student, Miss Carter? Are you also an aficionada of fine art?"

She laughed.

It was a small laugh, but it startled Jonas. He'd never heard her laugh before—or he supposed he had, once; he thought he remembered seeing her laugh with McBride. But he hadn't *heard* it then, and now the sound of it galvanized him, made him feel light-headed and strange.

"I try to understand what little I can, Mr. Tremaine," she said. "Though sometimes I'm not sure it's fine art I'm seeing."

Tremaine chuckled. Jonas stared. He hadn't expected her to have the presence to hold her own with these people. He remembered suddenly that she'd come from an upper-class family in Nashville; she'd probably spent hours at her parents' parties, had no doubt learned all the niceties of conversation. But he'd forgotten that, had seen that upbringing only in how cosseted she was, how protected.

And now here she was, not just smiling but conversing. Captivating Tremaine the way she'd captivated him, and looking as if she wasn't sure whether to be confused or delighted by the critic's attention. It was charming—it was more than that. It was so innocently erotic that it paralyzed him. There it was, the mystery he'd been looking for, shining from her so brightly he couldn't believe the others didn't see, that they weren't blinded by her presence.

"An honest woman," Tremaine said, taking off his

glasses and shaking his head as he tucked them back into his pocket. "My compliments, my dear." He looked at Jonas. "She is quite perfect, sir—I look forward to seeing her in paint."

And then, with a quick good-bye, Tremaine disappeared again through the crowd.

"Well." Anne turned with a smile. "Congratulations, Jonas, you've captured Davis's attention."

"An easy enough feat when you've any intelligence at all," Rico commented dryly. He smiled at Genie. "You've another fan, Miss Imogene."

She smiled back, but it was frayed at the edges, distracted and self-conscious. "Another fan," she repeated, the words so soft it was as if she spoke to herself. She looked at Jonas. "What do you suppose he meant—about seeing me in paint?"

And it was gone. In that second, the mystery fell away, and she was ordinary again, the colorless girl who had walked into his studio two weeks ago.

But that was the masquerade, and now he knew it— and knew what he had to do to find the mystery again.

"Perhaps some wine," he said, looking to Childs.

Rico smiled, a knowing light in his pale blue eyes. "Ah, yes, some wine." He held out his hand to Genie. "What do you say, Miss Imogene? Shall we have a glass?"

Chapter 12

She watched him the way everyone in the room watched him, and for the same reasons—because it was impossible to look away. He was mesmerizing, intoxicating. A god, almost, Imogene thought, seeing the religious zeal in his expression as he talked and gestured. Though a group of people surrounded him, he stood out from them, tall and finely made, his intense green eyes and flashing smile hypnotizing. He gestured with his glass, but not a drop of wine spilled, and though he drank it almost as quickly as he spoke, his movements were graceful and alluring.

Tonight, the entire room seemed to spin around him. People flitted to him like moths to a flame, and he kept them there, circling his orbit, flushed and laughing. She could imagine their dazzling repartee even though she couldn't hear them, could imagine the sheer brilliance of their ideas, the sharpness of their wit.

She wanted to be one of them.

It was a ludicrous thought, she knew. She could not keep up with them. She was no Bohemian thinker; she was barely an artist. Her father was right, after all, when he told her she needed steel instead of milk and water. But still . . .

She forced her gaze deliberately to the women who stood beside him. Anne Webster seemed to sparkle beneath the onslaught of his gaze; her dark eyes were vibrant and shining, and her laughter rang through the room. How beautiful she was, flushed with his attention, alive in the sound of his words. And the woman on his left, a woman elegantly clothed in green satin and black velvet, was equally lovely. A woman who smiled into his eyes and hung on his every word. A beautiful, interesting woman.

Imogene's throat tightened. She was nothing like them. She'd already proved it once tonight, when she'd tried to charm Tremaine, when she'd tried to impress Whitaker, impress them all. She flushed with embarrassment when she remembered the way she'd stammered, offering her father's opinions instead of her own, mangling them in her usual way. When she remembered Tremaine's patronizing comment. *"An honest woman. My compliments, my dear."* He'd been laughing at her—even Childs's kind attempt to camouflage it hadn't hidden the truth.

She heard Whitaker's laugh across the room and winced. She wondered why he'd even brought her here. Earlier tonight, in the carriage, she had hoped maybe—just maybe—they were on their way to someplace special, that he wanted to show her something magical, to give her some insight into his art. And that hope had lasted until they stepped into the Websters' glittering parlor, and Imogene realized this was no special place at all. It was only a salon, like all the others she'd been to, like the ones her father had held when Chloe had been alive—a sparkling collection of literati and artists that left her feeling out of place and alone. She could not compete with their wit then, and she couldn't now.

This time the failing was more painful than ever. More disappointing. Because Whitaker had brought her here and she wanted to impress him, wanted that magnetic gaze turned on her. She remembered what Peter had said, how he'd told her that when Whitaker was in a certain mood, he was brilliant, a shooting star. She understood what he meant now. A shooting star. Yes, Whitaker was that.

How did one capture a shooting star?

She wished she knew. She had the feeling that if she could get close enough, if she could wait for just a little while, he might be able to help her understand the things the rest of them all took for granted. Maybe he could make her feel—for even a moment—the sheer exaltation of philosophies and ideas, or give her again the vision, the blinding passion, she'd felt the other day. The vision she had always wanted, the vision that everyone but she seemed to access so easily.

She saw him lean close to Anne Webster, whispering something in her ear, and Imogene felt a longing so strong it took her breath—and then the quick, hopeless drop of resignation. She would never get that close to him. He would never whisper in her ear that way, or laugh with her the way he was laughing with Anne now. What a silly wish it was. What a silly, stupid wish.

Still, she couldn't help thinking it, couldn't help the enticing little voice murmuring in her ear, *Oh, I wish he would smile at me that way.*

Imogene turned away, taking a desperate sip of wine before she started through the crowd again—away from him, though every step putting distance between them felt painful. She heard snippets of conversations, the glib and abstract flood of thought: *"But as Swedenborg said . . ." ". . . he claims to be a Transcendentalist, but I have my suspicions . . ." ". . . if all men are capable of divine inspiration, then shall we consider that 'sin' is simply a lack of spiritual development . . ."*

She maneuvered around the crowd, smiling a smile that felt pasted on, murmuring hellos to people who were nothing more than strangers, drifting away again before they could involve her in a conversation she could not maintain. She drank her wine until her first glass was empty, then a second, until her smile was no longer such an effort to keep up even though the room felt too close and too hot.

But she could not ignore him. In this mood he was too irresistible. She searched for a place where she could watch him surreptitiously, without interruption, and found it—a corner where the musty-smelling, heavy drapes were pulled back from the entryway. She settled into the shadows and glanced toward him, expecting to see him gesturing enthusiastically to one of the others.

He was gone.

Anxiously Imogene glanced through the crowd, looking for his tall form, for Childs's bright blond hair. They had simply disappeared. She stepped away from the curtain to scan the room more closely.

"More wine, Miss Imogene?"

She jerked around so quickly her head spun. Childs was standing beside her, a smile on his face as he held out a bottle of wine. Right behind him stood Jonas Whitaker. They'd come from nowhere; it was impossible that she hadn't heard them. It disconcerted her that she hadn't, but her confusion faded in the sharp, soaring joy of their company.

Childs poured more wine into her glass. "You'd best drink up," he said, nudging it toward her. "God knows you'll need it. Tremaine's readying to torment us with a poetry reading."

She looked down at the glass, trying to keep from grinning like an idiot over the fact that they'd searched her out. "A poetry reading?" she asked.

"We're hoping Tremaine knows more about literature than he knows about art," Whitaker said. He leaned close, smiling at her, his green eyes warm and beguiling. "How about you, Genie?" he asked. "Do you like poetry?"

He was teasing her; it made her feel strangely giddy. "Some poetry," she managed.

"That's a greater appreciation than Tremaine has, I'll warrant," Childs said dryly. "The last rhyme I heard him read began 'There was a young lady from Nice.'" He grinned audaciously at her. "And he mangled that."

Whitaker laughed. "Your polish is slipping, Rico."

"Says the man who never had any to begin with." Childs lifted his glass in tribute. He nodded at the goblet in her hand. "Miss Imogene, you're falling behind."

Obediently she took a sip. The wine tasted better than it had all night, rich and spicy and dusty on her tongue. It relaxed her now, and along with the light in Whitaker's eyes, and Childs's quick tongue, the wine took away her isolation, made her feel warm, as if she suddenly belonged. She wanted to stand here and talk with them all night—in fact, she wished she could. Because in this moment, the specter of her father's words, her own inadequacies, faded away. Standing beside them, she was touching the star.

She laughed at the thought.

Whitaker's smile broadened. He curled his fingers around her arm, and then he was bending close, whispering in her ear. "Come with me."

Come with me. She would not have refused even if he'd given her the chance, and before she knew it, Childs was at her other side, and she was being led through the crowd so quickly the flickering lights of the candles made her dizzy, the hot, fragrant smells of beeswax and perfume stole her breath. It took her a moment to realize everyone was moving, the little social cliques were breaking up, heading toward the far end of the room. The piano music grew louder, the chattering voices sang in her head.

Then Whitaker stopped so suddenly she stumbled. She felt his hand tighten on her arm to steady her. They were standing at the front of a half circle of chairs, and she realized the room was already set up for the poetry reading Tremaine had promised. Five minutes ago, she would have taken a seat in the back and listened in silence, feeling out of place and alone. But now everything was different. In five minutes, Whitaker had changed it, and his hand on her arm, his smile, was such a startling acceptance she felt dazzled and a little winded.

"That's the way." Whitaker spoke in her ear, the words sounded strange, breathless and shivery. "You know, you're beautiful when you smile."

The comment startled her. Imogene looked up at him, sure she was hearing things, sure he could not have said the words. It was the wine. It was all illusion.

He laughed and motioned to a huge chair covered in burgundy brocade.

"Sit, Genie," he said, and his voice was deep and smooth and tantalizing. The room seemed to sway to the sound of it, the smooth, deep reds of the furniture and the drapes seemed to shimmer and pulse with light and dark shadows.

You've had too much wine, she thought, sitting, but it felt good—decadent and somehow enlightening. It reminded her of how she'd felt the day she modeled for the class—that powerful, seductive feeling, and when Childs came to stand at the other side of her chair and poured more wine into her glass, she didn't protest. Nothing felt real. It was as if she were in a dream, a beautiful, enticing dream. She watched the people taking their seats, their exaggerated gestures and expressions, the fine satins and velvets of their clothes glimmering, their skin golden and beautiful in the light. The vision elated her, embraced her.

A laughing Anne Webster tore herself away from a group of people and moved to the front. "We've a special treat tonight," she said, beaming. "Mr. Davis Tremaine has offered to read from Walt Whitman's new poetry collection. It's a stunning achievement, I understand."

"Quite stunning," Tremaine said, ambling over to stand beside Anne. "And quite shameless, I might add."

"All the better." Anne laughed. "Please, Davis, the floor is yours."

Tremaine smiled. His frock coat was unbuttoned to reveal a gold-embroidered waistcoat, the shiny threads glinting in the glow of the candles. He reached into a pocket and took out his glasses, settling them on his thin, pointed nose before he reached for the book lying on a nearby table. Though the intricate, tendriled lettering was hard to read through her unfocused eyes, Imogene made out the words *Leaves of Grass* stamped onto the dark green leather cover of the thin chapbook.

"Which one shall you read, Davis?" Anne asked. "I must confess I've barely read it myself, but I've heard such scandalous things."

"Which is precisely why you decided you had to own it," Leonard Webster teased from his place against the far wall. He toasted his wife with his glass. "Find Anne the most decadent poem, won't you, Tremaine? If you don't, tonight's conversation could be most dreary."

"The one thing Anne isn't is dreary," came a voice from the crowd. "Scandalous poems or no."

Laughter greeted the remark. Imogene heard Childs's chuckle just behind her. He was leaning against the right side of her chair, with Whitaker flanking the left, and the two of them made her feel oddly safe—her own archangels, guardians of the gate. She laughed at the thought.

Far too much wine, she thought, looking down into her glass and knowing she should put it aside. But almost as she had the thought, Childs poured more, and there was such a sense of companionship in his gesture, such an engaging smile on his face, that she took another sip just to please him.

"Perhaps this one," Tremaine said, pausing as he leafed through the pages of the book. He read a few lines silently and then looked up at his audience with a smile. He adjusted his glasses and spread the volume wider and cleared his throat.

" 'I sing the body electric . . .' " he began, his tones slow and lilting. " 'The armies of those I love engirth me and I engirth them . . .' "

The room was hushed, the rise and fall of breathing pulsed around Imogene. She saw the rapt faces of those listening, the flushed cheeks and glittering eyes.

" '. . . And if the body does not do fully as much as the soul? And if the body were not the soul, what is the soul?' "

She took another sip of wine, and another. She thought the glass was almost empty, but when she looked down again it was full, and she wondered if she'd really been drinking it at all, or if she'd just imagined it, too caught up in the words of the poem to remember the drink. She blinked, looking up at Tremaine, who gestured softly while he spoke.

The words were so pretty, graceful and full of sound, like a lullaby. Imogene closed her eyes and leaned back in her chair, feeling drowsy and warm and good, feeling herself sway to the cadences.

" '. . . You would wish long and long to be with him, you would wish to sit by him in the boat that you and he might touch each other . . .' "

The poem was seductive—innocently so, the way a spring day was seductive—full of light breezes and sunshine smells. His voice encompassed the rhythms of the words, and she got lost in the sounds and forgot to hear the meaning. It was so easy to fall into it, into darkness and song, to drink the soft, soothing wine and feel her limbs grow heavier and heavier, and listen the way they all did, enraptured, one collective breath, connected by the fine mesh of words and music.

" 'This is the female form . . . it attracts with fierce undeniable attraction . . .' "

She wished it could go on forever. In the caressing melody of the words, in the heady warmth of Whitaker's care, she almost believed she wasn't plain Imogene Carter. She almost believed she was really part of this night, a Bohemian artist like the rest of them, a philosopher. For the first time she felt capable of offering an opinion on something, on the beauty of Whitman's words, the sublimity of his vision. Yes, she could tell them that. She opened her eyes, feeling a rush of excitement, and leaned forward, ready to speak at the first opportunity—

" 'Hair, bosom, hips, bend of legs, negligent falling hands all diffused, mine too diffused, Stung by the flow and flow stung by the ebb, love-flesh swelling and deliciously aching, Limitless limpid jets of love hot and enormous—' "

The words were razor sharp, startling and so lurid they scattered her thoughts, sent heat flooding her face. She caught her breath, heard the sound echo in the stillness of the room, too loud, too shocked. It cut Tremaine short.

There was dead silence.

Tremaine took his glasses off to look at her. From the corner of her eye she saw Anne lean forward, felt the combined breath of anticipation. Imogene felt suddenly sick. In a matter of seconds, she was a pretender again, an outsider who didn't belong and never would. It was ludicrous that she'd thought she could talk to them. She was a fraud, nothing more. A fraud who was shocked at a few lines of a poem they accepted as inspiration. Lord, what a fool she'd been to think she could belong here, how horribly, horribly naive.

"Shocked, my dear?" Tremaine asked with a smile. She stared at him, unable to answer. He seemed to be wavering against the red and gold wallpaper, the edges of his body blending into it, soft shadows, blurred details.

Anne laughed breathlessly. "You were right, Davis, it is quite . . . scandalous. I loved it."

"Nothing like a little decadence to brighten up an evening," Childs drawled quietly. "Is there, Anne?"

Anne flushed, her eyes hardened, her smile was too bright. "I'm surprised you didn't like it, Frederic," she said brittlely.

"Oh, I think we all liked it," Tremaine cut in. "Except perhaps for Miss Carter."

Imogene flushed. She felt their eyes on her; bright, expectant eyes, and she was immediately tongue-tied. "I—it was fine," she whispered.

"Except for those last lines," Tremaine insisted. "Didn't care for those, did you?"

"Down, Tremaine," Childs said wryly from his place behind her. "Be a good boy."

Davis Tremaine glared at Childs, and then his gaze slid back to Imogene. She felt its scrutinizing heat against her skin.

"For discussion's sake, what was it that offended you, Miss Carter?" he insisted. "Assume you're familiar with the human form—I know you've seen Homer—"

"And having seen Homer, was offended by its simplicity." It was Whitaker's voice, soft and firm and fast with feeling. "Art offends, great or otherwise."

"You're saying if it didn't, it wouldn't be art?"

"I'm saying we all see art differently," Whitaker said. He surged forward, his eyes glittering, his body tense with feeling. "You see it in 'Women with Sheaves,' and I see it in—" He twisted around, and before Imogene could move or think, he grabbed her hand, pulled her to her feet. "I see it in this."

She stood there, too confused to move, too uncertain to comprehend what was happening, or why Whitaker had brought her forward. She was dimly aware of Childs taking her glass, but mostly all she saw was that they were staring at her—all of them.

"Careful, *mon ami*," Childs said. His voice was soft and chiding.

Whitaker ignored him. "Look at her. Look at her and tell me you don't see art." He talked quickly, his words falling over themselves. "It's as Kant says, everything is point of view—how we see something gives it significance. When I look at her I see art in all its finest forms—art that encompasses the entire universe. Look at her, Tremaine, and tell me you don't see it. Tell me you don't see the whole of life in her face. She is much more than eyes and hair and breasts—she is . . . like music—like the parts of a symphony. Think about it—every instrument is separate, every note, but together they shape the music—they *are* the music. It is only separateness that offends—sex without interpretation, naked limbs without reference. The notes without the symphony. I can take her clothes off and offend half this room, but it won't change the essential truth of her, and it won't make her any less a work of art."

"Good Lord," Tremaine said eagerly. "And beauty is the same, then? Just an interpretation?"

"Or essential truth?" Anne asked. "Do you think . . ."

Their voices swirled around Imogene; she felt dizzy and strange, sick with wine and confusion. She looked at them all around her, at their avid faces, their lips flushed with wine. She looked at Childs leaning languidly against the chair, watching them talk with that lazy, too-jaded gaze, and at Whitaker, who had forgotten her in the heat of discussion, and she felt bewildered and oddly humiliated, an outcast again. She stared numbly at the others. They were gathered around each other now, talking wildly, eyes intense, words fired with inspiration.

She did not belong here. The thought slammed through her, a painful revelation that hurt doubly now, because she knew what it felt like to be part of things, because she'd had those first few minutes of basking in his sun. Misery made a knot in her stomach, pressed behind her eyes in the ache of tears. Slowly, carefully, she made her way through the crowd, slipping past the others until she reached the entryway and then the hall. It was an old habit; during her father's parties she'd often sought refuge in empty rooms. There was a reassuring familiarity in the quiet, in the sound of distant talk echoing from the salon. Now she needed that solitude, needed the comforting stillness to creep inside her until she could tell herself it didn't matter, until her tears disappeared along with her illusions and she became plain Imogene Carter again, a woman who was tired and hungry and wondering what time it was.

Imogene took a deep breath, looking at the rapidly dwindling row of cloaks and mantles and coats hanging on the pegs near the door. It felt late; perhaps she could find a place to lie down. Just for a while, just until Whitaker and Childs were ready to leave.

She wandered down the hall, feeling graceless and clumsy from the effects of wine. The candles only went as far as the foyer; the rest of the corridor faded to darkness. She stumbled along it, exclaiming with pain as she bumped into something. A settee. She reached out and felt the slippery hardness of satin and wood. With a sigh of relief, she sank into it, pulling her legs up and leaning her head back, closing her eyes. The upholstery was slick and hard, and combined with the slickness of her gown, it was difficult to keep her balance. But she was so tired, and her limbs felt so heavy, and her mind was befuddled with drink and confusion. She couldn't think, not about tonight. Not about Tremaine or Whitaker, not about anything. But sleep—sleep sounded good now, a way to forget her humiliation, her failure. She let her head fall back, let her hands drop. Just a short nap, just until they came for her—

She heard the step in the hall an instant before the dreams came. Imogene opened her eyes.

Whitaker was standing there, holding a single candle —a candle that sent light glowing around him like a halo. It turned his skin to gold and put colors in his hair, touched his deep-set eyes with radiance and sent his black-clad form disappearing in shadow. For a moment, she thought he *was* a dream—a vision conjured by her wine- and sleep-befuddled mind. For a moment, she felt no surprise at all, only a warm, reassuring acceptance.

Then he spoke.

"Genie," he said. "Don't run away from me." And his voice was a deep, soft whisper that floated on the soundless air, a voice that hinted of temptation and the dark, secret places of night. A voice that belonged to every nightmare she'd ever had.

And every fantasy.

Chapter 13

She groped for something to say, an "I'm not running," or even a simple, composed "hello." But the words seemed suddenly unnecessary, superfluous, and instead she just stared at him as he moved toward her, a mysterious man of shadow worlds and dream places, a man who existed far better in her imagination than in reality.

A small smile touched his lips as he stopped in front of her. "You look frightened," he said, and his voice was low and sensuous and touched with amusement. "Are you frightened?"

"No." It was true. He didn't frighten her. He never had. He filled her with a sense of promise, of potential, and the only frightening thing about that was the thought that she might not fulfill it. "I'm not afraid."

His smile broadened. He knelt before her, setting aside the candlestick, and took her hand, enfolding her fingers in his long, elegant ones. "I want to show you the world, Genie," he whispered. "Ah, what a ride it will be. . . . Will you come with me?"

There was an urgency in his words, a harsh persuasion, and she realized that he believed she might refuse him. As if she could refuse him anything. His words shivered inside her, an echo of the ones he'd spoken to her earlier, a promise that hovered in the air and made her weak with longing. All her uncertainty, all her questions, faded away, and she no longer cared why he paid her so much attention or what he wanted from her. It was enough that he *was* paying attention to her. It was enough that he wanted anything from her at all. No one had ever wanted her for herself. Not even Nicholas. Especially not Nicholas.

She looked up into Whitaker's eyes, shadowed as they were by the dim light of the candle. "Yes," she said. "Of course I'll come with you."

He laughed, a short, exhilarated sound, and stood, pulling her to her feet, leaving the candle to burn unattended in the hallway as he led her down the hall. His step was fast. She stumbled over her skirt and gripped his hand for support, but he didn't slow, not until they were almost to the foyer and she looked up to see Childs waiting by the door, holding her mantle and Whitaker's hat in his hands.

"So you found her then," he said as they approached. "Hurry along, *chérie,* before Tremaine finds us again. He's taken quite a fancy to our brilliant friend here."

Whitaker only smiled. He dropped her hand to take the hat Childs offered, and she shrugged into her mantle, barely having time to fasten it before they hurried her through the door and out into the clear, chill night.

At the bottom of the stairs, Whitaker stopped short, his whole body stiffening as he stared up at the sky. "Christ," he murmured. "Look at that."

She followed his gaze. The night was beautiful; the

clouds that had brought the rain earlier were gone, the
sky was clear and dark blue, scattered with thousands
of stars that twinkled like chips of ice in the freezing
air. Imogene hugged herself against a sudden breeze,
saw her breath, frosty and smoky in the darkness.

"What am I looking for?" she asked quietly.

"The gods," he said, and then, before she could ask
him what he meant, he laughed and grabbed her hand
again, striding with great, quick steps to the carriage
Childs was hailing. "Hurry," he urged. "The night is
disappearing."

Childs gave him an inscrutable look. "We've hours
yet," he said, standing back from the door so she could
climb inside. When she had pulled her skirts around
her, he took the seat opposite, lounging in the corner
with his usual indolent grace. "You may want to provide Miss Imogene with a meal, *mon ami*," he said
when Whitaker settled into the seat beside her. "I
imagine she's starving, since we took her from her dinner."

The moment Childs said the words, Imogene realized he was right. She'd forgotten all about dinner,
and now that the wine she'd drunk was settling poorly
in her stomach, she felt the faint but growing pangs of
hunger.

Whitaker blinked as if Childs's words confused him.
"A meal?" he repeated blankly. He looked at her, his
gaze boring into her as if he could somehow assuage
her hunger with a glance. "We've no time to stop," he
said, and there was a faintly accusing tone in his voice,
as if he blamed her for needing something as prosaic
as food.

"I'm all right," she said quickly, not wanting to anger him, afraid he would leave her behind if she admitted to hunger. "I don't need anything, really."

"Don't humor him, *chérie,*" Childs said dryly.

"I'm not," she protested. "Truly, I'm not hungry."

Childs didn't believe her, she knew, but he said nothing as the carriage started. The jerk of the springs forced her against Whitaker, and he grabbed her hand and kept her there, anchoring her to his side, not releasing her even when the carriage swayed and it was obvious he could not support himself with his false hand.

She wondered why he didn't just let her go. It would be so much easier for him. But she was glad he didn't, even when she saw how he pressed his feet into the floor to keep from falling into her on the turns, even when she felt the flex of his hand, the tightening grip of his fingers. And when he looked down at her and said, "So how did you like our little party, Genie?" she had the absurd feeling that he cared about her answer, that her opinion mattered.

She hesitated, struggling to find the right thing to say, something worthy of his respect. But his regard was too new and too unfamiliar, and she couldn't concentrate. Finally all she said was, "Your friends are very interesting."

From the corner, Childs snorted.

Whitaker laughed. "Friends? Ah, no, darling Genie, I wouldn't exactly say they were friends. Acquaintances, more like. There are more vipers in that room than in the whole of South America, I'd warrant." He looked at her, his eyes gleaming in the passing light. "But some of them are brilliant. Their philosophies are interesting even if their morals aren't. These people can make gods or destroy them, darling. And we were making gods tonight."

She stared at him in confusion. "Making gods?" When he didn't explain, she turned questioningly to Childs, who shrugged but made no attempt to answer. Yet his expression was strangely thoughtful; he watched Whitaker with a careful scrutiny that was somehow disturbing.

She had no time to discover why. Within moments the carriage stopped, and when she looked out the window she saw they were in front of the studios. Imogene felt a quick stab of disappointment. It was too soon. Whitaker had led her to believe he was taking her someplace else, someplace special, and she wanted that—oh, how she wanted it. But now it was obvious the night was already over. Her throat tightened; she tried not to show her frustration as they got out of the carriage.

She gestured toward Thomas's brougham, which still waited by the curb. "I should go now," she said politely, reluctantly. "You must have—"

Whitaker spun around so quickly she faltered.

"Are your promises so easily broken, Genie?" he demanded. "Or are you frightened after all?"

"No," she said. "No, I—"

"Then send your man away."

"You're safe enough, Miss Imogene," Childs drawled softly, glancing at Whitaker. "Though it may not seem like it."

The relief that surged through her was overwhelming.

"Rico, tell him to go on home, won't you? We'll send Genie later."

Childs smiled wryly. "I'm sure he'll be ecstatic."

Whitaker ignored him. He urged her toward the steps and the front door. "Hurry now, we're wasting time," he said, his hand a gentle pressure at her waist. He opened the door and nearly lunged inside, ignoring the people crowding the huge open room of the gallery, propelling her toward the stairs at the back of the room as if the other artists and their guests didn't exist.

She glanced behind her, searching for Childs, but when she saw him enter they had already reached the stairs—she had just enough time to see him follow a man into another room before Whitaker pulled her with him up the steps so quickly she could barely catch her breath. She had no chance to worry about the fact that Childs had left her alone with Whitaker. They were upstairs before she knew it. It felt as if her feet barely touched the ground as Whitaker led her down the hall to the door of his studio.

He released her long enough to open the door and usher her inside. Then he was grabbing her again, pulling her with him toward the tapestry-covered doorway at the far end of the studio.

His bedroom.

Imogene tensed. His words came flooding back. *"I want to show you the world, Genie . . ." "Ah, what a ride it will be. . . ."* Suddenly she thought of the way he'd pressed against her all those days ago, the way his hand stroked hers, the rough desire she'd felt, and fear washed over her, making her throat tight and her mouth dry.

He gripped her hand tighter and turned back to give her a sensual smile. "Don't tell me you're afraid now," he said gently, in that low, charismatic voice. "Not now."

She stared at him, unable to speak. Her heart raced, she felt the tingling of a strange anticipation in her stomach.

"Come along," he said, and even in her fear she couldn't resist. He pushed aside the tapestry and went inside, and she saw the newel-posted bed in the corner, rumpled and unmade, its threadbare quilt slipping to the floor, saw the paint-stained clothes he'd abandoned in tousled piles, and before she realized what was happening, he was dragging her past them, through a small doorway half hidden by the bed, up a narrow, dingy flight of stairs.

"Wh-where are we going?" she asked, stumbling behind him.

"To the roof," he said. He paused at the top, where the passage was barred by a beaten, rickety door, and released her hand. "Here we are," he said, satisfaction filling his voice. He flipped the latch, pushed open the door. She felt the instant rush of cold wind. "There are whole worlds up here, Genie," he said. "Come and see them with me."

Then he plunged through the door and disappeared.

It seemed to take her an eternity to follow him. Jonas stood outside the door, throwing off his hat to feel the cold breeze in his hair, to feel the night brush his skin and welcome him. He shrugged off his frock coat, loosened his silk tie until it hung limply around his neck, dragged at his shirt so the chill, crisp air caressed his chest. God, the world was beautiful from up here. He hurried to the edge of the roof, looking at the street three stories below, at the gaslights casting their glowing halos onto the flagstones, painting highlights on horses and carriages that moved like dark shadows in the night. The silhouettes lengthened before his eyes, a kaleidoscope of sound and movement. Ah, yes, so beautiful.

He was so caught up in the vision he didn't hear her when she finally stepped onto the roof, not until she was right behind him.

"What are you looking at?" she asked softly.

He turned to face her. It was only a quarter moon, yet the night was clear enough that its light touched her face. He saw the way she looked up at him, the dark luminosity of her eyes, the way her lips parted, and it was so much like his vision of the courtesan he was momentarily stunned.

She gave him a small smile and glanced away. "It's a lovely night."

Her movements were so delicate, so fragile. He stared at her profile, drinking in the sight of her, the line of her jaw, the straight, short nose, the slope of her chin. He watched the shadows shifting on her face, each movement accenting something else, a highlight on her skin, her mouth, her eyes. He saw the way the moonlight glanced off her bonnet. Christ, that bonnet. It was the ugliest thing about her, the ugliest thing about the whole evening, and he grabbed at the ribbons, ignoring her startled jump as he jerked the hat from her head. He heard her "oh" of surprise when he tossed it over the side of the building.

Then it was only a shadow in the darkness, catching the wind and fluttering to the street, startling a carriage horse, who nickered and shied away. The shout of the driver echoed in the night, the reins jangled as he brought the horse sharply into line.

Jonas looked back to her. Her hand went to her

head, she pushed back strands of hair that had loosened with the bonnet, escaped from the barely held-together chignon. She tried vainly to straighten it, tucking tendrils back into the bun, shoving at pins.

"Take it down," he said.

A startled breath again. She stopped midmovement, looked at him with wary eyes.

"Take it down," he whispered.

She hesitated. Then she licked her lips and looked away, and he waited while she pulled the pins from her hair, loosening it a little more with each movement, until she held a handful of pins and her hair was falling around her shoulders, straight and heavy and glinting silver and gold in the moonlight.

"I've been wondering what it looked like," he said.

She gave him a funny little smile. "Why?"

"Why? Ah, why?" He laughed, seeing the confusion on her face, a wistfulness that was charming and innocent. The little moth was turning into a butterfly before his eyes, and he wanted more, so much more. He grabbed her hand and pulled her to one of the thick chimneys breaking the shadow plain of the roof, sitting near it and urging her down beside him.

He leaned his head against the brick and stared up at the sky, at the thousands, millions, of stars, and before his eyes they began rushing at each other, falling stars, streaks of light that reminded him of the gaslights passing by the carriage windows, and suddenly he had the thought that they *were* the street lamps, that all the lights of New York were gliding through the night, bent on collision.

"Genie," he said. "Tell me what you know of the world."

"What I know?" She laughed lightly, self-deprecatingly. "I'm afraid I know precious little."

"Oh? And how is that?"

"I—" She looked down, plucked at the fabric of her gown. "I have not gone many places."

Her voice was soft, so soft he had to strain to hear it. Jonas looked back at the stars. "There is traveling and there is traveling," he said. "Shall I tell you something about the world? The truth of it? One man travels to a hundred places. He knows the scenery in Africa and the canals of Venice, he knows the Pantheon and the pyramids of Egypt. And in each place, he sets up his tent and drinks his tea and orders his servant to press his clothes. Another man lives in Nashville. He stands back and watches the crowd, and he knows what each man's voice sounds like and how to read a face and the smell of every woman's perfume. Tell me, darling, which of them knows more of the world?"

"But the one knows only Nashville," she protested, and Jonas heard the confusion in her voice, and something else, an exclamation of alarm, or . . . surprise, or perhaps it was only his imagination.

"Broaden your mind," he said. "See the whole of it, the complexity. Knowing the world is understanding what you see. Apply that to your art and you have all of life before you—all of God." He stared up at the stars, the street lamps of New York. "A world of gaslights," he murmured.

"Gaslights? I'm . . . sorry. I'm not . . . as worldly . . . as your friends. I'm afraid I don't understand."

He heard the confusion in her voice, the painful reluctance in her admission, and it cut through his vision, erased the beauty of the stars. She thought she was something less than those fools she called his friends, those vipers at the salon, and the realization stole his breath, made his heart hurt, made him want to tell her how wrong she was, how shallow and insipid they truly were. It made him want to show her . . .

Ah, yes, *show* her.

Quickly he reached behind him, grabbing the frock coat he'd abandoned moments ago, digging through the inside pocket until he found the small sketch pad he always carried, and the charcoal pencil. When he had them in his hands, he turned back to her, smiling at the confusion in her expression.

"Let me tell you what I think of my 'friends,' " he said, opening the sketch pad to a blank page. He grinned at her. "Let's start with Anne, shall we?"

She gave him a puzzled, uncertain smile. "I don't understand—"

"Ah, but I suspect you understand very well, Genie," he teased. "For example, tell me about Anne."

"I barely know her."

"You don't need to know her to see her," he said. He poised the pencil over the paper. "Describe her to me."

"But—"

"Describe her."

"Well . . ." She paused, staring thoughtfully off into the night before she turned back to him. "I don't know." She shrugged. "She was very beautiful."

He leaned forward with a laugh, brushing her cheek with the end of the pencil. "Such easy words, Genie. Words that mean nothing. Let me show you what I mean."

It was an easy talent, one he had possessed since he was very young, one he rarely used now. He drew quickly, a few lines only, but when he was finished, Anne Webster was before him on the paper, her round cheeks a bit too round, her doe eyes very wide and unblinking, her short nose a mere wisp of line. With a flourish, he handed the pad to Genie, who took one look and laughed out loud.

"A caricature," she said, and he heard the breathless surprise in her voice, the delight. "Oh, how ridiculous you make her look."

"She *is* ridiculous," he said, feeling a rush of pleasure at Genie's laughter. "They all are." He grabbed the pad from her fingers and drew another—Davis Tremaine this time.

She grinned when she saw it. "You've been too kind," she said, pointing to the wisp of beard, the huge bug eyes behind absurdly tiny glasses. "He's much more pompous than you've shown him, don't you think?" She gave him an arch look and lowered her voice in an attempt at mimicry. "'. . . Yes, of course, Miss Carter. It's the perfect sculpture for those too lazy to interpret truly great art.'"

She did it so perfectly he laughed out loud, and the pure pleasure of it coursed through him, intensified when she laughed along. Her eyes lit in the darkness, he heard the ring of her laughter—soft at first, then more confident, huskier, *happier*—and suddenly he saw her with a clarity of vision that stunned him. He looked at her and he saw again the woman who had posed for his class. The self-confident beauty who had held her chin high and lowered her dress.

And in that moment he realized how wrong he was about her. He had thought she was his goddess, his courtesan, but she was much more than that—good God, so much more. There was something else in her too. Something he'd never allowed himself to see before, something that made his soul cry out in yearning. Honesty. Strength. Safety.

Safety . . .

It frightened him, how pure the thought was, how reassuring. Safety. Christ, when was the last time he'd thought that about anyone? Had there ever been a time?

His laughter died abruptly, he found himself trembling. And then slowly, slowly, she stopped laughing too, and he saw the sudden bewilderment in her face when she turned to look at him.

"Jonas?" she asked. Then she gave him that uncertain smile again, that crooked, beguiling hesitation. It was not as beautiful as her laughter, but he was mesmerized by it all the same. By that, and by the soft touch of her fingers on his hand, the uncertain caress.

"Draw me another one," she urged. "Show me who they are to you."

It was all he could do to speak. "Is it truth you want, then?" he asked.

"Yes." She smiled, and he heard the relief in her voice. "Yes."

But he was no longer sure of the truth. He had lost something—or gained it, he wasn't sure which. He was confused when he looked at her, confused by the things he saw in her, by a reality that jibed strangely with his fantasy. Who was she? Who was she really?

He put aside the pad and leaned forward, wanting reassurance, wanting badly to look at her and see only the woman of his fantasy. She was staring at him, her forehead creased with concentration, and he saw she was trying to comprehend him; he imagined the wheels turning in her brain, the ceaseless search for answers. She was curious and alive and open. There was no dissembling here, he realized. Nothing but the cocoon cracking open little by little, showing the first bit of brilliant color. A color different from the one he'd expected. A color that tempted and cajoled him, that had him bending toward her.

She was a marble statue coming to life beneath his artist's hand, Galatea to his Pygmalion, and he wanted to touch her, to make love to her here on the hard roof, with only the light of the stars and moon shining down on them. He wanted to hear her moan, wanted to see the sensual knowledge come into her innocent eyes, the self-awareness, the celebration of intimacy.

But mostly he wanted the safety of being with her. The salvation he dimly sensed. He wanted her strength, because he had none of his own . . . .

"You want truth," he whispered, touching her hair, letting the heavy strands fall over his fingers. He felt her stiffen and then relax when he drew away again— an infinitesimal relaxation, a subtle pause—and then he touched her again. He touched her mouth, felt the soft, warm swell of her lips, the moistness of her breath.

"Let me show you what I know of it," he murmured. "Your mouth can be considered a hundred ways. Rico would look at it and he would see the light and shade; Byron Sawyer would see the color; yet another artist might see the line. A hundred truths, and not one is wrong. There are no original ideas, darling, only original visions. Each of us would draw your lips a different way, yet none of us could capture the complete essence of them." He paused, hearing her hushed, rapid inhalations, seeing the frosty steam of her breath in the cold night air. "There is only one way to find real truth."

"How is that?" Her voice was hushed. It sent a shiver through him.

He smiled, cupping her jaw in his hand, leaning forward. "Taste it for yourself," he said. And then he kissed her.

Christ, she was soft, so soft and so warm, and just the mere touch of her lips aroused him, the quiet eroticism of her hesitation. He expected her to pull away, so he tried to hold her closer, felt a surge of frustration at the lack of strength of his false hand, the uselessness of it. But in the same moment he realized she was not drawing back, was not protesting with maidenly affectations and trembling hands the way he'd anticipated.

But she was not kissing him back either. She was stiff and awkward against him, and he drew away and looked into her eyes and saw her uncertainty and her longing. *Longing.* It nearly undid him. He saw her in colors suddenly, bright blues and pinks that suffused her skin, that played with luminescence in the moonlight, fell into her hair in rainbow prisms. Ah God, his butterfly . . .

"This way," he whispered, and he bent and took her mouth again, tracing her lips with his tongue, hearing the hush of her breath with his body, the soft sound in her throat. He released her chin and grabbed her hand, bringing it up to his shoulder, feeling a numbing relief when he felt her fingers touch his hair tentatively. It inflamed him, that simple touch, and he pressed her mouth open, pressed deeper, wanting the heat of her, the taste—wine and sleep and sweet, humid warmth. She was nothing like he'd imagined, everything like he'd imagined. As rich and heady as he'd wanted, more giving than he had expected, and he unfastened one of the frogs of her mantle, eased his hand between the heavy wool folds, warm from the heat from her body, felt the hard wrap of her corset beneath the satin of her dress, the armor that kept him from touching her ribs, from cupping her breast. Ah, God, how frustrating, that cocoon of safety, as frustrating as the courtesan, as incomplete.

And he wanted completion, wanted to hold her soul in his hand, to press into her body and feel her convulse around him, to know he'd possessed her as no one else had. The truth of her, the essence, would be his tonight, the way her thoughts already were.

He broke the kiss, pulled back. She opened her eyes slowly, as if drugged, and then she blinked and looked away, laughing slightly, a nervous, shaky sound. She touched her hand to her swollen lips.

"I suppose . . . I suppose you think—"

"Come with me." Jonas barely heard her words. He lunged to his feet, pulling her with him. He felt the vibration in his body. It was burning him up, using him, and he wanted to slake it in her now, wanted to feel the strength of her soul caress his, to take her breath and wrap himself in that hair of hers. Christ, he couldn't wait.

He heard her footsteps behind him, heard the harsh rasp of her breath, but he didn't slow, kept his grip firmly on her hand. He strode to the door, down the stairs. She stumbled once against him, and the press of her body nearly had him turning around to grab her, to take her right there on the steps, but he waited until they reached the bottom of the narrow stairwell, waited until they were safely in his bedroom, and then he backed her against the wall and held her prisoner with his body.

"Tell me you want me, Genie," he said. He wanted her to say the words, ached for her to say the words. He looked down into her eyes, eyes that seemed suddenly infinitely deep, infinitely dark. Eyes that held the secrets of the world. Eyes that held salvation. *"I want to know what it's like to be you,"* she'd said once, and he thought that this would do it, that he could show her now what it felt like, the elation of climax, the uneasy peace of repletion.

She hesitated. One second, and then two, and he thought he would go crazy then, thought he would tear off her clothes and take her without consent, without caring. But he couldn't do it. He wanted the words. He needed the words.

He heard the ache in his voice. "Please. Tell me."

Her breathing was deep and labored. She swallowed and looked away, and he saw the uncomfortable tightening of her jaw, the indecision. Then she looked back at him again, and he saw the *yes* in her eyes, the answer he wanted. The answer he suddenly felt he could not live without.

She opened her mouth to speak. "I—"

"So there you are, *mon ami*."

It was Childs's voice. Light and teasing, taut with amusement. It was like ice water crashing over Jonas, and with a sound of frustration he released her and whipped around to face his friend, who was leaning against the door jamb, a steaming bowl in his hand. "Christ, Rico—"

"The hair down is a stunning look for you, *chérie,*" Childs said, ignoring him, stepping fully into the room. He held out the bowl to Genie and smiled. "Care for some dinner?"

——— Chapter 14 ———

*J*mogene watched him as he paced, his long hair flying out behind him, his movements restless, violent. His words cascaded like a waterfall, sounds bubbling and twisting as if he couldn't get the ideas out quickly enough, and though he paused now and again, laying his hand flat on the table, leaning forward to nod at her or Childs for emphasis, the moment was always gone so soon Imogene was left wondering if he'd truly stopped at all, or if she'd simply imagined it.

She did not understand him. Imogene looked down into her half-eaten *boeuf bourguignon,* suddenly losing her appetite. Her stomach twisted, the smell of wine and beef nauseated her.

She did not understand herself.

She thought of where she'd been less than an hour ago, pressed against Jonas Whitaker's body, her hands in his hair, his taste on her tongue. She thought of how she'd almost given herself to him, how she'd wanted to give herself to him, wanted that passion, that intensity, touching her everywhere. Like a mesmerist, he had cast a spell over her, and she had been ready to say the words he wanted, had been ready to say "I want you," knowing that there would be no turning back if she did, no escape, no reprieve.

But the interlude ended before it began, and she wasn't sure how she felt about that, couldn't help thinking of where she would be if Childs had not interrupted them, if he had not done as he promised and protected her from herself. The images pressed into her mind, tantalizing, erotic. Lying in Whitaker's arms. Touching him. Holding him. Kissing him.

And then what?

Then what?

The question burrowed into her, an uncomfortable reminder. Suddenly the memories came flooding back, images from a time she tried not to think about, a time too painful to remember. She saw the morning sun streaming through a window, the breeze blowing fine muslin curtains as the man beside her pulled away and swung out of bed. She saw him wince when he looked at her, the regret deadening his fine blue eyes. She heard his voice, heavy with self-recrimination, angry with a loathing she still wasn't sure hadn't been directed at her. *"Imogene, I'm sorry. God, you'll never know how sorry. . . ."*

She clenched her jaw, pushing the memories away. She glanced at Whitaker, at his rough pacing, his scattered talk, and felt the same longing she'd once felt for Nicholas, the same hope that intimacy would somehow give her a piece of him, an understanding she could not find on her own. That it could change plain Imogene Carter into someone brilliant and talented. Someone like Chloe.

Yes, it was just the same, and just like with Nicholas, Imogene knew how it would end. Jonas Whitaker was so intense, so brilliant, a man with a genius that far surpassed anything she had ever seen. A man like that didn't need someone like her. A man like that would take his pleasure because he could, would use her until he tired of her.

And then he would leave her behind.

The thought pierced her heart, a sharp, desperate pain. She remembered how it had been when Nicholas left her, remembered the ache that stayed with her for months afterward, for years. Even then she'd known it couldn't last, had known he would never stay with her, that she could not hold him. She'd told herself it wouldn't matter.

But it had mattered. And it had hurt much more than she wanted it to. Lord, it was still hurting.

She wondered sometimes if it would hurt forever.

You could not survive it again. The voice slid into her mind, a mocking reminder, a relentless murmur. *You would not survive it.*

No, she would not, she knew. She should leave now. Should run far away from him and never look back. Because she was so close to destruction—she knew too well the feel of it, the smell. It was there, waiting for her, tempting her—

". . . isn't he, Genie?"

She jerked, her thoughts splintering at the sound of Whitaker's words. He was regarding her impatiently, but he turned to Childs before she had a chance to say anything, and kept speaking as if he'd never posed a question at all.

"You soothe yourself with mindless platitudes," he said, gesturing at Childs. "I've heard you, Rico, and I tell you it's nothing but prattle. You say: 'God in His wisdom has a purpose, *I* have a purpose, all this is meant to be. . . .' God has no reasons. He sits on His throne and plays chess with all of us—a checkmate here, a nothing little pawn there. And why is that? I'll tell you why. Because He has no equal, that's why. No friends, no lovers. How jealous He must be of man, who actually has someone to talk to, someone who understands. No wonder man irritates Him. No wonder He torments us." He flashed a warm, meaningful smile at Imogene that made her blush. "God cannot make love. He cannot have companionship."

"I've heard this before, *mon ami.*" Childs grinned and tossed back the final sip in his wineglass, barely pausing before he poured some more. "So how does that theory explain the great works of mankind? Why would an envious God let art survive, for example? Or doesn't God have the capacity to appreciate Da Vinci?"

"Da Vinci is God."

"Really, Jonas, you go too far—"

"No, Rico, think. God created us; doesn't it make sense that there is some of Him in everyone? A bit of divinity, a way to fight the devil—"

"There is the argument that if there's a God there can't be a Satan."

"Of course there can be a Satan. Temptation is the devil, if nothing else. What do you call the urge to torment Anne Webster the way you do?"

Childs smiled and lifted a brow. He glanced at Imogene and winked. "Ah, so I'm Anne's personal devil? How appealing."

Imogene laughed.

Whitaker whirled to face her. "Like Genie there," he said, pointing to her. "Divinity shines from her.

She's a butterfly with a goddess's face come to earth. . . ." He paused, frowning. "Perhaps that's the secret then. Yes. Yes, it must be. . . . Of course, Aphrodite was as much a whore as a goddess . . . like God."

Childs frowned. "What the hell are you talking about?"

Jonas laughed. He put his hand on the table, leaned forward. "Creation, Rico—don't you see? Creation comes from evil, from temptation. From that green darkness."

Imogene tried to make sense of his words. *Green darkness?* He was looking at them as if they ought to know what he was talking about, and she tried to understand him, stared at him as if she could divine the meaning from his expression.

She licked her lips. "Of course," she said, searching for something, anything, to say, wanting badly to be a part of the conversation even though she could barely follow it. Something to soothe him. "Of course it must come from evil."

She felt an overwhelming relief when his eyes lightened. He smiled at her, a quizzical, puzzling smile that sent a shiver running deep inside her, made her heart race. "Ah, I see your colors, Genie," he said softly.

"I see your colors." It sounded like a compliment, but she wasn't sure, had no idea what he meant by the words. But then again, the words didn't matter. He was looking at her as if she belonged here, in this room, this conversation. As if her comments were important, as if she were someone extraordinary.

The warnings came trembling back, the small voice in her mind: *You would not survive it,* and she realized suddenly that she didn't care. Because on the roof he had looked at her and she had seen herself reflected in his eyes, and she had looked beautiful there. Because right now he made her feel like she belonged. He made her understand things she had always wanted to understand. There was so much she could learn from him, so much, and though she knew he would hurt her, knew she could not satisfy him forever, that pain would be a small price to pay for feeling his passion, for learning whatever tiny bit of knowledge he cared to teach her. Whatever sacrifice he demanded, she would make it. Lord, she would make it a hundred times if he asked her.

The decision took the weight from her shoulders. She smiled at him, feeling warm and beloved in the heat of his answering grin. He turned to Rico.

"Do you see it?" he asked. "Look at her face and tell me you see it."

Childs took a deep breath and leaned back in his chair. Slowly he looked at her. "See what, Jonas?"

"Aphrodite."

Childs chuckled. His eyes were warm. "What I see is a very tired Miss Imogene. Perhaps we should send you home, eh, *chérie*? Your godmama will be furious with us."

"*No,*" she said, and she heard the thin edge of desperation in her voice. "No, please . . . I'd like to stay awhile longer."

"But—"

"But I'd like to stay." She grabbed her glass of wine and took the last sip, pushing the empty glass toward him to fill.

"No, no, she must not go," Whitaker said, laughing a little. He said it again, singsongy this time, emphasizing the rhyme. "No, no, she must not go. No, no, she must not go."

Childs hesitated, and she saw his concern, a thoughtfulness that turned quickly to resignation. With a sigh he poured more wine into her glass. "There goes my commission," he said dryly. "Ah, well, I suppose the night's still young."

"Too young to give to sleep," Whitaker agreed. He lifted his glass from the table, downed the contents in a single gulp and poured some more. "We've hours yet to dance with the spirits, but then they must go away. No doubt they'll take Genie with them. So tell me, Rico, do you think Caravaggio's angels were simply manifestations of spirits? Religious visions? I've heard it said, but there's such evil in their faces, it grounds them too much in earthly things, in man. But perhaps it's only the models he used. Whores and thieves . . . You know Millet used to say there was divinity in the peasants. . . ."

It was the light that woke her. It streamed into her consciousness, god-beams that caressed her eyelids, the faint light of dawn.

Imogene opened her eyes, blinking in the brightness, momentarily disoriented when she saw the un-curtained windows. For a split second she had no idea where she was, and then she saw the half-empty wine-glass before her, and Rico Childs sprawled, sleeping, in a nearby chair, and the memories of last night came flooding back, along with an instantaneous panic. Good Lord, it was morning. Morning, and she was still here in the studio, still with Jonas Whitaker and Childs.

She was wide awake in an instant, struggling from the clumsy arms of the chair she'd fallen asleep in. The last thing she remembered was the taste of deep red wine and an argument Childs and Whitaker had been having over Rembrandt. She didn't remember falling asleep, didn't remember even thinking that she should go.

Imogene scrambled to her feet. Her stomach twisted with anxiety when she thought of how worried Thomas and Katherine would be, what they would think when she arrived back home now. Oh, Lord, what they would think. . . .

She took a deep breath, anxiously searching the room for Whitaker. Childs was snoring softly in a chair, but Whitaker was nowhere to be seen. There was no time to look for him. She had to get home.

Imogene grabbed her mantle and hurried as quietly as she could through the studio, out the door. She nearly ran down the hallway, down the stairs, a hundred excuses flew through her mind. She felt a growing sense of panic when she stepped outside and realized how late it was—a panic that turned to guilt the moment she saw the brougham waiting. Whitaker had ordered Childs to send it away, but Thomas's carriage was still here. Waiting for her.

She winced and hurried quickly to the door, opening it to find Henry curled in what looked like a supremely uncomfortable position on the seat. He woke the moment she opened the door, sat up with a groan, blinking at her.

"Oh, pardon, miss. I—I didn't mean to fall asleep."

She felt sick. "Don't be ridiculous, Henry," she said. "I'm so sorry. I thought they'd sent you home. I didn't know you'd been here all night."

He rubbed his eyes. "I did go home," he said, frowning. "It was Mr. Thomas who sent me back this mornin'. Said I was to fetch you home an hour ago."

Imogene's heart seemed to stop. "I see," she said quietly, standing aside for the driver to climb out and then getting inside herself, sitting stiffly against the seat.

It seemed to take only minutes to reach Washington Square, and her godfather's house. The carriage jerked to a stop, and when Henry opened the door and helped her to the walk, Imogene's mouth was so dry she couldn't swallow. She struggled for calm as she went inside. In the quiet of the foyer she stopped and closed her eyes, inhaling deeply, searching for strength and explanation.

"Genie."

Thomas's voice came before she was ready. Imogene's eyes snapped open. She saw her godfather standing at the door to his study, his white hair rumpled as if he'd run his fingers through it many times, the circles beneath his eyes evident.

She felt immediately guilty, horribly contrite. "Oh Thomas," she babbled. "I'm so sorry. I didn't mean to worry you, or Katherine. I just . . ." She let the words trail off when he gestured wearily.

"Have you eaten?" he asked.

Her stomach twisted. "I'm not hungry."

He nodded. "Then perhaps you have a moment to talk?"

How calm he was, how reasoned and low his voice. It confused her; she'd expected a lecture, anger that she richly deserved. But then again, she'd never seen Thomas really angry, not in all the years she'd known him.

The thought gave her pause, she felt worse than ever. A tirade would be better. Punishment would be better. But this disappointment that hovered around him like a fog, this strange disillusionment, was somehow harder to bear.

She tried to swallow the lump in her throat. "Of course," she said, shrugging out of her mantle and hanging it on a peg behind the stairs before she followed him into his study. Her dread grew when he carefully closed the door; guilt made her chest tight as she watched him make his way heavily to a chair.

He waited until she took the seat opposite, until she nervously smoothed her skirts and lifted her chin to look at him. Then he sighed.

"Your father has been my good friend for more than thirty years," he began. "I wonder if you can imagine what that means? I wonder if you understand the trust he has placed in me? You are his only child now, Imogene. He would be inconsolable if I allowed anything to happen to you."

Imogene tried to imagine her father grief-stricken over her. It was an impossible image. Anger, she could visualize. Disappointment, yes. But grief? No. Chloe had been the one her father grieved over. Still grieved over. Imogene looked down at her hands.

"I must confess I don't understand what happened last night," Thomas went on. "You've always been such a level-headed girl."

Imogene swallowed. She looked up at him, meeting his eyes. "I'm sorry, Thomas."

He frowned. "I'm not sure that's enough, Imogene. If it gets out that you spent the evening—the night— with Whitaker, your reputation will be in tatters. I doubt I can do much to save it."

"I don't care about my reputation."

"Perhaps." Thomas looked thoughtful. He hesitated, and she saw the question in his eyes, knew he was debating whether to ask it.

She decided to save him the trouble. "Nothing happened, Thomas," she said. "They took me to a salon, that's all, and then we came back and we . . . we talked. I fell asleep—in a chair in the studio."

He made a soft sound, a wry laugh. "Whitaker didn't touch you?"

She wondered how to answer him, felt uncomfortable with the lie she knew he wanted, the safe answer, the *"He was a perfect gentleman."* But she couldn't just lie outright, and more than that, she wanted to talk to someone about Whitaker, wanted some insight into what had happened last night, wanted to understand herself. And since she had been very small, Thomas had always been someone she could talk to— the only one.

But she was afraid if she told him the truth, he would forbid her to see Whitaker, and she couldn't bear that either. Not yet.

So all she said was, "I feel . . . special . . . when I'm with him."

Thomas's thick white brows came together in a frown. "Special?"

Imogene leaned forward, her words falling over themselves in the rush to explain. "I'm not sure how to describe it, but it's like he's—he's changed. Overnight. He was brilliant before, but now he's like . . . like a shooting star. And he's interested in *me*, Thomas. *Me*, not Chloe, not anyone else. He wants to teach me things, and Thomas . . . Thomas, I want to learn them. I want to learn anything he cares to show me."

"Things? What things does he want to teach you, Imogene? Hmmm?"

She flushed and looked down at her hands. "I'm talking about art," she said quietly.

"Oh, my dear, I'm sure you are." Thomas sighed. He leaned forward, took her hands in his. "But surely you realize Whitaker has a reputation. I don't mean to be indelicate, my dear, but Jonas has always had an eye for the ladies—and he is never in a relationship for long."

"You think he'll seduce me and leave me," Imogene said flatly.

Thomas's gaze never left hers. "I think he'll try, if he hasn't already."

She pulled away.

"I'm sorry," he continued evenly, "but I must admit I don't know what to believe. A month ago you never would have done this. You never would have disappeared for an entire night, you would have considered your reputation and our worry. I can't help but wonder just how much Whitaker has to do with this change."

"I've told you—"

"I know what you've told me." Thomas took a deep breath. "I would like to ask you not to see Jonas for a while, but I understand these lessons are very important to you. So for now, I will simply warn you—as your guardian, as your friend. Jonas is an artist; he lives in a different world from you and me. He would think nothing of ruining you. Do you understand me, Imogene? He cares nothing for your future. You are not the kind of woman who could escape him unscathed."

"I'm not like Chloe, isn't that what you mean?" she asked bitterly.

Thomas looked at her steadily. "That is not a failing, my dear," he said gently.

His words startled her. They took her anger and left her with a sadness that seemed to reach deep into her heart, a sadness so deep she could not respond to it. All she could do was give him the answer she knew he wanted, the promise he was hoping for. "I'll consider what you've said," she said slowly. "I'm sorry for putting you through this."

He met her gaze, and she saw the scrutiny in his eyes, had the feeling she wasn't fooling him at all. And when he spoke, when he said, "Consider yourself forgiven, my dear. I merely want to protect you," she was doubly sure that was the case, because though his words were carefully neutral, she heard the chill beneath them, heard the unspoken threat in his reminder.

"I merely want to protect you," he'd said.

But what if she didn't want to be protected?

Chapter 15

When he came back, she was gone. He froze, looking around the studio, wondering if she'd gone into his bedroom or behind the changing screen, but he knew she hadn't. There was a feeling of vacancy in the room, a sense of emptiness, even though Rico was there, still sound asleep, his long form folded into a worn and overstuffed chair.

No, she was gone. Jonas felt a sharp stab of disappointment; he clutched the tube of color in his hand so tightly the paint bulged. With a sigh he glanced down at it. Vermillion, to put life in the courtesan's skin—the same life that pulsed in Genie's. He wanted to find a way to re-create that soft strength in her soul. To show the spirit in her heart. He ached to try. Now. This morning. So he'd borrowed the color from Byron Sawyer, thinking it would take too much time to go to Goupil's to buy it, and more than that, Jonas was afraid she would leave in the time he was gone.

But still he'd been gone too long, though it had been only minutes. Hadn't it? He glanced at the window, trying to gauge the time, and then gave up and looked

back at the chair where he'd left her. Her face burned
in his mind, the erotic tranquility of her sleep—Damn,
how dare she leave him? How dare she abandon him
now, when his entire masterpiece, his entire career, de-
pended on her? With a curse he threw the tube of
paint aside. It thudded against the wall.

"Temper, temper." Rico's soft, lazy voice came from
the chair.

Jonas turned to see Childs watching him from half-
lidded eyes. "Where the hell did she go?"

Rico raised a brow and struggled to sit up, groaning
as he did so. He glanced at the chair beside him.
"She's left then?" he asked, pushing fine blond strands
back from his forehead. "Home, I imagine. How unfortunate. I'd hoped to take her back myself and explain. No doubt Gosney will be furious with her."

"Who gives a damn about Gosney?"

Rico looked faintly surprised. "Why, you should. Especially if you intend to keep the girl close. I can't
imagine he'll approve, given your reputation."

Jonas frowned.

"I would expect a visit from him today if I were
you," Rico went on, his voice deliberately, annoyingly,
casual. "To ask what your intentions are." He slanted
a startlingly blue glance at Jonas. "About which I am
also quite curious. What *are* your intentions toward
the charming Miss Imogene?"

Jonas felt a surge of irritation; he wasn't sure if it
was because of Rico's question or because of the way
he used her name. *The charming Miss Imogene.*
Charming. Yes, she was that. Among other things.
Many other things.

He glared at Childs. "My intentions are none of your
business."

"Come, come," Rico said impatiently. "You forget who you speak to, *mon ami*. I'm not blind. That was no innocent *tête à tête* I interrupted last night."

Jonas felt irritation again, pulsing through his blood, igniting his temper. "Get the hell out, Rico."

Childs didn't budge. "You cannot run away from it, Jonas," he said reasonably. "Think about who she is. The goddaughter of your patron, an innocent. She is no Clarisse. You cannot simply seduce her and toss her aside when you're tired of her."

"I have no intention of doing that," Jonas said angrily, though he had no idea if he did or not. He saw Childs's raised eyebrow, his cynical disbelief, and Jonas's irritation grew, a sharp anger that made his skin hot and his temples pound. "Damn you, Rico, leave me alone."

Rico hesitated. Jonas saw the wariness in his friend's eyes and suddenly he knew what was coming, knew the words before Rico said them.

"You are not yourself, Jonas," Childs said, and there it was, the phrase Jonas had expected, the look he'd seen a hundred times before—ah, God, the look. Compassion.

Pity.

"You are not yourself. . . ." "Because you must wish you still had it. . . ." "This is for the best, son, you must believe me. . . ." Rico's words. Genie's words. His father's words. They echoed in his mind, and it was like being in a room from which he couldn't escape, a prison in his brain that hurt—God, it hurt so damn bad. The pain infuriated him, filled him with a fierce, white-hot anger that overwhelmed reason and everything else.

It exploded in him, uncontrollable, undeniable, and

before he knew what he was doing, he grabbed an ivory statuette, a Chinese love toy he had treasured but that suddenly meant nothing, and threw it at Rico with all his strength.

He saw the rest with the fuzziness of illusion: the ivory spinning through the air, twisting slowly, one end over the other. Too slow, he thought, watching it turn. He wondered if it would ever reach its destination and then forgot what that destination was. He saw Rico's shock, saw his friend twist away, ducking his golden head. Saw the ivory miss Rico by inches, heard the sharp crack of it against the wall, saw it split and fall in pieces that scattered across the floor.

And all the time Jonas thought, *Stop this. You can stop this.* But he couldn't. The rage was still there, burning inside him, and when Rico jerked around to face him, Jonas clenched his fist, his whole body felt tight.

"Get the hell out of here," he said, and though he meant to simply speak the words, they came out in a scream—an otherworldly sound that echoed in the studio, that trembled within its walls. "Get the hell out."

But Rico didn't move at all. His stare cut through Jonas. It was too concerned, too caring, and it made Jonas want to lash out, to hurt someone, anyone. He grabbed another statuette from the shelf, readied to throw it.

"Why do you do this to yourself, *mon ami*?"

Jonas hesitated, and in that hesitation was salvation —he saw it, he tasted it. But it was too far away, too hazy to see clearly, and he struggled for an answer and realized he had no answer to give, no reason except that he couldn't help himself. Ah, Christ, he couldn't help himself.

"Get the hell out," he shouted, throwing the statu-ette to the floor instead, watching it clatter over the stained boards. "Leave me alone."

And he told himself not to care when he saw the way Rico considered him, saw the way his friend took a deep breath and started to the door. He told himself he had a right to be angry. Rico had no right to tell him what to do, no right to insinuate . . . what?

Christ, he couldn't remember. The only thing left was the anger.

And it was only anger that remained when Rico went out the door. Jonas was suddenly left alone in the mess of his studio, alone with his thoughts and his temper. Alone with his vision.

His vision. Ah, yes, his vision.

He looked at the canvas. At Genie.

Genie.

The thought of her immediately calmed him.

It was late. So late there were only a few patrons left in the posh Park Row gambling den known as The Red House. Late enough that Jonas had forgotten his ear-lier anger, as well as the reasons for it. After six hours of working on the courtesan, he'd been filled with the undeniable urge to socialize, to laugh and talk and play, and to that end he'd searched Rico out again, had brought him a bottle of very expensive French cognac as an apology and begged him—cajoled him—into go-ing out on the town.

And now Jonas felt at peace with the world—more than that. He felt . . . in harmony. Yes, that was it. In harmony.

He smiled and sat back in his chair, tapping his fin-

gers restlessly on the table, breathing deeply of the ci-
gar-scented smoke hovering in the room, the musky
scent of men's cologne. He glanced at George Teck,
who sat opposite him. The man stared at the cards in
his hand as if he could somehow divine the world's
secrets from their faces.

"Do you think you could make up your mind before
the year is out, George?" he asked impatiently.

George glanced up. "Just a moment, just a moment.
Stop that infernal tapping, won't you? It's deuced dis-
tracting."

Beside Jonas, Childs yawned. "It's getting late," he
said. "Let's finish this hand, shall we?"

"All right, all right." George smoothed his heavy
brown mustache and threw a voucher into the pile.
"Fifty dollars."

William Martinson took another sip of his bourbon
and shook his head. "Too rich for my blood, boys," he
said, folding his cards. "I'm out."

George looked at Jonas, raising a heavy brow.
"Well?"

A rush of adrenaline surged through Jonas, a restless
excitement. He didn't bother to look at his cards again,
kept them folded on the table, and tossed a voucher
into the center of the pile. "I'll raise you fifty."

"*Mon dieu.*" Rico exhaled in surprise. He leaned
forward, his voice low and concerned and a trifle wary.
"Careful, my love. You were poor as a parson yesterday. Since when did you become Croesus?"

"Don't worry." Jonas waved his friend's concern
away. Nothing could go wrong tonight. The world was
safe and warm; the men who sat at this table with him
were his best friends. He loved them like brothers. Perfect men, as perfect as the fine wine they drank. He

thought of buying another bottle—two or three, perhaps. Nothing was too good for his friends. He would give them everything he owned if they only asked for it. He grinned. "Luck is with me tonight."

"It most certainly is not," Childs contradicted. "By my count you've lost over two hundred dollars."

"Let him play if he wants," George protested. "You're not his guardian, Childs."

Jonas watched with amusement, seeing the avariciousness shining from George's eyes, as well as Rico's worry. It made him laugh. "But he is my guardian, George," he said. "My guardian angel. Rico, surely you know it's my turn to win."

"I know it had better be," Rico said dryly. "Or you'll be living out of my pockets for the next month."

Jonas ignored him. He glanced around, at the flickering gaslights illuminating the room, glinting on the rosewood furniture and sparkling off the gilt mirrors. It was too bright in here, too bright and too polished. The reflections in the mirrors showed every face in the room. He saw them all; they filled his consciousness, and for a moment all those reflected faces took on the snouts and ears and eyes of animals, and he imagined he was seeing every man's true nature revealed in his face: wolves and foxes and dogs—like those unpleasant dogs of his father's—two spaniels who traipsed around the property as if they owned it, trampling the gardens and the roses. The image made him think of his mother, as well as an old lover who smelled so strongly of roses it had given him a headache to be with her, and that brought back the memory of his old schoolmaster, who had a rosewood settee in his office —just like the rosewood chair in the corner here. Jonas wondered where rosewood came from. Was it wood from rosebushes? The bushes seemed hardly big enough for a chair, but perhaps they grew that way. He thought he remembered a fairy tale where the rosebushes had covered the castle walls, making it impenetrable. Or were those brambles?

"Here you go, then." George set his cards on the table, fanning them so Jonas could clearly see the two pairs, jacks and sevens.

Jonas laughed and spread his own cards. "They're all red," he said.

Childs leaned over, studying Jonas's hand. He heard Rico's sigh of exasperation. "All red, yes. Hearts and diamonds and nothing. *Nothing, mon ami.*" He looked up. "Did you not look at them, Jonas? You've just lost another hundred dollars."

Jonas shrugged, already forgetting the loss, but the sense of well-being melted away, and suddenly he was too restless to sit still any longer, wanted to leave this place and the upper-class gambling houses of Park Row and go down to the Bowery, to see the outpouring of life the theaters released into the streets, the whores and the gang boys and their little red-booted girls. Life in all its diversity, more honest than the lavish gambling dens here, more honest than the conversations he and Rico had been part of earlier tonight, the ones held over oysters and cheese at the Century Club.

"Let's go," he said, pushing back his chair and getting to his feet. "Come, Rico."

Rico glanced up at him. "It's late, Jonas. Let's go to bed."

"Bed? No, no, no." Jonas laughed. He caught sight of a woman near the door, a lithe and lovely girl clothed in the colors of burgundy wine. "One moment," he said, heading toward her.

Childs was at his side so quickly Jonas wondered if he'd flown there. He felt the touch of Rico's fingers on his arm, a firm grip that stopped him in his tracks.

"No," Rico said. "Come along. It's late. Almost morning already. You've done enough damage for tonight. Let's go home."

"I'm not sleepy," Jonas argued. He looked again for the girl, but she was gone already, and then someone opened the door and he saw the thin light of dawn, the beginning pearlescence of the sky, and he forgot all about her. The door shut again, and he felt suddenly stifled. The smoke and wine, the scent of gaslights, the muffle of heavy velvet curtains—they felt oppressive, and he wanted to be outside, wanted to feel the air on his face.

"Very well, let's go," he said, not waiting for Rico's answer before he headed for the entrance. He was across the room in moments, wrenching open the door and striding out into the cold quiet of early morning.

"I'll hail a carriage," Rico said, coming up beside him and then stepping down the stairs.

"No." Jonas stopped him with a word. He looked around, at streets where that brief quiet time was just beginning—that time after the gambling halls closed, just before the business of the day started. He saw the men rushing into the streets like flushed rats, settling their hats on their heads, hurrying home to complacent wives or compliant mistresses. "No carriage," he said, breathing deeply of the salt-tinged air. "Let's walk."

Childs sighed heavily. He shook back his golden hair and frowned, glancing down the street. "It's a long walk, *mon ami.*"

"Come with me, Rico. I need your company." Jonas smiled. He started walking.

"You would be happy with any company," Rico noted, following.

"Ah, but you're so pretty I like to look at you."

Childs's grin was wry. "Pretty is as pretty does."

"Pretty is as pretty does." Jonas's mind flew with the phrase, spiraling out in all directions. Pretty doves. Pigeons. Flocks of them that pecked the street, looking for handouts the same way the girls of the Bowery did, those low-class whores masquerading as upper-class women, wearing jeweled dresses that set off their skin and colors that shone in the lamplight like precious stones. Flashing like the few brooches and rings left in the windows of the shops he and Rico walked by tonight. Diamonds and rubies and sapphires, some as fake as a portrait smile, others—others . . .

He saw it as he passed. It caught his eye, flashing a code meant for his eyes alone, a message from God. A brooch in the window, sparkling with pinks and golds and purples, with amethysts that winked in the soft light of dawn. A butterfly.

Jonas jerked to a stop. He turned, pressing his hands against the window, leaning down to look at it, at the delicate filigree, the jewels hung suspended within it. Ah, God, it was just like Genie, just like his vision. The colors that were muted in the dimness, quiet and dull until they caught the light. But then—ah, then—they were vibrant and alive and beautiful.

"Rico," he breathed. "Rico, look at this. Look at this."

He heard Childs step up behind. Rico's shadow fell over the window, throwing the stones into darkness again.

"Look at what?"

"This." Impatiently Jonas stood aside to let back the light, pointed to the brooch.

"A butterfly." Childs shrugged. "A pretty little bauble."

A pretty little bauble. Oh, so much more than that. So much more. Jonas thought of her wearing it, thought of it next to her skin, glittering on a low décolletage, thought of how it would bring out the colors in her hair. Christ, he wanted that brooch, wanted to hold it in his hands, to give it to her and see its sparkle reflect her eyes. The thought was so compelling he hurried to the door.

"Open up!" he called, pounding his fist on the wood, rattling it so the sound echoed in the quiet streets. "Hey there, open up!"

Rico was at his side in an instant. "*Mon dieu,* Jonas," he said in a harsh whisper. He grabbed Jonas's hand, stilling it. "What do you suppose you're doing?"

"Buying the bauble." Jonas laughed, yanking his hand away. He pounded again, called louder. "You inside! Come out! You've paying customers!"

He felt Rico pawing his sleeve, heard his friend's careful, soothing voice. "Let's go, shall we, *mon ami*? The bauble is hardly worth the trouble. It is not you. And it's barely dawn."

"But it *is* dawn, my friend, and stores should be open for business." Jonas didn't stop. "Hey there! Is anyone home?"

"What do you propose to buy it with? The rent?"

"You scold like an old woman." Jonas said. "And it doesn't matter. I must have it. Genie must have it."

"Genie?" Rico stepped back, frowning. "You can't

be serious. It is—" He grabbed Jonas's hand. "It's inappropriate for her. Come along now. Let's go home."

Childs's words irritated Jonas, along with his friend's calming, humoring tone—the kind one would use with a child. But it didn't anger him as much as Childs's hold on his wrist. Annoyed, Jonas wrenched away. "Don't touch me again, Rico," he warned. "I want the goddamned brooch."

"You can buy it later. This evening."

Cajoling now. And there was that familiar veiled look in Rico's eyes, that look from this morning, the amusement that twisted into concern, into worry. That look he'd seen on the faces of his family a hundred times, the suspicious musing, the silent questioning: *"Are you mad?"*

It put a sick lump in his stomach and irritated him at the same time. Of the two he preferred fury, and he grabbed it now, felt the hot flush of it rush into his face. Without hesitation, he turned away from Childs and pounded on the door, yelling at the top of his lungs.

He was yelling so loudly he didn't hear the footsteps behind the door. He saw the rattling of the knob and thought it was from his pounding until the door was wrenched open before him, and he was suddenly staring into the sleep-drawn, angry face of the shopkeeper —and a leveled shotgun.

"Mon dieu." Rico's voice was a shocked whisper.

"What the hell's goin' on here?" the man asked. He looked from Jonas to Rico and back again.

Jonas started toward him.

"Don't move," the man said, "or I'll blow you straight to perdition."

"We're sorry to wake you, *monsieur,*" Rico said quietly. "My friend here has had a bit much to drink, I'm afraid. I was taking him home."

The man looked at Jonas. "Drunk, eh?"

"In ways you only dream about, old man," Jonas said. He nodded toward the window. "I want the brooch—the butterfly. How much?"

"We're not open."

"You are now. How much?"

"I said—"

"I don't give a damn what you said." Jonas felt his irritation rising again, and the restraining hand Rico put on his arm only made it worse. "Sell me the damn brooch."

The man glanced at Rico. Jonas felt his friend shrug.

"Sell it to him, *monsieur,* if you will," Rico said. "I'm afraid there'll be no denying him this morning."

The storekeeper hesitated, considering, and then finally he relented. He lowered the gun and opened the door to let them in, and Jonas was swept with a relief so intoxicating he wanted to laugh out loud, an elation so swift and complete it was all he could do not to run singing into the streets while Rico and the shopkeeper haggled over the price.

He was barely aware of paying, had no idea how much the piece cost him. All he knew as the clerk handed him the small package was that it was his. His now, and then hers. Soon he would see it glittering on her breast, glowing against pink satin—or, no, not pink satin. Not pinks or lavenders or pale blues. None of the sickly pastels she wore now. No, he would make sure she had velvets by then. Winter colors of dark greens and bronzes and deep, passionate yellows. Midnight blues and rusts and golds to match her hair and warm her eyes.

Ah, yes, he could imagine it. Imagined her hair down, imagined her wrapped in velvet while she lay against the bed and posed for him. The vision was so strong his fingers itched. He thought of the canvas, waiting at the studio, and it beckoned him, a siren song that burned in his blood. God, he wanted to get back to it. Wanted to paint. . .

He shoved the wrapped butterfly in his frock coat pocket and started off, out of the shop without even a good-bye, back to the street where the sunlight was growing stronger and stronger. He was halfway down the block before Rico caught up with him again and grabbed his sleeve and said, "No more, my love. We're hailing a coach."

He looked at Rico in surprise. "Of course," he said, smiling. "Of course, of course. And we should sing too, Rico. Sing to the dawn. That old hymn, you remember? That beautiful old song. What was it called? —I hardly remember." He looped his arm through Rico's, pulling his friend down the street, feeling as if his grin might split his face. He laughed out loud; the sound echoed in the eaves, rose up to heaven. "Ah, the world is good, don't you think, my friend? The world is very good indeed."

Chapter 16

Her heart was pounding as she made her way up the stairs. She wasn't sure what she would find when she reached the studio. She hadn't seen or heard from Whitaker since the night of the salon, but he haunted her nonetheless, his image filled her days.

Invaded her dreams.

Oh, Lord, her dreams. . . . The thought of them brought heat to her face, made her mouth dry. The last three nights she'd awakened covered with sweat and trembling, aching for something. Something that had to do with Jonas Whitaker's kiss, with his touch, with the taste of him.

And no amount of logic made it go away, just as wisdom and good sense hadn't dissolved her resolution to take what he offered, whatever it might be.

Still, her longing for him made her anxious. Still, she was aware of what she risked by coming here again. Just looking at him was enough to make her abandon morals and propriety, and listening to him erased any lingering resistance. He could control her with a word, and she wondered if he knew it and suspected he probably did.

She wished she cared more, but it was hard to care when the tempting little voice inside her, the demon voice, kept whispering, cajoling *"Take what you can. It's all you'll ever have."*

All you'll ever have. It was that voice that kept her from turning and running down the stairs. That voice that had her lifting her chin and hurrying up the last flight as quickly as her skirts would allow. Her heart raced as she went to the last door on the left and knocked. She couldn't bear to wait more than a moment before she pushed the door open and went inside.

There was no one there. Imogene hesitated and glanced down at the note in her hand, the note he'd written telling her that class resumed today. The time was right, as well as the date, but she had expected to find the others here. She was late; Peter, Daniel, and Tobias should already be working away.

But instead she was alone.

Her throat tightened; it was suddenly hard to swallow. Her gaze swept the room, taking in the scattered paints and brushes, the hastily colored canvases. If possible, the studio was in worse shape than the last time she'd visited, littered as if he'd been painting only moments ago, as if he'd just gone out. The smells of turpentine and linseed oil were strong in the room, and suddenly she realized he *was* here. She felt his presence as powerfully as if he stood before her.

Almost as if he'd heard her thoughts, he stepped out from behind the tapestry doorway of his bedroom. Imogene's heart seemed to stop; her breath caught in her throat. She waited, feeling foolishly hopeful and horribly awkward at the same time. Images from the last time she'd seen him flashed through her mind, erotic visions of her hands tangled in his hair, his hips pressed against hers. Her nervousness grew. It seemed an eternity before he looked up and saw her there.

"Genie," he said. Relief surged through her when she saw the grin crinkling his face. He came hurrying toward her. "I've been waiting for you."

Her last doubts fled, her nervousness melted away. No one had ever said such a thing to her before, and the simple phrase left her speechless, defenseless. She tried to remember if anyone had ever looked so happy to see her, and couldn't think of a single person. Lord, not one.

He stopped before her, his eyes burning. She motioned to the empty room. "I—I expected to see the others here."

"Did you?" He raised a dark brow. His grin was mischievous, charmingly wicked. "Yes, well, I had to say something to see you again, didn't I?"

She felt breathless. "You could have asked."

"And you would have come, just like that?"

"Yes." The word came out on a sound, a long rush of breath. "Yes, I would have come."

He leaned forward, and before she knew what he was doing he brushed her lips with his own, a light touch, a tingle of feeling that was so quick she wasn't sure if she'd felt it, if he'd kissed her at all. And when he stepped away from her, striding purposefully across the room, it was suddenly cold where he'd been, freezing where before the air had been too hot. She buried her hands in the folds of her heavy mantle, feeling bewildered, and . . . and excited. A thin frisson of anticipation shivered along her skin.

"What—what are you doing?" she asked.

"Getting ready to paint." He grabbed a canvas from the pile against the wall and settled it on an easel. "Take off your wrap, Genie. Come join me."

Her excitement grew. Quickly she did as he asked, hanging her mantle on the peg beside the door and taking off the pink bonnet she'd bought to replace the one he'd tossed away. She touched a hand to her hair and started toward him.

He was moving feverishly around the room, setting out paints and brushes so quickly it hurt her eyes to watch him. But she did watch him, it was impossible not to. Impossible not to notice his frenzied energy or the too-bright shine of his eyes. She frowned, noticing for the first time how drawn he looked, how tired. As if he hadn't slept. As if he were running on reserves of strength but little else. She wondered fleetingly if he'd eaten.

It worried her suddenly. She hadn't seen him for two days. What had he been doing in that time besides painting? She remembered the night at the salon, the fact that she hadn't seen him eat a thing, the fact that when she'd awakened, Childs was sleeping but Whitaker was gone. Had he slept that night at all? Had he slept since then?

The questions nagged at her, but then Whitaker looked up and met her eyes, and his unexpected, blinding smile made her worries seem suddenly foolish. Lord, even Childs, beautiful as he was, was no match for the man who stood in front of her now, his charisma seeming to energize the very air around him. How could she have thought he looked tired?

He stood back from the easel. He motioned for her to come up beside him. "Are you ready?"

She hurried over to stand next to him. "Ready for what?"

"Ready for art," he whispered in a voice that sent shivers running down her spine. "Not charcoal today, Genie darling. Today you paint."

She looked at him in surprise. "You want *me* to paint? I thought you said I wasn't ready."

His gaze caressed her face, his smile was slow and heart-stoppingly seductive. "You weren't, then," he said, and she had the strange and unsettling feeling that he wasn't talking about art at all. "There are things only paint can teach you," he said, his voice deepening. "Or are you afraid?"

That dark voice brought back the images from her dreams, the erotic fantasies she told herself it was indecent to have. Suddenly they didn't seem indecent at all. No, not indecent, but tempting. Compelling. Inescapable.

"No," she said quietly, not taking her gaze from his. "I'm not afraid."

She saw the fire in his eyes, a flame that leapt and then died away again, that banked-coal look. It made her whole body feel tight; she was not completely sure that her movements were her own as she swallowed and glanced away. "What am I to paint?" she asked hoarsely.

He laughed then, a light chuckle, and moved away. She watched as he walked around the room, quickly grabbing things and shoving them under his arms so he could carry more than one, then arranging them on a table before her: an opalescent vase, a silver cigar case, two red-veined apples and a blue velvet ribbon.

"This," he said, gesturing at the display. "A true study for you, Genie. An artist's test." He came to her again, reached around her for the paints he'd scattered on the table, pulling dishes and tubes of color into place. "These are the colors we'll use."

She felt the brush of his breath against her cheek, was mesmerized by his nearness as he grabbed a tube in the palm of his hand, uncapping it with a practiced, one-handed motion. He squeezed the color onto a palette—vermillion—and she watched as he added the rest: white lead and ultramarine, a touch of ivory black, burnt umber, yellow ochre, and a small pool of Naples yellow.

"Now, Genie," he said, stepping back—a tiny step, one that left him close enough that she still felt the heat from his body. "Paint."

Paint. As if it were easy, as if the colors alone would tell her what to do. Imogene felt the freezing touch of panic; it made her fingers stiff as she reached for a brush. *Paint,* he'd said, but for her painting had always been little more than an exercise in futility. Watercolor sunsets and houses. Yards with flowers. Washes and tints and pale colors without body or substance. It was all she knew how to do.

But he was waiting. She felt him there beside her, felt his impatience, felt that fierce energy. She looked at the still life in front of them, at the opalescent glass, the swirls of pearly color. Saw the silver case and the muted shades of the blue velvet and the delicate green of the apples. She felt a wave of frustration, of hopelessness, that coursed all through her. She would never be able to do this. In a hundred years, she would never be able to do this. She was not Chloe, she was not an artist. She was a fraud.

Then she felt him move behind her. She felt his hand on hers, his gentle pressure urging her to the pal-

ette. "Paint, Genie," he whispered, directing her to the
first color, to ultramarine. She watched her hand dip-
ping the brush, pulling color out, mixing it with white
until she had a pool of pale blue, a base color. She
watched him take her hand to the canvas, watched the
vase take shape—vague still, nothing but a start, a
wide bottom and a narrower neck, the slash of a wide
lip. And all the time she felt him behind her, around
her. Felt the press of his fingers on her wrist, his moist
breath at her ear.

She felt mesmerized again, completely lost. Completely his.

"Pearly tints," he said. "No palette knife, Genie.
Mingle the colors with the brush—ah, that's right.
Make them sparkle."

She did as he asked without a word, dipped the
brush, let him lead her motions, and the opalescent
glass began to shimmer on the canvas.

She heard his voice in her ear, a quiet brush of
sound. "Sfumato here," he whispered, and under his
direction she softened the lines, with his help she
painted film upon film, creating hazy, smoky shadows.

"Impasto," he murmured. "Not so much. Slower.
That's it, darling. Slower. Slower."

Like a seduction, his words. He stroked her with
them, beguiled her with sounds instead of caresses.
Sfumato, impasto, chiaroscuro. And when she was
lost, when his words had taken away her will and her
strength, he added the touches. He let his hand slip
down her wrist until he was covering her hand, until
the paint that marked her fingers spread to his, until
she felt the gorgeous, buttery feel of it between their
hands, the smooth, thick slickness of it spreading over
her skin. So delicious. So erotic. She watched, frozen,

her mouth dry and her heart pounding, as he dragged his fingers back again, over hers, over the back of her hand, her wrist, leaving color behind, a streak of blue against her skin, marking her.

Branding her.

She caught her breath.

And then she heard the hushed whisper in her ear.

"I want you, Genie," he said. "I want to be inside you."

Oh, Lord, the images. The wicked, wicked images.

"Tell me you want me." Those words again, the soft, barely spoken words. "Tell me."

Unbidden, other words flew into her mind. Thomas's warnings. *"Jonas has always had an eye for the ladies." "He would think nothing of ruining you. . . ."*

She felt Whitaker's fingers on her hand, her wrist, felt the sensual friction of paint.

"I want you, Genie. I want to be inside you."

She wanted it too. She wanted—oh, Lord, how she wanted—to touch the shooting star. She wanted to burn within it.

She wanted the magic.

"Yes," she said, and she heard the harsh whisper of her voice, the desperate crack. "Yes."

She closed her eyes, afraid to see his face in that moment, afraid of what she would find there. She heard his breathing, as hoarse and ragged as her own, felt his heat against her. Then she felt him move, and she knew he was in front of her, felt the gentle touch of his fingers as he lifted the brush from her hand, heard the soft *click* of it as he set it aside.

Then she felt his hand in her hair, and it was suddenly impossible to breathe at all as he loosened the

pins that held it. She heard them clink to the floor and
scatter. She felt the heavy mass of her hair falling free,
over her shoulders, down her back.

"Genie," he said.

She opened her eyes.

Lord, he was too beautiful. He was too beautiful for
her. Too fine for her. She did not deserve him.

But as he stared at her with those smoldering green
eyes, those thoughts melted away, replaced by a yearning so strong she could barely stand to look at him
even as she could not tear her gaze away.

He grabbed her hand, brushed it against his lips.
"Frightened, Genie?" he asked.

The question was familiar now—and so was her answer. Imogene licked her lips, shook her head. It was
all she could do to say the one word. "No."

"No," he repeated softly, and then, "Yes," and then
he took a step closer and threaded his hand through
her hair, keeping her in place as he bent to brush his
lips over hers—a simple touch, an erotic tease. But this
time he didn't pull away. This time he pressed closer,
slanting his lips across hers, and she opened her mouth
for him, tasted him, humid and sweet, brandy and
smoke. It was intoxicating, captivating, and when he
kissed her more deeply, when she felt the thrusting of
his tongue, the imitation of intimacy, she melted
against him, heard a moan coming from somewhere—
from her.

"Genie." He breathed the word into her mouth,
pulled back before she could stop him, leaving her
limp and wanting, too dazed to move, too aroused to
do more than stare at him as he traced the line of her
jaw, her throat. His exploration stopped at the edge of
her collar, his fingers touched the cut-out lace, slipped

over the onyx buttons of her bodice. She felt the
warmth of him through the fabric of her gown, even
through her corset.

"Green," he mused, glancing at her dress. "Pale
green."

"R-reseda green," she managed.

A small smile curved his mouth, amusement danced
in his eyes. "Reseda green," he repeated. And then, in
a voice that sent shivers up her spine, he said, "I don't
like you in reseda green, Genie. And I don't like you in
pink or lavender or watered blue. In fact, I think I'd
prefer you in nothing at all."

He reached for a button. She was caught in his eyes
as he undid it, a practiced movement, an easy con-
quest. She didn't move as he unfastened another and
another, and she felt her dress loosening as her breath
grew tighter and tighter. Then it was open to her
waist, and she watched as he eased the material down,
over her shoulders, down her arms. She felt the hardness of his gloved hand. The leather was cool, quickly
heated by her skin, soft and rigid, an erotic contrast.
His good hand traced her—her collarbone, the hollow
of her throat, the lace edging of her chemise—and she
followed his movement with her gaze, her breath coming shallow and fast as she saw the paint he left behind, mapping the trail of his touch. Blue and red and
yellow, marking her skin. She had the sudden, seductive thought that he was painting her, that he was
bringing her alive with color and caresses, making her
real where before she had been just illusion.

And when his hand slipped beneath the fabric of the
chemise, when she felt his fingers on her breast, she
knew he *was* bringing her alive. When he lifted her
from the confines of her corset, bending to touch his

mouth to her skin, to kiss the swelling of her breast, Imogene pressed into him, closing her eyes and throwing back her head, gasping as his mouth closed over her nipple, suckling her, arousing her until she could only stand there helplessly, bracing her hands on his shoulders, arching back to press harder into his mouth, feeling the erotic pull and nip of his tongue, his teeth.

"You're as beautiful as I imagined you, Genie," he whispered against her, looking up at her with those incredible eyes, and though she knew the words were a lie, Imogene felt a strange heat work its way through her, from her stomach to her heart, into her face. Embarrassed, she glanced away, but he drew back, grabbing her chin and forcing her to look at him again, and the drowsy, intimate way he looked at her made her feel swollen and tight and beautiful.

His hand dropped from her chin; she felt it suddenly at her thigh, and then he knelt in front of her. She felt his hands beneath her skirts, on her legs, felt the gown and her petticoats moving up and up and up as he rose with them. Slowly, slowly he pressed into her, backing her up, step by step, until she felt the hard edge of a stool at her buttocks. And then he was lifting her, seating her on the stool, and she grabbed its edge, trying to hold her balance as he moved between her legs.

His hand was tight on her hip, his body hard against hers. "Kiss me, Genie," he murmured, the intense green fire of his eyes burning through to her heart, beckoning her. "Kiss me."

She couldn't deny him, didn't want to. In the end she had no choice but to lean into him, no choice but to kiss him the way he'd asked her to, to touch her tongue to his and tease him the way he teased her.

His fingers gripped her hip, he moaned deep in his throat, and she was lost. She let go of the stool, wrapping her arms around his neck, trusting him to keep her from falling, pulling him closer. His hair was heavy against her fingers, heavy and soft and sinful. The feel of him, the taste of him, pulled at something deep inside her.

It was the magic she'd yearned for, the burning touch of the shooting star. She was alive with it, inflamed with it, and she wanted it to go on forever, to never end.

It seemed as if it never would as he kissed her throat, the tender spot behind her ear, moved lower still until she felt his kiss at her breasts, laving and teasing. She pressed into him, felt the smooth touch of her hair against her back, felt it tangling over her shoulders, and it was erotic too, as erotic as the warmth of his hands through the thin cotton of her drawers, all heat and temptation. She felt his thigh between her legs, against her very center, a burning touch, and involuntarily she raised her hips, wanting him harder against her, wanting . . . something. Wanting—oh, Lord, wanting.

"Slowly, darling," he whispered against her; she felt the words rather than heard them—heated, moist breath against her nipple. "Slowly, slowly." Then he was moving away from her again. The cold air caressed her breasts, danced across the moist kisses he'd left on her skin.

She moaned in protest, and he quieted her with a touch, quieted her by moving his hand from her hip to her inner thigh. Imogene held her breath, gasping when his hand eased through the slit in her drawers, when she felt his fingers tangle in the curls there, when she felt the heat of his caress. She couldn't help herself; she arched into his hand, her fingers digging into the hard wood of the stool.

"Please," she heard herself begging. "Please. . . ."

Before she knew what he was doing, before she could even begin to imagine it, he was kneeling before her, and his mouth was where his hand had been, kissing her, tasting her. She jerked against him, trembling, embarrassed, but he didn't stop. His kisses deepened; suddenly her embarrassment fled in the rich flood of sensation. Suddenly she didn't want him to stop, wanted nothing but this feeling, this building pressure, this ache that spread through her as his tongue played over her, tormenting and hot, wet kisses that left her trembling and straining.

She shook against him, yearned to grab on to him. She could not control herself, and the pressure was spiraling, spiraling . . . She heard herself moan, felt herself waver, and then he stroked her deeply with his tongue, and she cried out, nearly falling off the stool with the force of the climax that ripped through her.

But he was there, his arms around her, holding her steady. She heard him whisper something though she didn't hear the words, and suddenly he was inside her too, a swift, deep thrust that eased the throbbing of her body and intensified it at the same time, a fierce, sure possession that had her arching against him. He caught her moans with his mouth, lifted her slightly, eased her forward, and then he was moving against her, long, slow thrusts, exquisite torture—a torture she craved, a torture she wanted. She looked into his eyes and saw him watching her, felt scorched and sensuous and beautiful—Lord, yes, beautiful, as she'd never been before. Not ever.

She clutched his arms and pulled him closer, wanting to drown in him, wanting to be a part of him, wanting to *be* him. Imogene wrapped her legs around his hips and rocked with him, wanting him all over her, aroused by the feel of satin against her thighs, the rub of corset and the lace of chemise, aroused by his taste and scent and feel.

"Slower," she said, gasping, wanting the pleasure never to end. "Slower."

He smiled then and kissed her, slowing until she felt that building pressure again, circling his hips against hers until she was mindless with need and yearning, until she was twisting against him and calling his name.

Then it collapsed around her, and Imogene heard herself groan—in repletion or denial, she didn't know, didn't want to know. She shattered in his hands, arching into him, jerking against him. Then he was thrusting hard inside her, and she heard the hoarseness of his voice, felt him stiffen. She felt the harsh expulsion of his breath against her throat, and he was collapsing in her arms. She felt him throbbing inside her, the soft echo of his rhythm, and he was finally still.

Imogene swallowed, holding tightly to him, wrapping her arms and legs around him, keeping him still against her. It was over.

She closed her eyes and waited for that inevitable moment, that same moment that Nicholas had taught her to expect, the afterglow that faded in recrimination and blame, in shame too great for tears.

The moment she became plain Imogene Carter again.

Chapter 17

He was aware of nothing so much as her stillness. She was wrapped around him, her arms tight across his back, her knees locked about his hips. He heard her soft, shallow breaths, a little rushed, a little panicked—as if she were afraid her breathing would rouse him, as if she were afraid it would break the spell.

Jonas stirred himself, pulling away from her, hearing her little sound of protest as her arms fell away to allow him to move. She was still warm and wet around him, and he eased himself from her body, fastening his trousers before he looked at her.

She was beautiful—as beautiful as he'd known she would be. Her cheeks were flushed and her hair was loose and falling over her shoulders, partially shielding the breasts he'd freed from the confines of her corset. The pale green dress pooled at her waist, her hips, and the modest white cotton of her drawers shielded the rest of her from his gaze. Still inviolate, even though he'd been inside her only moments before, even though her moans still echoed in his ears. She had folded her wings now, but he knew what they looked like spread, knew the colors that lurked there, the same colors he'd smeared on her skin—ultramarine and vermillion. Naples yellow.

It took him a moment to realize she was watching him with wary eyes. Wariness. How silly it was, as if what had transpired between them were ordinary at all, as if it were anything like it had been with Clarisse or any of the others. Those times had always been quick and hasty, leaving him restless and unsatisfied. Never had he left feeling so rejuvenated, so alive. He felt as if he could make love to Genie all day, but there weren't enough hours.

He grinned at her, saw the slight ease in the lines creasing her brow—lines that disappeared completely when he leaned over and kissed her lightly, lingeringly, on the lips.

"How lovely you are," he whispered against her mouth.

She flushed and turned away, straightening her corset and chemise, pulling up her bodice. But he saw the slight smile caressing her lips, the pleased curve of her mouth, as she slipped into the sleeves and buttoned the dress.

Buttoning away her secrets. The thought made him regretful, but only for an instant. He reached over, brushing hair from her face. When she looked up in surprise, he said, "Are you ready?"

She smiled uncertainly. "Ready for what?"

"Come with me, Genie," he said, grabbing her hand, pulling her off the stool. Her skirt fell in folds back down to her feet, the cocoon again, soft propriety. She stumbled a little against him.

"Where are we going?"

"To a place I know," he said, taking her with him across the studio, to the door.

He felt her hesitate. "But my hair—"

"I like it down," he said, turning to her. He pulled her into his arms, gave her a hard, intemperate kiss. "You look like a princess—what was her name? Rapunzel. 'Rapunzel, Rapunzel, let down your hair. . . .'"

She laughed, and he released her, opening the door and then grabbing her hand again. He strode quickly down the hall, the stairs, so quickly he barely saw the two or three other artists haunting the lower gallery. In moments, he had her outside. The cold air felt good against his thin shirt, the late-autumn breeze fluttered his hair.

"Christ, I love this," he said, flinging out his arms to embrace the chill, turning to her with a grin. "Don't you love it, Genie?"

She was hugging herself, her honey-colored hair blowing back from her face, and she gave him a stiff little smile. "Aren't you cold?" she asked.

"Cold?" He laughed. "No, not cold. Invigorated. In love with the world." He swung back, wrapping his arm around her waist, pulling her close. He whispered against her ear, "Half in love with you, I think."

He saw her startled glance and released her, striding to the curb. He hailed a carriage, waited impatiently for Genie to get in and settle her skirts around her. "Delmonico's," he told the driver.

Beside him, Genie gasped. "Delmonico's?" she asked. "You can't be serious."

"Why can't I?" he said, feeling a touch of irritation at her question.

"But I couldn't. . . ."

"You couldn't?" His annoyance fled in quick amusement. "How can you not, Genie, when the world lies before us?"

She looked at him uncertainly, and then she laughed slightly and glanced out the window. "The world," she said softly, and he heard wistfulness in her tone.

"It opens up to you if you let it," he said. He leaned close, nuzzling her hair, and immediately caught her elusive perfume again, that soft almond fragrance. Only this time it was more beguiling, because along with almond he caught her scent—that warm muskiness that spoke of darkened rooms and skin on skin. With a groan he leaned over and tangled his hand in her hair, wishing his other hand weren't so useless, wishing he could catch her up and hold her completely still. She made a sound of protest—a little half murmur—and he captured her mouth and swallowed the sound, tasting her, running his tongue over her lips, exploring her mouth, feeling the hot flush of desire as she responded and pressed into him.

The sway of the carriage rocked him against her; he imagined it was the rhythm of lovemaking, the soft thrust of bodies meeting, the gentle slap of skin and wetness. He grabbed her skirt, easing it up over her legs, her knees, pooling the fabric along with her petticoats until he could run his hand up her inner thigh. Christ, how erotic: cotton and lace and heat. He searched for the slit in her drawers, found it, ran his fingers through the curls there, and then caressed her, stroked her. He felt her wet dewiness on his fingers, felt the involuntary jerk of her hips against his hand, heard her small moan.

The squeak of the wheels, the clop of the horses, the swaying gait—ah, it was heaven, as close to ecstasy as he'd ever found. She was open to him, her head thrown back, her eyes half closed. His innocent virgin, his butterfly, was so easy to arouse. There was such beauty in it, such radiance in the flushed pink of her cheeks, the melting in her eyes.

"Come alive for me, Genie," he murmured, stroking her, circling her, watching her. "Come alive, darling. . . ."

She did. She grabbed his arms, twisting into his hand. He heard her gasp of surprise, the half-spoken words, the groan that could have been his name. Then she was throbbing against him, breathing heavily, lax and limp and sated. He wanted to take her then, would have taken her if the carriage hadn't jerked to a stop.

He saw she was too dazed to realize they'd arrived. Quickly Jonas backed away, pulling down her skirts, smoothing her hair. By the time the driver opened the door, she only seemed a bit distracted. Charmingly distracted. Jonas wondered if he could talk the waiter at Delmonico's into one of the private rooms on the third floor, someplace where he could take her, make love to her. . . .

"Are you sure we should be going here?"

Her voice broke his train of thought. Jonas turned to look at her. She was shoving at her hair, working hard to retain some semblance of dignity. For the first time he noticed the paint streaking her hair and the bright red smear of vermillion at her jaw, the last vestige of the color he'd streaked her breasts with, a hint of her secrets.

"Leave it," he whispered, leaning close. "You look beautiful."

She looked down at the ground, he saw the beginning of her protest. He swung his arm around her waist before she could speak, bringing her up firmly against him. She glanced up, a small, surprised smile on her lips—Christ, what wonderful lips. He kissed her quickly, hurried her up the stairs until they were at the door of the posh restaurant.

He'd eaten at Delmonico's before, though not often. It was a place for businessmen and visitors, too expensive for him most of the time, too staid the rest. But now he wanted badly to be here; he wanted to show her off to the world, to flaunt her in the face of respectability, to show them all how boring it was. She had been a part of that upper-class respectability, and he'd changed her. Already he'd changed her. She was his creation now, vibrant and alive, a laughing, beautiful testament to his talent.

The doorman stood aside to let them pass, and when Jonas saw the man's gaze rake over Genie and himself, saw the lift of eyebrow, he felt a rush of exhilaration. Already people were seeing his brilliance. Christ, even a doorman realized how stunning she was, how perfect. He felt her slight tug at his hand, and he gripped her closer, afraid to let her go for even a moment, afraid someone might steal her away. There were a thousand villains in this city, a thousand opportunities for one to claim her for himself—Jonas saw larceny in every interested gaze that turned to them, saw envy in every eye.

He hurried to the maître d'.

"A table for two in the café," he said.

The man frowned. He stared at Genie, a slow, burning gaze. The sight of it took away Jonas's fear, elation spread through him again. The man saw his artistry, recognized true genius. Even as Jonas realized it, he felt her shrink into his side, and he wondered why.

Couldn't she see the admiration in the waiter's eyes? Didn't she know how perfect she was?

Jonas grinned. "I see you understand a work of art when you see it," he said, winking broadly.

The maître d' hesitated. "Mr. Whitaker," he said. "We are certainly grateful for your patronage, but may I suggest the dining room instead?"

Jonas felt a stab of surprise at the man's recognition, a surprise that faded in sudden self-assurance. Of course the man knew him. Everyone knew him. He was Jonas Whitaker, famous artist. No doubt the moment they saw Genie they knew who he was. After all, she was his greatest work of art.

". . . after all, we do have certain standards—"

He heard Genie's rush of breath, saw her flush.

"Of course you do," Jonas agreed. "And I appreciate your willingness to keep those idiots at bay. But the café will be fine. Just do me a favor, won't you, and don't let the art fanatics hound us while we eat—or the critics. I'll wait to see their opinions in the newspapers."

The maître d' frowned again. "But, sir—"

"Any table will do." Jonas searched the restaurant. The first-floor café was filled with the usual lunch crowd of businessmen, but there was an empty table in the middle of the room. He raised his false hand in its direction. "That one, perhaps."

He felt Genie's tension; she was so stiff he thought she might break. No doubt it was all the attention. She wasn't used to it, not the way he was. He turned to her and smiled. "Relax, darling," he said. "I'm sure we'll be well taken care of here."

She threw a halting glance at the maître d'. "I'm not sure—"

"I am," Jonas said. He smiled at the man standing so sternly in front of them. "Please, my good sir. The table?"

The maître d' hesitated, and then he nodded briskly at a hovering white-shirted waiter. Within minutes they were seated at the table Jonas had wanted, where everyone could see them without crowding around. He grinned at the few heads turned their way and ordered an expensive bottle of bordeaux. It was time to celebrate.

He leaned over the table to whisper to her. "Look at the way they stare. They can't believe what they're seeing."

She licked her lips nervously, cast a quick glance around the room. "Perhaps we should go."

"Go?" He laughed. "I don't think so. They'd mob us if we tried." He reached over and grabbed her hand, folding her fingers in his and squeezing. "I can see I've a few things to teach you about moving in art circles, Genie."

She looked supremely uncomfortable. "Yes, I suppose you do," she said.

He released her hand, following her gaze to a man who sat a few tables away. Some scion of a prominent family, no doubt, Jonas thought. The man looked a bit like Henry Wolford—his son, probably. Certainly he was as foppish as his father, and as easily impressed. The younger Wolford was ogling Genie and whispering something to the other man at his table.

Jonas smiled. "I didn't think Wolford's whelp had such taste," he said. "No doubt he'll be pounding on my door tomorrow, demanding a portrait."

She gave him a strange look, one he couldn't interpret. "Will you paint him?"

"If he interests me." Jonas shrugged.

"You can afford to be so selective?"

"Ah, Genie." He sighed. "I can't afford not to be. Portraits are not art. Portraits are merely ways to waste time."

She frowned. "But certainly there are techniques to study. My father used to say—"

"Let me explain something about portraits, darling," Jonas said. "Painting a portrait is like ordering Nathaniel Hawthorne to write a novel about the next person who comes into his office—whether that person interests him or not. There is no art involved, no vision. Techniques can be learned in much more challenging ways."

"But Chloe always said there was so much to see in a person's face."

"Chloe?" Jonas looked up as the steward brought the wine. He motioned for the man to pour. "Who the hell is Chloe?"

She seemed to cringe before him. "My sister."

"Your sister—ah, yes, the artist. An optimist, no doubt. Probably she would have been one of those idiots at Barbizon, finding God in every peasant."

He was gratified by Genie's small smile. "She admired Millet."

"Millet. Of course, who did not? Even I did for a while—until I realized I didn't want to glorify dirty poverty and illiterate stupidity."

She took a sip of wine. "You didn't find the purity everyone talks about?"

"You mean 'the noble savage'?" Jonas laughed. "Hardly. Few men would choose to live like that, Genie. And there are other ways to portray the best of humanity, you know. Take Rico, for instance. There is divinity in every still life he paints, a glimpse of heaven or hell, a subtle violence in his arrangements. Isn't that as noble? In the end, an artist's job is to transform experience however he can, to transcend the material, to elicit emotion and religion. Otherwise we are nothing more than one of those photographers—copying nature so men have pretty pictures to hang on their walls."

She was staring at him, her eyes wide. "You are astounding," she whispered.

Christ, he wanted to devour her. That adulation in her gaze, the soft innocence of her face, the dawning awareness. He felt he could expound for hours, talk to her about everything: God and heaven, morality and martyrdom, spirituality and pure love. He wanted to keep that look on her face—ah, how precious it was—understanding without wariness, reverence without fear. She was looking at him as if he were God, and in that moment he felt as if he were. He was God, and she was his Eve, more perfect than Adam had ever been, more interesting. He wanted to shout it to everyone in the room, to run out onto Broadway and bring in the promenaders to worship at her feet.

"Divinity is in so many things," he said in a low voice. "You, for instance."

She gave a startled laugh. "Me?"

"Yes, you," he said. "I see it every time I look at you, Genie. God had perfection in mind when He made you."

"I don't think so." A warm flush moved up her cheeks, she looked away. "Perhaps Chloe, but not—not me."

"You think not?" Jonas smiled. "It shines from your eyes. Did Chloe have such beautiful eyes?"

"More beautiful." She took her wineglass in her hand, swirling the dark red liquid inside the globe. "Hers were blue. The color of the sky."

"But she didn't have hair like yours."

She made a small sound of protest. "No. She had golden hair."

"I imagine she didn't have paint in it," he teased.

Genie gasped and put her hand to her hair. "Oh, no. No wonder—"

"It's quite charming," he told her. "Much more charming than I warrant your sister ever was."

"No," she protested. "You don't understand. She was perfect. In everything."

"You're describing a paragon," he said gently. "And paragons are notoriously boring."

She looked up at him with eyes that were distressingly blank. "Chloe was never boring."

He heard the longing in her voice, the resignation, and it moved him, twisted his heart in some strange and fascinating way. "Ah, Genie," he said softly. "You are so beautiful."

She looked away. Her fingers tightened on her glass. "I'm not," she said. "I know I'm not. You needn't keep saying it."

There was something about the way she said it, a distress, a despair, that was more than yearning or acceptance—much more. It seemed to come from deep inside her, and it startled him, sent a flash of anger stabbing through him. Jonas leaned across the table so quickly the glasses rocked, the silverware scattered. He grabbed her chin in his hand, forcing her to look at him.

The look in her eyes stole his breath, sent his blood racing. There was pain there. *Pain.* Those beautiful eyes were brimming with it, with a misery that said more clearly than words what someone had once done to her. She had no idea of what she was, he realized suddenly. She had no idea of her beauty or her desirability. She was as naive as he'd first thought her. Naive and newborn, just as he'd once wanted to see her. And someone had hurt her. Someone had put that expression on her face.

The thought infuriated him. "Who was it?" he said harshly, gripping her chin so hard she winced. "Who told you that you weren't beautiful? Tell me and I'll kill him."

She made a sound, a half laugh, a breath of despair, and tried to pull away. "No one," she said.

"I don't believe you."

She swallowed. "It doesn't matter."

"Like hell it doesn't."

The waiter was suddenly at the table. "Sir, please—"

Jonas ignored him. He released her quickly, jerking to his feet. He knocked the table; her wine overturned, spreading across the white tablecloth like the blood that pounded in his head, like the rage swirling through him. He heard her gasp, felt the waiter's restraining hold on his arm.

Jonas wrenched away. "Goddammit!" He pushed past the waiter, hearing the man's frenzied words and Genie's protest with some part of his mind, the part that screamed reason, that screamed for control. *Stop this, stop this, stop this. . . .* But it was too late; anger thrummed in his veins—it felt as if his head might burst.

"Listen to me! Damn you—all of you—listen to me!" he shouted, spreading his arms until he saw every eye in the restaurant on him. He jerked his hand at Genie. "Look at her. She's beautiful, isn't she? Isn't she?"

There was dead silence. It enraged him. He saw Wolford's son turn to whisper to his partner, and Jonas's fury exploded. He grabbed the bottle of bordeaux, slamming it to the table, soaking the stained tablecloth, feeling the wetness of it course over his arm, his shirt. Wolford jerked back again, startled.

Jonas pointed to him. "You," he said. "You there. Look at her. What do you see?"

The man blanched. "I—"

"I said look at her! What the hell do you see?"

The waiter advanced. "Sir . . ."

Jonas brandished the half-empty bottle. "Get the hell away from me." He felt a grim satisfaction when the waiter retreated. Jonas turned back to Wolford. "Well?"

"She—she's quite lovely."

Pacifying words. Insincere words. For a moment Jonas was so angry he couldn't see. "Damn you for a coward," he screamed. "You fucking cowards! All of you! Don't you see it? Can't you see a goddamn thing? All of you—"

"Please, Jonas . . ."

Something tugged on his arm. Jonas jerked away. "You're looking at a goddess! Damn you! A goddess!" He took a step, holding the bottle, spilling the rest of the wine over his pants, his boots. He pointed to Wolford. "How dare you even look at her, you fucking bastard! You don't deserve to see—" He faltered as he noticed the look in Wolford's eyes, the way the man turned back to his friend, shaking his head. It confused

Jonas, distracted him. "Damn you," he said. "You son
of a—"

"Jonas."

The voice was so soft it seemed to come from inside
his head. He could barely hear it. Desperately he tried
to hold on to his anger. "Dammit! You're all . . .
you're all—" The rest of the sentence eluded him. He
forgot what he was going to say. "You—"

"Jonas . . ."

It unsettled him, that voice. So soft, so strong. Bewildered, feeling suddenly lost, he turned in its direction.

And saw Genie. Genie, her pale skin splashed with
red wine, marked with paint. Genie. There was something in her face that puzzled him. Something—oh
Christ, what? He tried to remember, but his heart was
beating so fast he couldn't hear, could barely see. . . .
She reached out; he felt her hand on his arm, a warm
caress, a comforting touch.

"Please, Jonas . . ."

Ah, the way she said his name—so quiet, a breath of
sound, the soft *s* that faded into the rhythm of her
voice. It wrapped around his heart and comforted him,
took his anger and his will, and he found himself staring at her, getting lost in those deep brown eyes, in the
distress of her expression. Distress. Christ, he didn't
want that. It made his heart ache to see that look on
her face.

His butterfly was opening up to the world, and he
wanted to protect her suddenly, wanted to keep those
still-wet wings folded inside the cocoon, to let them
out only bit by bit, to make sure she was safe before
she flew away. It bothered him that he hadn't succeeded, that someone had got to her first, that some-

one had already wounded her—and wounded her in a way he couldn't quite fathom.

He wanted to understand it. He wanted to ease it.

The yearning took his anger and the last of his strength, fed his confusion. He fell to his knees in front of her, buried his face in her lap, exhausted and dazed and ashamed. Christ, so ashamed.

"Oh, Jonas," she whispered. He felt her hand on his hair, smoothing it back from his face, caressing him.

"Madam." The waiter's voice, stiff with disapproval and wariness. "I'm afraid I must ask you—"

"We're leaving," she said, and there was such authority in her voice, such a tranquil strength, it silenced the waiter. "Please send me the bill." She stopped her stroking; Jonas heard the scratch of writing, knew she was giving the man her address, but he couldn't lift his head from her lap to protest. Christ, he felt so empty, so helpless.

He heard the waiter's retreat, and then the restaurant was quiet. Not even the tinkle of silverware on china. He felt her touch on his hair, felt the warmth of her sigh, and he waited stiffly for the words he'd heard a hundred times before, the words he knew he deserved. *"You're mad. Good Lord, you are quite mad."* In a way he even wanted to hear her say them, wanted the bleak comfort of knowing he'd disappointed her too. He had ruined everything. This interlude with her was over, along with the waiting—he felt a dismal relief at the knowledge. He'd finally done it, finally disgraced her the way he ultimately disgraced everyone. *Say it,* he thought. *Go ahead, say it.*

But instead, all she said was "Oh, Jonas" again, and there was a gentleness in her words that astounded him, a serenity that called to him through his torment, a promise of redemption. Then, most surprising of all, he felt her bend closer, felt the brush of her hair against his, heard her soft whisper in his ear.

"Let's go, shall we?"

She got to her feet before he knew what she was doing, took his arm and helped him to his. And then his paint- and wine-stained beauty smiled—a small, determined smile—and twined her arm through his. She walked with him through Delmonico's with her head held high, as if she were truly the goddess he'd told them all she was, as if he hadn't lost his temper and his mind in the finest restaurant in New York City.

As if he weren't truly mad.

But he was. *He was.*

And now she knew it too.

Chapter 18

She left Jonas sleeping. He'd been morose and silent on the trip home, and once they returned to the studio he collapsed in a chair, ordering her to leave as if he couldn't stand the sight of her. She had not gone. She'd waited the few minutes until his eyes closed and she heard his steady breathing, and then she carefully went out, hurrying across the hall to Childs's studio. There was no answer when she rapped on the door. Feeling numb and bewildered, not knowing what else to do, she settled herself on the floor to wait for him.

It seemed like hours before she heard his step on the landing. Imogene caught her breath, not relaxing until she saw the top of his golden head through the railing.

He caught sight of her almost instantly; she saw him stiffen in surprise, saw his sudden worry.

"Miss Imogene?"

She rose, smoothing her skirts. "Do you think I might have a word with you?" she asked softly.

He frowned and glanced at the door to Jonas's studio.

"He's sleeping."

"Sleeping?"

"Yes."

He seemed to relax slightly. "Well, in that case, *chérie*," he said, opening the door to his studio and motioning her inside, "please come in."

She stepped into the room, stopping in astonishment as she caught sight of the splendor of his studio. It was nothing like Jonas's. Where Whitaker's was sparse, furnished with old furniture and littered with paraphernalia, Childs's was opulent. A huge centerpiece of a bed covered with brocaded pillows and dark, highly polished tables made it look more like a wealthy man's bedroom than an artist's workspace. If not for the canvases and painting implements set up near the windows, she would never have known it was a studio at all.

Childs chuckled as he closed the door. "You look surprised," he noted. "Surely you didn't think I lived in squalor."

"Not squalor, no," she said. "But this—"

"A rich father who died young," he explained. "And a mother who remarried money and feels guilty."

"I see.

He smiled. "You look distressed, *chérie*," he said, changing the subject with smooth aplomb. "And as flattered as I am by your visit, something tells me it's not my company you crave. What has you so worried, eh? What made you wait in the hallway for me?"

Imogene took a deep breath, wishing she knew exactly what to tell him, how she could explain that it had seemed somehow right to come to him, that she had wanted comfort and answers and she'd hoped he could provide both. She felt unsettled and vulnerable, unsure what to do, how to feel.

All she knew was that she couldn't stop the question that chanted ceaselessly in her brain. It had consumed her while she waited, impossible to ignore, too strong to push away. She looked at Childs, trying to decide how best to word it, what to say. In the end she simply said it.

"How mad is he?"

Childs didn't look the least bit surprised. "Mad enough. But I expect you know that already."

His answer didn't soothe her. She sighed. "We were just at Delmonico's," she said.

Childs raised a brow. "Delmonico's?"

"I'm not sure why he took me there." The words rushed out, falling over themselves before she had time to think them through. "It was . . . he had a temper tantrum . . . or . . . I'm not sure what to call it really."

"He broke a bottle of wine, I take it?"

Imogene looked at him in surprise.

He motioned to her skirt. "It's all over you. Along with an interesting amount of paint. I'm almost afraid to ask."

She felt heat move into her face. Imogene looked away. "I don't think he knew what he was doing."

"Which time?" Childs asked softly. "At Delmonico's, or when he made love to you?"

Startled, she jerked around again to face him.

"It's quite obvious, *chérie.*" He paused, studying her with a detachment that made her uncomfortable. "What would you like me to say? That you're wrong, that he knew what he was doing when he kissed you?" He shrugged dismissively; his indifference seemed painfully deliberate. "I can't tell you that. I don't know. You'll have to find your reassurance elsewhere."

His words angered her. Imogene forced herself to hold his gaze. "You're not normally so cruel," she said. "I thought we were friends."

He gave her a bland look. "You don't know me that well."

"I know you well enough," she insisted. "I know you care for him. I've seen the way you protect him. You've even protected me."

"And succeeded admirably, as you can see," he said wryly. "As a result of my 'protection,' you have been seduced, assaulted, and abandoned. I am overwhelmed at my success."

"No," she said quietly. "I'm not so fragile as you think. If he seduced me, it was because I wanted to be seduced. The way you describe it—that's not how it happened."

Childs's gaze swept over her, disbelieving, a little cynical. "No? Suppose you tell me how it was then."

She licked her lips, trying to put her thoughts in order, wondering what she wanted from him, what she'd expected. Perhaps it was reassurance, as he'd said, or maybe it was simply hope—something to soothe her scattered emotions, to ease her confusion. She wanted to know what had happened to turn Jonas Whitaker into a madman. She wanted to understand.

"I thought I understood what people meant when they said he was mad," she began hesitantly. "I thought I did. Now I realize how stupid that was, how impossible it is to understand unless you see it for yourself. He was—" She stopped, searching for words. She saw Jonas before her, the wild rage in his eyes, his stiff anger. She saw spilling wine and expansive gestures. She heard his harsh, condemning words. *"You're looking at a goddess! Damn you! A goddess!"*

Now those words echoed painfully in her mind. He'd wanted to convince her she was beautiful and instead he'd shown her something else. Instead he'd shown her that he didn't truly see her at all. To him she was only some vague ideal, some visionary goddess that had little to do with who she really was.

And the words he'd murmured in her ear only convinced her further. *"Half in love with you, I think."* The words of a man who had loved a hundred women. A man used to making people look better than they were, to finding beauty in everything. A man who made his living from illusion. What had he said today? That an artist's job was to transform reality, to transcend the material. That was what he did with her. In his mind he transformed her into someone he could be proud of, someone worth his time. But he didn't really see her. He did not know her at all, or he would never have said the words.

She closed her eyes briefly, pushing away her sadness, forcing herself to remember Childs, who was waiting for her to finish. She swallowed painfully. "He was in his own world."

She saw sympathy in Childs's expression. "What shall I tell you, *chérie*? That he is not always so difficult? That he is easy to love? Is that what you want?"

She looked at him steadily. "I want the truth."

"The truth?" He laughed lightly. "The truth is that there is nothing you can do. The truth is that he goes from mood to mood the way others change mistresses. And you are not even seeing the worst, I'm afraid. As much as I love him, I find myself escaping him once a year—to Paris, for sanity." He gave a bitter, self-contemptuous laugh. "As ludicrous as that is."

His admission made her uncomfortable. It was so intense, so painful. In a way she understood it too well. She wished there were simple answers, but she had the feeling nothing would ever be simple with Jonas Whitaker.

Lord, she wished she understood him, wished she understood herself. She wished she knew why she wasn't running from him as fast as she could. A reasonable person would. After all, he was a madman. He was everything they'd ever told her he was.

She looked at Childs, working to keep her voice steady. "You said it gets worse."

Childs took a deep breath. "Yes. It gets worse."

She waited, her chest tightening.

"You have seen his charm . . . this . . . this mesmerist he becomes, this—"

"Shooting star," she said.

Childs nodded. "A shooting star. Yes, he is that. But there is another side to him too, a side not everyone sees."

"Like last spring."

Childs shook his head. "You don't know all of it," he said quietly, and then he hesitated, a pause so long that the sounds from the street intruded on the silence, the thunder of carriages, the strident *whoas* of the drivers. Normal sounds. Day-to-day sounds. They made Imogene suddenly sad, as if things were changing so quickly she might never hear the rumbling clatter of wheels on cobblestones again, as if she were entering a place where nothing would ever be the same.

Finally, Childs looked up. "Last spring was . . . ah. . . ." He closed his eyes briefly, hanging his head, and his next words were weak and pained. "He tried to kill himself," he said bluntly. "If I had not been here, he would have succeeded. It was not . . . the first time."

Childs looked at her, his expression bleak. "Now do you understand, *chérie*? Now do you see?"

Imogene hesitated. Her throat was tight, her lungs felt paralyzed. His question chimed in her mind. *"Now do you understand,* chérie? *Now do you see?"* and she knew what he was really asking her, heard the words as clearly as if he'd said them. *Can you love him now for me too? Can you help him?*

She squeezed her eyes shut. "Don't ask me," she said softly. "Look at me, Rico. I'm nobody. He won't . . . he can't . . ." She took a deep breath. "I'm not a fool. He won't want me long, I know. I'm not his kind."

"Perhaps you'll become his kind."

She laughed, hearing unfamiliar bitterness in the sound, and glanced back at him again. "You don't believe that, I can hear it in your voice."

"I don't know what I believe."

"How world-weary you sound, Rico."

He glanced up at her. For the first time his handsomeness didn't shine from his features, didn't overwhelm her. He looked drawn and somber, ascetically, bleakly beautiful. He sighed. "Perhaps. Perhaps I've simply lost the will to deal with him any longer."

She felt a stab of fear. "You don't mean that."

"Don't I?" He gave her a slight smile. "Should I consign him to your care, *chérie*? You've survived him once. You've still a good hundred times or so left within you."

"He won't stay with me."

"I think you underestimate yourself."

Imogene folded her arms over her chest, shook her head. "You don't know. You don't know me at all."

"Then perhaps you should tell me who you are, eh?" Rico sank into a well-padded chair, steepling his fingers, watching her. His tone was cajoling, charming —the same beguiling voice he'd used on her before. "Tell me about Imogene Carter, Genie."

"Genie," she repeated, feeling the name roll off her tongue, the quick thrust of it against her teeth. "You and Jonas keep calling me that." She didn't tell him that the name made her feel warm inside, somehow beloved. She'd never had a nickname before. Never a name that implied intimacy. She'd never been called anything but Imogene. Imogene Elizabeth Carter. A staid, steady name. A name heavy with the implications of inviolate spinsterhood, rigid with propriety.

"It's Jonas's name for you," Childs said. "Not mine."

She looked down at the floor. "Oh, Rico," she sighed. "I—I know he's using me. I know he won't be interested for long. But I thought—I thought perhaps I could learn from him while he was. I thought he could teach me how to be somebody"—she laughed self-consciously—"somebody important. It's a silly dream, I know, but—"

"What makes you think you're not already important?"

The question bewildered her. She looked up at him with a frown. "Because I'm not. I'm nobody. Just another art student, and not even a very good one."

Childs looked at her thoughtfully. "You think so? I—"

"Geenniiee!!!"

The shout came from the hallway, a loud, anguished cry that followed the slamming of a door, running footsteps.

Jonas.

Imogene's head snapped up. Rico stiffened in his chair.

"Genie! Geeennniee!"

"Mon dieu!" Childs shot from his chair, stopping her with a gesture. "Stay here," he warned.

She shook her head, hurrying across the studio. "He's calling me."

"I can't keep you safe."

"Geenniiee!!!"

"I don't care." Imogene surged toward him, halting when he blocked her path. "He won't hurt me."

Rico's eyes blazed. "Don't be so certain."

"Genie! Genie!"

"Rico, he's calling me!"

Childs muttered a curse beneath his breath. "Be careful, then," he cautioned. He turned back to the door, wrenching it open so hard it crashed against the walls. He raced into the hallway. Imogene was right behind him.

Jonas was at the far end, toward the stairs. He was screaming; harsh, jarring shouts she could barely understand. It took her a moment to make out the words, and when she did, they startled her so much she froze against the doorway, her heart thudding in her chest.

"They've taken her away! Christ, I knew they would. Those bastards—"

"Jonas, please . . ." Rico was hurrying toward him, almost sliding in his haste. "Jonas—"

"Where the hell is she, Rico? Do you have her? Goddammit, I'll kill you for that!" He lunged at Rico.

There was the sickening sound of crunching bodies, the thud of a punch. Rico went sprawling to the floor.

"She's fine," he shouted, scrambling to his feet, blocking the hall so Jonas couldn't get by. "She's right here—*mon dieu,* Jonas—" He ducked Jonas's second punch and came up spitting, his golden hair flying into his face. "Look for yourself, you fool! She's just up the hall!"

"Jonas!" she called. "Jonas, I'm right here!"

He looked up, his eyes blazing, and even though he was looking straight at her, she had the feeling he didn't see her at all. He shook his head and glared at Childs. "You liar," he said. "Do you think I don't know you're trying to fool me? Do you think I don't know?"

"It's no lie," Rico protested. "It's Genie."

"You think I'll fall for such a trick? I can see right through her, you bastard! She's not real! You've taken her and you don't want me to know." Jonas was wild-eyed and raging. "Where is she? What have you done with her? Geenniiee!" He lunged at Childs again, but just as he made the move, there was a commotion on the stairs. Several artists from the building were clambering en masse to the landing, shouting and laughing.

Jonas whipped around, crying out when Rico took his chance and tackled him.

"What have you done with her, you bastard? Genie!" Jonas twisted from Childs's grasp, shouting at the top of his lungs. He crashed against the wall so hard his false hand went through it. Plaster flew. Then Childs was on him again, clinging to him, trying to hold him still.

The other artists didn't budge. They watched with unconcealed interest, as if it were an entertainment put on for their benefit. As if they'd seen its like before. For a moment Imogene almost expected to hear them lay down bets.

It was more than she could bear. It was inhumane, the way they watched him, like spectators at a cock-fight. A sob caught in Imogene's throat as she picked up her skirts and ran toward them. "Jonas!" She called his name, nearly screaming it, heard the thud of bodies against the wall, the hard smack of a blow.

She wanted to touch him. She had the feeling he would hear her then, if she could only touch him, if she could only prove to him that she was here, that she was no illusion. She reached out, but before she could touch him he swung around, slamming Childs into the wall. She heard Rico's grunt of pain, heard the crack of his shoulder.

"Ah, God," he groaned.

"Where are you hiding her?" Jonas's shouting echoed into the rafters, reverberated against the walls. "Damn it, where is she?"

She couldn't get close, couldn't touch him. He was flailing too desperately to see her, yelling so loudly she knew he couldn't hear her call his name. Desperation rushed through her. Desperation and worry that made her voice crack when she called to him, that had her nearly crying in an attempt to make him hear.

"Jonas, I'm here," she shouted. "It's me! I'm here!"

She tried to move closer, caught Rico's desperate glance and couldn't help him at all. Jonas lunged and jerked, trying to dislodge Childs, crashing into the walls.

"Geenniiee!" he screamed.

All she could do was scream back at him. All she could do was shout "I'm here," over and over again, until it was a ceaseless prayer in her head, a desperate litany. And then finally, when her voice was hoarse with shouting, when she was sure she couldn't calm him at all, he spun around. His eyes were dark with fear that faded the moment he saw her. Fear that simply melted away. He quieted. Suddenly. Completely.

"Genie," he said, and his voice as hoarse as hers, heavy with relief and something else.

Joy, she thought. She heard joy.

"I thought you'd gone," he said, sinking to his knees, sliding from Childs's arms. Rico backed warily away. "I thought you'd gone."

"No," she said. "I'm right here." She moved closer, reached out to touch his hair, to smooth it back from his face. "I'm right here."

He leaned into her, sighing, pressing his face against her stomach. She heard the sounds of the others going downstairs, talking among themselves, laughing as if it had all been a great show, a huge joke. She threaded her fingers through his hair and glanced up at Childs, who was rubbing his shoulder and watching, a strange expression on his face—startled curiosity, puzzled surprise.

"You're not important, eh, *chérie*?" he asked softly.

Chapter 19

*J*onas woke the next morning safe in his bed, with no idea of how he'd got there. For a half second it didn't matter. For a moment he saw the cracked plaster of his ceiling and felt the relief of waking, the peace just before realization set in. Then the memory—or lack of it—came crashing down, crushing his soul, half illusions and craziness and disbelief. He struggled to remember; the old familiar dread came slamming back. *What have I done? Christ, what did I do?*

It had happened again—the thought filled him with desperation, a terror so pure he shook with it. God, it had happened again, and he didn't know why, didn't know how to keep those good feelings from spiraling so completely out of control, from turning on him, from destroying him. And the worst part was he couldn't remember, at least not completely. There were just bits and pieces that floated back, like those from a particularly inexplicable nightmare, an alcoholic fog. There was a night—somewhere, a night—where he and Rico had gambled at The Red House.

Yes, he remembered that, or parts of it anyway. But after that there was nothing. After that there was . . .

After that there was Genie.

Jonas closed his eyes. His heart raced in sudden panic and bleak desperation. He had done something to Genie. Christ, what? What unpardonable sin had he committed this time? He couldn't remember. God, he couldn't remember. There was a dark pit in his mind, hovering, waiting, and he knew it was where his memories were. His memories and his reason, hiding from him. Taunting him. Baiting him.

You're mad. The voice whispered to him, a haunting murmur. *You're as mad as they've always said you were.* . . .

No. Jonas fought the thought, forced himself to push back the covers, tried to control his shaking. His false hand hit the edge of the bedstead, and he looked down at it in surprise, wondering why he hadn't taken it off for the night, trying again to remember getting into bed. The memory was truly gone; in its place was exhaustion and despair. Wearily, aching in every bone, every muscle, he undid the straps to his hand and let the appendage fall to the mattress, feeling too weary to pick it up, not caring enough to wear it.

Clumsily, slowly, Jonas got to his feet. He stumbled to the tapestry guarding the door and pushed it aside, blinking at the gray light coming through the studio windows. It was raining outside. Pouring. For a moment he stood there, staring at it, feeling the dampness ease into his heart, his soul. The autumn was gone. It was winter now. Coldness, bleakness. Months of weather to match his spirits. *Don't think of it.* But he couldn't help himself. He couldn't stop the images from crowding his mind: barren trees and frozen mud and colorless horizons. People died in the winter. They froze to death in their little shanties and were buried in the hard, cold ground. Nothing saved them. Not faith, not prayers. In the end God made fools of them all.

Just as He's made a fool of me. The thought weighed upon him, heavy and unrelenting and merciless. Jonas shuffled to the window, sinking into a chair and staring out at the grayness, at the slashes of rain streaking the glass. Dead leaves caught in the wind, ripping from branches, spiraling crazily to the walk, leaving trees that were bare and dark against the wet stone of the buildings across the street. It was cold; he could feel it through the glass, and he thought he should start a fire to warm the studio. He couldn't summon the energy to do it, so instead he just sat there, cold and shivering, watching the sleeting rain and wishing . . . wishing what? Wishing he were normal? Wishing he weren't so damned lonely?

Wishing Genie were here with him?

He laughed mirthlessly. Genie was never coming back again, he knew. He'd driven her away, like the others. Like Rico, who abandoned him every year, searching for friends in Paris, friends who weren't so demanding, friends who didn't embarrass and scandalize and hurt. No doubt she felt the same way.

The thought filled him with sadness so stark he couldn't bear to feel it. He tried to concentrate on the swirling leaves instead, but the words kept intruding, increasing his misery and his pain with every repeat. *She's not coming back. She's not coming back.*

That voice was so loud he barely heard the footsteps in the hall or the tap on the door. When it finally did intrude—a relentless knock that pounded in his head —he couldn't bring himself to answer it. There was no one he wanted to see. Rico would only look at him with those sad, too-knowing eyes, and Genie was gone forever. And there was no one else. No one.

The rapping stopped. He waited for whoever it was to go away, waited for the tread of steps over the creaking floor. The sound didn't come, and he was just telling himself he'd missed it when the lever clicked and the door jerked open. It *was* Rico, he thought without turning around. No one else would dare—

"You're awake." It was Genie's voice, rushed and out of breath.

No, it couldn't be. It's a lie. It was not her. It could not be her. Slowly he twisted to look.

She stiffened at the sight of him. He'd shocked her, he realized. He saw it in her face, in her frozen little smile, the attempt to school her expression. He wanted to take offense but he couldn't. She looked so flushed and radiant and wet. Rainwater dripped from her pink bonnet, darkened the matching wool of her mantle. She set aside a net bag of food and quickly lifted off her bonnet, shrugged out of the coat, hanging them both on the pegs by the door. She was wearing a pale green dress.

Reseda green.

Memories came flitting back, jagged puzzle pieces that barely fit together. Her body twisting beneath his, her rapid breath, the feel of her hair. White-shirted waiters and carriages and screaming in a hallway. The images were terrifying, humiliating, and he pushed them away, too afraid to give them life, too afraid to remember.

"I wanted to get back before you woke," she continued, an almost desperate rush to her words. "I'm sorry it took so long. I imagine you're hungry."

Christ, what had he done? He shook his head. "No."

"No? But you haven't—"

"Why are you here?"

She blinked. Wariness slipped into her expression, a hint of despair that made him angry with himself, and that anger twisted inside him, mean-spirited and ugly. Because of it he wanted to be more hateful, to drive her away because he could not stand himself, and she was so perfect. So beautiful and innocent and young. So incredibly strong.

He turned back to the window before she had a chance to answer him. "Get the hell out."

He expected her to go. Expected to hear the click of the door.

Instead, all he heard was her soft—too-soft—voice. "No."

"No." Her answer startled him. The unexpectedness of it increased his anger.

"Decided to brave the monster, have you? How courageous you are." He heard the biting sarcasm in his words.

"Is that what you think you are?" she asked. Her voice was very calm, very even. "A monster?"

"What else would you call it?"

"I'd call you a genius."

"Ah, a genius." He laughed self-deprecatingly. "Don't lie to yourself, Genie. Geniuses don't scream like madmen or rape innocent women."

He heard her gasp—a short, startled sound. "Rape?" she asked. "You raped someone?"

He turned to look at her then, saw the paleness of her face, the blackness of her eyes within it. "Didn't

I?" he countered bitterly. "Or did you strip your clothes off willingly for me?"

Her lips tightened; he saw the flex of her jaw, and he waited—again—for her to run. But she stood her ground, met his gaze. She wasn't afraid of him, and he wondered when she'd learned that. Certainly she had every reason to be afraid. The memories tangled in his head. He remembered screaming her name somewhere —ah, where? He pushed the half memory away. Suddenly he didn't want to know. He really, really didn't want to know.

"I was willing," she said firmly. "And I'm not young. Or innocent."

He barked a laugh. "No, of course not."

"I'm twenty-six years old," she said, lifting her chin —as if she were braving a monster after all. "And I'm not . . . a virgin."

"Not anymore. I made sure of that."

"Before then, even."

"Oh?" he asked scornfully. "Someone kissed you once, perhaps?"

"Is it so hard to believe?"

He shrugged. Her words wounded him for some reason he couldn't fathom. He felt the sting of irritation and was unsure whether it was because he didn't understand himself or because he hated the idea that she had made love to someone else. The thought annoyed him further; again he felt the tug of mean-spiritedness, the need to push her away. He knew how cruel his words were before he said them and didn't care, wanted to hurt himself by pushing her away and punish her for letting him.

"Is it hard to believe that you kissed someone? No. But I'll warrant you haven't had a man between your legs before. I haven't seen that kind of innocence since I was thirteen."

She took a step back as if he'd slapped her. Jonas waited to feel the touch of satisfaction and was startled when he only felt more depressed, more angry. He jerked back to the window, back to the stark New York winter, to barrenness, and told himself she would leave now. She would leave because he'd hurt her, because he'd crushed her the way hopelessness was crushing him.

Leave, he thought. *Leave before I hurt you more.* And then, to guarantee it, he said, "Better watch out, Genie, the monster has teeth. I told you to get the hell out of here."

He heard nothing. Not a single sound. Not a step or a sigh. It was so quiet he wondered if this were all an illusion, if maybe she wasn't here at all, if he'd imagined the whole thing.

"His name was Nicholas," she said softly. "I thought I loved him."

"How sweet," he said cynically.

She went on as if she hadn't heard him. "But he—he loved someone else."

A pause. He sensed her pain hovering between them, filling the air, and he refused to let himself feel it. If he felt it he would cry. If he felt it, he would get down on his knees and beg her never to leave him. And then he would be the one who got hurt. Because she would leave him. The moment she realized what a burden he was, she would go, the way they all did. In a way he wanted that. In a way he wanted her to leave so he could sink deeper and deeper into that darkness that waited for him, so he didn't have to make any effort to elude it. If she left, he could go back to bed and stay there, give in to sleep and restless dreams and forgetfulness.

"Life is like that," he said. He meant to stop with that, just that clean, cynical statement, a hurtful declaration. But despite himself, the other words spilled out, the words he'd never meant to say—and especially not to her. "What do you want—a guarantee? There aren't any. People say they love you and then they leave. They say they'll stay no matter what happens. But they don't." He paused, feeling the pain well up so strongly inside him that he spoke the last in a whisper. "They never do."

There was silence again. So much of it, and so long, that his words seemed to reverberate within it, a ceaseless rhythm, a painful reminder. *They never do.* Not his mother or his father, not his sister or his brother Charles. Not Rico. No one.

Then he heard her step behind him, felt her hand on his shoulder. A calming touch, a steady one. So tranquil it hurt him—physically hurt him—even as it soothed him, even as he felt her strength pouring into him.

"I won't leave," she said. "Not as long as you need me here."

The unsaid words floated between them, twisting out of his reach, sucked away by that awful blackness. *People say they love you and then they leave,* he'd said, and he wondered if her answer held the first part too, if she thought that she loved him but was too afraid to say. He wished she'd said it, though he knew he wouldn't believe her. Hell, he didn't believe her now. He never believed anyone.

Because of that he didn't give her an answer. Because of that he said nothing. But even so he felt himself stiffen beneath her touch, a too-revealing response, one that gave him away. He stared at the window, trying to ignore the feel of her hand on his shoulder, the strong, gentle heat, the only warmth at all on this cold, dark, rainy day. Christ, he felt cold to his very center. Cold and barren.

And suddenly he was glad she hadn't said "I love you." Glad because he couldn't have said it back, because his heart was heavy and empty and he didn't know if he could care about anything anymore.

She waited a few moments, and then she eased away, leaving a chill at his back. He heard her moving around the studio, and the comforting sound of her movements only made him more miserable. He thought he heard her humming, and he closed his eyes and listened to her, growing more desolate with every wavering note. She reminded him of all the things he would never have: a wife, a family, a normal life— God, a normal life. Was there such a thing? He thought of all the people he knew, of the way they talked. Planning for two weeks from now, a year, five. . . . They talked about the future as if it were a guarantee.

He wished he knew how they did it. Even planning for the next day was beyond his capabilities. He didn't understand how to think that way, how to plan, and he wanted to. He wanted to understand how people mapped out their lives, how they went so easily through a day. How they managed to keep from destroying the people around them, destroying themselves. He looked down at his arm, at the too-smooth stump, the thick pink ridge of scar. Christ, how did they do it? How did Genie do it?

"Genie," he said. His voice was hoarse and rough, it

didn't sound like his. But the moment he spoke she stopped, he heard the silence.

"Yes?"

He tried to read her tone. Was it wariness he heard? Concern? He didn't know, couldn't decide. He continued anyway. "Genie," he said again. "Tell me—tell me how you plan your day."

"How I plan my day?" She sounded confused now. "I'm not sure what you mean."

"Do you . . . do you have a schedule?"

She gave him a funny little smile. "A schedule? Yes, I suppose you could say that."

"You know what you're doing each day."

"Yes."

He took a deep breath and looked away from her. "How do you know?"

"Well . . . There are just things that need to be done. And people who expect you for things. Dinners, for instance. And parties. And school. Just . . . things." She moved across the room; he felt her presence behind him, and then she was in front of him, leaning against the window. He wondered if she was cold, and then realized the fire she'd started had warmed the room. But he was still cold. Freezing cold.

She gripped the sill with her fingers and shook back her hair. She was wearing it loose. It fell over her shoulders and down her back, light brown strands clung to the satin of her dress.

"Just things," he managed.

"Yes. Things like . . . I went to Atkinson's every day for lessons. Always. Unless I was too sick to go—"

"Too sick?"

"Yes, well, I—I was often ill." She rushed through the admission as if it embarrassed her. "Before Chloe died, they were going to send me away, to a hospital. But then she died and . . . and I didn't go.''

The name sent anger spearing through him and he tried to remember why. "A hospital? What kind of hospital?"

"I don't remember," she said quietly. "Does it matter?"

No. No, of course it didn't. He shook his head. "Go on."

"Go on?" She paused, cocking her head as if she were trying to remember. "Well . . . my father was a great scheduler. He loved his salons—we probably had one or two a week. People came from all over the state. Writers and artists. . . ." She closed her eyes and smiled as if she were recalling a precious memory.

He wondered how she did that. How did people have memories that were precious? He had none. Only things he would rather not remember. Despair and embarrassment and pain. All of his memories were like that.

She opened her eyes. "Hiram Powers was there once."

"Ah, yes, he did the sculpture you disliked. 'The Greek Slave,' " he said.

"Yes. I wasn't lying when I told Mr. Tremaine I'd seen it."

"I never supposed you were," he said. That night at Anne Webster's came back in hazy detail. It seemed a hundred years ago. He hadn't even planned that, he remembered. Had just gone and expected to be welcome—and was.

He sighed, feeling drained. "I don't understand schedules," he said bluntly. "I've never had one. I don't know what will happen from moment to moment. Some days are good. Some . . ." He shrugged, letting the sentence fade into nothing, letting her draw her own conclusion, waiting for the look of arrested sympathy on her face, the pity he hated and wanted at the same time.

"Oh, Jonas." She came to him, all soft compassion and healing words that frightened him, pained him. But he didn't try to pull away when she knelt before him, between his legs. She reached out to take his hands, grabbing one, stopping short just before the other. He saw the moment she saw the stump, saw her startled shock, the quick way she tried to hide it.

His embarrassment numbed him, his self-hatred sprang to life. Deliberately he grabbed on to it, held it.

"Does it shock you?" he asked hoarsely, not sure what answer he wanted her to give, whether he would prefer the truth or a lie.

"Yes, a little," she admitted, holding her ground. "I've—I've just never seen it before. I was surprised."

"Surprised." He laughed humorlessly. "Not as surprised as I was when they took it. I woke up alive and without a hand. I didn't expect either one." He lifted his arm again, staring at the artificial smoothness of the flesh, the rounded hump of a wrist, the ridge of still-pink scar that marked the sutures. And then he turned over his other hand, wrist up. There it was, the companion scar that marked it, a thin white scratch, barely noticeable but there nonetheless. He eyed it casually. "Odd, don't you think, that I could cut one so deep and not the other?"

It took a moment for her to understand his words. He knew the precise moment she realized his meaning, felt a tingle of satisfaction at her gasp. She had given him the response he wanted finally, the one he expected. Revulsion. Horror. The same reaction his father had. The same look he'd seen on the face of his roommate at Barbizon, who'd found him bleeding and semiconscious and wanting to die. Jonas had screamed at them to leave him alone, had fought them when they tried to take him to the hospital, fought until the blood loss make him weak, until he passed out in the wagon.

And when he'd awakened it was to the stench of cauterized skin and the coppery scent of blood. It was to horror so intense he'd thought he would never see its like again.

But that was before he'd gone home.

That was before Bloomingdale.

He looked at Genie with smug satisfaction. She was like all the others, after all. Her horror was proof of it. Like them, she was only willing to love him, to stay with him, until she found out the truth. Madness was an easy thing to deny when it meant only brilliance and temperamental behavior. It was not so easy when it meant playing God.

"My father sent me to the Bloomingdale Lunatic Asylum after that," he continued, his voice light and nonchalant, as if he were describing a promenade in the park. "You know it?"

He looked at her expectantly. She was staring at him the same way those inspectors had, the men who toured the facility every few months, studying the lunatics as if they were animals in a zoo.

"I've heard of it," she said in a whisper.

"I was there for four months," he said, going on, wanting to shock her into terror, into flight. "A madman. They told me I was insane."

"Were you?"

He looked at her challengingly, daring her to run. "You tell me."

She met his gaze. For a moment she just looked steadily at him, and then she licked her lips and shook her head, a slight shake, a quick denial.

"You can't make me leave, Jonas," she said softly.

He laughed bitterly. "Don't make promises you can't keep."

She took a deep breath. He saw the rise and fall of her breasts, felt the warmth of her sigh on his face. But she said nothing, only squeezed his hand and got to her feet. He heard her move back across the floor, to the stove.

"Dinner will be ready soon," she said, "I hope you're hungry." Her voice was light—as if she didn't have a care in the world.

And perhaps she didn't, he thought. Perhaps she simply didn't understand what he'd just told her, the kind of man he was.

But he knew in his heart that she did.

And it scared the hell out of him.

Chapter 20

She told herself she was right to stay with him. She told herself he needed her. She reminded herself of it whenever she wavered in her determination—like this afternoon, when he'd tried to drive her away. There was no one else to stay with him, and she couldn't leave him alone. Especially not after today.

Imogene sighed and turned back to the bed, watching him sleep. She remembered how Jonas had collapsed once she and Rico managed to get him inside yesterday, how he'd curled into a ball, turning his back to them and falling into a restless slumber soon after. She had meant to go then, even though it bothered her to leave him that way. But Rico had given her a look that dissolved her intentions and said simply: "I'll send a message to your godfather and tell him you're here."

She'd known then she wouldn't go, at least not that night. Besides the fact that she didn't want to leave Jonas alone, she was afraid he would wake and start screaming for her again. If she wasn't here to soothe him. . . . It made her stomach knot to think of what might happen. For some reason her presence calmed him, and she thought he needed calm. So she didn't leave. She spent the night perched in an old ladder-back chair she pulled up beside his bed, and this morning she woke early, stiff and weary and determined to go home, to try to explain things to Thomas and Katherine, to leave the dangerous Jonas Whitaker to his own devices.

She'd meant to go. She'd meant to make him breakfast and run away before she could change her mind, before he changed it for her. But the moment he said, *"They always leave,"* it was too late. She'd seen something . . . fear, despair, *something* . . . behind his gruff and cynical facade, a pain that seared into her very soul, that pinned her there like a caught butterfly.

It only made it worse to see the scar on his wrist. Then she knew she could no longer simply walk away. Imogene sighed, staring at his shadow, listening to the strong and steady rhythm of his breathing, the rustle of his movements. The sounds were reassuring in the darkness, more comforting than she wanted them to be. They meant he was alive. As long as he was breathing, as long as he moved, he was alive—funny, how important that seemed now. She couldn't stop thinking of that scar on his wrist, and she couldn't help wondering why he'd wanted to kill himself, what sorrow had been black enough, bitter enough, to make him want to end his life.

She told herself not to care. She told herself all the reasons she shouldn't: He wouldn't stay with her, she couldn't survive him, he didn't truly see her. But that contrary rhythm in her heart, that singular beat, made it impossible to turn away. In the end, there was only one reason to stay, and it had nothing to do with logic or good sense. It had nothing to do with her own survival.

He needed her.

Three simple words, yet they held more power than any of her arguments for leaving. He needed her and she had never been needed before. She had never been important to anyone. It was such a strange feeling, one too startling, too alluring, to deny. She didn't care if he needed her only to make his dinner or to keep the fire going. It didn't matter why. The only thing that mattered was that he did, and she couldn't turn her back on that, not yet. She would wait until he was stronger, until that despair was not so dark and pitiless in his eyes. She would stay as long as he needed her. It was not much of a sacrifice.

Except it was a sacrifice, and she knew it. Staying here would cost her her reputation. Her godfather's position was strong enough to withstand the scandal, but Imogene knew hers was not. The gossip would follow her all the way back to Nashville. She would no longer be considered respectable. She would no longer be accepted in polite society.

And suddenly she wondered if being ostracized might free her in a way she'd never been free before.

She thought of Jonas's questions today and about her answers. About schedules that filled days but never fulfilled them. About churning away at watercolors that didn't inspire and only made her feel more useless and untalented than ever.

Imogene looked again at the man on the bed before her and thought of her childhood, of all those hours spent alone in her sickroom, listlessly watching life pass by the windows. So lonely she had even welcomed the visits of the doctor, with his uncomfortable prodding and poking and his vile nostrums.

That loneliness had lasted even when the illnesses grew less frequent, even after she could leave her sickroom. She had haunted the halls of her father's house, afraid to make friends, preferring to stay in the background and live vicariously through her sister. She had been afraid to do more, afraid that if she tried people would look at her the way her mother did, with that thinly veiled revulsion, that rejection, in their eyes.

That loneliness had never left her. Until now.

Imogene took a deep breath, hearing the rhythm of Jonas's breathing mingle with her own, a companionable, reassuring sound. She thought of the last few days, the last week. Of the salon and the night on the roof. Of Jonas's caresses and his mouth on hers.

And she knew, suddenly and completely, that if redemption meant giving up this last week with Jonas Whitaker, if it meant giving up the world he had shown her, then she would rather be damned.

Jonas Whitaker had helped her touch the world she had always been on the outside of, one in which she had never belonged. And if that was all she ever had, it would be enough. For it, she was willing to pay the price of scandal. He had made her feel alive, and she had no other way to thank him than to stay, no other choice but to give some of that life back to him now. She owed it to him.

She owed it to herself.

Imogene rose, feeling comforted suddenly, as if a great weight had been lifted from her shoulders. Her anxiety faded, along with her uncertainty. Her life was changing, but she would be ready for it. She would—

The knock on the door startled her. Imogene frowned, her thoughts scattering in sudden apprehension. It was late; who would go out visiting at this time of night? The answer came to her quickly. Rico, probably, she realized with a surge of relief. No doubt he was stopping by to check on them.

She hurried through the drapery covering the bedroom entrance, calling "I'll be right there," as she went to the door. She flung it open, a greeting ready on her lips.

It wasn't Rico.

It was Thomas.

He stood there, holding his hat and wearing a forbidding expression. His face was heavily lined with weariness and worry, along with a stark disapproval that froze and numbed her heart. She had expected condemnation, but not this soon, and not . . . not this way. But when she looked at Thomas's face she knew all her worst imaginings had come true—and that she had not really thought they would. Somewhere in the back of her mind she had expected Thomas to understand. In her imagination this discussion would be like the one they'd had the morning after the salon. Compassionate, sympathetic.

But she had forgotten Thomas's warnings then, and she knew by the expression on his face that she shouldn't have. The realization made her heart sink into her stomach. She felt suddenly ill.

Imogene struggled to hide her discomposure. "Thomas," she said softly. "I didn't expect you."

"Of course not," he said stiffly. His sarcasm was so heavy it seemed to deepen his voice. "Why should you? You send a messenger to the house carrying a note written in someone else's hand, telling me not to worry, that you're with Whitaker for a few days. Of course I'll understand. How absurd that I wouldn't."

"Thomas, I—"

"What did you think? That you could spend the night—two, from the looks of it—in the home of the most notorious womanizer in the city and no one would care? Could you possibly be that naive?"

His words reverberated down the hall, too loud, too condemning. Nervously Imogene swallowed, backing into the studio, motioning him inside. "Perhaps we should talk about it in here."

Thomas stiffened. "Where the hell is he?"

"He's—he's sleeping."

Thomas's eyes turned to ice. "Sleeping."

"It's not what you think."

"No, of course not."

Imogene bit her lip. "Thomas, please listen to me for a moment."

"I think not." He stepped inside, closing the door firmly behind him. "I think it's time you listened to me, Imogene. I have, I think, been very understanding. I have tried hard to be. But this behavior is . . . it's beyond reasonable. I'm afraid I have no choice but to insist you return home with me. There may still be time to minimize the damage." He motioned to her mantle. "Come along."

She had never seen Thomas look so forbidding, never so angry. But the worst of it was that she'd hurt him. She saw the ache in his eyes, and she knew he regarded her behavior as a betrayal. He was right, it was. She had led him to believe she would follow his suggestions. She had taken advantage of his love and his support, of his understanding.

But she'd had no choice. She remembered Jonas

screaming her name in the hallway, collapsing against her. How did she have a choice?

She moved behind a chair, grasping the back of it so tightly the blood left her fingers. "I'm sorry I've hurt you, Thomas," she said carefully. "It was the last thing I wanted to do. You have to believe that."

His lips compressed; the skin around his nostrils turned white.

"I'm sorry," she said again. "But I . . . can't leave. And it's not what you think. He needs me right now. There's no one else—"

"He has friends."

She thought of the salon. She thought of the artists gathered on the landing. She thought of Rico, and Paris. "No," she said quietly. "He doesn't."

"Let him find some then, instead of corrupting you."

"He's not corrupting me," Imogene said. She stepped around the chair, toward him. "Do you remember when I was telling you what Peter McBride said? That Jonas was mad? Do you remember what you told me?"

He regarded her warily.

"You asked me if I was afraid of it. You told me you had the feeling it tortured him. Well, I've discovered something, Thomas. I *am* afraid of it, and I know it does torture him." She swallowed. "I'm not just afraid for myself, Thomas. I'm afraid for him."

His face didn't soften. "Let him find his way on his own," he said slowly. "I don't want to sacrifice my goddaughter to him."

"It's not your choice," she said stubbornly.

"Imogene, I can't believe you've thought about this." He frowned. "I heard about the scene in Delmonico's—did you think I wouldn't? I told everyone it couldn't be you. And when I got the message you sent, I told myself you would see reason, that you would come home. I wanted to come right away, but I gave you time. You've always been such a reasonable girl—"

"Hello, Gosney."

Both Imogene and her godfather whirled around at the sound of Jonas's voice. It was low and tired, barely audible, but it seemed to cut through the tension like a knife. He was leaning against the door frame of his bedroom, the tapestry draping over his shoulder, his deformed arm hidden. He looked terrible; tired and drawn, his hair tangled and unkempt, the beard-shadow heavy on his jaw in the dim lamplight.

She heard Thomas's intake of breath. She saw the shock in his eyes, the surprise.

"Good God, Whitaker," he said softly. "You look wretched."

Jonas's gaze flickered over him. "I suppose so," he said dully. "Sorry. I wasn't expecting visitors."

Thomas's mouth tightened. Imogene saw her godfather struggle to compose himself. Then he nodded toward her.

"I'm not here to visit," he said. "I'm here to take her home."

She thought she saw Jonas flinch, thought she saw despair flit through his eyes, but it was soon gone, leaving in its place a resigned detachment.

He shrugged. "Take her then."

"No." Imogene shook her head. "I'm not going."

Thomas didn't shift his gaze from Jonas. "What have you done to her?" he asked. His voice was too calm, too controlled. "What have you done, you bastard?"

At the words, life glinted in Jonas's eyes. He gave Thomas an insolent stare. "Afraid I'll ravish her, Gosney? Don't worry. I already have."

Her godfather's gaze richocheted to her. Imogene felt the heat of a blush move up her throat, over her cheeks.

"Well?" Thomas asked. "Has he?"

She licked her lips. "You don't understand—"

"You bastard." Thomas whirled back to Jonas, spitting the words. "You goddamned bastard. I trusted you. I asked you not to . . . you bastard."

Jonas's face tightened. "Just living up to my reputation," he said heavily.

Thomas lunged.

Imogene rushed forward, grabbing her godfather's arm, pulling him back. "Thomas, please," she begged. "It's all right, really. Please."

Anger made his body rigid and his features sharp, but he stopped, his fist clenched at his side, his breathing harsh. He jerked away from her. "I can't believe you would defend him," he said raggedly. His disappointment was a palpable, horrible thing. "I want you to come home with me," he said.

"I—I can't," she said helplessly. "You don't understand. He doesn't know what he's saying."

"I know exactly what I'm saying," Jonas interjected. "Go with him, Genie. I don't want you to stay."

She knew it was a lie. It wasn't his stance that told her, or his voice, or even his eyes. But there was something there, something that reminded her of earlier today, of his too-sad words. *"They say they love you and they leave."* And though she'd never told him she loved him, those words hung between them; she felt his dejection and his despair, hidden as it was by his dismissal.

Thomas touched her arm. "It's settled then—"

"No." She pulled away.

"What spell has he cast on you, Imogene?" Thomas's voice was edged with frustration and exhaustion. "What the hell has he done to you?"

"He's done nothing," she said slowly. She took a deep breath and licked her lips. "Just a few more days, Thomas. Please." She dropped her voice to a whisper. "Just give me a few more days."

Thomas expelled a harsh sigh. "You leave me no choice, my dear, you know this."

Her stomach tightened. "Yes," she said. "I know."

"And you'll still defy me?"

"I'm not defying you. I'm asking you to understand."

"I do understand. I understand that he's taking advantage of you. I understand that you're—you're obsessed with him somehow." Thomas spun on his heel, heading for the door. He grabbed the lever and jerked it open, pausing to look at her. "Imogene—" he said, and she knew he was giving her one last chance. One chance for forgiveness. One for absolution.

One last chance.

She gave it back to him. "I'll keep in touch, Thomas," she said.

She winced at the slamming of the door, trying to gather her composure as she heard him stomping down the hall. She thought she heard the crashing of the front door clear up to the third floor.

"You didn't have to do that." Jonas's voice drifted

over her, soothing and soft, gravelly with fatigue. "You should have gone with him."

She turned to look at him. "Probably."

He regarded her through bleary eyes. "You'll regret this, you know."

"No."

"Yes, you will." He rubbed his hand over his jaw. "You think there's something you can do, but there isn't. There's nothing anyone can do."

His words were self-pitying and sad and vaguely annoying. Imogene said nothing.

He turned back to the bedroom. "I'm going back to sleep," he said dully.

She felt desperate and isolated. Thomas had always been her only friend, and without him she had no one. No one but Jonas. She wanted, needed, reassurance that she had done the right thing. She needed someone to sit up with her for a while, to talk about—oh, about art and its place in the world, about Caravaggio's angels. She needed the Jonas of two nights ago.

But he was gone.

She wanted him back so badly she could barely stand it. "Wait," she said, and when he stopped and looked over his shoulder at her she babbled on, unable to stop. "Stay up with me, won't you? Please? We'll drink some wine. We'll talk."

"Talk?" he repeated. "About what? The human condition? The fleetingness of life?" He shook his head and turned away, shuffling back into the bedroom. "I'm not in the mood to talk," he said, disappearing through the curtain. "I'm going back to bed."

And she was alone again. Just as she always was. Just as she was afraid she would always be.

Chapter 21

He wanted her to go. He was afraid she would. He couldn't stand the sound of her voice, but when she was silent he nearly went crazy in the quiet. He couldn't bear her presence, but he hated being alone more. Because when she was silent, and when she was gone, he had no choice but to look inside himself, and what he saw there terrified him. Hopelessness. Blackness. Madness. A despair that wouldn't go away. He was mad; his father had always said it, everyone had always said it. And every year brought that insanity closer, until now it was hovering just beyond him, baiting him, threatening him. One day he would wake up and it would all be over, he knew. His mind would be consumed by the blackness. There was only a thin wall keeping it from him now. A thin wall.

Genie.

He turned to look at her. She was sitting just beyond him, looking stiff and uncomfortable in one of the rickety ladderback chairs he'd bought from some relocating artist. She'd pinned her hair back again, but it

was escaping from the chignon to dangle about her
cheeks and against her neck, and the honey-colored
strands warmed the paleness of her face, the colorless-
ness of her lips. She looked surprisingly serene, unac-
countably tranquil. She was reading an old book with
a split and discolored leather cover, and her lips
moved slightly as she read, as if she were memorizing
every word.

He tried to remember making love to her. Tried to
remember how her skin had looked, what it had tasted
and felt like. He wondered if he'd kissed the curls at
the apex of her thighs, if he'd watched her cry out in
climax. He wanted to remember. He wanted to remember not just the act but how he'd felt afterward,
wanted to know if her touch had calmed him the way
her presence did, if she'd looked at him with gratitude
or with pleasure.

But all he could remember was bits and pieces; the
sight of a breast and the feel of her nipple against his
tongue, how she threw her head back and how dark
her lashes looked upon her cheeks. And he thought he
remembered repletion and its accompanying joy.
Thought he did, though that last got tangled up with
his memories of waiters and red wine, and he wasn't
sure which was real and what was illusion.

He wondered if that was what was making her stay.
God knew there was no other reason. He couldn't
fathom why she'd disobeyed her godfather, why she
was braving the condemnation of society to stay with
him. Surely they'd all told her about his reputation,
and she certainly knew he lived up to it. "Mad" Jonas
Whitaker, he'd heard people call him, and it was true.
She knew it was true. So why the hell was she here?

Why did she insist on staying? Didn't she know he would destroy her? Couldn't she see?

It made him crazy, the questions, the unanswerability of them. He wanted to ask her, wanted to frighten her into telling him, but he couldn't rouse the effort, so finally all he said was "What are you reading?"

She looked up in surprise, and it made him wonder how long he'd been silent. An hour? A day?

"This?" She lifted the book. "Oh, it's nothing. Poetry. Byron. I found it on your shelf, I hope you don't mind."

"Byron?" he repeated wearily.

She flushed and looked down. "I know, I know. I should be reading about art, I suppose. But this was so much more . . . interesting."

He couldn't wrap his mind around that. Didn't want to. She wasn't reading about art and she should be, and he didn't care.

He looked away. "Byron was mad," he said.

"He wrote beautiful poetry."

"But was it worth the price?" he murmured. "Was it?"

"I don't know." Her voice was quiet and even and calm. "His words move me. Is that enough?"

"Does it matter if you're moved?" Jonas looked back to her. "Who are you, anyway? Just some woman. You'll be dead someday, and then what will all of this matter? What does any of it mean? So his words live on in you. His immortality lasts only as long as you do."

"And my children," she said stubbornly. "Because I'll read it to them. And perhaps their children."

"A hundred years," he scoffed.

"His poems have lasted thirty years already," she said.

He shook his head. "It doesn't matter," he said, staring at the wall, at the cracking plaster, the water-stain that looked like a giant feeding spider. "Nothing does. We all strive to say something—as if it's important. As if there can be some lasting value . . . And yet we all know mankind is doomed to nothingness. Immortality." He laughed bitterly. "There's no such thing. There's no meaning to anything. We get up in the morning, we push through the day, we go to sleep. Day after day. Endlessness. Meaninglessness."

"God is playing games with us," she said softly.

He looked at her in surprise. Her words were a familiar echo; through his bitterness he remembered his conversation with Rico, the argument he was always making, that God was jealous, that life was nothing but a trivial amusement.

"Yes," he said. "Yes, that's exactly it."

She glanced down at the book, a small smile caressing her lips. "Maybe you're right," she said. "Maybe, in the long run, life is only a game. But does it have to be something else? Does there have to be meaning?"

He stared at her, puzzled. "Yes, of course."

"Why?"

Why? Her question rattled him. He couldn't think of an answer, and there had to be one. Had to be because he couldn't conceive of life without meaning, because then it fit too closely what he was feeling right now, bleak hopelessness, nothingness. If there was no meaning, then it didn't matter if he allowed the madness to take over, and he couldn't bear that. Christ, it terrified him to consider it.

"You . . . you can't mean that," he said hoarsely.
"I've seen life without meaning. I've seen it."

"At Bloomingdale."

He squeezed his eyes shut, his throat grew too tight
to swallow. "Yes," he breathed.

"Tell me," she said, "why it frightens you."

He didn't want to answer her. His head hurt, his
body hurt. He didn't want to remember. But there was
something in her voice, a genuine interest, a need to
understand, and he was selfish enough to indulge her,
selfish enough to want her to feel how hopeless and
dark he felt. Selfish enough to hurt her, because when
she hurt he had the upper hand. When she hurt, it only
reaffirmed what he knew about himself: that he destroyed everything he touched, that he deserved to be
alone.

"There . . . are times," he said unemotionally,
"when I wonder if I'm real, when I can't feel my body.
Once I . . . cut myself . . . to see if I would bleed. I
thought if I bled, it meant I was real. It meant I was
alive." He looked at her, letting his despair shine from
his eyes. "Can you even begin to understand that?"

She didn't flinch. She didn't look away. She swallowed, and he saw the sadness enter her face, a sadness so poignant he recognized it even through his
own.

"Yes," she said. "I understand that."

He stared at her in shocked surprise. "How can
you?"

She glanced down at the book, flipping slowly
through the pages. "My father wanted to send me
away. My mother couldn't stand the sight of me. Until
Chloe died I was nothing." She looked up at him, and
the pain in her eyes was so stark it sharpened her fea-

tures. "I used to walk into rooms and they would talk right through me as if I weren't there. As if I were invisible."

Her words sank inside him. Despite the sorrow in her expression, they were so matter-of-fact, as dispassionate as his had been. They reminded him of something she'd said yesterday. Something about a man who loved someone else. A man . . . Nicholas. Unexpectedly Jonas realized he wanted to know about him. For some reason it seemed important that he know.

"What about Nicholas?" he asked. "What about him?"

She shook her head.

"Tell me," he urged, unsure why he wanted it so badly, unwilling to think beyond the fact that he did.

"I already told you," she said. "He was in love with someone else."

He waited.

She clenched her jaw, and he saw he'd cracked her composure at last, that the tranquility he'd wanted to take from her was gone. He saw the vulnerability in her face even though she wouldn't look at him. He'd wanted to hurt her. He'd wanted to prove to her that he would destroy her, and he'd done it with a word, with nothing more than a name.

He hated himself for it. Hated himself for hurting her. Christ, this was not what he wanted at all.

"Genie—"

She shook her head again, stopping his words in his throat.

"It's all right," she said. Then she swallowed, and he saw her struggle to regain her self-control. "It—it doesn't hurt any longer, truly it doesn't."

He didn't believe her, but he said nothing.

She kept her eyes fastened on the book. On Byron. Her finger traced the lines as if she were reading it, but he sensed she didn't see the words at all. "Nicholas was my sister's fiancé," she began, her voice so low he barely heard her. "And he was my friend. He used to talk to me. I couldn't believe he even noticed me, but he was always so kind." She paused. "I didn't mean to love him. I didn't want to love him."

"But you did," he prompted.

"Yes." She nodded. "I did. And when Chloe died . . . I wanted him to love me. I was willing to be Chloe to make him love me. So I tried to be her. I made myself as like her as I could."

"Did it make a difference?"

She slanted him a glance. "No," she said. "He left me anyway."

They were quiet. He was thinking about her words, about her wish to be Chloe, and he had the feeling she'd told him that before, and that there had been the same sadness then too, a sorrow that needled him— that leapt beyond his own pain, beyond his fear and his despair. Her pain had nothing to do with him at all, but it hurt him just the same. He was afraid for her. Afraid for her simple beauty and her heart. Afraid of all the things that could hurt her in this life, the things that already had. He wanted suddenly to comfort her, and it was such an alien feeling it made him pause, such a strange notion he had no idea what to say or what to do. Finally he said the first thing that came to mind.

"He was using you, you know."

"Yes," she agreed softly. "I know."

With her admission his reticence melted away. The urge to protect her, to take care of her, grew stronger, and it nearly made him laugh. He couldn't protect her. Hell, she needed someone to protect her from *him*. He was the most dangerous thing of all.

But still he couldn't keep from holding out his hand. Still he couldn't stop himself from saying "Come sit beside me, Genie."

And when she did, when she took his hand and settled on the bed beside him, leaning into his side and drawing her legs up so the pale green satin flowed over his, Jonas felt comforted in a way he couldn't remember feeling in a long time, maybe ever. Comforted and safe. The blackness in his mind retreated just a little. He felt her warmth, her tranquility, ease into him, a pale yellow light, a soothing presence.

He held her tightly against him and looked up at the ceiling, listening to the rain.

She had been there three days before she decided to take him to the market with her. She thought he was better. Not good yet, but not so silent, not so hopeless. He was still quiet, and it seemed to hurt him to move and gave him headaches to think. He couldn't make a decision about anything, and so she made them all. She told him what to eat and how much, she told him when to wash and when to get out of bed. But mostly he stayed in bed and mostly she sat beside him, reading from Byron, or Tennyson, or one of the other books of poetry he had. She'd tried once to read to him from the "The Crayon," but he'd stopped her after two paragraphs, claiming he didn't want to hear about art.

She wondered if maybe that wasn't so true, if he had rejected the new art journal because he'd seen through her careful attempts to appear interested. Though she had been forced to read art journals and criticisms since Chloe's death three years ago, Imogene had never really understood them; she had never been interested enough to care what they said.

Why had that been so hard to admit before now?

She didn't know, and she tried not to think about it too much. Just as she tried not to think of anything too much. It was easier to go through the days with Jonas without wondering when they would end, or what would happen to her when they did. It was easier to concentrate only on him, on their short but intense conversations, on the things she was beginning to learn about him. Little things, like the fact that he drank his coffee very strong and that his right arm needed massaging in the evening to ease the strain of bearing the burden for two. Things like his shelves, which were scattered with knickknacks from all over the world, strange little toys she didn't understand, and that he liked her to sit beside him on the bed so he could twirl his fingers through her hair.

Little things. Things that made her feel alive and precious. Things that made her feel real.

She told herself it was only fleeting, that this time would come to an end, and with it all these little intimacies, these strange and tender familiarities. He would get better, and she would return to Nashville. It would end. He needed her now, but he would not always need her. It was something she reminded herself of every single day.

Because she was growing attached to him, and it frightened her. Because at night she fell asleep curled beside him, and in the mornings she was still there, cradled against his body. He liked her there because she soothed him, she knew. No other reason. He never made a single attempt to kiss her or caress her. He never spoke of the one time they'd made love.

No doubt he wanted to forget it. The thought made her sad, but it was a reality she was used to, one she could accept. At least Jonas Whitaker had never professed false love. He didn't try to make her believe something that wasn't true. He was temperamental, and he was . . . touched, but he was honest, and as the days passed she found more and more to admire about him. More to care about.

And though she told herself it was wrong, in a way she secretly hoped he wouldn't get better. She wanted to stay. She wanted to care about him. She wanted him to keep needing her. The longing was dangerous, and she knew it, but every day that passed made it grow a little stronger, made the sense of dread within her a little sharper.

With a sense of desperation, she tried to remember how long Rico had said this mood would last. A week? A month? She didn't remember, and she wished he were around to ask. But Rico had disappeared, and though she checked his rooms daily, there was never any answer, and no one ever picked up the notes she left pinned to his door.

Finally she'd sent a note to Peter. He'd been around last spring, surely he knew how long this was likely to last. But there was no answer from him either, and she had the needling suspicion the gossip had already reached him. No doubt the whole city knew of the incident at Delmonico's, and certainly it was no secret she was staying in Jonas's studio. She wondered what the gossip was, whether they were assuming she was his mistress or his model or both. Probably the former, she decided distractedly, but she couldn't really bring herself to care. Time enough for that later.

For now, she wanted to get him outside, into the fresh air. The rain had gone this morning, though the clouds were still hovering, heavy and gray in the sky, and it was cold enough to threaten snow. Still, she thought taking him to the market would do him good. The one time she'd been there, it was invigorating, and she wanted something invigorating, something to grab his interest, since he seemed to take no interest in anything here.

She sighed at the thought, ladling out a steaming bowl of porridge and taking it into the bedroom. He was still asleep, curled on his side, his hair hiding his face. Hesitantly Imogene glanced at the pocket watch dangling from the bedstand. Seven o'clock. It was early. He usually slept—albeit restlessly—until nearly noon.

There was no choice but to wake him. If they were going to the market, they had to be there early, else the best would be gone. She set aside the bowl, touching his shoulder, shaking him gently.

"Jonas," she whispered. "Jonas, wake up."

He barely moved.

"Jonas." She shook him again.

This time he groaned and shrugged off her hand. "Go away," he murmured.

"No." She gripped his shoulder more firmly. "It's time to get up. We're going out."

That got his attention, she noted with satisfaction. He rolled over, opening one bleary eye to look at her. "Out? You're leaving?"

"I need to go to the market—"

"No." He rose, shaking, to one elbow. She saw

panic in his eyes. "You said . . . you said you wouldn't go."

"You didn't let me finish," she said patiently. "I was going to ask you to come with me."

He looked confused, the fear didn't leave his expression. "I can't," he whispered.

"Why not?"

"I can't."

"Of course you can." She reached for the bowl of porridge and held it out to him, waiting patiently for him to adjust himself to take it. But though he sat up, he didn't do more than make a cursory glance at the bowl. "Please," she urged. "We'll have fun."

"Fun?" He gave a short, mocking laugh. "I don't think so. I'm staying here."

"You'd rather sit in here and rot."

"Yes!" he shouted. "Yes, I'd rather rot." He held up his useless stump. "Hell, I'm halfway there already."

Her patience snapped. She started to slam the bowl of porridge on the rickety nightstand, then stopped herself, fighting for composure. "I won't let you make me angry," she said slowly, forcing her breathing to calm. "Do what you like. I'm going to the market."

She spun on her heel, hurrying from the room before he had time to stop her. She heard his muffled curse, heard the dull thud of something hitting the wall, but she ignored it. She would not go back in there, not while he was in this mood. He was aching for a fight, and she didn't want to give it to him. She didn't want to hurt him. She didn't want to be hurt.

But she felt the sharp pang of disappointment as she fumbled with her hair and grabbed her bag from the table. She went to the door, reaching for the mantle that hung on the peg beside it, trying not to think of the things he could do in the hour she'd be gone.

"Wait." His voice was low and steady.

She turned. He was leaning against the wall beside his bedroom door, holding his carved hand by the straps. It dangled against his leg. He held it out to her.

"I'd like to go," he said, and she saw the effort it took him to say the words, the fear and wariness in his eyes. "But I . . . I can't seem to get this on. Do you think you could . . . will you . . . help me?"

The last words faded off, a whisper of sound. In spite of her relief, Imogene said nothing. She set aside her coat and went to him, intensely aware that he watched her as she took the wooden hand from him. She had never touched him like this, had never performed such an private task, and the intimacy of it made her nervous. She had to work to keep her fingers from trembling as she settled the pad over his wrist and buckled the straps about his forearm.

She looked up when she finished, inadvertently meeting his eyes and the measuring look in them. He was testing her, she realized, and she felt the heat move into her cheeks. She looked away, wondering if she'd passed. Hoping she had.

"Your glove?" she asked.

He nodded toward the table. "Over there."

Imogene grabbed the glove quickly and handed it to him. "Are you ready?"

"No," he said. He pulled the glove slowly over his fingers, looking tired and beaten. He glanced up and met her gaze, and a strange quirk curved his lips. Almost—not quite—a smile. But it lightened his expression nonetheless, and Imogene found herself smiling back.

"It's cold out," she said. "Don't forget your coat."

He didn't, but he did forget his hat, she noticed when they finally stepped outside into the cold. She thought about sending him back inside for it. It was truly freezing. Her lungs burned with every breath. The clouds were gray and heavy, and there was a sense of expectation in the air, the kind of muted light and muffled sound that promised snow.

She saw the dullness in his eyes and decided not to worry about the hat. It was enough that he was standing out here with her, his hands buried deep in the pockets of his overcoat, his loose hair trailing over his shoulders, strands fluttering into his face. His chin was buried in his collar. He was unrelievedly black, she thought. Black hair, black coat. His pale skin merely accentuated it. The only color to him at all was his eyes, and they were such a flinty green this morning that they barely qualified.

He stood there waiting while she hailed a carriage. He said nothing as they got in, and only stared out the window when the carriage moved off toward Washington Market.

As early as it was, the market was crowded. Wagons bottlenecked the streets leading up it, clogging the entrances so the driver had to leave them more than a block away. Even then, there were so many people and horses in the streets that it was difficult to maneuver around them. Imogene tucked her arm through Jonas's, leading him through the chaos until they reached the wagons and stands of the main area. The scent of the Hudson River mixed with the odors of fresh fish and seaweed, sawdust and horses and pigs.

Imogene took a deep breath, her eyes watering in the stinging cold. "Isn't it wonderful?" she asked.

He shrugged. "I've been to the market before, Genie," he said. "Look at these people—most of them don't have a penny to their name. There's nothing but poverty here, look around you."

Obediently she did, and wondered what he was really seeing, why he didn't notice what she did—the fresh produce nearly tumbling from overfull wagons, plump, ivory-skinned chickens hanging from their feet, baskets filled with seaweed and oysters and speckled lobsters. Certainly there was evidence of poverty. Small children with dirty faces and torn clothes angling to nab an apple or a cabbage, girls in tight dresses and thin shoes, women whose worn scarves accented tired, lined faces, but she wondered why he wasn't seeing everything else, everything that made the scene before them a beautiful, vibrant painting. Yellow pumpkins from Valparaiso next to bins of dark green, leafy kale. Pale round cabbages and bright red apples. Men and women wearing burlap aprons and colorful scarves and frayed hats, their beefy hands shoving potatoes into bags, their eyes bright as they tried to convince a customer of the freshness of a whitefish.

Imogene sighed, feeling a stab of disappointment as she pulled him with her from stand to stand. He was sullen and silent as she haggled with the vendors, but at least he helped her get a better price. His very forbiddingness made the merchants think twice before cheating her, and he didn't even have to say a word.

Dejectedly she left the poultry-seller, dodging past a horse blanketed against the weather and two small children playing hide and seek. The milk merchant was her last stop. After that they could go back to the studio. She felt a tug of desperation at the thought, a sense of hopelessness. Today hadn't helped him at all,

and she wondered if anything could—if she could.
There had to be something more she could do. Something more than sit beside him on the bed and read to
him, something to help ease his misery and despair.
But she didn't know what, and she was struck with the
dull knowledge that Chloe would have known what to
do. Chloe would have been able to make him laugh.

Imogene tried to swallow the lump in her throat,
and tightened her hold on her bag. Lord, she was so
ill-equipped for this, so damned useless—

"Wait."

She was so involved in her own thoughts it took
Imogene a moment to realize Jonas had pulled her to a
stop, that he'd spoken. Confused, she looked up at
him.

He was staring at a wagon loaded with bolts of fabric: bright velvets and satins, jewel-toned silks,
sprigged muslins and pale mousselines. The peddler
hovered nervously, pulling a heavy sheet of canvas
over the more delicate fabrics, muttering as he looked
up at the sky.

"What is it?" she asked.

In answer, Jonas strode toward the wagon, pulling
her along with him, seemingly oblivious to the people
in his way. He stopped at a bolt of dark green velvet,
releasing her and pushing aside the gray canvas to
touch it. His long fingers smoothed over the fabric,
lingeringly, caressingly.

"This," he said in a low voice. "This is the color I
want to see you wear."

His words sent a stab of yearning plunging through
her, a sharp and dizzying pang of desire. Imogene
swallowed, surprised to see how intense his eyes suddenly were, how incredibly green. Like the velvet, like

they'd been the night of the salon, when they'd gone onto the roof and he'd made her laugh at his cartoons.

After so many bleak days, his expression was startling and wonderful. Imogene looked down at the fabric, mesmerized by the movement of his hand. "I—it's lovely," she managed.

"It would be lovely on you," he said, and there was a wistfulness in his voice, a longing, that seemed to pierce straight through to her heart.

"Are ya int'rested in that, sir?" The merchant pushed forward, his sharp gaze scrutinizing Jonas. "I c'n give ya a good price on it."

Jonas hesitated. "I'm sure you can," he said finally. He drew his hand away, shoving it in his pocket. "Perhaps some other time."

He moved off, away from the wagon, back into the crowd, and Imogene saw the disappointment in the vendor's eyes—the same disappointment she felt, though she didn't know why. As lush and beautiful as the fabric was, it didn't matter to her. What mattered was that look on Jonas's face, the yearning in his voice. What mattered was the way he'd looked at her and said *"It would be lovely on you."* She had the feeling he would have said something else, something more, if the vendor had not questioned him. She had the feeling he wanted to say something. But now she would never know what it was, because she wouldn't ask, and she knew already that the moment was gone.

He was waiting for her in the crowd, and her disappointment grew when she recognized his expression. It was disinterested, detached. The same look that had been on his face for more than three days, that had disappeared only for that one split second when green velvet had reflected itself in his eyes.

Imogene sighed. The touch of wetness on her forehead and her nose surprised her. It was beginning to
snow. Soft, big flakes. It was sticking in Jonas's hair,
white against black, light against dark for that brief
moment before they melted into transparency.

Slowly she made her way toward him. "I suppose
we should leave," she said. And then, unnecessarily,
"It's snowing."

He said nothing, and she tucked her arm through
his, starting back to the street. He didn't move with
her.

She looked up at him, puzzled, startled to find that
he was staring at her. Staring at her with a softness
she'd never seen on his face before. With a pang she
realized that his eyes weren't expressionless, as she'd
thought. They were brilliant and thoughtful and a little
sad, and gently he reached out, smoothing a strand of
hair back from her face.

"You've snow in your hair," he said, and then he
leaned down and kissed her, a soft, brief kiss, a brush
of lips that left her mouth tingling. "I'm sorry."

"Sorry?" she asked, confused. "Because there's
snow in my hair?"

Something that might have been a smile touched his
lips. But it was gone so quickly she couldn't be sure.
"No. I'm sorry I couldn't dress you in green velvet. I'm
sorry because I've disappointed you."

"You haven't—"

"Yes I have," he said slowly. "You wanted today to
be . . . fun. Isn't that what you said?"

"Jonas—"

He pressed a finger to her lips, stopping her before
he let his hand drop again to his side. "I can't make it
fun for you, Genie. I wish I could. I wish I could give

you everything you deserve. I wish I could thank you for trying."

"You could," she said quietly. "You could thank me."

He shook his head. "No, I—"

"You could kiss me again."

Her own words surprised her. They seemed to jump out of her mouth, and Imogene didn't realize until she'd said them how much she wanted it. A kiss to make her feel wanted and cherished.

But mostly—oh, mostly what she wanted was to keep that light shining in his eyes, to kiss away the darkness and keep it away. Forever, if she could.

He looked down at her, and she felt his hand at her waist, felt his heat through her mantle, through the cold damp air. The snow fell into her eyes, catching on her eyelashes and melting there so she saw his face in prisms.

"A kiss," he murmured, and with a sharp stab of relief she saw that radiance grow even stronger in his eyes, blinding her, dazzling her as he bent and brushed his mouth against hers. And when he pressed deeper, when he drew her closer and urged her lips apart, and she heard the soft desperation of his moan, she leaned into him and wound her fingers through his snow-wet hair, hearing the gasps around them and not caring, not caring at all as he kissed her senseless in the open air of the Washington Market, there for everyone to see.

Chapter 22

$\mathcal{J}$t made his heart hurt to look at her. Jonas turned back to the cold window, staring at the falling snow. He heard her moving about the room, putting a chicken on to stew, chopping onions, and he could picture her in his mind: the pale green, wine-stained skirt shifting about her feet, the stretch of satin across her shoulder blades, the strands of hair caressing her cheeks.

Ah, yes, he could picture her all too well. Just as he couldn't erase the image of her at the market this morning, staring up at him with wide brown eyes, snowflakes gilding the loose strands of her hair, drifting onto her eyelashes. She was so beautiful, and this morning had been so ordinary—

He caught himself on the thought. No, not ordinary, that was the wrong word. Normal, perhaps. Yes, this morning had been normal in a way things in his life had rarely been. He had not been able to stop watching her as she moved from vendor to vendor, so self-assured, so at ease. She had bargained and smiled and talked about inconsequential things. *"Oh, see those bananas—why, they're from Cuba,"* and *"The oysters look good today, don't you think?"* Silly things, things people talked about every day, things to fill the silence.

He had treasured them. In his life there were so few silly things, so few trips to the market, so few smiles. And he found he loved her smile. It brightened her face, lit her eyes. He loved the way it whitened that tiny scar at the top of her lip, the way it squared her jaw. Her smile made him ache for all the things he'd never had, never thought he wanted. A wife, children, a home.

Christ, it frightened him. Everything about her frightened him. He had wanted to turn her into a butterfly and she had exceeded his wildest dreams. She charmed him and soothed him. She eased the pain in his soul. She kept a door closed on the darkness. She was everything he'd ever dreamed of. And today, when he'd kissed her, he'd lost himself in her the way he'd never imagined losing himself before. He had wanted her so badly, badly enough to keep her chained by his side, to trap her with lies and caresses, with pregnancy if he had to. Anything to make sure she didn't leave him.

And that was what frightened him the most, because he destroyed whatever he touched. He had never been able to maintain a friendship—Rico was the closest he'd come to that, and even now he wondered how long that would last, how long it would take for Rico to tire of him completely enough to leave for Paris and never return. Jonas's family had disowned him long ago, had sent him off to Bloomingdale with barely a prayer for his soul. And though there'd been women, they were always temporary. A night, a week, a month, but never through the madness, or the depression.

Christ, even Rico couldn't endure it more than once a year.

Genie had survived it. The thought haunted him, tormented him, surprised him. She was so strong, the strongest person he had ever known, and that strength tempted and cajoled him. *She could bear it,* the voice whispered in his ear. *Maybe she would stay.*

With effort he ignored it. It didn't matter if she could endure him or not. It was unfair to ask her to. She deserved someone who could give her a normal life. Someone who could have fun at the market. Someone who could buy her the green velvet she would look so beautiful in. Not someone like him. Not someone who had no idea how he would be from day to day. Normality eluded him. Money slipped through his fingers. What kind of life was that to promise someone? To promise her?

He should send her back to her godfather, he knew. Gosney would do his best to smooth over the scandal, and Genie was strong—stronger than Jonas had ever imagined she could be. She would endure it and go on. She would find someone who would treat her well.

The thought made his chest tight. Not seeing her again, not touching her. . . . It was absurd how desperate it made him feel. But there was no choice, and he knew it. He knew what happened to the people who stayed with him, God knew he'd seen it a hundred times before. He could picture it in his mind, knew that eventually he would see a painfully familiar look in her eyes, the same look he'd seen in those of his family, of his friends. The dull expression, the fear, the pain. And finally, the good-bye.

"They say they love you and then they leave."

Well, it was true. It had always been true. And he

suffered for it not just because he was losing them, but because he knew he'd beaten them down, because by leaving they were only trying to survive.

He owed her more than that, more than a life chained to a man who would eventually destroy her, who would whittle away at her strength until it was gone, who would test her every day. He owed her a life away from him. He owed her freedom.

Give it to her, the voice inside him said. *Give it to her now.*

He grabbed the moment before he could talk himself out of it. "Genie," he said, surprised to hear how hoarse his voice was, how rough. "Genie, come here."

The sound of chopping stopped. He heard her rinse her hands, and then her footsteps behind him, felt the air from the swish of her skirt as she came up beside him. Her presence was like a tonic, invigorating, comforting.

"What is it?" she asked, kneeling beside him, grabbing the arm of his chair for support with one hand, reaching out to touch him with the other. Her skin was cool, still damp. The perfumes of parsley and bay clung to her, mixing with that elusive scent of almond.

He couldn't look at her. It was hard enough to feel her, to smell her. He wanted to take her in his arms and hold her tight. He wanted to kiss her again, to make love to her. If he looked at her he would. So he focused on the window, on the snow, until it was nothing but a blur of white and slate before him, until he felt nothing but the cold.

"Jonas," she said, and he heard the concern in her voice, the worry. She squeezed his hand. "Are you all right?"

"I'm fine," he said. "Much better, thanks to you."

"Much better," she repeated hesitantly.

She withdrew her hand; his skin was suddenly cold where she'd touched him. He felt her guardedness even though he wasn't looking at her, and it hurt him —God, it seemed to pierce right through his heart.

He couldn't say anything. He wanted to tell her she should leave him, that he wanted her to go, but when it came down to it, he couldn't say the words, couldn't make the sacrifice. All his noble thoughts, and yet it came down to selfishness after all. Christ, he couldn't even do this, simple as it was.

As it turned out, he didn't have to. She released her hold on the chair and sat back on her heels in a swish of satin.

"You want me to go," she said bluntly.

He heard the detachment in her voice and the pain behind it. Pain, even though he wanted so badly to spare her from it. He squeezed his eyes shut. Felt her movement as she got to her feet.

"Of course," she said, taking a deep breath. "Of course. I expected you'd want to be alone once you felt better. I—I'll just get my things, and—"

"Don't." He surprised himself with the word. It was harsh and raw, and before he knew it he lashed out, grabbing her wrist, gripping it so tightly he heard her startled gasp. "No."

Then he made the mistake he'd told himself not to make. He twisted in his chair to look at her.

Her eyes were large, bright with tears she fought to blink away. Her jaw was clenched, and her mouth was tight, and it dawned on him that he'd seen that look on her face a dozen times before, that he knew the emotions she was trying to keep at bay, the strength she was struggling to find. She wouldn't look at him, but stared out the window the way he had done only moments before, to the snow and the empty street, to the barrenness that only accentuated pain and didn't ease it. He saw her smooth skin and her soft hair and the trembling of her mouth, and he wanted to kiss it away, to forget that he would hurt her, that she would leave. To show her the only way he could how much she meant to him. But he knew he couldn't. He had to let her go. There was no other choice. But if he could make it easier . . . Christ, he'd give his heart to make it easier.

He released her hand and rose from the chair, quickly, before she could step away. Then he moved in front of her and cupped her chin in his fingers, gently bringing her around to face him. There was wariness in her eyes along with tears and . . . embarrassment. With a little laugh she wiped at her eyes.

"I'm sorry," she said. "I knew it was only a matter of time before you tired of me—"

"I'm not tired of you."

She frowned. "But you want me to go . . . don't you?"

"Yes."

She tried to look away again, but he held her there.

"Look at me, Genie," he said. "Look at who I am. Surely you know you can't stay here."

She didn't try to misunderstand, she didn't protest. She hesitated, and then she nodded slowly. "Yes," she said. "I know."

And those were the saddest words of all. He felt them clear into his soul, and though they made his sacrifice easier, they only increased his need to touch her one last time. He couldn't help himself, he leaned forward and kissed her, feeling relief and completion when she melted into him, when her mouth opened beneath his and he heard the small moan in her throat. He let go of her chin, shoved his hand through her hair, loosening it, letting it fall over his fingers, smooth and heavy, wanting to feel it the way he'd felt it before, against his body, tangling in his hair.

Then the memories returned. All the things he'd denied—her taste, her scent, the feel of her—all those things came rushing back to him, along with the images of the last time they'd made love. He knew when she would whimper, he knew how she would arch back when he touched her breast. He knew how she looked, breathless and flushed and beautiful, when he came inside her. He knew all those things, and he wanted to know them again, wanted them, if not forever, then at least tonight, at least right now.

But the last time he'd taken her on a stool, and she deserved better than that. Jonas pulled away, hearing her little murmur of protest, smiling when she looked up at him, puzzled and unsure, her lips swollen from his kiss.

"Let's go to bed," he whispered, pulling her with him across the studio, past the steaming pot on the stove and a pile of chopped onions, through the uneven path left by dozens of unfinished canvases. Together they dodged the tapestry that covered the door, into the darkness of the bedroom. Darkness, where he wanted it to be light. For the first time in days, he wanted light.

He released her hand and went to the beaten leather trunk against one wall. Its surface was dotted with candles, short stubby ones that had half melted into wax pools. There was a box of matches on the floor beside it, and he took one and lit each stub until the

glow they set off suffused the room, a gentle light.
Then he turned to her again.

She was standing in the doorway, watching him, and
her eyes were dark, her emotions hidden. But they
wouldn't be for long, he knew. With two short strides
he reached her, pulling her to him, sinking his hand in
her hair and pressing his tongue into her mouth. She
tasted of parsley and tea, along with a sweetness that
was pure Genie, a sweetness that intoxicated him. And
when she touched her tongue to his, when he felt her
tentative exploration, he groaned and pressed deeper,
wanting all of her, wanting to eat her alive, to bring
her so far inside him she could never go away.

He struggled with the buttons on her dress, slipping
them through the tiny openings, finally loosening the
gown far enough to push it down over her shoulders.
He felt her corset against him, hard and inviolate,
keeping her safe, and frustration made him impatient.
He could not undo it, not without two hands, and so
he was forced to pull away.

"Take it off for me, darling," he whispered.
"Please."

She smiled then, a smile he couldn't remember seeing before, soft and worldly wise, that woman-smile
that spoke of power and seduction. It made his insides
twist, sent a rush of heat into his loins. He had never
felt this way before, never so out of control, never so
aroused. Always before he had been removed, always
before he had wanted sex and nothing more. But the
look in her eyes and the feel of her and the exquisite
sweetness he felt when he touched her—ah, God, it
was more than he could bear.

He watched as she stepped out of her gown, leaving
it pooled on the floor. He ached to touch her, but he

waited, letting his desire build with every movement of
her hands. Slowly, as if she savored it, she unhooked
her corset and let it fall, and then she was standing
before him in only a creased cotton shift that clung to
her breasts, its shapelessness and simplicity only accenting the indentation of her waist, the curve of her
hips.

She lifted her chin. That knowing, sensual expression was still in her eyes. "More?" she asked softly.

Christ, so erotic. He couldn't speak. Only nodded.
She was made for flirtation, he thought, even though
he'd never seen her flirt before. But the way she untied
the string of her chemise, the way she shrugged so it
fell enticingly over one shoulder and then the other—
ah, God, it was flirtatious, it was seductive. She let the
chemise fall, leaning forward to unroll her stockings.
The waterfall of her hair shielded her breasts from his
view. She stood again and looked at him, a question in
her eyes that he answered with a nod, and then she
untied her drawers and slid them over her hips, down
her legs, until she was naked before him.

"Lie on the bed," he said hoarsely, forcing himself
to stand still as she did so, feeling his breath catch in
his throat. He wouldn't let himself move as she lay
back against the pillows. He wanted to look at her, to
see her with his artist's eye, with the palette he used
every day. A wash of color and chiaroscuro, ivory and
peach, soft pinks and dark swatches of bold shadow.
In the candlelight she was a mystery to him, her eyes in
shadow, her hair spread against the quilt, glinting with
gold. Fine stray hairs caught on her arms—one spun
across her breast, a lone gold thread, a spider's web
that glittered near her nipple. She was beautiful.
Small, full breasts and a slight waist and hips that were

wide and softly rounded. All this hidden by clothing and propriety. All this passion disguised by tranquility. Such a contradiction, and he wanted to see it illustrated for him, wanted her legs spread and him between them. Wanted to see her push against him and moan the way she'd done before, to thrash in climax. Wanted to devour her.

He undid his shirt quickly, clumsily, shrugging out of it and throwing it aside, sending his pants to follow. And then he padded to the bed and bent over her, leaning down to kiss her gently, first her mouth, and then her throat, her collarbone, her breast. He heard her sigh as he captured it, as he teased and laved her nipple, as he brought it to a peak against his tongue. This, ah, yes, he remembered this. Remembered it all, and he dipped lower and lower, hearing her moans in his ears and feeling her body twist beneath his touch.

Genie. Her name sang in his mind, magical and enduring. *Genie, Genie, Genie.* He touched her and she responded. He kissed the curls at the apex of her thighs, felt the softness against his mouth, the slight jerk she gave when he dipped lower still.

"Shh," he whispered against her. "I won't stop."

"I . . . I don't want you . . . to stop," she said, a sensual heaviness in her voice, a delightful breathlessness.

He slid his hands beneath her hips, lifted her with one and with whatever strength he had in the other, brought her closer to his mouth and kissed her there, licked her, teased her. She thrashed beneath his assault, and he felt her hands tangling in his hair, pulling him closer, holding him prisoner against her. She was trembling, and he wanted her to tremble. He wanted to taste her when she climaxed, he wanted to remember her taste forever. She was on the edge, he knew. He felt the tension in her body, and he licked deep and then up, heard her cry out the same moment she stiffened, the moment he felt her throb against his mouth.

"Ah, Genie," he murmured. "Genie, my love." Slowly he moved up, kissing her belly and her waist and her breasts, looking down into her face. Her eyes glinted in the half light, and her smile—ah, her smile was everything he wanted, everything he dreamed of. He kissed her and sheathed himself in her at the same moment. Her body welcomed him, she was wet and hot. Without moving she nearly sent him to climax. He felt her hand on his chest, her fingers sliding through the dark curls there, pulling gently, an erotic pain. She was thrusting against him, and he reached down and held her hips steady, bringing her up to meet him as he sank inside her and pulled out again, over and over, a slow and tantalizing dance, an arousal that grew more painful and more sweet with every thrust.

She was his—the thought spun through his mind, growing louder and louder, as undeniable as everything else about her. He clutched her to him, rocking against her, hearing the soft slap of flesh and her equally soft cries, feeling her hands on his shoulders and his hair. She was his and he couldn't bear to let her go—God, how could he let her go?

But with every thrust, with every movement that brought him closer and closer to repletion, he knew he had to release her. She was his for the next moments and that was all. Until he climaxed, she was his.

And so he prolonged it. He slowed his thrusts and tasted her mouth and reveled in the sweetness. He worshipped her body with his own and kissed her with hot, open-mouthed kisses that made his blood pound in his ears. But too soon he felt the sharp sweetness of culmination. *Too soon . . .*

"No," he gasped. "God, no."

But he couldn't stop it. His release crashed through him, a mercy and a punishment, washing over him with a headiness he'd never felt before, had never even imagined. He heard her cry join with his own, felt her throbbing again around him, soft convulsions, and he cradled her in his arms, pulled her to him as closely as he could.

They lay there that way for only moments. Long enough for his breathing to ease, for his heart to slow. It was then he felt the hot wetness against his chest. Tears, he realized. She was crying. He was so startled by the knowledge that he didn't respond when she pulled away from him. She was off the bed before he knew what she was doing, grabbing her clothes from the floor.

"I'll put the onions in the stew," she was saying, her back to him. "It should be done in a few hours. Then you won't have to cook for yourself for a day or so."

Jonas struggled to one elbow. "Genie—"

"I bought some bread too. It's on the table." She stepped into her drawers and tied them, then pulled her chemise over her head.

Desperation washed over him. Panicked, he stood up and reached for her. "Genie, don't."

She turned around at his touch, and he saw the tears she'd been trying to hide, streams of candlelight that trailed over her cheeks. But when she spoke, her voice was devoid of sorrow or pain or any kind of emotion at all.

"Don't what, Jonas?" she asked. "Don't go? We both know I have to. You don't want me here, not really, and I—" She paused and took a deep breath, and then she looked away again. "And I don't want to stay."

He knew it was a lie. He knew it, but he couldn't do a thing about it, because she was right. Because he had meant to send her away. Because he was mad. Because he would destroy her.

But, oh God, how he wanted her to stay. It took everything he had to stand back while she finished dressing, every ounce of control he could muster to keep from running after her as she went out of the bedroom and gathered up her things.

And when she finally went to the studio door and paused, her hand on the lever, he had to bite his lip to keep from calling her back, had to turn away as she opened the door, as she left him without a word, without even a glance back.

She was gone, just as he'd intended. He told himself it was best. He told himself it was what he wanted.

But he couldn't stop the echo of her footsteps in his head. He wondered if he would ever forget the sound.

Chapter 23

She knew the way back to her godfather's by heart. She knew every single turn, knew the feel of every cobblestone. There was a pothole on Ninth Street, just where it turned onto Fifth Avenue—she knew exactly when the carriage would hit it, exactly how much it would jostle her. And at the corner of Washington Square North, there was a rut the wheels always caught on.

It was easier to concentrate on those things, on the sway of the coach and the rattling of the wheels, on the passing brownstones. Easier than thinking about the man she'd just left and the terrible lie she'd told him. *"I don't want to stay."* God, how untrue that was. The most untrue thing she'd ever said. What she wanted was to be wrapped in his arms, reveling in the warm afterglow of lovemaking. What she wanted was to love him.

Imogene squeezed her eyes shut, clenching her fist in her skirt. Lord, what a fool she was. She had known he would hurt her, she'd told herself not to fall in love with him, and yet she'd done it anyway. She'd stayed

with him these last days even knowing how dangerous
it was. Just this morning she had told herself it was
time to leave, before it was too late.

But it was already too late.

She opened her eyes again, staring out at the thin
blanket of snow laying over the city, at bare trees
frosted with white. Jonas Whitaker was not for her;
she'd known that from the beginning. She'd known he
would eventually tire of her, that he would use her and
let her go. So why had his rejection been so painful?

*Because you hoped he might need you forever. Be-
cause you mistook need for affection.* Just as she had
with Nicholas. Imogene winced at the thought. She'd
fallen for Nicholas simply because he needed her comfort, and she'd vowed never to be so stupid again. But
here she was, just as foolish as she'd been three years
ago, loving the first man who needed her.

It was why she'd let Jonas touch her, why she'd
dropped her dignity and her pride and let him make
love to her one last time. She had wanted a memory to
hold on to through the bitter days ahead, to give her
strength when she was nothing again. She had wanted
just once more to touch the shooting star.

Instead, it only made her realize just what a failure
she was. Deep inside she had wanted things to be different. She had wanted to be the one who could help
Jonas through his nightmares, she had wanted to believe she could be important to him.

But he didn't want her, and it was time to face that.
It was time to return to her old life. She tried to convince herself it was what she wanted, but when the
carriage jerked to a stop and the gothic facade of her
godfather's town house loomed up through the window, Imogene wondered how she could ever do that.

How did one forget a man like Jonas Whitaker? How did a person get used to being without that intensity? How could she live without him?

There was no other choice, she reminded herself. Jonas had sent her away. He didn't need her any longer, and she knew he was trying hard to be kind with his rejection, to not hurt her. But all the same she hurt. All the same, she couldn't help wishing . . .

Imogene took a deep breath, banishing the thoughts. There was no point in torturing herself. It was over. *Over.* She chanted the word in her mind, forced herself to repeat it as she stepped determinedly from the carriage, into the falling snow. She paid the driver, and then she made her way up the stairs, holding on to the rail to keep from slipping. Out of habit she grabbed the knob to go inside, stopping just before she turned it. She wasn't even sure she was welcome here, not anymore. Slowly she uncurled her hand from around the doorknob and knocked.

There were rapid footsteps on the other side. The door swung open, revealing Mary, the housekeeper, whose mouth fell open in surprise.

"Miss Carter!" she said, her ruddy face growing redder. "Come in, do, outta the cold. Why it's snowin' and ye forgot yer hat!"

Imogene frowned, putting a hand to her hair, realizing for the first time that she'd left her bonnet at the studio. It sent an odd little surge of pain through her; she wondered briefly what he would think when he found it, what he would do. She wondered if he would keep it as a reminder of her. The thought made her chest tight; she blinked back sudden tears.

"Y-yes," she stammered, struggling for control. "Yes, I—I left in a hurry, I'm afraid."

Mary backed away from the door, motioning her inside. "Yer just in time. They're all in the dining room. Just sat down to dinner, they have."

The words eased Imogene's apprehension. At least she wouldn't have to face Thomas alone, not yet. She didn't really feel up to handling his anger or his disappointment tonight, and Katherine was so very good at soothing him.

Distractedly Imogene took off her gloves and her mantle and handed them to Mary. Then, forcing a calm she didn't feel, Imogene walked to the dining room. She heard the sound of voices just before she got there, deep masculine tones that contrasted with Katherine's light chatter, three voices instead of two. They had company. All the better. Imogene stopped at the side of the doorway, mustering her courage, closing her ears and her eyes for one short moment, struggling to gather her composure. Then she raised her chin and stepped inside.

She stopped short. At the table was the last person she expected to see.

Her father.

Samuel Carter sat at Thomas's table as if he owned it, his shirtsleeved elbows splayed on the polished surface, his wineglass clutched in his pale, square hand. He was gesturing to Thomas, and laughing, his bushy gray mustache bobbing.

Abruptly Thomas's words from three days ago burst through her shock. *"You leave me no choice, Imogene, you realize that."* Of course. She should have remembered. She had known the moment he'd said it that he was planning to contact her father, but she'd forgotten. And now Samuel Carter was here, in New York City. Longing and pleasure warred with wariness—and a sense of dread she tried desperately to squelch. She had nothing to fear, she told herself. Her father had spent the last three years wanting her to take Chloe's place in the art world, and now she was there. In love with an artist, as much a bohemian as Chloe had ever been. He would be happy about that, surely. It was what he'd always wanted.

Still . . .

She eased into the room, forcing a smile. "Papa," she said.

The single word was explosive. The conversation snapped to a stop. In unison the three people at the table turned to look at her. But Imogene didn't take her gaze from her father. With relief she saw a smile spread over his face.

"Imogene," he said, rising. He hurried over, holding her out at arm's length while he studied her. His smile faded a bit when he took in her dirty dress, her straggling hair, but still he leaned forward and gave her a brief, dry kiss. "I was certain you would show up, girl." He threw a smug look to Thomas. "Didn't I tell you, Tom, that you were mistaken? Imogene and Whitaker . . . what a preposterous idea."

Imogene went suddenly cold. "Papa—"

"Why, Imogene's never committed an indiscretion in her life," he went on jovially. "She doesn't have the spine for it. Now if you'd said Chloe—well, *that* girl was so full of life I would have believed anything you told me."

At the table, Thomas looked supremely uncomfortable. He set aside his wineglass and leveled her a regretful look. "I'm sorry, my dear. I felt he should know."

"You should learn how to nip these scurrilous rumors in the bud, girl." Samuel barely acknowledged that Thomas had spoken. "God knows you're so damned meek you're prime fodder for gossipmongers."

Imogene throat was too tight to swallow. "Papa," she said quietly. When he went still beside her, she forced herself to continue. "What Thomas told you . . . it's all true."

Samuel Carter frowned. His fingers tightened around her arm almost painfully, the furrow between his heavy brows deepened in confusion. "You don't know what you're saying, Imogene," he insisted. "Do you even realize what your godfather told me?"

Imogene nodded. She had to fight to get her voice out. "I imagine he told you Jonas Whitaker and I were . . . having an affair."

Her father's frown grew; his gaze swept over her. She knew too well what he was seeing: mousy hair and pale skin and mud-brown eyes. She knew without hearing the words what he was thinking. *Whitaker interested in her? I don't believe it. It couldn't be true.*

She saw the moment his confusion eased. His frown changed to a smile, and he barked a laugh. "An affair?" he repeated, shaking his head with amusement. "Good God, girl, you must be mistaken. I'm sure you *thought* he might harbor an interest in you—after all, I've taught art a time or two myself, I know what it's like. It requires great attention, but that's quite different from romantic intentions." He patted her shoulder reassuringly. "Jonas Whitaker is a famous artist, a man of great discernment. If you consider that for a moment, I'm sure you'll realize this 'affair' is only in your imagination. I mean really, Imogene, doesn't it seem odd that he would notice you?"

How easily he did it. How easily he turned her into nothing again. Imogene felt immediately foolish and naive, the doubts he planted grew and spread in her mind, insidiously corrosive. Maybe her father was right. Maybe she was imagining that Jonas needed her. After all, he'd told her to go. He'd told her—what had he said? *"Look at me, Genie. Look at who I am. Surely you know you can't stay here."*

The words danced in her head, joining with her father's mockery, and Imogene winced and turned her eyes away, swept with a fierce, unrelenting pain. Jonas had told her to go, and though she could deny the reasons forever, it didn't make them any less true. Jonas wanted someone else, that was clear enough. Someone more beautiful. Someone he wouldn't be embarrassed to have beside him. Someone to match people's expectations—

"I don't think she was imagining Whitaker's intentions, Samuel," Thomas said dryly.

Samuel ignored him. He bent slightly, holding Imogene's gaze. His smile was slightly off-kilter, but it was reassuring nonetheless, begging confidences. "Let's be realistic, girl," he said softly. "Maybe you wanted him to kiss you, but he never did, did he? He never touched you."

He wanted her to tell him no, she knew, and Imogene found herself wanting to say it. He would forgive her if she told him Whitaker hadn't touched her. Her father would still love her. The longing for that rose up so sharply her heart ached. But then she thought of how he'd pushed her to study in Nashville, how he'd brought her into his salons and walked away in disgust and disappointment when she wasn't witty or charming. Her quiet listening had only angered him.

And she realized he didn't really want her to say no. He didn't want a milksop daughter; he never had. He wanted a Chloe, a woman who could captivate an artist. If she told him what he expected to hear, she would only disappoint him again. But if she told him the truth . . . if she told him the truth, he might love her at last. He might respect her.

She met his gaze. "He touched me," she said simply. "He kissed me."

Samuel froze. The silence stretched between them, and Imogene waited for his surprise and his praise, waited for his ringing, boisterous laughter and his admiration. The things he had given Chloe without hesitation, the things he had never given Imogene. And in the split second before he dropped her arm, she thought she might have it. She thought he might finally say *"Dammit, girl, but you're just like Chloe, after all. You've made me proud."*

But then he released her and stepped away, and she knew in that moment he wasn't going to say the words —and that he was horribly, terribly angry. It was so familiar, the look in his eyes, the tension in his body. Lord, she'd seen it a hundred times before. Her hope withered in sheer, desperate disappointment. She waited for the attack.

She didn't have to wait long.

His eyes flashed. "Your sister," he said slowly, each word a dozen little knifepoints stabbing into her heart, "would never have behaved this way."

"Papa—"

"She was a true artist." His eyes narrowed as he drove his point home. "That's the difference between the two of you, Imogene. Chloe would have taken this opportunity to study art, not to spread her legs for her teacher."

Imogene flinched.

"Samuel," Thomas interjected.

Samuel turned to him. "Well, that's what she's doing, isn't it? All this fine education I provide her, and what does she do with it? She becomes some artist's whore." He glanced back at her, his mouth tight with anger. "What was it, girl, couldn't you learn anything Whitaker had to teach you? Was that it? I suppose you thought you could seduce him into giving me a good report."

Imogene gasped. His words slammed into her so painfully she stepped back. "Papa, no—"

"At least you've found your true talent," he sneered, ignoring her protest. "God knows you've never been much of a painter. Just a milk-and-watercolorist, and not even a good one."

"That's enough." Thomas's quiet voice cut through the bitter aftermath of her father's words. "Samuel, I must ask that you not talk to her that way."

"She's my daughter, Gosney," Samuel retorted. "I'll talk to her however I damn well please."

"Not while you're in my home."

At the end of the table, Katherine rose and put her hand on her husband's arm. "Darling," she said softly. She gave Imogene a sympathetic glance, a glance that helped soothe her humiliation, and then Katherine looked back to Thomas. "Perhaps we should leave Samuel and Imogene to discuss this alone."

Thomas frowned. "I don't—"

"It's all right, Thomas," Imogene said quietly, wishing it were true. She saw her godfather's embarrassment and regret, but the thought of him further witnessing her humiliation was too much to bear. "I'm fine."

Samuel gestured impatiently. "Yes, leave us, won't you?"

Imogene backed against the wall, feeling the smooth yellow silk wallcovering beneath her hands, taking strength from its reassuring solidity. She heard her father's harsh breathing, knew he was struggling to keep his temper under control while Thomas and Katherine left the table and moved to the door. Just before he stepped out, Thomas stopped, touching her arm with a gentle concern that hurt as much as it reassured.

"My dear," he began.

Imogene cut him off with a shake of her head. "I'm fine," she said shortly, seeing the regret in his eyes. She wanted to say more, wanted to punish him, to be angry with him for bringing her father here, but she couldn't. Thomas had only been worried, she knew. He'd wanted to protect her. She could not condemn him for that.

When he and Katherine left the dining room, pulling the heavy brocade curtains across the doorway to give them privacy, Imogene only felt more alone than ever. Thomas's presence had given her support, if nothing else. Now she was alone with her father, and she knew his tirades too well to believe she would be all right. He wouldn't hurt her—not physically, anyway—but emotionally. . . .

She licked her lips and turned back to face him, steeling herself. "Papa," she said, "I—"

"Don't you dare speak to me," he said, glaring at her. "Not until I'm finished with you."

She swallowed and pressed harder against the wall. He closed his eyes and pinched the bridge of his nose, taking a deep breath before he looked up at her again. "Do you realize," he said slowly, "what a scandal this will cause? No, of course you don't. Just as you didn't even wonder what the hell it was Whitaker wanted from you. Why did you suppose he would he even look twice at you? Hmmm? Did you think it was your looks he was after?"

She shook her head, forcing back the tears, feeling his verbal blows clear into her soul. "No," she whispered. "Of course not."

Her father paced the room. "Well, at least you're that intelligent. Dammit, no doubt I'll get a message from him in a few days, demanding money or something. And he'll get it too, because if Nashville hears about this we'll never get you married off."

Imogene swallowed. "He won't do that," she said. "And I—I don't want to be married off."

"I don't give a damn what you want." Samuel jerked to a stop. "I had hoped that, given enough education, you might develop some of your sister's better points, but to my disappointment, that hasn't happened. It's clear you don't have talent to give the world. The best you can do is find a husband somewhere and hope you stay well long enough to give him children."

The harshness of his words paralyzed her. She felt skewered to the wall, pierced through with his bitterness. "I haven't . . . been ill . . . for a long time," she managed.

He didn't seem to hear her. He put his hands to his head, running them through his bushy gray hair, pressing on his skull as if the motion could somehow calm him. He stopped pacing, lumbered heavily to the table and sagged into a chair. "Well, there's no help for it,"

he said on a sigh. "I'll meet with Whitaker and see
what he wants. But then—" He turned to her, his eyes
shooting sparks. "Then we're going back to Nashville,
and once we're there you'll do exactly what I say. Is
that clear?"

Imogene's fingers curled into fists. With effort, she
nodded. There was no point in disagreeing, after all.
She had no other choice. "Yes, Papa. I understand."

"Good." He took a deep breath and leaned his head
back, closing his eyes. "Oh God," he murmured.
"God, why not you?"

He spoke under his breath, but Imogene heard the
murmured words as clearly as if he'd screamed them.
Words she'd heard a hundred times before. And even
though he hadn't said them, she heard the words that
followed, too, the ones she knew were in his mind.
"Why didn't God take you instead?"

Why not you?

She had no answer for him, because she wondered
that herself, had wondered it since the day the cholera
took Chloe. And just as she had since the day her sister
died, Imogene felt guilty that she had lived. She should
have traded places with Chloe somehow; she should
have been the one to die.

She wondered if her father would have loved her
any better if she had.

The thought knotted her stomach. Deep inside she
knew even that wouldn't have made a difference, and
it bothered her that she cared so much, that her father's love was so important. He'd never done anything but hurt her. He'd never looked at her. He didn't
really see her at all.

Like Jonas, she thought, but the words didn't ring
true any longer; she didn't quite believe them. Maybe

once that had been the case, but things had changed. She remembered this afternoon, heard again the melody of Jonas's soft words, saw the tenderness in his eyes. *"Ah, Genie. . . ."* His whispers came winging back, tender and haunting. *"Genie, my love. . . ."*

She grabbed on to the memory, holding it like a bulwark against the world, against her father's hurtful words, against his disappointment and his illusions. In it, she found strength—enough strength to walk away from her father, to escape through the heavy curtains into the hallway and pass by Thomas, who waited anxiously at the foot of the stairs. She clung to it as she climbed the stairs to the safety of her room, where the reassuring scent of her almond soap awaited her, where the armoire welcomed her with its scores of pastel dresses. She could bear this, she told herself. She could bear it all, if only she could keep hold of the memory of those precious nights with Jonas. If only she didn't forget the things he'd taught her.

But then she saw the sketch hanging on the wall, the crumpled and smudged drawing of a half-dressed woman with a mysterious smile. A beautiful woman. A woman who was not her at all, and her father's voice came back to torment her, a truth she couldn't run away from no matter how hard she tried.

"Why would he even look twice at you? Did you think it was your looks he was after? Hmmm?"

The good memories melted away. Imogene collapsed on the bed and cried.

Chapter 24

He missed her so terribly he couldn't sleep. Not that he'd been sleeping well anyway, but that first night without her was interminable. He watched the seconds tick by, watched the shadows grow and change on the studio walls, and told himself it would be all right. The longing would ease, and in a few days he would be fine. Things would be fine. When dawn finally came, he forced himself to set out his paints, to grind colors. The day-to-day routine eased him somewhat—at least he was doing something. But he couldn't banish her face from his mind, not her compassionate brown eyes or her delighted smile or her soft vulnerability. And the restlessness her presence banished was back again with a vengeance.

Jonas cursed as he prepared his pallet and began to paint. She'd barely lived here a week; it should be easy enough to erase her from the studio. It was only a matter of time until he forgot her. In a few days the smell of her perfume would waft away; the long golden-brown hairs he found in his bed would vanish. One morning he would wake up without even thinking of her. One morning soon. Soon, he knew it.

He wanted to believe it. He *had* to believe it. Jonas tightened his fingers around the brush, swirled a pool of lead white into one of ultramarine. He'd never thought so much about a woman, never felt so . . . so dependent on one. But Genie—ah, she was hard to forget. Hard enough that he found he was constantly reminding himself why he had to let her go. *You did the right thing,* he told himself. *For once, you did the selfless thing.*

Now if only he could make himself believe it.

The knock on the door startled him—it had been so long since he'd had a visitor. He felt a swift surge of relief and pleasure, the unreasoning hope that it might be her. He forced himself to calm down, to think. It wasn't her. It couldn't be her. Still, he couldn't banish the thought. He tried to keep his voice as steady as he could.

"Come in."

The door opened the second he said the words. He saw the top of a blond head, and his heart raced in the split second before he realized it was Rico. Rico, back from the dead, or wherever the hell he'd gone.

Childs dodged inside, a wide grin splitting his features as he closed the door behind him. *"Bonjour, mon ami,"* he said amiably. "I've missed you."

Jonas snorted. "Where the hell have you been?"

"Here and there." Rico shrugged. "I had a little business to take care of in Bridgeport. Besides, I wanted to give you some time alone with your little butterfly." His gaze scanned the room. "Where is she, anyway?"

Jonas ignored the stab of pain that seared through

him. He tried to speak as tonelessly as he could. "Gone."

"Gone?" Rico raised a brow. "You're developing a real talent for obscurity, my love. What do you mean, gone? Is she out for a walk? Gone to market?" From the table he grabbed the pink bonnet she'd left behind, dangling it from its strings. "She didn't go far, apparently."

"Far enough," Jonas said. He focused his attention on his pallet. "She's not coming back."

"No?" Childs sat on the edge of the table, spinning the bonnet in his hands. His voice was mild, nonchalant, but Jonas heard the question beneath it, the sharp curiosity—and something else he couldn't identify. Concern, maybe. Or . . . or sadness.

"No," he repeated firmly. "She left two days ago."

"Hmmm." Rico stared at the hat thoughtfully. "And you let her go?"

Jonas dabbed paint forcefully on the canvas. "I didn't have a choice."

"Which I take to mean that you asked her to leave," Rico said.

Jonas clenched his jaw. He focused on the painting, smudged a shadow here, and here, smoothed a line. Perhaps if he ignored Rico long enough, he would leave. But then he heard Childs sigh, and Jonas's chest tightened. He took refuge in anger. "Spare me the lecture," he said between clenched teeth.

"No lecture." Childs rose from the table, setting the bonnet aside, and strode with languorous ease to where Jonas stood. "I'm just surprised, that's all."

"She's an innocent," Jonas said. "The most naive woman I've ever known."

Childs said nothing.

Jonas flashed him a glance. "Christ, Rico, you saw her. You *know*. All I had to do was look at her and she crumbled."

"That's not what I remember," Rico said calmly. "And I don't think you believe it either."

"You weren't here," Jonas said. He clutched the brush hard in his hand. "You didn't see."

Rico leaned against a stool, crossing his arms over his chest. His pale blue gaze was too cool, too measuring. "Don't lie to me, Jonas," he said softly. "Did you think I would leave her with you if I thought she couldn't handle it? Did you think I would have simply abandoned you?"

Childs's words cut into Jonas's heart, along with guilt. He closed his eyes, struggling for breath, for words that pushed away, that protected. "You've done it before," he said.

"Never when you were like that," Rico reminded him—a little insistently. "Never when I knew you needed help. Afterward, yes. After."

Jonas said nothing. He couldn't force the words, and he didn't know what to say anyway. There was no way he could tell Rico the truth: that he hadn't missed him during these last days, that Genie's presence had been enough to distract him. It would only hurt Childs if he knew, and there was enough pain in this room already. Jonas let the silence grow.

Childs sighed. "You're right, of course," he admitted finally, his words heavy with regret. "I have not always been here for you. I'm afraid I am not as . . . altruistic . . . as I'd like to be." He laughed self-deprecatingly. "I have not always been the best of friends to you, *mon ami*."

Jonas took a deep breath. There was something so

sorrowful in Rico's words, an admission Jonas wasn't sure he wanted to hear, a guilt he wanted to ignore. He took a deep breath, wanting to offer comfort, but the words that came out were painfully inadequate. "I understand," he said.

Rico gave him a wry look. "Do you?" he asked. He glanced away, to the frost covered window and the snow that fell outside. "I'm going away for a while," he said. "A few months, probably."

Jonas tried to banish the dread that rose with Rico's words. He worked to keep his voice light. "Back to Paris?"

Childs shook his head. "No. Paris has lost its charm for me." He smiled ruefully. "Perhaps south somewhere. Maybe even California—the land of gold and wickedness. I imagine I'd enjoy that." He shrugged. "Somewhere that isn't cold."

"I'll miss you," Jonas said, forcing nonchalance. His heart felt heavy. Genie was gone, and now Rico. Already he felt too damned alone.

Rico straightened. "You flatter me," he said. "But I doubt you'll be lonely."

Jonas gave him a weak smile. "I'll be heartbroken."

"You are heartbroken, my love," Rico noted gently. "But not over me."

Jonas's smile died. He turned back to the painting. "Don't be absurd."

Childs shook his head. "You know, when I first saw her, I thought she was one of those nameless debutantes who had a *tendre* for painters. She was irresistible; so shy and helpless, with those big doe eyes." He chuckled at the memory. "I could not help myself. She was ripe for teasing. I expected her to run screaming from the room, and I believe she wanted to do just that."

He looked at Jonas with a soft smile. "But she didn't run, *mon ami*. She was so serious, but she didn't run, and she didn't play those silly games women play with fans and eyelashes. I was half in love with her myself at that moment."

"So I remember." Jonas wanted the words to be wry, but his throat was too tight, and they came out sounding strained and hoarse instead.

Rico continued as if he hadn't heard. "When she was there a second day, and a third . . . well, it became clear she was not at all what I'd imagined."

"No," Jonas whispered. "She wasn't."

There was silence. Jonas stared down at his palette, but instead of seeing ultramarine and vermillion, he saw her face. Her face the way she looked when she walked out the door. He saw the sadness in her eyes, the loss, the determination. Christ, the determination. The intensity of it almost made him weep.

"Why are you afraid of her, Jonas?" Rico asked quietly. "What makes you want to push her away?"

Jonas squeezed his eyes shut. "I'm not afraid of her," he said, but he knew it was a lie. He was afraid of her. Afraid that her strength was an illusion, that he would crush it as easily as he'd crushed so many others, that he would see it crumble around her. He was afraid of her because the thought of her pain made him weak, and he knew if she stayed with him he would see too much of pain. He couldn't bear it. He couldn't stand to watch her tranquility fade, or her trust. It was as selfish a reason as any, but he couldn't run from it, couldn't deny it.

And in the end, he couldn't admit it either. "She's not that strong," he lied.

"She's the strongest woman I've ever known."

"It's not enough."

Rico let out a harsh sound. "Nothing's ever enough for you, is it, Jonas? *Mon dieu,* I've seen you throw away things before, but never anything this good. Never anything that could help you so much. *Jésus,* do you think my leaving was an accident?" He shook his head. "Don't be a fool, Jonas. I left because she is so much better for you than I. She is the only woman I've ever been jealous of, because in only a few days she calmed you the way I never could. And unless I miss my guess, she's in love with you—which is damned convenient, given that you're in love with her as well."

Jonas couldn't help it; he felt the plunge of desperation at Rico's words, as if he were poised over a paper net, ready to fall through it to the ground. Nothing was safe. *"You're in love with her as well."* The words spun back to him, a demon truth, and he wanted to deny them, to protest with every breath, long and loudly. *No, I'm not. No, I'm not. No, I'm not.*

Except he was. He was, and he hated it. Hated the desperate way it made him feel, hated his vulnerability. Loving her didn't matter. Nothing mattered but the madness and what it would make him do to her. A week was nothing; it was the months that would destroy her, the days, the hours. Living with him, loving him. . . . Christ, it was a curse he wouldn't wish on his worst enemy, and certainly not the woman he loved.

The woman he loved. Ah God, not that. Anything but that.

He swallowed and turned away. "I don't love her,

Rico," he said, forcing a detachment he didn't feel, could never feel. "I would . . . destroy her."

Rico looked at him with compassionate eyes. "I think she might surprise you."

Jonas shook his head. "You don't understand. I . . ." He inhaled deeply. "You don't know. You've never seen . . . that look."

"What look?"

Jonas closed his eyes, remembering. Remembering pity and wariness and fear. Remembering his brother's expression when he'd left the asylum, that blankness, the dearth of emotion. "Can I even describe it to you?" he asked softly. He paused, trying to find the words. "When I—when I left the asylum, my brother came to see me. Like a fool I thought he wanted to know what I'd been through. And I . . . I wanted to talk about it. I . . . needed to. But he didn't want to listen. He pretended it hadn't even happened, that I hadn't been locked up in that hellhole for four months. And he wasn't the only one." Jonas opened his eyes, staring helplessly at his friend. "A conspiracy of silence. It got so I wondered if I'd even been there. There were times when I thought it was just another illusion, just a bad dream."

"Jonas—"

Jonas silenced him with a shake of his head. "I don't know what's wrong with me, Rico. I don't know if I'll ever escape it. I don't know what I would do if I did. All I know for sure is that I can't condemn her to this life. Don't you understand? I can't do it."

Rico held his gaze. "It's not your choice. It's hers."

Jonas let out a bitter laugh. "Well, she's made it then. She's gone."

"It would take only a word to bring her back."

"I don't want her back." Jonas fought for composure, for wryness and sarcasm and simple denial. He gestured with his brush. "Leave me to myself, Rico. All I want are my paints and a canvas. Given enough time, I'll forget all about her. I'm halfway there already."

"Oh?" Rico smiled, a crooked, ironic smile. "Then why is that her face I see on your canvas, *mon ami*?" He came around, peering over Jonas's shoulder. "Ah, I see you're right. You've forgotten her quite well. That scar on her lip was never there before, was it? Or that mole on her jaw. Yes, I do believe you're suffering the throes of amnesia even as we speak."

Jonas shrugged away in irritation. "Damn you, Rico. Leave me be."

"Certainly." Rico leaned back against the wall. His expression was knowingly smug. "I'll be happy to, as soon as you admit what a damned fool you are."

"Rico—"

"She won't wait forever, you know," Childs said, gently needling. "She'll go away and marry someone else. Someone who isn't you. She'll be kissing someone else, Jonas. Having someone else's children—"

"Goddammit, shut up!" The words spilled out before Jonas could stop them, he clamped his mouth shut and turned away, struggling to regain control. "I've explained it to you, Rico," he said, his voice dangerously shaky. "I've told you—"

"You've given me nothing but excuses." Childs shook his head. "If you don't love her, Jonas, why are you painting her? Why is it that canvas over there is fully sketched with her image? Your masterpiece, you said. She was to be your masterpiece."

Galatea to his Pygmalion. The words came floating

back, an echo of memory. Jonas took a deep breath. His masterpiece. Yes, she was that, but not a painted one. She had come to life beneath his hands, had given him something he'd thought was lost to him forever. Peace. Hope.

Love.

He dropped the brush, hearing it clatter to the floor, and covered his eyes with his hand. "My masterpiece," he murmured with a bitter laugh. "Tell me, Rico, who was more changed when Aphrodite turned Pygmalion's statue into a live woman? Pygmalion or Galatea?"

"Must it be one or the other?" Rico asked. "Couldn't it be that they were both changed? Life is not as simple as you make it, my love. Things are rarely black or white."

"Perhaps."

Rico leaned close. "You can't protect people from hurt, Jonas. You can't protect yourself. If you try, you might as well commit yourself to Bloomingdale now, because it's where you'll end up."

"A cheerful thought," Jonas managed.

"Yes, well, I'm known for my optimism," Rico said dryly, backing away. He clapped his hand on Jonas's shoulder, a reassuring touch, a connection that warmed him. "Now, come have a cognac with me, won't you, *mon ami*? Help me celebrate new horizons. I'm off after the National Academy showing." Rico's voice was deceptively bright. Jonas heard the strain of their conversation beneath it, and he knew Childs was deliberately trying to lighten things. Jonas thought about ignoring the attempt, punishing his friend with harsh silence, but the truth was he wanted the forgetfulness of cognac and the comfort of companionship.

He wanted to talk about stupid, trivial things. He wanted oblivion.

He put aside his palette and his paints and followed Childs to the door. "You're going so soon?" he asked.

"I'd leave sooner," Rico said, "but I'm dying to see that masterpiece of yours." He grabbed Jonas's coat from the peg by door and threw the garment to him. "You still mean to finish it, don't you?"

"I'm not sure." Jonas fumbled with his coat. Clumsily he pulled it on, reaching inside to straighten the lining, halting when his hand knocked against a heaviness in the inside pocket. He'd left something in his coat again. With any luck it would be money. God knew he needed it. He reached inside, his fingers tangling in the torn lining before he felt inside the pocket, and knew the moment he touched it that it wasn't coin. It was covered in tissue, an awkward shape—

"Are you coming?" Rico stood at the door impatiently.

"Just a minute. There's something in my pocket . . ." Jonas wrapped his fingers around it, pulling it loose. "Christ," he muttered, looking at the heavily wrapped lump. "What the hell is this?"

With a frown Childs came over. "What's what?" he asked. He glanced at the package, and his frown gave way to a rueful smile. "Ah. I'd forgotten all about that," he said. He nudged Jonas's hand. "Go ahead, open it."

Hesitantly Jonas placed the package in his false hand, lodging it between two fingers for leverage. Then carefully, curiously, he unwrapped it. The paper unfolded awkwardly beneath his fingers, the white tissue easing away bit by bit, revealing the shine of gold filigree, sparkling amethysts.

A butterfly.

Jonas stared at it. The gold caught the light from the window and reflected it back into his eyes, for an instant making the piece look surreal and oddly alive. A shining, beautiful, delicate butterfly, one he could not crush in his clumsy fingers, one he could not harm.

Jonas stared at it, and the memory came trembling back. Red brocade and cards and the thin light of dawn. Walking with Rico up Park Row and onto Broadway. Little shops with their windows closed and their expensive wares shut up tight.

Except for one little shop, and a brooch that had cost him the last of his rent money. A butterfly. For Genie.

He closed his eyes. "Christ," he murmured. When he opened them again, Rico was staring at him, a resigned look on his face, a strange sadness in his eyes.

"Forget the cognac, *mon ami*," he said with a sigh. "Go paint your picture. Paint your masterpiece. Try to get her out of your mind—if you can."

And then he turned on his heel and headed for the door, disappearing into the growing darkness of the hall, leaving Jonas alone.

Chapter 25

"It's absolutely invigorating!" Samuel Carter burst through the entryway of the parlor, bringing with him the smell of snow and a draft of cold winter air. "I tell you, there's nothing like New York. It's worth a visit for the Century alone." He peeled off his gloves, slapping them together in his palms before he shrugged out of his coat and held them out to Imogene, who sat by the fire. "Here, daughter, make yourself useful."

Slowly Imogene put aside her embroidery and rose, fighting a surge of resentment as she took her father's things. In spite of the rancor that had been between them this last week, she forced herself to speak with cool courtesy. "Did you enjoy the club, then?" she asked, folding the wet coat over her arm.

"Of course I did," he said. "I just said so, didn't I?"

From a chair on the other side of the fireplace, Thomas looked up from his book. "My letter of introduction served you well?"

"It was perfect." Samuel swept his hat off his head and set it on a side table, where droplets of melted snow slid to the polished wood. He grinned widely. "Ah, the clubs of New York! Nowhere else in the world are they as fine—except for London, perhaps."

"I thought you hated the clubs in London," Thomas said.

"It's not the clubs, it's the people I abhor," Samuel sank into a mohair-covered chair. "A bunch of foppish snobs is what they are. At least New York has intellectuals. True philosophers. And artists . . ." He leaned his head back with a sigh of delight. "London pales in comparison, and Nashville . . . God, Nashville. . . ."

"Well, there aren't many artists there, certainly," Thomas commented.

"Couldn't make a living if there were." Samuel smoothed his bulky mustache distractedly. "As it is there's nothing much to paint but a bunch of prize-winning cows, maybe a dour farmwife every now and then." He sighed again. "No, much as I wish it, Nashville isn't destined to be an artistic center. I can't patronize 'em all, you know."

"Yes, I know," Thomas said wryly.

"Still, I do what I can. Maybe one day." Samuel glanced up as if he'd only just realized Imogene was in the room. "What are you standing there for, girl? You make a damned bad coatrack."

Imogene flushed with angry humiliation, but she swallowed the retort that rose to her lips and clenched her jaw. There was no point in angering him, even if this last week and a half had been unbearable. Her father obviously wanted to punish her; he berated her constantly, he seemed to take joy in humiliating her. And she knew she wasn't imagining that secretive glint in his eyes. He was waiting for something, planning something, and with a growing sense of dread she wondered what it was.

Though she would find out soon enough, she was sure. In a way, it would be a relief to know—Lord knew she was ready for this all to be over. She wanted to return to Nashville, wanted back her safe, normal little life, with its tightly scheduled days, its long nights. She wanted to put this all behind her. To put Jonas behind her.

Jonas. She closed her eyes, pushing the thought away, just as she'd been pushing it away since she'd left him. At least Nashville would help her forget him. At least there she wouldn't wonder if he was sitting by his windows watching the snow fall—or wonder who was watching it with him. At least Nashville didn't hold a hundred little things to remind her of him.

It doesn't matter. It's all over now. It's over. Imogene forced the words into her mind as if they could comfort her. As if they could sweep away the hurt and kill the yearning. But as long as her father was here, she needed the words. If nothing else, they helped her pretend everything was fine, helped her keep a hold on her self-control, however tenuous. For now it was too dangerous to think of Jonas. For now it was easier to imagine it was some faraway dream, a fantasy. Later perhaps, when she was safe in Nashville again, she would let herself think of him. When she was far away from here and the temptation to fall on her knees and beg him to take her back had eased. If it ever did.

She sighed, hanging her father's coat on the hook behind the stairs, draping his gloves across the collar. Then she took a deep breath and returned to the parlor.

And immediately wished she hadn't. Her father swiveled in his chair, his dark gaze resting on her with an unsettling speculation, a scrutiny that made her feel suddenly cold. He was finally going to tell her what he was waiting for, she knew. What was that old saying? *Be careful what you wish for. . . .*

"There was a reason I went to the Century Club today," he said, and though his tone was nonchalant, she heard the calculation beneath it. He smiled—not a pleasant smile at all—and with a twinge of surprise she realized that once even that smile would have made her happy. She had always craved his attention so badly that even his anger was welcome. But now that same anger only left her feeling embittered and resentful. She wondered when that had changed. When had she started to notice the contempt in his expression? Had it always been there?

He tapped his fingers on the well-padded arm of the chair, not taking his eyes from hers. "I went looking for Whitaker."

The name seemed to drop into her heart. Imogene struggled to maintain her composure. "Oh?" she managed.

" 'Oh?' " he mimicked. "Is that all you have to say for yourself, girl? Don't you wonder why I went looking for him?"

"Wouldn't it be more direct to visit his studio?" Thomas asked.

Her father turned, thoughtfully shaking his head. "He's avoiding me. I thought I might run into him at the Century, take him by surprise, so to speak. You did say he was a member."

"Yes, but—"

"I've sent two notes already, asking for a meeting."

Imogene's stomach knotted. "You sent him notes?"

"Of course I sent him notes," Samuel snapped. "What kind of a father would I be if I didn't demand satisfaction? He despoiled my daughter, for God's sake. Your reputation is at stake."

"My reputation," she repeated disbelievingly. She laughed bitterly. "Since when have you ever cared about reputations? You're the one who sent me off to study with an artist to begin with. Wasn't that scandalous enough?"

"There's a difference between education and scandal, Imogene," he shot back. "You would have been perfectly safe studying under him if you acted like a lady instead of some . . . some trollop."

"That's enough, Samuel," Thomas said softly. "Tell me, what will you do if Whitaker agrees to a meeting? Demand marriage?"

Imogene stared at her godfather in horror. "Thomas, no—"

Samuel lifted a brow. He turned to look at her. "Well, Imogene," he said coldly. "Would he marry you?"

It was those words that hurt, far more than Thomas's suggestion that Whitaker be forced to marry her, far more than anything else her father could have said. Because he knew the answer to that question as well as she did. It was humiliatingly obvious. She looked down at her hands, hearing the rest of his talk through a heavy buzz in her ears.

"I know what he's doing," he said to Thomas. "Biding his time. No doubt he's waiting for the right opportunity."

"The right opportunity?" Thomas frowned. "To do what?"

"To make his demands, of course. Do you think he hasn't a reason for ruining my daughter? Certainly he does. He wants something, just you wait and see."

"Are you suggesting he would blackmail you?" Thomas asked, raising his brows in surprise. "Really, Samuel, I don't think Whitaker—"

"Well, he's not above *being* blackmailed, is he?" Her father asked, throwing Thomas a knowing look. "I'd think he'd jump at the chance to turn the tables."

She was slow to understand his meaning. She heard his words, one by one, drifting through her humiliation and pain, but finally it wasn't the words at all that she understood, but the way her father said them, the edge of accusation. Imogene looked up. She caught her godfather's helpless glance, and everything fell into place: the way Jonas had taken her on even though she obviously lacked the skill level or talent of his other students, his anger at the beginning, the way he tried to drive her away. Of course. She couldn't believe she hadn't known it before. Thomas and her father had forced Jonas to teach her. They'd made it impossible for him to refuse.

She waited for the hurt to penetrate. She expected to feel pain and betrayal. Instead, all she felt was anger, and for Jonas's sake, not her own. She had never thought Jonas Whitaker could be forced to do anything. The knowledge that he had been was anathema to her. Thomas and her father had trapped him, had forced him to sacrifice his integrity—God, the thought was so ugly. It was ugly the way a trained bear was ugly, a proud and beautiful animal baited to do tricks for a crowd. She hated the idea. Lord, she hated it.

She felt frozen as she turned to Thomas. "What was it you offered him?" she demanded. Her voice was so cold it sounded like a stranger's. "What was it he couldn't refuse?"

"Imogene." Her godfather opened his palms in supplication. "My dear, you must see I meant no harm. You wanted it so badly . . ."

"Tell me. Was it money? Or was it something else you threatened him with?"

"Calm down, girl," Samuel said. "You're overreacting. It was nothing more than a little judicious pressure."

"Judicious pressure?" she repeated. She threw a baleful look at her father. "I know what your definition of judicious pressure is, Papa. You used it on Chloe often enough. You've used it on me. But I don't imagine Jonas cared much about losing your love, so what was it you told him?"

His eyes blazed. "Don't you use that tone with me."

"I'm not a little girl anymore, Papa," she said evenly. "You can't just tell me to be quiet when you don't want to hear me. What you did was wrong." She turned away, to Thomas. "I can't believe you would be a part of this," she said to him. "I can't believe it. You knew how I felt—"

"I knew you wanted to be an artist," Thomas said quietly. "That's what I knew. I wanted to give you that. I could give you that. I didn't think about right or wrong." He paused, running a freckled hand through his white hair, looking at her with a sadness that seemed to sink into her soul. "I told him I would withdraw my patronage if he didn't take you on. It was enough at first. But you know him, my dear. You know that could only hold him for so long. If he didn't want you there, eventually it wouldn't have mattered what I said."

His words were oddly comforting. Perhaps it was only that she knew they were true.

"I wanted you to have the best, that's all," Thomas continued. "I have always wanted you to have the best."

"Good God, this is maudlin," her father broke in. "You shouldn't coddle her, Tom. She's got to face the truth sooner or later. Whitaker's an opportunist. He saw a chance and grabbed it. He's probably thinking of ways to strip me of my fortune as we speak."

"He's not like that," Imogene said.

Her father frowned. "I'm only trying to protect you, girl. You don't know the world like I do—"

"He's not like that," she repeated.

"He's a painter, for Christ's sake."

"He's an *artist*," she corrected angrily. "Listen to yourself, Papa. You've spent years telling me the difference between craft and art, and yet you can't even see it yourself. Jonas Whitaker is brilliant. He's the most brilliant man I've ever known."

"Brilliant enough to know what side his bread's buttered on, obviously," her father retorted. "Don't waste your breath defending him, Imogene. He was using you. If you had the sense God gave a goat you'd know better than to fall for the first man who tells you pretty lies."

"Papa," she protested. "You don't understand—"

"It's you who doesn't understand," he said. He lurched from his chair, stopping only inches away. "You want to see the truth, girl, you'll come with me tomorrow to the National Academy's exhibition. I'll show you. Whitaker won't answer my notes, but by God he'll answer me—and you'll see I'm right."

Imogene shook her head. Things were pressing in on

her, too much, too fast. He was controlling her, just as he always had, and she felt a growing sense of desperation, of an anger she couldn't restrain. "I won't do it. I don't want to go."

"Dammit, girl, you'll do as I say, and don't you forget it," he said angrily, his face close to hers. "You *will* be there. If I have to carry you bodily into that hall, you'll be right beside me. I wonder if you'll still be singing your lover's praises when he tells me how much money he wants to keep quiet."

Imogene jerked away. "I'm not going."

"We'll see about that," he muttered, spinning on his heel. "We'll just see." He left the parlor so quickly she felt the breeze of his movement. The buzzing in her ears grew louder.

For moments she just stood there, trying to catch her breath, to quiet the noise in her head. She was aware of Thomas standing on the other side of the fireplace, watching her, one hand resting on the back of his chair. She felt his silent scrutiny, but it was minutes before she could look up at him, minutes before she spoke.

"He's so wrong," she said helplessly. "About everything."

Thomas nodded. "He just wants the best for you, my dear."

She snorted softly in disbelief.

He smiled. "He does, in his way. Just as we all do. The question is, what will you do about it?"

She frowned. "What can I do? He's my father."

"Yes." Thomas looked down at his fingers as he traced the patterns on the brocade upholstery. "But you're not a little girl anymore, Imogene. You're a grown woman. Perhaps it's time you think about what you want out of your life, instead of what your father wants." He paused. "Have you . . . have you given any thought to going back to Jonas?"

Her heart caught. Imogene laughed shortly. "It's all I've thought about," she said. "But it doesn't matter. He doesn't want me."

"Oh?" Thomas looked up. "Are you sure?"

"Yes," she said. "You know him, Thomas. You . . . you know what he's like. He needs someone who can charm him. Someone like . . ."

"Like Chloe?" he put in.

Her throat tightened. She shook her head. "I don't belong with him. I don't belong in that crowd. I'm as out of place as a moth among butterflies."

"You're a pretty little moth," Thomas teased gently. Then, when she didn't smile, he said, "I think you undervalue yourself, Imogene. Where is the woman who turned me away from the studio a week and a half ago? Have you forgotten her already?"

She looked away. "I haven't forgotten. But Jonas needed me then. He doesn't need me now."

"I see."

His voice was so thoughtful she glanced at him again. "He asked me to leave," she said.

He nodded, but that thoughtful look didn't leave his eyes. "I think you should go to the exhibition with your father," he said.

She stared at him in surprise. "Why?"

"Because, my dear," he said gently. "If you don't go you'll always regret it. You'll always wonder if you should have." He smiled, a soft, encouraging smile, the smile she'd loved since she was a little girl alone in a sickroom. "Go to the show, Imogene," he urged. "If not for yourself, then for me. Go for me."

He couldn't avoid it forever, he knew. Jonas stared at the note hanging from his fingers, at the fine ivory stock embossed heavily with the letters SGC. Samuel G. Carter. Genie's father. Without unfolding the sheet Jonas knew what it said. He had it memorized. Carter wanted a meeting, and Jonas knew exactly why. In the back of his mind he wondered why he hadn't expected it. He had ruined her, after all, and the whole world would expect him to pay the price. *Marry her,* the voice inside him said. *Do what her father wants. Marry her.*

And in a way he wanted that. Wanted to be forced into marrying her, into loving her. Wanted no decisions and no sacrifices. Wanted to be able to say *"I tried to save you. God knows, I tried, but your father forced my hand. . . ."*

Yes, that was exactly what he wanted. An excuse to keep her beside him. An excuse to love her. Ah, God, he wanted it.

But he couldn't have it. He couldn't have her.

He stared at the butterfly glittering on the table beside him, at the gold that shimmered in the cold winter light. The only light in his darkness, just as Genie had been. And without her the darkness was creeping closer now. Without her it would overtake him. He knew that. He knew it more certainly than he'd ever known anything in his life.

Over the last two weeks he'd made a valiant attempt to forget her. He'd done what Rico suggested; he'd thrown himself into painting her. And now the painting was done and hanging in the gallery, ready for the exhibition tomorrow. He'd been right, it was a master-piece. His masterpiece.

But it didn't help him forget her. It didn't ease the pain of being without her.

He struggled to keep his mind clear. Struggled to remember why he could not have her, what he would do to her. He picked up the jeweled butterfly and tried to crush it in his hand the way he would crush her. But the gold only bent slightly, held in place by amethyst and solder. Things that would not break, would not bend. Not like flesh and blood, not like tender feelings and gentle souls. How easily they were broken. How little it took to destroy them forever.

No, he could not marry her, and he knew in his heart there were only two things that could keep her father from forcing the issue. Two things.

Jonas stared at his wrist, at the fine scar. He closed his eyes and thought of what it had felt like, that first cut so long ago. The quick pain and then the throbbing ache, the numbness. He thought of how his fingers had trembled when he'd cut the other wrist, the way he could barely hold the razor through the blood on his fingers. The clumsiness of it, the lack of grace or beauty. In the end, suicide was just a lack of courage, he knew that now. Genie had taught him that, just as she had taught him that there was hope in the world—something he'd given up on long ago. Hope. Such a small word, but how strong it was. How much it sustained him now.

And because of that, death was no longer a choice. But the other. . . .

He thought of what Rico said, the words that had been spinning in his mind for days. *"You can't protect people from hurt, Jonas. You can't protect yourself. If you try, you might as well commit yourself to Bloom-ingdale now."*

Bloomingdale. He thought of it, and he thought of what was waiting for him without her. Nights without end. Blackness that would advance day by day. There was no point in fighting it. In the asylum he wouldn't have to. It was the best place for him now, the only place. He would go mad without her anyway. It was his gift for protecting her. His reward. Madness for her safety.

It seemed a fair bargain.

He stared at the window, at the falling snow. And he thought of how she'd looked standing in it, of snow-flakes melting on her skin, sparkling in her hair.

After tomorrow, he promised himself. *Just give me tomorrow, and I'll go.* Back to where they would make sure he didn't break his promises. Back to where they could keep him safe from himself.

Chapter 26

She dressed for the occasion. It took her hours to go through her armoire, to dismiss one gown after another. She had a rainbow of pastels, yet when she held each one to her body and looked into the mirror, she realized Jonas had been right. Pastels did not become her. Pastels were colors for true blonds with blue eyes. Chloe's colors, not hers.

But she had nothing else. Finally she'd gone to Katherine, who had searched her own wardrobe, picking out a gown that was too small for her but perfect for Imogene. It was three years old, and slightly unfashionable, but Imogene could forgive that, because it suited her so well. It was simple and beautiful, with an open caraco bodice of bronze velvet and a flounced skirt of matching brocade. When she put it on, the color warmed her skin and brought out the highlights in her hair, made her eyes seem a mysterious golden brown instead of the muddy color she knew they were.

She looked attractive in the dress, if not beautiful, and Imogene took care with the rest of her toilette, pinning up her hair with two golden combs and clasping on earrings of gold filigree to dangle against her cheeks. She wanted to look beautiful. She wanted something to help her be strong, because the little bit of courage she'd shown her father yesterday had faded, and she knew it was because of Jonas, because she would soon be seeing him, and she was afraid of herself. Afraid she would lose her dignity and her self-respect completely. Afraid she would beg him to take her back.

She told herself there were a hundred good reasons to stay away from him: He was as mad as they said. She would never survive him. She didn't belong in his crowd. They were the right reasons for leaving him, the practical reasons. She could pick any one and feel she'd made the right decision. Just one would allow her to keep her dignity.

Imogene squeezed her eyes shut. She heard the front door open downstairs, heard the bustle in the foyer, and she knew it was time to go. Time to brave the crowds at the gallery, to pretend nonchalance and composure when inside her heart was breaking. She did not know if she could look at him again. She did not know if she could survive seeing that regret in his eyes—or worse, seeing nothing at all. She wondered if she would even be able to walk away once she'd seen him.

Slowly she went to the door. Her hands were trembling, and she forced herself to calm before she turned the knob and stepped out into the hallway. They were waiting for her at the bottom of the stairs: her father, Thomas, Katherine. She saw them turn worried eyes upon her—except for her father, who only looked at her with contempt and turned away again. She wondered why that didn't hurt. It should have. It always had before.

"You look lovely, my dear," Thomas said.

Imogene gave him a weak smile.

Her father was holding her mantle for her. She came down the stairs and took it from him, putting it on, buttoning the wool collar tightly about her throat and then tying the ribbons of her hat, pulling on gloves. The movements were mechanical, and though she heard the others talking as they readied to go, Imogene felt too detached to answer.

It was so cold outside it nearly took her breath away. Though it had stopped snowing, the sky was still heavy with clouds, the streets frozen with hard-packed mud and ice. It would be better to stay home, she thought, and wished her father and Thomas would look at the road and agree, but they didn't, and Henry was already waiting at the curb with the carriage.

"It'll be 'ard goin' today," he warned as he opened the door. "We'll take it nice 'n' slow."

Thomas smiled and stood back to help Katherine inside. "Good enough," he told Henry. "We're in no hurry."

Imogene climbed in beside Katherine, echoing Thomas's sentiments with relief. They were in no hurry. There was plenty of time to arrange her thoughts. Plenty of time to decide just how she would greet him when she saw him again. Calmly. Coolly. With just a touch of disdain. *"Why hello, Jonas. How nice to see you again. Have you met my fath—"*

Good Lord. Her father. She glanced at Samuel from the corner of her eye, noting his serious expression, the thin lips beneath his mustache. She had forgotten her father's reasons for going. She had forgotten about his desire for retribution, his notes to Jonas.

She sat back in the seat, closing her eyes, wishing she could fade into the leather. This was going to be a nightmare. She listened to the carriage wheels slipping and sliding on the icy streets, and she wished a rim would catch, or the horses would balk—anything to keep them from arriving at the National Academy Gallery.

But nothing happened, and before long the carriage was pulling up in front of the building that housed New York City's finest art school.

"Crowded tonight," Thomas noted, looking out the window. "Though it always is, I suppose."

He was right. The National Academy of Design's yearly exhibition was a well-attended event. There were people everywhere, clogging the walks, thronging the stairs, casting shadows against the lighted windows lining the front of the building. They had to wait their turn at the curb, and once they were out of the carriage, they joined those huddled against the cold. It took a long time to get in, and a brisk breeze only made the wait more uncomfortable, but once they were inside, Imogene wished she were still on the walk, still battling the cold.

She had been to exhibitions before, of course. Her family had gone whenever one was held in Nashville. Her father especially had loved those exhibitions. He had lived for the opportunity to socialize with neighbors and enter into long and intricate conversations about "art" and its "value." But Imogene had the feeling he liked this one more, and for different reasons. Samuel looked expectant. Readying for a fight.

Her heart sank. She moved away from her father,

following Thomas and Katherine up the low stairs that led to the first of the six galleries. It was a large room, its high ceilings leading to skylights that opened the space and lit it during the day. But as open and large as the room was, people nearly filled it, and the scent of the many gaslights mixed suffocatingly with those of perfume, wet wool, and warm bodies. It was hard to breathe, hard to even hear oneself over the excited buzz of talk, and it was so crowded that they were forced to move with the throng, circling slowly past the many paintings paneling the walls, forced to linger agonizingly by each one.

Imogene scanned the room, wanting to see him, afraid to see him. She didn't know whether to feel relief or disappointment when she saw only the backs of heads and feathered hats and voluminous cloaks. With a stab of dismay she realized she would come upon him suddenly, without time to prepare herself, to compose herself. There were simply too many people to see beyond the next bend, or even the next painting.

"Where is he?" her father demanded impatiently from beside her. "Show me where he is."

Thomas tried to smile. "Patience, Sam. We'll come upon him in time." He pointed to a large landscape that took up a good portion of a wall, bounded on either side by smaller canvases showing a similar scene. "What do you think of that one? I think he's a promising young artist."

Samuel gave the painting a cursory look. "Fine, if you like that sort of thing." He grabbed Imogene's arm, holding her tightly against him, as if he were afraid she would run off. He leaned down to whisper in her ear. "I want no nonsense from you, daughter, do you hear? When you see Whitaker, you point him out to me. Let me take care of it."

She slanted him a glance, pulling away from his grip. "Of course, Papa," she said stiffly.

They moved from painting to painting, following the crowd from one gallery into another, and then to a third. She heard the talk around her distractedly. *"Oh, Jeffrey, I love it! Such fine colors . . ." "Luminism is evident in every brushstroke, my love. Mark my words, this man will go far . . ." "I don't see it. I simply don't understand what all the fuss is about . . ."* The voices pounded in her head. The paintings wavered before her, each one blurring into the next, a mix of style and color as confusing as the feelings crowding her heart. Anticipation, fear . . . She wasn't sure what she should be feeling, was afraid of what she would see in Jonas's eyes when finally she saw him. She tugged at the collar of her mantle, feeling too hot where before she'd been cold. She undid the frogged fastenings, but even that didn't help. Her lungs felt tight, her throat swollen. She could not silence the question chanting in her head. *Where is he? Where is he?*

"This is lovely," Katherine observed, stopping before a still life of peaches and grapes. "Oh, Imogene, look! This is by that friend of yours, that Mr. Childs."

The name startled Imogene. She had not expected to hear it. Already Rico seemed to come from a past so long ago it was almost forever. Imogene stared at the painting, her heart racing. She'd thought maybe he'd gone back to Paris. Obviously not.

Katherine grabbed her husband's arm. "He brought a message to the house a few weeks ago, darling. I thought I might commission him . . ."

Her godmother's words trailed off, blending into the sea of voices. Anxiously, nervously, Imogene looked around, trying to see through the faces. Rico was never far from Jonas. She wondered where Childs had been, where he was now. Was he taking care of Jonas? Was anyone—

"Good heavens, it's her. Gerald, look, it's her."

The hushed sentence was close by her ear. Frowning, Imogene looked over—into the narrowed eyes of an older woman in pale apricot silk.

The woman was staring, but when Imogene caught her gaze, she flushed and turned away, pulling her startled husband with her through the crowd.

How odd. Imogene glanced back at Katherine, but she and Thomas were still bent over Childs's painting, her father close beside them. Impatiently Imogene stepped back, but the crowd jostled her, and she drew back farther, looking up just in time to see a man in a tall beaver hat staring at her. He tipped it to her, smiling a smile she found vaguely disturbing. Not just friendly, but . . . but *too* friendly.

Flustered, Imogene looked away. When she glanced back, he was gone, but there was another group, a woman who looked at her with sharp, beady little eyes before she leaned over and nudged the woman walking beside her, whispering into her ear. The other woman glanced up, and her fine features drew into a tight little mask; she turned to her friend with words whose harshness carried over the noise, even if what she said didn't. The two of them bustled away.

Self-consciously Imogene checked her gown. Her bodice was buttoned tight against her throat; she was hardly indecent. And surely the dress wasn't all that dated. She adjusted her bonnet. Only a few loose hairs escaped her chignon, nothing more.

Disturbed, she moved to where the others stood. "Katherine," she said quietly. "Do I have something on my face?"

Her godmother turned from the painting. "No," she said. "You look fine."

"People are staring at me."

Her father frowned. "You're imagining things."

"No, I—"

"Nervous, are you, girl?" He grunted in satisfaction and took her arm, giving a cursory nod to Thomas. "Let's get on then, shall we? We can come back to look at these if you like."

He tugged on her arm, pulling her with him. Imogene scanned the faces they passed, telling herself that the stares she received were only in her imagination, as her father said. Certainly the whispers weren't about her, they couldn't be. But still her cheeks burned. She gripped her father's arm more tightly, feeling more and more flustered with every step they took.

She heard the giggles first. Nervous, embarrassed laughter, scandalized half words. A murmur of talk with a slightly hysterical edge. It was just ahead of them, and she knew without looking what it signified; she'd been to enough art shows to know.

She glanced at her father, who lifted his brow and smiled. "Ah, there's something scandalous ahead," he noted, interpreting the hushed talk as she had. "What shall it be this time, I wonder? Which artist?"

Imogene's heart raced. *Which artist?* The whispers pounded against her ears; she heard everything, each word was too loud, too distinct. *"Shocking!"* *"Who is* she?" "How dare he?" "My dear, it's obscene. Isn't it obscene?"

She knew who it was before they came upon him, before the crowd parted slightly to reveal a huge canvas painted with the figure of a woman. She barely glanced at it. Instead, her gaze went unerringly to the man beside it.

Jonas.

He stood back, leaning negligently against some small still life, his shoulder nudging the frame, angling it so the painted pheasant within looked ready to roll off its table. His dark hair was loose, falling over his shoulders in defiance of fashion, seeming black-black against the blue coat he wore. He was talking to Rico, who stood beside him, the perfect blond foil to Jonas's darkness, and Imogene was reminded of the first time she'd seen him. He'd been so vibrant then, a dark sun, a mysterious, frightening man. He was not so mysterious now, and not at all frightening, but the vibrance was still there, emanating from him so strongly she wondered why everyone was staring at the painting instead of him, since he was far more stunning.

"Sweet Christ." Her father's voice was a harsh whisper in her ear. "Jesus Christ, what the hell have you done?"

Startled, she tore her gaze away from Jonas. Her father was glaring at the painting before them, his face tight, his nostrils pinched with anger. She glanced at the portrait.

Her heart stopped. Imogene gasped. The painting glistened in front of her with a delicate luminosity, all shades of white except for the background, which was shadowed and dark, nearly black. It was a woman reclining on a stack of white pillows, her pale skin vi-

brant and alive, the lines of her nude body obscured
and yet somehow made more clear by a diaphanous
white scarf. She was a mystery of shapes: small
breasts, rounded hips, a triangular hint of shadow at
the juncture of her thighs. Her hair was a soft golden
brown, falling over her shoulders, strands curling
against her cheek. It was a shocking portrait. Too
alive, too erotic, too beautiful. But those things
weren't what made it shocking. What made it shocking
was something else, something far more elemental.

It was a portrait of her.

Imogene felt as if the floor had tilted beneath her. It
was her, and though she tried hard to deny it, she
couldn't. It was her face—those were her eyes looking
dispassionately at the crowd, that was her chin. And
that tiny mole just below her mouth was hers too. All
her. Good Lord, it was her. Except for one thing. The
woman in the painting was alluring and beautiful. She
was everything Imogene was not, everything she'd ever
wanted to be. Vibrant. Exotic. Sensual.

Her father's fingers dug into her arm; Imogene
heard him say something, heard the rage in his voice.
But it barely registered. She could not look away from
the painting, not until she heard her name, not until
she heard Jonas's voice cutting through the gleeful
murmurs of the crowd.

"Genie."

That was all, just her name, a hush of sound, a rush
of breath. She glanced up, catching his gaze, and his
eyes seemed impossibly bright, impossibly green. His
face tightened; he clenched Rico's arm as if the motion
gave him strength. But he didn't move. He just stared
at her, and it seemed his features were more finely

etched than she'd ever seen them, taut with something, some emotion . . . despair?

"Jonas," she breathed. She stepped toward him, but her father's grip held her tight, pulling her back. She turned to her father. "Let me go," she said, trying to wrench free. "Papa, please. . . ."

She trailed off when she saw her father's face. It was white with anger, his brown eyes flashed with it. His fingers bit more deeply into her arm, so painful she cried out.

"Are you mad?" he asked in a harsh whisper, shaking her so hard her head snapped back. "What did you think you were doing, posing for him this way? Wasn't it enough that you blackened my good name by sleeping with him, you had to advertise it as well?"

She heard the gasps around her, the sudden tittering. Imogene swallowed. She caught a woman's avid stare and Imogene turned away, keeping her voice low. "Papa, no," she said, trying to soothe him. "You don't understand. Please, let's talk about this somewhere else."

"Goddammit, we'll talk about it now!" He shook her again, his voice rising steadily until even those yards away turned to stare. "You didn't seem to mind the attention when you posed for this . . . this filth! You wanted to show your nakedness to the world, so be it! Let them hear this too!"

He flung her away so violently Imogene went sprawling. She fell painfully to the ground, sliding against a woman's skirts, jamming her elbow on a man's leg. Stunned, she tried to rise, tried to grab her father's arm. "Papa, please—"

He shook her off, sending her falling again. "Get out

of my sight. You're no better than a whore, and no daughter of mine!"

The rest happened so quickly Imogene saw it in a blur. She heard a curse, heard: "Damn you, that's enough!" and then she saw someone—Jonas—rushing her father, she heard the crack of a fist on a jaw, the loud shout of pain. She gasped, and she saw Jonas turn, saw him look at her and shout, "Get her the hell out of here!" and then hands were on her, pulling her to her feet, surrounding her, closing in on her. She thought she saw Rico in the crowd, and Thomas, thought she heard the sound of a struggle, but it was so confusing, and she couldn't see. Her head was spinning; she tasted blood on her lip from the fall. She tried to push past, but the crowd held fast, mad for the fight. She heard running footsteps, and she turned to see men in black coats dodging the crowd, racing toward the commotion.

"Jonas!" she shouted, trying to move closer. "Jonas!"

But he didn't hear her. No one heard her, she couldn't get close, she couldn't see. Desperately Imogene pushed through the crowd; it eased just enough so she wedged herself between two men, just enough so she could see Rico grabbing for someone, his blond hair falling into his face, a red mark on his cheekbone.

"Rico!" She cried. "Jonas!" And then she heard his voice, a hoarse shout, a desperate cry.

"Get her out of here! Dammit, I told you to get her the fuck out of here!"

And suddenly there were arms around her, pulling her back, wrenching her away.

"No." She struggled against them, fighting to stay, to get to Jonas, to stop her father. "No!"

But they were stronger than she was. And the voice, the weary, anxious voice, was stronger too.

"It's all right, Imogene. Imogene, please, my dear. Come with me."

It was Thomas. Thomas looking harried and worn and dispirited. "The authorities will intervene. There's nothing we can do. Come with me."

She didn't want to go. She tried not to go. But the crowd was yelling now, and the men in black coats were forcing their way through, trying to quiet the mob. Thomas was right. There was nothing they could do. Nothing at all.

She looked up at her godfather, seeing Katherine just behind, a kind and sympathetic look on her face. And in her mind, Imogene heard Jonas's desperate words again, called through a crowd. *"Get her out of here!"*

She surrendered, letting Thomas and Katherine guide her from the hall, into the cold winter night. And when Thomas helped them both into the carriage and told the driver to take them home, Imogene said nothing, leaning her head on Katherine's comforting shoulder, hearing the jeering of the crowd echo in her ears as the carriage jerked forward, skidding through the icy streets of New York City, taking her away.

Chapter 27

*J*onas shoved his hand deep in the pocket of his overcoat. The cold air stung the cuts on his face, the tender bruise on his jaw. A quiet breeze blew his hair into his face; the strands caught on the roughness of dried blood marking his cheekbone and his eye. He shook his head, closing his eyes against the glowing gaslights and the bright reflection of the gallery windows shining on the snow.

He had wanted one day. One more day to think about her, to stare at her portrait and wish she were beside him. One day, and it had shown him more irrevocably than ever what a danger he was. He had lost control, had lunged at Samuel Carter without a thought as to who he was or where, had been mindless and aching, wanting only to punish the man for the things he'd said to her, wanting to kill him for the things he'd said. If Jonas needed any more proof that he should be locked away forever, tonight had given it to him. He'd been an animal. A madman. He was everything his father had called him that long-ago day in Cincinnati.

But the worst thing was not the fight. The worst thing was that he had been so caught up in his obsession with Genie that he hadn't stopped to think about what it would do to her. He'd painted that portrait and known it was a masterpiece, but he had not expected the crowd's reaction to it, or hers.

He had turned her into a pariah. The good people of New York City might have accepted her as his mistress, but as his model—his nude model—she was labeled no better than a whore. It was ludicrous and hypocritical, but it was the way things were, and he should have known. She would be shunned by the very circle that paid his bills, that purchased his paintings. They would buy the portrait, they would stare at her naked body hanging from their walls, but they would revile the woman who had posed for it.

It didn't matter that she hadn't posed. It didn't matter that he'd painted her from memory. He had ruined her.

Christ, he'd ruined her.

Jonas opened his eyes, staring blankly around him, hearing the rattle of carriages on Broadway, the muffled talk from those leaving the gallery. Truthfully, he had not expected her to come to the exhibition, though he knew her father was in town. He had not expected to see her ever again. He had told himself he wanted it that way. But the moment he'd seen her, he'd known he was lying to himself. She was so beautiful in that bronze gown, with the rich color accenting her hair and eyes, and the sight of her brought such a pure, all-encompassing joy, such a overwhelming gratitude, it was all he could do to keep from running toward her. He would have, he thought. He would have crushed her to him and never let her go if she hadn't looked away from the portrait at just that moment. If he hadn't seen the stunned expression on her face and the unshed tears in her eyes. Those things had stopped him dead, had left him feeling bereft and uncertain. They were feelings he hated, and so when he heard her father's condemnation, he had gratefully turned to the safer emotion of anger, had let it overtake him.

And had ruined himself as thoughtlessly as he'd ruined her.

Jonas raked his hand through his hair, taking such a deep breath of the frigid air it burned his lungs. Ah, what a mistake he'd made. What a terrible mistake. He belonged in Bedlam, belonged with the other lunatics, the dream-crazed creatures who couldn't be trusted to not do damage to themselves or to others. He belonged in solitude, where his uncontrolled rages and rabid joys would be witnessed only by silence and darkness, where he could let his despair give in to madness and no one would care. He deserved it. He needed it.

He told himself he wanted it.

But what he really wanted was her.

In the near distance a woman's laughter sparkled over the snow, along with the clack of bootheels and an answering baritone chuckle. And for just a moment Jonas allowed himself to wonder what it would be like to have her. What it would be like to have a normal life, to do normal, everyday things. To go to an exhibition on a cold and snowy night and see the gaslights reflected in the snow and the jewels glittering on the ears and throats of every woman there. To walk arm in arm and laugh breathlessly together, whispering secrets and exchanging small flirtations. To go home with her and pull her laughing up the stairs, to take her in his arms and kiss her and know she was his forever, that together they could survive this madness, that with her he could withstand his pain and temper his joys.

It would be like living a fairy tale. Prince Charming and Sleeping Beauty. But in fairy tales the witch was always killed at the end. In fairy tales evil was banished. And Prince Charming never turned back into a frog.

Jonas sighed, leaning back against the wall. There was no point in thinking about it anymore. Genie would never be his. She would go back to Nashville. As Rico said, she would find a nice young man and settle down. She would have children. She would be happy.

Happy. Yes, that was what Jonas wanted for her. It was all he wanted.

"Ah, there you are."

Rico's voice came out of the darkness, disembodied and strange but hardly a surprise. Jonas turned to see his friend standing at the corner of the building, huddled against the cold.

"Yes," he said calmly. "I'm here."

"I finally got Carter settled down. He's decided not to press charges."

Jonas nodded. "Thank you."

Childs came toward him. Jonas heard his friend's footsteps crunching in the frost-covered snow, heard the deep tenor of his breath. Then he felt Rico's warmth beside him, a reassuring presence in the cold night.

"You had no choice," Childs said. "What that man said to her was criminal."

"She's his daughter."

"That doesn't give him leave to abuse her." Rico

leaned back against the building, his shoulder close to Jonas's. "You were a brave man to attack him, *mon ami*—or incredibly stupid, I can't decide. He had the advantage, after all."

Jonas laughed bitterly, holding up his false hand. It jiggled loosely on his wrist. A broken leather strap dangled down his arm. "Next time I'll think twice before I take on an angry father one-handed."

There was a pause. Then Childs said, carefully, "I would like to think that this is the end of your father-fighting days."

"It's not as if I've made a career of it."

"That's not exactly what I meant." Rico sighed. "You realize, my love, that it would go a long way toward mending things if you simply married the girl."

Jonas said nothing. The pain that speared through him at Rico's words was too great to fight.

"You're not going to, are you?"

Jonas shook his head. "No."

"Will you tell me why?"

He'd already given Rico all the answers. There were no others. Jonas angled his head back, staring at the black sky, wishing he could see the stars tonight, needing to see the stars. A pinpoint of light in the darkness, as bright and elusive as the hope Genie had given him. The hope that was slipping away from him now, slipping through his fingers like water. He let it go, not knowing how to keep it, afraid to try.

He heard Rico sigh again beside him, heard the catch in his breath.

"You're going to do it, aren't you?" Childs asked quietly, a murmur of sound on the breeze. "You're going to let her go."

"Yes."

"And then what? What will you do then, Jonas? Commit yourself? Lock yourself away?"

He knew Rico expected a denial, that he wanted one. Deliberately Jonas kept quiet, kept looking at the black, black sky, at the ineffectual glow of the streetlights against it.

Rico exhaled in disbelief. "That's your plan, isn't it? Dammit, tell me I'm wrong. Tell me."

Slowly Jonas turned to look at him. Childs's eyes sparkled in the darkness, dark and luminous. His face was lit in planes of shadow and light.

"I'm going tomorrow," he said.

"What if I told you I wasn't leaving?" Rico demanded sharply. "What if I told you I'd stay? Would it make a difference?"

Jonas smiled. Tenderly, he touched Rico's shoulder, clasping it tightly, feeling the warmth of his friend's body through the heavy coat. "No," he said softly. "It wouldn't make a difference. Not this time."

He pulled away and started walking, away from the glittering windows of the National Academy, into the gaslit shadows of the night, leaving Rico standing stunned and silent behind.

The clock in the hallway chimed two a.m., but Imogene stood at the window of her room, watching the snowy street below. There were still people up at this hour, couples dashing home late from parties and distractions, lovers sharing illicit kisses in dark corners.

Any other night she would have liked watching them. Any other night, she would have made up stories in her head about where they'd been and who they were. But not tonight. Tonight, she could not stop thinking about Jonas, about the painting.

About herself.

Imogene shivered, drawing her arms closer about her chest, feeling the brush of the earrings against her jaw, the smooth touch of the bronze velvet against her knuckles. The trappings of beauty. Jewelry and velvet and brocade. Tonight she had put on this dress and felt that she was pretty. She had seen the way the hue heightened her color and added honey to her hair and she had thought, *now he'll want me. Now he won't be so ashamed.* She had wanted to impress him with fine things, and instead he had shown her how unnecessary such things were. Instead, he had created beauty with nothing.

With nothing.

She had not even posed for him. He had created a vision from memory alone, had transformed her into a woman who was beautiful and alluring. A woman she had always believed she could never be. At least she had believed that, until tonight. Until she'd looked at the painting and seen in that woman the same things she saw in the sketch hanging above her washstand. Beauty and grace. A subtle eroticism. Tranquility. And something else. Something familiar.

Herself.

Yes, she was the woman in his painting. She knew it when she thought of the way she'd been with Jonas, when she thought of how she'd lain in his arms and cried out for his touch. She had come alive beneath his hands, had felt vibrant and beautiful and sensuous. And perhaps . . . perhaps feeling those things had made them true. Perhaps she had been wrong about who she was, perhaps her father had been wrong. She had spent her life comparing herself to Chloe, and it was true that in comparison to her sister, Imogene was not as pretty, not as talented. But now she wondered if they were really the things that mattered.

She thought about the things she'd always wanted, things that had been defined by Chloe. Talent and beauty and attention. Imogene had wanted, more than anything, to be like her sister, to be the belle of the ball.

Or she had wanted that, once. But wanting those things had become a habit more than anything else. Over the years, over the last weeks, they had somehow lost their attractiveness. Instead of remembering the way Chloe had bloomed beneath the admiration, Imogene remembered the mindless flirtation and superficial talk, the attention that had smothered as much as it flattered.

Chloe had not been able to go anywhere without men falling over themselves to talk to her. She had grown to expect it, had relied on her beauty to give her whatever she wanted. Imogene had always thought her sister was defiant and rebellious, but suddenly she wondered if that wasn't it at all, if maybe Chloe hadn't been a bohemian, or a rebel.

If maybe she had simply been spoiled.

The thought was startling and disconcerting. In death, Chloe had become what she had never been in life: a perfect sister, a glowing talent. Death had given her a heroism, a sharp focus that wasn't blurred by reality or faults. Grief had turned her into a myth, a fantasy.

Imogene had been struggling to become an illusion. For years she had wanted a life that had never existed. She had wanted love—her father's love, her mother's,

Nicholas's. She had wanted to be beautiful to someone. She had wanted those things so badly she had given away her own life to have them.

But still no one had given her those things. No one had ever loved her enough to believe she was beautiful or special.

No one except Jonas.

Except Jonas. She thought of how it felt to lie in his arms, to press her cheek against his chest and hear the rumble of his voice, the steady beating of his heart. And she knew that Chloe would never have fallen in love with Jonas. Chloe would have dismissed him and walked away, because she had no compassion and less understanding. She would never have wanted to try.

But Imogene was not Chloe. She was no artist, and she was no beauty. Except in the eyes of one man. A man who made her believe anything was possible. A man who made her believe she could be the woman in the portrait. A man who looked at her and saw beauty and tranquility.

A man who loved her.

She knew that too, as irrevocably as if he'd told her. And it hadn't been the pain in his eyes tonight that had told her, or the way he'd defended her against her father. It had been simply that he had painted a portrait of her from memory. That he saw her as beautiful. She'd been wrong when she thought he didn't really see her—she knew that now. He not only saw who she was, he made her more than she'd ever thought she could be. His words from the other night came rushing back to her, haunting and doubly painful now, because now she understood what he'd been saying. Now she understood.

"Look at me, Genie. Look at who I am. Surely you

know you can't stay here." Not because she wasn't good enough for him. Not because he was tired of her. But because he was afraid of himself. Because he was afraid. God, how simple it was.

And yet the worst thing was that she had misunderstood and so had done what everyone did. She'd left him. Because she had undervalued herself, she had given her life away a second time, was once again surrendering what she wanted without a fight. She was giving up happiness. She was giving up love.

Thomas's words came trembling back to her. *"You're not a little girl anymore. You're a grown woman. Perhaps it's time you thought about what you want for your life, instead of what your father wants."*

What you want. . . .

Imogene opened her eyes, staring out again at the golden glow cast by the gaslights onto the snowy streets. She heard the muffled clatter of carriage wheels, saw a hired carriage pull up in front of the house. The door opened, and Thomas and her father came stumbling out. Samuel was hunched into his cloak, and though he shook his head when Thomas tried to help him down, he did not shrug off the steadying hand her godfather placed on his arm. She watched as the two of them climbed the stairs, watched until she heard the unlatching of the front door, until they disappeared inside and she heard them in the foyer, stumbling and talking as they went down the hall.

She let the curtain fall and stepped back from the window, then slowly she walked out her bedroom door and down the stairs. She heard their murmurs in Thomas's study. Without hesitating, she went to stand in the entry.

Her father was slumped in a chair, his head resting in his hand. At the other end of the room, Thomas was pouring brandy. He looked up and saw her. Slowly he set the brandy aside and restoppered it. He picked up two half-full glasses and walked to Samuel.

"If you don't mind," he said, handing her father a glass, "I think I'll take mine upstairs. It's getting late."

"Not that late," Samuel protested. He turned in his chair as Thomas started to the door. "For God's sake, man, I—" He caught sight of her and stopped. "Imogene. Good God, girl, why aren't you in bed?" He waved her away irritably. "Leave us be."

Thomas paused as he passed her. He smiled reassuringly. "Good night, my dear," he said softly.

She caught his gaze. "Good-bye."

She saw the flicker of surprise in his eyes, surprise that turned to sudden comprehension. His smile grew; she felt his joy in his quick squeezing of her arm. "Be happy," he whispered.

"I will be."

He nodded, and then he turned away, saying loudly, to Samuel. "Good night."

Imogene heard her father grumbling as Thomas left the room. She waited until she could no longer hear her godfather's footsteps, and then she walked over to where her father sat, staring into the fire. She stepped in front of him, blocking his view of the flames.

"I'm leaving," she said softly. "I just wanted you to know."

He looked up at her, frowning. The motion made the swelling of his cheek seem worse, accentuated the cut on his chin. "Of course we're leaving," he said, obviously annoyed. "We're catching the early train tomorrow, so be ready. I only hope Nashville hasn't already caught wind of all the trouble you've caused."

She shook her head. "I'm not going back to Nashville."

"What the hell—" He stopped short, his expression clearing, his confusion replaced by disbelief and contempt. "Ah, I see where it lies now," he said slowly. "You'd best get that thought out of your mind, girl. You think you can just run back to Whitaker, eh? Well, you can't. He won't take you back. He's got what he wanted."

Imogene shrugged. "Maybe that's true. I won't know until I ask him."

"He's a madman. He'll end up in jail one day, you mark my words."

"Then I'll be there to bail him out."

He laughed shortly. "No doubt you think you love him. That's it, isn't it? Good God, girl, you're so naive. I'd lay odds ten to one he doesn't love you."

Imogene said nothing.

Her father fingered his glass. He sat up a little straighter, his dark eyes narrowing, his lips thinning in a straight line. "You'll be sorry," he said. "The scandal will destroy you, and don't think you can come running to me for help. Even though you've shamed both me and your mother, I'm willing to take you home tomorrow. We'll do what we can to help this thing blow over. But if you go to him, you can forget about your family. If you defy me again, I won't lift another finger to help you as long as I live."

Imogene looked at him thoughtfully. "I understand," she said. "And I'm sorry."

He stared at her as if she had turned into a stranger before his very eyes. "I'm not joking," he said harshly.

"I'm warning you, Imogene. If you do this, I'll never forgive you. Your mother will never forgive you."

She nodded, wondering why his words didn't hurt. Wondering why she didn't feel anything at all. "I'm sorry for that too."

He watched her steadily. She saw the anger in his eyes fade. She saw his disappointment. And suddenly she felt the sadness she'd been waiting for. This was the man whose love she had wanted so badly she changed her life to please him. The man she'd always thought of as strong and vibrant, as charismatic and refined. But his love came at too high a price, she knew, and now when she looked at him she only saw a weak, angry old man. A man who could not forget the daughter he loved, and because of it was losing his other one.

She felt sorry for him suddenly, felt sorry for herself. In a way, she would have preferred to remember him without his weaknesses, would have preferred to remember him as the man who had entertained artists and philosophers, the man who held Nashville in his hands. He had shown her a world of sophistication and brilliance, but that was not the same thing as being a father. He had never been a father, not to her, and she wished he had been, even one time, because that was the memory she wanted. It was a memory she would have never given away.

"Your sister would never have done such a thing," he said, fixing her with his gaze.

Imogene didn't look away. "I'm sorry, Papa," she said. "I'm sorry I'm not the daughter you want me to be. But I want my own life. Not Chloe's. Not yours. I hope you can understand that. I pray that you can."

Her father closed his eyes. He took a deep breath.

When he looked at her again, there was pain in his expression, something that looked like regret—whether for himself or for her, she didn't know. And she didn't care. He had abandoned her long ago. He no longer deserved her sacrifices. He never had.

"You'll regret this, daughter," he said dully. "You'll be knocking on my door in a month, I know you will."

She shook her head and smiled and leaned over him, kissing his forehead, feeling his dry skin beneath her lips. He didn't move. He didn't try to kiss her back. When she straightened, he was looking at the fire.

"Give my regards to Mama," she said softly, and then she turned away, leaving him with his brandy and his pride. Leaving him to stare into the fire—forever, if he wanted to.

In the hallway, the grandfather clock chimed three. The night was slipping away. It was time to go.

Chapter 28

He could not sleep. He didn't want to. This would be his last night of freedom, and he had intended to make the most of it, had thought to walk the streets until dawn, to take great deep breaths of this city he loved, to smell its salt smell and the clean freshness of snow, to breathe Broadway's scents of manure and smoke and riches.

But in the end those things meant nothing to him. In the end, nothing mattered at all, and nothing was precious. The streets, the docks, the studio . . . they were all as meaningless as the stone walls of the asylum. He had lost his vision. He had lost his passion.

He had lost her.

And so he had come back to the studio. There was a sketch of her on the table, one of the many studies he'd done before he painted her portrait, and he propped it onto the windowsill where he could see it without moving and stood there, feeling the cold and staring out into the dim yellow glow of the street, waiting for the night to pass.

He waited a long time. So long, he didn't know what

time it was when he heard the creaking on the stairs.
The sound encroached upon the silence—soft, hesitant, unsure. So quiet he thought it was his imagination at first, but then it grew louder, turned into footsteps, and he heard them coming down the hall and
waited for them to pause. At Byron Sawyer's door, at
Paul Ellston's, at Rico's. But they didn't halt at any of
those rooms. They kept coming.

And then, at his door, they stopped.

There was quiet. For minutes, it seemed. Long
enough that he was convinced he'd imagined the steps
after all. Then the door to his studio opened. Slowly,
hesitantly. The hinges screeched in protest.

With one part of his mind Jonas thought it must be
morning already, that the men from the asylum were
here. The thought brought a surge of pure panic. But
then he remembered they weren't coming for him. He
was going there. And it was still dark. Still so damned
dark.

"Jonas."

He knew then that he was hallucinating. It sounded
like her voice, soft and lilting, but it couldn't be her.
Goddammit, it couldn't be her. She had left the exhibition and gone home. She was safe in bed. It was too
damned late. Dawn was still hours away.

"Jonas."

The door closed. He heard her breathing. An illusion, he told himself, but even knowing that, he
couldn't resist. Even knowing that, he welcomed it.
Slowly, afraid it would vanish if he moved too quickly,
he turned around. The studio was dark, but he saw her
form against the door, saw the dim light from the
streets glance across her face, whisper against her hair.
She was holding something large and bulky, a bag of

some kind, and when he turned to look at her she let it
fall to the floor with a thud and moved toward him—
so quickly, so gracefully, he was sure it *was* an illusion.
It seemed her feet didn't even touch the floor.

Suddenly it was more than he could take. He backed
against the wall, covering his eyes with his hand. His
heart was racing. "Christ," he breathed. "Ah, Christ,
don't torture me. Not this way. Please . . . not this
way."

It was quiet. He let his hand drop, expecting her to
be gone, expecting to face the empty nothingness of
his studio, afraid that he would. He looked up.

She was standing there, in front of him. A mere foot
away.

She was no illusion.

He closed his eyes, feeling a surge of pain so raw
and desperate it took his breath, and then opened
them because not looking at her was more painful. He
wanted to savor the sight of her, to burn this memory
onto his brain, to not wonder why she was here or
remember that he had to send her away. He just
wanted to look at her, at the shadows of her eyes and
the litheness of her body, at the strength in her face.
And she let him look. Her breathing was her only
movement, and he felt it pulsing in the air between
them. Giving him life where he had none. Making him
weak. Giving him strength.

He swallowed, forcing out words—God, such inadequate words. "You shouldn't be here."

"No?" She smiled, a tiny motion in the darkness.
"Where should I be then?"

"Genie—"

She came toward him. The very surprise of her
movement stopped his words in his throat. She

stopped only an inch away, perhaps two. He felt the press of her warmth, caught her scent.

"I love you," she said.

The ache stabbed through him. He looked away. "Go home," he said, and his voice was harsh and raw. "I want you to go home."

She paused, an infinitesimal hesitation. Then, "This is my home."

The words sank into him—a promise, a curse. "No," he said, his voice hoarse, his heart hurting so badly he could barely breathe. "Genie, you don't understand. You can't understand. I . . . I don't know what's happening to me. I don't . . . I don't know why. I've spent my life—Christ, my whole life—wondering if this . . . madness . . . will ever go away. And now . . ." He took a deep breath, trying to gather his thoughts, trying to harness the pain growing, spreading like a disease within him. "Ah, God, now I don't think it will. I don't think it ever will."

He heard her voice, a soft whisper in the darkness. "I don't care."

"But I care," he said. "I care. I would hurt you, Genie. You think I won't, but I will. Over and over again. I can't ask that of you. Don't make me ask it."

"Don't make you ask it," she murmured, repeating his words thoughtfully. "Does that mean you want to?"

The question speared him. He looked at her helplessly. "Genie—"

She stepped forward—a half step was all it took— and slid her arms around his waist, holding him captive, a sweet prison. Her body was cradled perfectly to his; he smelled the warm, sweet perfume of her hair. He tried to keep from touching her, but he could not.

He wanted to touch her, he ached to. He laid his hand tentatively against her hair, felt its satiny softness, closed his eyes and breathed deeply of her, as deeply as he could, and for the first time in days he felt connected, he felt . . . alive. Since she'd gone, he had not felt this way. Not since she'd gone.

But still he fought it. Still, he tried to push her away, forced himself to say the words hovering in his mind. "You can't save me," he whispered. "No one can save me."

She pulled back only enough to look up at him. "Jonas," she said softly. "Jonas, I don't care about any of that. I don't care. I've spent my life making sacrifices for other people. I've spent my life hiding in corners. I don't want to do that anymore. Oh, Lord, I . . . I never felt alive until I met you. I never felt . . . anything. Please don't ask me to give that up. I can't. I won't. I want to stay here . . . with you." She reached out, touching his face, cupping his cheek in her palm. "You made me beautiful," she whispered. "Now let me do something for you. Let me keep you safe."

"Let me keep you safe."

The words sank inside him, a benediction, a prayer, a wish, and it struck him suddenly that if anyone could do that, if anyone could keep him safe, it was Genie. Christ, she already had. She kept away the darkness, she made him feel whole the way he'd never felt before. *"Let me keep you safe,"* and he realized it was what he wanted more than anything in the world. To be safe, yes. To be loved. She had seen him at his worst, and she had stayed. She had looked into his eyes and seen his hell and she had touched him and smiled at him. She had loved him. Despite everything, she had loved him.

Had he ever been loved like that before? Had he ever thought he could be?

He felt her touch against his cheek and it warmed him. Clear into his soul, it warmed him. The cold in his heart eased, dissolved, and through the bleak darkness inside him, he felt a light—the hope she'd given him. The hope he thought he'd lost forever. It shone before him, weak at first, then growing stronger and stronger. A lone star in the night, a beacon he turned to, one he needed. Because he knew suddenly that without her he would disappear. Without her, he would give in to the darkness forever. And he was so afraid of it. Christ, he was so afraid.

He was trembling, and he grabbed her wrist, holding her hand tightly to his face, afraid she would stop touching him, that she would back away. He thought he would die if she did. "Ah, Genie," he murmured. "You don't know what you're getting into."

"Don't I?" she asked in a whisper. "Maybe you're right. Maybe I can't save you. But I can love you. I can love you, Jonas. Isn't that enough?"

The words were haunting, so soft and tender they took his fear and his pain—and brought him something else instead. Something he'd always wanted, something he never thought to have.

A future.

It shivered tremulously before him, weak and wavering, but it was a future nonetheless. A future where before he'd never had one, where before there had been nothing but . . . nothing.

Jonas swallowed. He wrapped his arms around her and pulled her more tightly to him, burying his face in her hair, needing to feel her solidness and her strength, wanting to hold her so tightly that everything she was became part of him. He wanted her compassion and hope and tranquility. Her beauty and her strength. Her love.

God, he wanted her love most of all.

And it was that, finally, that he surrendered to. There was no denying it, not anymore. He loved her. He wanted her. Forever, if she would have him. He wanted to feel her beside him all through the night, wanted her calming presence during the day. She'd said he made her feel alive, but the truth was just the opposite. The truth was that without her he had no life at all. Without her, there was no peace and no future and no happiness. Only loneliness and pain. Only that.

He tightened his hold, clutching her with desperate strength. "I love you," he whispered against her hair. "Christ, Genie, I love you so much. Don't ever believe anything else. Please, no matter what happens, believe that one thing. Believe I love you, and—please—don't ever stop loving me."

She looked up at him.

"I won't stop," she said. "I love you."

"I hope it's enough," he said quietly.

She smiled then—that soft, wonderful smile—and pulled him closer, and he saw the conviction burning fiercely, beautifully, in her eyes. "It will be," she promised. "It will be."

And for the first—the only—time in his life, he believed maybe it would.

— Author's Note —

*J*n the mid- to late-nineteenth century, New York City was the American artists' mecca. The areas along lower Broadway and Greenwich Village were filled with art dealers and studios, and the affluent sponsored and patronized artists as much to prove the measure of their taste and success as for investment purposes.

The National Academy of Design was the preeminent art school and gallery in New York at this time, and every year it held a very popular exhibition for local artists. Though the exhibition was always in the late spring, readers will note I have changed it to the autumn in my story. Because of the nature of Jonas's illness, and several other factors, it served my purposes better to take some creative license with the timing.

Jonas's sufferings from bipolar illness (commonly called manic-depressive illness) are not atypical. Those diagnosed with bipolar illness experience mood swings that range from mild euphoria and depression to extreme life-threatening and psychotic episodes. Though lithium and other medications can sometimes be used with great effectiveness in controlling the cycle, there are those who are not treatable—or who refuse treatment.

In the nineteenth century, there was no choice. The only "treatments" for bipolar illness were alcohol or drug abuse, confinement to asylums, or suicide. In spite of that, many of those who suffered did survive to contribute lasting and beautiful works of art—among them Lord Byron, Samuel Taylor Coleridge, Robert Schumann, Robert Lowell, and Vincent van Gogh.

Though a small number creative artists are actually bipolar, studies have shown that artists as a group have a higher percentage of bipolar illness than the general population, and recent studies have explored this link. For those wishing to read further, I recommend Kay Redfield Jamison's excellent book on creativity and manic-depression, *Touched with Fire.*

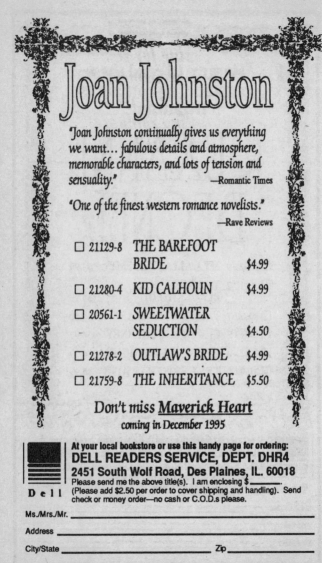